Audrey McCormack

D0810171

Emma's Gift

Emma's Gift

A Novel

LEISHA KELLY

Fleming H. Revell
A Division of Baker Book House Co
Grand Rapids, Michigan 49516

In memory of
Juanita Lane,
with special thanks to Mom and Jan for all your help.

ONE

Julia

December 19, 1931.
Joe Hammond came racing up our lane in his father's wagon. I'd never seen their team move so fast, and it set my heart to pumping. Something was wrong. Before the horses half stopped, Joe jumped down and came flying toward our front door like he'd seen a ghost. Samuel opened the door for the boy, and Joe sucked in a giant breath of air before he could manage to say what had brought him here in such an awful hurry.

"Mama's sick again," he said, looking nearly as pale as the white winter sky. "I come to fetch Emma. And you too, Mrs. Wortham, if you'll come."

I dried my hands and pulled off the bib apron. Of course, we'd go, though my stomach was already wrenching sideways. Emma would never refuse to help the neighbors. Not ever. No matter how sick she was feeling.

Emma set her teacup on the table. "Don't you be wor-ryin', Joey. Sit down and catch your breath while I get ready."

That was it. Calm as a May breeze. Emma Graham never refused to answer a call.

She shoved her clunky wheelchair away from the table and waved my husband back when he offered to help her. "Go get m' coat an' boot, if you don't mind," she told him. "You'd be quicker'n me about it. Not every day Wilametta asks for help." She sounded awfully hoarse. "What is it she's complainin' of?"

"Mama didn't ask," Joe said, twisting his dingy blue stocking cap around in his hands. "Pa sent me."

Emma didn't answer him right away. George Hammond asking for help was surely worse, and she knew it as well as I did.

"I'll get my coat," I told them. "What else do we need to bring along?"

"Lap robe for the wagon," Emma answered. "An' your doctorin' herbs, 'case they ain't got what we need over there. Do you know what it is ailin' her, Joey?"

The wiry thirteen-year-old glanced at the door and then down the hall where Samuel had gone. "Pa said nerves, but it was never this bad before."

"She been outta bed today?"

"No, ma'am. She don't look just right for color, neither, I don't think." He hadn't sat down. Wasn't about to. I turned to the kitchen cupboard and started pulling down jars.

Samuel came rushing back with Emma's coat and mine. God bless him, he knew how to rise to an occasion better than I did sometimes. Robert and Sarah followed him and stood there looking at me. "Don't worry," Samuel said as he gave me my coat. "We'll be fine till you get back."

I stood for a minute, at a loss for what to say.

"No tellin' how long it'll be," Emma told us. "'Specially if the snow keeps up. If you wanna stay, Juli, I'd sure understand."

"I'm coming." I hadn't even noticed that it had started to snow, and I barely gave it a thought. I just looked at Samuel's deep gray eyes and started pulling on the coat.

It ought to be Emma staying home. She'd been so weak lately that it scared me, her going out at all. Surely I could handle whatever was ailing Wilametta. But there'd be no talking Emma out of going. She'd known Mrs. Hammond for twenty years, and she'd sooner die than not come when there was a need.

It was snowing thick by the time we got outside, making it hard to see down to the road. We bundled Emma up in her fur-lined coat, and Samuel lifted her into the wagon seat. She looked so small sitting up there. Like a child, but for the thin gray hairs showing under her woolly hat and the deep lines defining every inch of her face. I spread one quilt on her lap and another around her shoulders.

"Don't fuss on me, now," she scolded us. "We gotta be going."

Samuel set my bag in the back of the wagon, and I turned to the porch long enough to tell Sarah and Robert to stay in while I was gone.

"Don't worry," Samuel told me again. "We'll be all right here."

Tears filled my eyes as soon as he said it. Of course, they would be. There wasn't any reason to doubt it. But I was scared pitiful nonetheless and not about to say so.

Snowflakes were circling down and falling on my gray wool skirt. I climbed up beside Emma and pulled the edge of the old quilt over my lap too. Joe Hammond hardly waited till I got sat down—we were off down the lane as quick as he could make those old horses go, and I held onto Emma with one hand, the seat with the other.

George Hammond was out to meet us. He didn't say anything at all, just reached Emma down off the seat and started for the house with her.

I jumped from the back of the wagon, my mind whirling and trying to pray. *Lord, heal Wilametta. Keep Emma strong.*

George hadn't waited for me and neither had Joe, who ran ahead of his father to open the door. They both went busting in without slowing down. I hurried behind them with my bag.

Inside that house was a wilder scene than I could ever have dreamed up. Three-year-old Bert was standing by the door, bare from the waist down in the draft and hollering at the top of his lungs. His brother Harry was sitting on the floor in a puddle of something, twisting up a dishtowel he was probably supposed to be cleaning up with. Two boys sat at the table, managing to slurp down some gray mush and argue with each other at the same time. They only hushed when one elbowed the other and pointed at Emma.

Lizbeth stood at the stove, wrestling a steaming pot away from the heat with one hand and holding her fussy baby sister with the other. The poor girl looked like she could cut loose and cry too. *Or maybe she had been, not long ago,* I thought. And there was one other boy, sitting on the loft ladder in a shirt twice his size, watching everything. He had puffy, hollow-looking eyes and the dirtiest cheeks you ever saw. Little Rorey was nowhere in sight, nor was the oldest boy, Sam, who was considerably taller than me.

George didn't pay the slightest bit of attention to the kids. He took Emma straight back to Wilametta's bedroom without taking the time to help her off with her coat. I followed after them, scarcely able to breathe. The whole house smelled like camphor and waste, stale food, dirty diapers, and a hundred other things. The Hammonds had always been a crazy household, wild and disorganized and loud. But today something different hung over the place. An angry kind of hopelessness.

Wila lay on the bed, sleeping or unconscious—it was impossible to tell. Six-year-old Rorey was beside her, stubbornly clinging to her mother's hand. As George set Emma down on the edge of the bed, most of the kids came clustering in, waiting to hear whatever she would say.

Emma pulled off her big winter hat and leaned real close, listening to Wila's breathing. She felt her forehead, then turned around to pull the blanket back and look at the woman's swollen feet.

"Juli," she said, "take your coat off. We're gonna be here a while."

Franky, the boy who'd been sitting on the ladder, pushed his way to Emma's elbow. "Whatcha gonna do?" he asked with his fingernail in his mouth. "Can I help?"

Joe looked at his brother in disgust. "Shut up! Nobody asked you to get in the middle of ever'thin'!"

Emma glanced at them as Lizbeth squeezed in behind me. "She was feverin' yesterday, an' I been bathin' her head," the girl offered. "She was awake a little bit, early this morning, but she ain't took in nothin' at all." In her arms, the baby, Emma Grace, squirmed and let out a cry.

Little Bert climbed up on the bed next to Rorey, and Emma looked them all over with a sigh.

"George," she said in a quiet voice, "Wila's gonna need some good solid rest. And quiet. I think you might oughta take the young'uns over to Samuel. Won't hurt 'em to be a while at my house again."

George didn't answer for a minute. He looked at Emma and his wife, then bowed his head and looked at the floor.

"We can be quiet," Rorey protested in a whisper. "Honest! I been real quiet."

But George shook his head. "Go get your coats. All a' you."

Lizbeth was horrified. "I need to stay, Pa. At least me an' the baby. And what about the snow?"

"The little one been drinking your goat's milk?" Emma asked.

"Yes, ma'am." Lizbeth had tears in her eyes. She hardly ever left home; she was always so busy helping her mother. And she sure didn't want to leave now.

"The little one'll be fine if you wrap her up good," Emma maintained. "If you got milk left from this morning, take it along."

"We got milk left," George said.

"But Pa—"

"You can't do no more right here," George told his eldest daughter. "You'll have to keep your brothers in line over there. Do whatever you can."

Lizbeth just stood for a minute, her lips quivering like she was all set to argue. But she took one more look at her mother, then one at me, and turned and fled the room.

Nobody else moved.

"Don't you worry," Emma told the rest of the kids. "I'll get your mama all fixed up. We just need some good, quiet space. Go on! You can play with Sarey an' Robert over there. They'll like that."

"Get your coats," George ordered again and then noticed his half-naked youngest son. "Willy, climb up and get your little brother's pants. And shoes. Get on, now. All a' you."

As the room slowly cleared of children, I wondered what Samuel would think of them showing up at our doorstep. I thought maybe Lizbeth should stay here after all, and I should be the one to go back home.

But no, I knew I needed to be here for Emma. We'd taken her canes, but she'd have considerable trouble getting around without the wheelchair Samuel had made. I had the feeling, anyway, that she wanted all the kids gone for their sakes as much as ours, so they wouldn't be here watching and worrying.

"Where's that big boy a' yours?" Emma asked George.

"Gettin' the stock in."

"I'm thinking maybe you oughta send him to take the younger ones for you and then go on into Belle Rive after the doctor." She said it real slow and quiet.

George looked at Wilametta. "She ain't good then, is she?"

I could see one muscle sprung tight and quivering in his lower jaw. He glanced out the bedroom door to see if any of the youngsters were close enough to hear.

"No, she ain't," Emma told him. "I'm thinking it's the dropsy, and I sure could use Doc Howell out here if you'll let 'im."

George had never hired a doctor before, not ever. And to my knowledge, Emma hadn't pushed for one. But he must've known this time was different.

"All right," he said. "But it'll take a while, goin' more'n ten mile with the snow out there. It's gonna get worse. The doc might not come."

Emma nodded. "He'll come if he can. But we'll pull her through, one way or the other. You tell your boy that, so he won't be in no reckless hurry."

George didn't answer but turned slowly and left the room. Emma started stripping off her coat. She kicked off her solitary boot and stood with one foot on the floor and the stump of her other leg balanced against the bed.

"I'll need you to steep me some red raspberry and some dandelion root too," she told me. "An' bring me a towel and cloth and a bowl of warm water." She leaned down close, steadying herself with her hand against the head of the bed. "Now, Wila," she said. "It sure would be a comfort to your family if you'd wake up and tell 'em bye."

She didn't wake up. I went to the kitchen and helped little Bert squirm into his pants and shoes, then wiped his nose and put on his too-thin jacket. It looked like there was a good three inches of snow on the ground already, and it was coming down so thick I could hardly see out to the barn. I began to pray that George's son would be able to make it through to the doctor.

"Tell Samuel not to worry," I said to Lizbeth. "Emma just wants your mother to have some quiet. Try to rest over there too. Looks to me you could use it."

She looked at me and shook her head. But I helped her wrap the squalling baby in blankets. "You're so awful good to your brothers and sisters," I said. "Your folks must be proud."

She didn't answer. She just grabbed what looked like nothing more than a spring sweater and headed back for her mother's room. I picked up little Emma Grace and held her till she calmed down. Then Joe took her so I could fish from my bag the "doctorin'" herbs, dried for winter use.

By the time Lizbeth came back out, the rest of the kids were dressed as warmly as they were able. I told them to bundle under the quilts, and they all headed out the door as I set on a pot of water to boil. There wasn't much wood in the wood box, but I threw a couple of chunks in the stove to keep it hot.

Wilametta gave a moan, the first sound I'd heard out of her since getting there, but it was no real comfort. I'd expected to find her fevering maybe, and miserable, but not like this. No wonder Joe had looked so scared.

In a few minutes, George came back in the house and told me he'd done what Emma had said and sent his oldest boy to drop off the kids and fetch the doctor. Then he went in the bedroom, looking pale and nervous, and I could hear him telling Emma that the kids would be staying the night at our place, even though it wasn't yet two in the afternoon. I hurried in when I had a bowl of water warmed up.

"Have you eaten?" I asked George.

14

"Don't want nothin'." He sat on a chair that looked homemade, his eyes on Wilametta's plump, pink face. She was sweating, and one of her eyes was half open, but she didn't seem to be seeing us.

"Can you help me sponge her down, Juli?" Emma asked, pulling back the covers just a little. Wilametta had always been chubby, but today she looked more swollen than usual. Pink and kind of mottled white—funny colored, just as Joe had said.

"I ain't never seen her like this," George told us. "She weren't this bad yesterday. Got up and cooked herself an onion. She says onion'll cure anything."

"It don't hurt," Emma assured him. "She knowed that much."

I started bathing Wila's face and shoulders while Emma rubbed one arm.

"This morning she was painin'," George said real slow.

Emma turned his way. "Where?"

"To the chest. She told me not to fetch you. Heard you been sick an' didn't want to have you over here fussin' for her again."

I thought of the last time Emma had been here, two months ago, when Wila'd been three days in bed. We'd heard it from the kids, and Emma had insisted on coming. I couldn't blame Wilametta, certainly. Then or now. But George should've had the sense to fetch the doctor before this.

The wind started whistling outside, and Emma asked George to light the oil lamp. It was getting darker, all right. In the middle of the day. I looked at the swirling snow and thought of the kids. They'd have a nasty time of it riding over to our house, though it was just over a mile by the road. I was glad I'd sent our quilts back with them.

Wilametta gave out another moan and suddenly opened her eyes. "Emma Jean," she whispered. "You come to see me?"

15

"I sure did." Emma turned to me. "Juli, get some drinkin' water. Those herbs ready yet?"

"Not yet." I got up and ran for the water bucket, nearly tripping over the broom somebody'd left on the floor. It didn't seem possible that it'd been used lately.

Wilametta drank a sip and closed her eyes. "Tell Lizbeth to fix you some tea," she said, all dreamy-like. "Ain't got a cookie in the house."

"You shush," Emma told her. "We ain't here to be pampered, now. You hurtin' anywhere?"

Wila looked around. "It's kinda quiet."

"Yup. Good'n peaceful. Lay still a minute." Emma laid her head against Wilametta's chest, listening, and then raised up and asked her again how she was feeling.

"Tired. You know. I'll be all right."

"That's what we're countin' on." Emma lifted the water and got Wila to take another sip.

"I'm gonna see that the cows got water," George said suddenly and rose from his seat.

"Got wood enough in?" Emma asked.

"No," I told them both, though I hated giving George another chore. It seemed to me that he ought to stay right here. But he wasn't minded in that direction.

It wasn't but a few minutes more and the red raspberry tea and root tonic water were ready. I carried them in, though I wasn't completely sure what Emma was going to do with either one.

She was rubbing at Wila's other arm when I came back in. She stopped to bathe the woman's face with the wet cloth. Wilametta looked to be asleep again, so soon.

"She doing any better?"

Emma shook her head. "I promised Lizbeth she'd be all right. How long you suppose it'll take the doctor, comin' from Belle Rive?"

"Oh, Emma, I don't know. It'll be a good while, the way it's snowing." Her question was a real worry. Sam Hammond had only just left with the kids. Surely she knew it'd be a considerable time before he even got to the doctor.

Wila coughed and seemed to sputter a little. "Emma Jean?"

Emma took her hand, massaging it carefully.

"My heart's a-flutterin', ain't it?" She sounded quiet, far away, like she was talking to us from the next room.

"It may be that," Emma said. "Does seem to be off a rhythm."

I set the herbs down on the bedside table, scooting Wila's Bible over to make a space. Emma picked up the raspberry tea, poured some of the dandelion root into it, and offered Wila a sip.

"I can't feel my toes at all," Wila said.

I felt the breath slide right out of me. But Emma answered calmly. "Don't worry about it. They's still there."

She turned to me and told me to rub Wila's legs some, not too hard. I sat on the bed and did what I was told.

Emma coaxed another sip of the tea into Wila. "Just think, Wilametta," she said. "Coming up this May, little Emma Grace'll be a whole year old."

"I dreamed she was gonna sing pretty as a bird," Wila said. "Her and Rorey too. I always did want my daughters to sing. They need more'n what we've had. You know?"

"I know," Emma said quietly. "I been prayin' on that very thing."

"Oh, thank you. Thank you so much." Wila was losing her pinkness, instead looking pale and yellow and slick with sweat. "Will you sing me a hymn? Will you do that?"

Emma turned to me, and I saw that she was sweating too, cool as it was. And there was something in her eyes I'd never seen there before. "Please sing, Juli," she told me. "'Blessed Assurance,' all right?"

17

Emma's Gift

It was all I could do to swallow a lump down and take another breath. They were scaring me, both of them. I could hear George come in to the kitchen, dump a load of wood in the box, and head back out. *He should be in here,* I thought again. But I couldn't say it. I hated the very thought of what it implied. Wila was fading. Dying. *Oh, God! A mother of ten!*

I couldn't shake the feeling of it as I started to sing, tears clouding my vision. I was slow and quiet, afraid to be otherwise and hoping for all the world that I was wrong. Emma's words went tumbling through my mind. *"I promised Lizbeth she'd be all right."*

Lord, help us! She's got to be all right. You wouldn't want it any other way!

I sang on, as much as I could remember, praying that I was just being foolish. The snow would quit and Wilametta would be back to her normal clamorous self by tomorrow, most surely.

"She sounds sweet as angels," Wila said, and I almost had to stop the song. "You know what the Good Book says 'bout heaven?" she asked.

"There'll be no sorrow there," Emma answered. "No sickness. No pain."

"I'll be glad for goin' there, one day. You tell Emma Grace an' all the rest it's a wonderful place. Will you do that, Emma?"

I stopped singing and went to rubbing her legs again, feeling heavy and cold inside.

George came in again, dumped a second armload of wood, and moved in our direction with his slow, even steps. He shook the snow off his coat and left it lying by the bedroom doorway. "She still awake?"

"Yes," Emma said. But that was all she said. She laid one hand on Wila's chest and left it there, moving her lips without making a sound.

18

"Good." George came and leaned over the bed, not seeming to notice that Emma was praying. "Wilametta Hammond," he said, "I called for the doctor. Folks that say I don't love ya, they ain't got a leg to stand on. I ain't never called a doctor for no one."

Wila looked up just enough to meet his eyes. For a moment she and George stayed like that, not a word between them. Then finally Wila smiled, just a little. "I love you too," she whispered, her eyes slowly closing.

George looked like he could jump out of his skin. "Emma!"

"She's still here, George. She's breathing just fine." Emma lowered her head down to Wila's broad chest, as if just making sure. "Don't you worry," she told us again. "She's breathin' fine."

George pulled his wet hat down off his head. "She just give me the awfullest scare." He curled at the brim nervously, sending little drips of half-melted snowflakes to the floor. "She's never been this bad," he told us again. "You say she'll be fine, though, ain't that right, Emma? Didn't you say she'll be fine?"

I looked from one to the other, glad it wasn't me he was asking.

"I believe it," Emma told him, solid as anything. "But it'd be a fine thing if you'd pray on it too, George Hammond. You got coffee in the house?"

"Yes, ma'am." He looked like a schoolboy just then, his too-long hair all mussed.

"Juli, go and make us some coffee," Emma ordered. "I'll set with her, but there ain't much more you can do while she's sleepin'."

I made coffee, enough to give to the whole family if they'd been there. Then I picked up the bowls on the table, some of them still half filled with the strange gray porridge. I moved the pot with the same gray stuff in it, heated most of the rest of the water, and did all the dishes. George would have to fetch more water in so we'd have some at hand for the evening.

When the dishes were clean and put away the best I knew how, I went about picking up all kinds of odds and ends that had been left lying on the floor. I could imagine the Hammond children playing with the strangest of things, like the broken shoelaces and mason's trowel I'd found, and then leaving them lie. Anything I didn't know a place for I stacked in a pile behind the loft ladder, which rose from one corner of the kitchen.

Emma sat by Wila's side, praying quietly or singing most of the time. I brought her some coffee and a fresh bowl of warm water a time or two, and she bathed Wila's face and neck and told me at least three more times not to worry.

I remembered what it'd been like when baby Emma Grace was born right in this bedroom, coming breech, with Wila sick as a dog. Emma had commanded every minute, telling us they were both going to pull through fine. And they did. It was no wonder the Hammonds trusted Emma. After she'd birthed nine of their ten kids, they must've thought she could do anything.

But right then I couldn't help noticing her sunken, weary eyes.

"There's a rocker out by the fireplace," I said. "You want me to bring it in here so you can rest while Wila's sleeping?"

She shook her head. "You cleanin's fine, Juli. But re-arrangin' furniture on my account's another matter. George might want that chair."

"He's in the kitchen. Patching a boot. I'm sure he wouldn't mind."

She didn't tell me anything else one way or the other, so I went and dragged the chair in next to the straight-backed one that George had been sitting on earlier. The two chairs together took up about all the floor space there was.

I helped Emma to the rocker and covered her lap with the first spare blanket I could find. It seemed to be growing even darker outside, and cooler too. And I wasn't the only one to notice it. I could hear George getting up to throw some more wood on the fire. The Hammonds' sitting room and kitchen were one open area, so with the fireplace at one end and the huge wood cookstove at the other, it wasn't bad for warmth. Better maybe than Emma's house, but a lot more cramped.

Wila was sleeping a long while this time, and George kept himself busy doing a little odd this and that. I went back to the cleaning that the house sorely needed, top to bottom. While sweeping in the kitchen, I stirred up so much dust and wood shavings that I set myself to coughing.

George looked up at me and shook his head. "You ain't gotta do that."

"I know. But I feel better making myself useful."

"Wila does that in the spring, when she can open all the windows and doors." He said it like he thought I ought to know this kind of thing. "That's why they call it spring cleanin'."

I stared down at the floor, wondering if he meant that she only swept in the spring. I could almost believe it, as sorry a shape as it was in. But she'd been sick, and you couldn't expect Lizbeth to keep up with everything. With seven boys, though, you'd think at least one of them would lend a hand with housework. Goodness, there was the awfullest crud on the floors and on the counters. Even the walls were a dingy, stained-up mess.

Despite the dirt, I set the broom aside before I was done, not sure if I was bothering George. I went to take a peek in the bedroom, and Emma looked to be sleeping in the rocker. I tried to back out, but she stirred anyway.

21

"Any change in Wila?" she asked me.

"I don't think so." I was wondering, and had been for quite a while, what she'd meant when she'd said that Wila was off a rhythm. So I worked up my nerve and asked her.

Emma sat forward, and I stepped closer in case she wanted to get up. She did. I helped her back to Wilametta's side, and she laid her head against the sleeping woman's chest. "Her heartbeat weren't regular, Juli. That's what I meant."

"What about now?"

She sat up a little. "Wila used to say she was strong as an ox. And she was too. Could lift like two men. And out-eat 'em, easy."

"Is she all right?"

Emma looked away toward the window and shook her head. "No. No, she ain't. But she's restin' in God's hands, and that's the best place for her."

I followed Emma's eyes past the frosty windowpane, where we could see the steady, driving snow. "It's getting pretty bad out," I told her. "George said you can't see the road anymore, even if you're standing on it. I doubt the doctor will be able to get through tonight."

"Then we wait till tomorrow," she said, her expression unchanging. "Don't fret for the children none. They'll make out just fine with Samuel over there."

It didn't worry me about the kids. So long as they'd gotten to Emma's, I knew Samuel would manage all right. He was good with kids. But before long, the whistling wind had picked up fierce and the snow began beating heavier against the window glass. It was a real storm, and there was no question in my mind that wherever any of us were, the doctor included, we were stuck.

Hours passed with everything just about the same. It came past time for supper, but nobody was interested in eating anything. Wilametta woke up twice more, both times briefly and barely long enough for us to get any drink down her at all.

Emma kept up her vigil, sponging Wila down, rubbing her arms and legs, talking to her when she got the chance. I tried to get Emma to rest some more, but she wouldn't do it. She let me take care of all the running between rooms, but that was all.

Later in the evening, I reheated the herbal concoctions and brought them just in time to see Wilametta stir awake again, this time coughing.

"George?"

I set down what I was carrying and turned around for the kitchen. But I didn't have to fetch him. George was just coming in the doorway. He got up close to the bed and squatted down, taking his wife's hand and lifting it up to his face. It was the first time I could recall seeing any physical affection between them.

"George," Wilametta was whispering. "You remember that necklace your grandmama give me?"

"I do," he answered slowly.

"You see that Lizbeth gets it, you hear? It's her right. She's been nothing but an angel to me, an' you know it."

"Uh, yeah. She's a good help, all right." George reached up and brushed away the frizzled stray hairs from Wila's forehead. "You oughta just give it to her yourself. She'd be real tickled—"

"I loved ya when I first set eyes on ya," she said, getting quieter. "Under that sycamore, acting the fool. A wonder we ever come together . . ."

"True enough," George said, nodding. "I reckon you shoulda knowed better."

"It's been good." She was whispering again. "Good enough."

And then she was quiet. She let out one little gasp and lifted her hand to touch George's flannel sleeve. Then the arm, looking leathery and unreal, slid slowly back against her pillow. She gasped again, and then there was no sound at all.

I saw the change in her face, the peace appearing at the same time as a chalky white. And I felt like running outside, anywhere, to scream for the God who was supposed to be watching and answering the prayers we'd been praying.

Emma jumped forward, rubbing at her again, talking, praying, trying to get some response. But finally she gave up and lowered her head down to Wila's chest. "Oh, Wila," she cried. "Not today. You ain't supposed to go today."

Never in my life have I heard anyone sound so absolutely weak and defeated. I could do nothing but stand and stare. It wasn't real. Couldn't be. I looked at George, afraid of what I'd see.

He was shaking his head, the set of his jaw making him look angry. "She ain't gone," he said. "She ain't, Emma. She ain't gone."

Emma closed her eyes, her head still on Wila's chest. She looked so tiny and broken. Suddenly she started shaking, and I wanted to pull her off Wila and hold her. "She's gone, George," she said, her voice far steadier than she looked. "God love her. She's gone."

Slowly she sat up, but just long enough to sink from the bed to the floor. "So sorry," she said, and I jumped up, hurrying to her side.

George bent over Wilametta, touched her cheek and her puffy, pale lips. He gave her a shake, tender and desperate, and I could hear his breath drawn out pained and slow. "She's gonna be hungry later, Mrs. Wortham," he insisted. "Oughta get a pot a' soup on, if you don't mind." He straightened himself. "Maybe if we put a poultice 'cross her chest . . ."

Emma was shaking in my arms, and he just stopped and looked at her. The silence right then was heavier than stone, and I could feel the weight of it pressing on my chest. George stood like a statue. Finally, he sunk down at Wilametta's side and bent to hold her. I turned my eyes away, hurting too bad to see.

"It can't be helped," Emma whispered.

"You said she'd be all right. That's what you said."

"None of us knows them things."

He was still a long time, lingering with Wila at the bed, not a single hair of him moving. "No," he finally said, barely able to get just the one word out.

"George—" Emma reached out her hand.

"No." He stood up and turned from us. I could hear his rapid steps as he moved to the door and then out, not taking the time for his hat or his coat.

"George!" Emma called again, pulling up straight and tense. "Juli, see if you can tell where he's gone! He oughtn't to be out in the storm in that frame a' mind! Oh, Juli, his heart's plumb broke."

She fell into sobs, and I didn't want to leave her. But I ran to the door like she'd said.

He hadn't even shut it. And there was no sign of him in the swirling snow. Already the whipping wind had covered his tracks.

"Mr. Hammond!" I screamed, knowing why Emma would worry. Blinded by grief and without his coat, he had no business being out in the bitter cold. I'd have gone after him if only I'd known which way to go. "Mr. Hammond!"

There was no answer but the howling wind and the distant, miserable lowing of one of George's cows. Shut in the barn but cold nonetheless, no doubt.

"Mr. Hammond!" I screamed once more. I thought about running toward where I knew the barn must be, just to see if he'd gone that way. But what if he hadn't? What if something lay out there under the snow that I couldn't see in the Hammonds' unkempt farmyard?

I knew he could be anywhere. He could even be trying to make it through the timber to his children over at our house. I was sorry about it, dreadful sorry for him, but I had to think about Emma inside the house, in the worst shape I'd ever seen her, weak and hurt for the loss of a friend. Wilametta Hammond. Strong as an ox. And gone in a moment. A quiet, cruel, devil of a moment.

Slowly I pulled the worn rope latch and shut the door.

T W O

Samuel

All ten of the Hammond children burst through the back door, covered in snow, too cold to wait for me to answer their knock. Willy was the first to say that Emma had shooed them out so their mother could rest.

"She'll be okay after she's had the quiet," Kirk offered. "Boy, if it was summer, we could just run outside a while."

Lizbeth took the baby straight in beside the fireplace, and the rest of the Hammonds followed her. I threw in more wood, all I could, to get the fire good and blazing. Lizbeth was solemn, too solemn. The littler girl and the two youngest boys cuddled close to her, their fingers and noses red with cold.

The oldest boy, named Sam like me, ordered all of them to take off their coats and stay by the fireplace. But he headed back to the door, pulling his old jersey gloves tight.

"You going back home?" I asked him.

"Yeah, and you should tell them so. But I got to fetch the doctor first."

The gravity of that did not escape me. George Hammond hadn't called a doctor when the baby came early. Didn't even consider it. And that had been decent weather.

"Son, I'm not sure you can make it through tonight in that wagon. And even if you did, I don't know that the doctor could reach her till morning."

He looked at me a minute, his black eyes deep and somber. "You're right," he said. "Come near stickin' the wagon in drifts just this far. With your permission, I'll leave it here, and ol' Teddy, and take Bird. She's the stouter of the two."

I wanted to argue with him, say that it didn't make sense to send a kid out in this storm. But I hadn't been there. I hadn't seen Wilametta. And they surely knew the weather as good as I did.

There was no persuading Sam Hammond. He was bound to go, no matter what I said, so I bundled him up better in my own coat and hat and the scarf Juli had made for me. I didn't know if he was much for praying, even though the family went to church, but I prayed before he left because it was the thing to do.

Robert came into the kitchen looking for me. His eyes were wide with questions. "Dad, are they staying the night?"

"They'll have to in this weather."

"Is their mom real sick?" He said it with a genuine worry. At ten years old, he was well able to consider what that could mean.

"Yes. I think so."

"What are we going to do?"

"Make everybody welcome."

I hunted cupboards for the cloth bag of popcorn we'd gotten from Russell Lowell, and the store-bought box of salt. I pulled out the biggest pan in the house and then ran out to the box on the porch and whacked off a chunk of butter.

"Anybody want popcorn?" I announced, hurrying back to the sitting room before the kids had time to get restless. Most of them were still soaking up heat, so much so that you couldn't even see the flame for all the kids gathered around it. But Bert and Harry, the two youngest boys, were already headed up the stairway.

"Paw-corn?" little Berty stopped to ask me, his rosy cheeks looking almost raw. "We get paw-corn?"

"Sure. If you want."

My own Sarah, sweet and innocent as a six-year-old could be, looked up with her smiling eyes and said, "Boy, this is better than a real live party."

Rorey Hammond was already at her side, and the two little girls ran upstairs after Sarah's rag doll. "I wanna be Emma," I heard Rorey say from the steps. "Your dolly can be Mama, and we'll fix her up right as rain."

Lizbeth stood to her feet, hugging Emma Grace, who was so quiet she must've been sleeping. The oldest girl took one look at Harry, already halfway up the banister, and shook her head disapprovingly. "Harry Beckwith Hammond, you get yourself down! That ain't no way to behave, and we ain't even been here a minute!"

The little boy looked at his sister, then at me, and as if daring both of us, swung his leg up over the rail and slid himself down to the post at the bottom.

"That's a trick, all right," I told him. "But I surmise Lizbeth to be your elder, and if you don't mind her good in my house, I might just set you out in the snow."

He cocked his head, as if trying to gauge if I could possibly be serious. He was nearly five, I guessed, and I'd never seen him when he wasn't in the middle of a mess or about to cause one. But his little brother suddenly sat down on the steps behind him and started to cry.

"Oh, no," one of the bigger boys lamented. "He's probably got to go outside. He hates the outhouse when it's cold."

"I'll take him," Joe said, looking no less anxious than he had when he'd been over here earlier that day. He was tall, lanky. I couldn't recall ever seeing him smile. He picked up his little brother, draped a jacket and one of the baby's blankets around him, and started for the door.

"Robert, why don't you show them the way?"

"Ah, Dad," Robert protested.

"I know where it is," Joe told us. "Not like I ain't been here a time or two."

A time or two was probably all, for Joe, anyway. Willy and Kirk and sometimes Frank came with Robert after school quite often, and we saw a lot of Rorey, who dearly loved the chance to run and play with Sarah. None of the Hammonds were strangers, but I felt pitifully unprepared as I looked at all the faces in front of me.

They'd piled their jackets in one giant heap beside a chair, and Frank had climbed up on top of it. The quilts were beside that, now damp with melted snow. I pointed to the line that stretched from the top of one window to the edge of the mantelpiece. "Hang up the quilts, somebody. We'll need 'em dry for bedding down everybody later."

Nobody moved at first, but then Robert got up, feeling duty bound, I supposed, after skirting one chore. Lizbeth handed the baby to Kirk and helped him while I shoved the pan down under the grate into the hot bed of coals to melt the butter. It was usually Julia that made the popcorn—and everything else around here. But I figured I could manage it, though hot as the fire was above, the corn might scorch pretty bad. Ought to wait a little while, I guessed.

With Christmas only a week away, I thought about suggesting a carol or two, but then considered that the timing might be rather sour. It might not feel like Christmas, poor as we all were, and their mother sick in bed. Lord, have mercy.

"Mr. Wortham," Franky spoke up suddenly, "do you have a mama? I know Emma don't. She's too old."

"I do. But she's in Albany, New York. Been a while since I've seen her." It didn't bear telling that she'd run me off the last time, liquor bottle in her hand.

"Does Mrs. Wortham have a mama?"

That wasn't something I wanted to discuss either. Telling them the woman had died when Julia was only five might just worry them unnecessarily. "Everybody's got a mother, at one time or another," I said, saying a silent prayer for Wilametta Hammond. Franky was just staring at me, his silvery eyes looking swollen. He was dirty, awfully dirty, like he'd been grubbing around someplace.

Sarah and Rorey came back down the steps, cradling raggedy Bess between them.

"I'll bet a onion'll help her," Rorey declared. "I just bet it will."

Lizbeth went to the window, looking out at the white fury beyond it. Harry snuck in right beside my elbow and poked at the popcorn bag. Willy was eyeing the box of checkers on the mantelpiece, and I took the game down for him. "You'll have to take turns," I said. "Winner take the next one."

Willy was just Robert's age, and pretty soon the two of them were setting their pieces out for a game, watched closely by twelve-year-old Kirk, who was still holding the baby.

Franky didn't look the slightest bit interested in any of that. He laid his head back into the pile of coats, still looking at me. "Do you sleep upstairs?"

"Usually, but as cold as it is, we probably all ought to stay down here tonight, closer to the fire."

"Good."

I wondered at him. He was only eight, and small for his age. Elvira Post, the schoolteacher, said he was slow. Like watching a stump grow, was the way she'd put it. But he was thinking tonight. He and Lizbeth. Like none of the others except Sam, and maybe Joe, he was seeing this day through eyes older than a child's.

Joey came back in with a thump of the back door. While he was still in the kitchen stamping snow off his boots, little Berty came running in, straight for the fire.

"Whoa, slow down, horsey," I told him. "Not too close." He was a little tike, for sure. And his nose was running like a pitcher pump. I pulled out my hanky and wiped at it, but he squirmed away, searching out his sister. Lizbeth picked him up when he tugged at the baggy trousers that might once have been her older brother's. But she just kept looking out the window, and this wasn't near enough excitement for a live wire like Bert. He wiggled till she put him down again, and he toddled off toward the stairs.

Baby Emma Grace woke up with a startling howl, and Kirk gladly gave her up to Lizbeth and covered his ears. I didn't think I'd ever heard a baby holler so loud. Lizbeth went straight for the kitchen and the bag she'd left there, pulling out a bottle of milk with a homemade nipple already prepared. She offered it to her little sister without even warming it, and the baby gulped it down greedily, not seeming to notice the slight.

"I got more," she told me. "Where can I put it so's it don't warm too much, nor freeze?"

"Basement steps," I told her. "I'll take it for you, just a minute." I pulled the pan with melted butter to the side a bit and took the Hammond goat milk in two mason jars to the basement. It didn't take me long to realize that Franky was following me, watching every move I made.

"I hope you're not worrying for your mama," I said. "She's in good hands. I know it's pretty strange, though, coming over here all of a sudden like this."

"It's okay." He held the basement stair rail with both hands. "We can be friends. Can't we, Mr. Wortham?"

"Sure, buddy. I'd like that."

He smiled and reached for my hand, a move that would've surprised me from any Hammond. They weren't much of a lot for kindly affections, or any touch, from what I'd seen. Except for Lizbeth, with the little ones.

"Can I stay by you?" Franky asked with a little tremor in his voice. He had the strangest eyes, pale and silver like the moon, deep and lonely like a forgotten soul.

"No problem," I told him, trying to sound lighter and more cheerful than I was really feeling. It hadn't bothered me one bit when Julia had left, that she'd be over there with the snow coming on. But that was before I knew it would be this bad, with the weather and the neighbor's need. I wanted to stop everything and pray, or better yet I would've liked to go for the doctor myself and let the oldest boy stay. But I had this houseful, and that's what Emma or George or Julia had wanted, and that had better be good enough for me. I had to trust them. And even with nine children, plus my own two here, I could scarcely doubt that it was me who had the easier job.

Franky squeezed my fingers and stopped at the top of the stairs. He didn't say anything, only stood there for a moment, looking in toward the kitchen and Emma's big clock on the wall. It struck the hour with a tinny sort of dong, a sound I'd grown pretty used to in the seven months we'd been here. But Franky seemed transfixed.

"Arthur Whistler says a clock stops when somebody dies." He looked at me with his strange eyes gone stormy, and I knew he was thinking of his mother. "Is that so, Mr. Wortham?"

"Can't see a logic to it, can you? I think it's just a tale."

"I broke Mama's clock last week." He turned his eyes back to Emma's old clock, his skinny shoulders drooping. "Didn't mean to. Just knocked it clean off the shelf. Couldn't fix it, neither. Glass was broke an' ever'thin'."

He looked smaller than he ever had, whipped and scared and not knowing what to do.

"Now, Frank, things get broke. It just happens. Can't say how many times I broke something when I was a boy."

"A clock?" He was looking hopeful that I could disprove his notion, and I couldn't tell him no.

"Could be. I'm sure I was a trial. Broke a lot of things. Don't remember what all. But I know one thing—if people forgive you, it doesn't affect them anymore, and things get pretty much back the way they were. Don't worry, okay? A clock's just a clock."

Franky didn't say anything, just let go my hand and went back to the sitting room and his pile of coats. That bothered me, but if any of his brothers or sisters had overheard our conversation, they didn't pay the slightest bit of attention.

Sarah and Rorey moved their doll right beside the checkers game, to be closer to the fire's warmth. Berty was peeking at them from behind a drooping quilt, and Harry was looking up at me with a sheepish grin. "I helped ya," he said, which brought my eyes immediately down to the popcorn bag he'd been so interested in. It lay completely empty and crumpled over his left shoe, its entire contents—about five pounds—dumped without ceremony into my buttered pan. It was a close fit, with only a half cup or so of loose kernels scattered across the hearth.

"All ready to pop," he said, smiling ear to ear. "Ain't you glad?"

I longed for a radio that night, just to have something to occupy their minds. We ate up every bit of Julia's soup and all the bread, and I opened three jars of homemade applesauce from the pantry too. At least there'd be no stomachs calling once we all got settled down.

Joe helped me drag Emma's mattress and the one from upstairs into the sitting room. It wasn't nearly enough space for all of us, but we could line up the youngest ones fairly comfortably at least. I made a little bed for Emma Grace in a pulled-out bureau drawer, emptied and padded with towels. Rorey declared it finer than what she had at home, which made me wonder where the baby slept over there.

Berty snuggled up in Lizbeth's lap, and when she started singing to him, Harry and Rorey pressed in beside her. Franky watched them a while and then turned his attention back to me. "Will you tell us a story? Like you did in October?"

That was the only other time they'd been overnight here, some of them. Their mother'd been sick then too. But not this bad. Not bad enough to call a doctor.

Kirk rolled his eyes at the mention of a story, obviously considering himself too old for such things. But Joe, who was at least a year older, gave me an approving nod. "Go ahead, if it's all right, Mr. Wortham, sir."

I searched my brain for a story for this group on such a night as this. Lizbeth, still softly singing, was looking away toward the window again, as if she didn't want me to see her face. Berty, nearly asleep, had stuck one thumb in his mouth. Sarah came and laid her head in my lap.

"Okay," I began. "I think I'll tell you about Bismark the Butterfly."

"Butterfly!" Willy exclaimed. "Criminy! How exciting is that going to be?"

Frank gave him a mournful expression, and Willy responded with a callous grunt. "Big baby!"

"Shut up, Willy," Joe commanded.

"I'm gonna be seven next week," Rorey informed me out of the blue. "Mama's gonna make me a real Christmas cake."

"Now that sounds like something special," I told her with a smile.

"We have one every year. Big deal." That was Kirk, suddenly scowling at his sister. "Maybe she won't want to do the same old thing."

"Yes, she will! She told me she would!" Rorey rose to her feet to face a brother nearly twice her size. "She's gonna make me a cake, and it's gonna have real icing and cherries!"

Kirk shook his head. "No frills this year. That's what Pa said. We ain't even gettin' a turkey. We'll prob'ly eat Patches instead."

I was glad for the knowledge that Patches was a hog, already butchered and the source of the smoked ham stored in the Hammonds' frigid attic.

"I don't care about that," Rorey maintained. "So long as we got my cake."

Lizbeth carefully shifted Berty down to the mattress and pulled a cover up to his chest. She was nearly as tall as my wife, but when she looked over at me in that dusky room, she looked no older than Rorey. "Why don't you all be quiet," she said, lying down between Harry and Bert. "Franky wants to hear a story."

Amazingly, the room became still. Lizbeth was boss, that was clear. At least at bedtime. Harry pulled his head onto her shoulder, and Berty snuggled against her side, squeezing her sleeve in his little fist. But she lay on her back, staring up at the ceiling, hardly seeming to be in the same room with us at all.

"Everybody ready?" I asked, feeling too empty to do a story justice. But I was committed to make an honest effort. "Bismark was a caterpillar once," I began. "You all

36

know that, right? He started out an egg, and then a caterpillar, and then he woke up a big, beautiful butterfly."

"Yeah. Is that it?" Willy questioned impatiently.

"He's just getting started," Robert defended. "Give it a chance." He surprised me, since he had been rather impatient with my silly stories himself lately. It was different, I supposed, in the company of others. But I might have expected him to reject my tale outright, especially since Willy and Kirk were none too enthused.

I tried again. "Bismark was a big butterfly, with very beautiful wings—"

"A monarch?" Sarah asked.

I petted her hair, and she looked up at me with a smile.

"Yes, a monarch. And a nice looking one too. But Bismark was not very brave. He was scared of just about everything, including other butterflies."

"Why?" Frank asked. He was on his belly, still on the coats, with his chin resting in his hands.

"I guess because he thought they all looked so big and fast. He thought they could all fly so much better than he could, because he never flew very much at all, unless he was hungry and had to get to a flower."

"This is a girl story," Willy complained.

"No girls in it," I told him. "At least not yet."

"It's for everybody, ain't it?" Rorey inquired.

"Everybody who wants to listen."

At that, Willy jumped up and got the checkerboard down again. He threw a chunk of wood into the fireplace, though it wasn't needed yet, and sat down in the fire's light to set up for a game. Kirk joined him after giving me a quick sideways glance. I just nodded to them and went on.

"One day when Bismark was flying to a flower, the sky got dark and gray. When he heard thunder, he was too scared to eat, so he hid beneath the flower's petals and waited."

Joe leaned his head back in a living room chair and closed his eyes. Sarah climbed all the way up into my lap, and Franky edged toward Robert, who was cross-legged at my side.

"It started to rain and rain," I told them. "And suddenly Bismark heard a terrible sound coming from far below."

"Was it a snake?" Rorey said, jumping up.

"No, not a snake."

"A lion," offered Harry. "They eat everything."

"No, it wasn't a lion, either." I took a deep breath. "It was voices. Many tiny voices, all of them calling for help."

"Why was that terrible?" Rorey asked.

"Because Bismark was afraid. He didn't want to go see who was calling. He didn't want to know why they needed help. He just wanted somebody else to come so he wouldn't have to move."

"Did somebody come?"

"No. Nobody. Not a butterfly or a dragonfly or a person. Nobody. So Bismark finally flew down, down, down, though he was very scared, to see what he could do."

"What did he do?"

I smiled at Rorey's persistent inquiries. "First he saw caterpillars," I explained. "Lots of caterpillars. They were so young they'd just hatched from their eggs. Some were still in their eggs. And they'd all fallen when the wind knocked their leaf down into a puddle."

"Caterpillars can't swim," Rorey pointed out.

"That's exactly the problem. That's why they were calling for help. So do you know what Bismark did?"

"Went to find their mama?"

"He would have. If he'd known where to look. If there was time. But there wasn't. So he flew down and picked one up and carried it all the way to safety."

"Just one?" This time it was Sarah.

"No. He went back over and over until he saved them all. But just when they were about to thank him, the wind blew very hard and blew him high into the sky, in twirling circles. He tried and tried to fly, but the wind was too strong. It blew him so far that he didn't even know where he was. But you know what? When he finally flew down again, there were many butterflies there and many other creatures, but Bismark wasn't afraid of any of them. He was bigger now, with big, bright wings just as fast and as strong as anybody else's."

"Where did he get new wings?" Rorey asked, her eyes glistening with the firelight's reflection.

"That's the point of the whole story," I told them. "Some say the wind gave Bismark new wings because he was a hero. But maybe his wings weren't new at all. Maybe he just looked at them differently because he knew what he could do now. He could help somebody smaller, and that made him feel big and strong."

"Maybe he died," Franky solemnly added. "Maybe the wind blew him into a rock, and he went to heaven and got better wings there."

The little boy's words struck me silent. Why hadn't I had the sense to anticipate such a thought? Franky wasn't slow, that was sure. He was quicker than I was tonight.

My little story hadn't lulled anybody to sleep, except the youngest two, who would've dropped off anyway. I made more popcorn, scooping it out of the mixing bowl where I'd dumped most of Harry's excess. We opened jars of home-canned grape juice, and with bellies full once again, the boys put up the checkers, and everybody lay down. Lizbeth's gentle voice floated over us, singing a lullaby I'd never heard before. I couldn't imagine how she could relax with three of her little siblings laying across her, but maybe she was used to it by now. Sleeping quarters at the Hammond house were probably tight. I stretched out on a quilt on the floor, and Sarah curled up beside me.

As I looked up at the high ceiling, I listened to all of their breathing around me, and I prayed like I scarcely remembered praying before, for that other Sam, off someplace in the blowing snow. And for Wilametta, Emma, and Juli. The howling wind outside sounded monstrous, large enough to pick up this whole house and everybody in it. Just like Bismark and his little monarch wings.

I felt somebody push up against me and found Franky seeking my hand. He didn't say anything, just clung to me with a finger in his mouth, the firelight dancing across his cheeks. I prayed for him too, and his brothers and sisters. They looked comfortable enough just now, dropping off to sleep, but they were lost in their own way, having nothing much in life but dirt and dreams, and gaining little so far from either one. It made me want to pray for George too, who'd told me more than once that he had too many kids. If there were only one, he'd said, he'd have something to give. But a little doesn't stretch very far across ten young backs.

That was easy for me to understand, since I'd found it hard enough just with the two I had. And my wife was well. *Lord, be kind to George Hammond. He needs your strength right now, your grace, and your love.*

THREE

Julia

We should fix her up, Emma insisted, because it'd just be harder later. So we washed Wila's body carefully, and I combed her long hair while Emma picked out the nicest dress she owned. We cut the back of it to make it easier going on, and it was one of the hardest things I'd ever done, as if taking the scissors to Wila's Sunday clothes in itself marked the finality of all this.

Emma set a couple of nickels on her eyelids, just to make sure they wouldn't open. She fussed about her hair a while and then decided if it was too nice it wouldn't be quite like Wila, who'd always looked like she'd been all day out in the wind. She folded Wila's hands together and smoothed the bedcovers, but she wouldn't cover her face. Not yet, because there wasn't family there to tell us so.

"Don't she look peaceful, Juli?" she said. "She's with the Lord now, can't you just see it?"

I couldn't say anything. Wila was a mother. Far from old. How could I rejoice?

"It should have been me," Emma whispered, gently touching Wila's hand. "God love 'em. It should have been me."

"Emma—"

"Don't tell me nothin', now. There ain't nothin' more to say."

"It's not your fault—"

"I shoulda knowed how to save her, Juli. I shoulda figured somethin' else to do."

She didn't sound like Emma anymore. Not the Emma I knew. Swallowed up in the death of that room, she seemed helpless and shriveled, and I was unable to respond.

She made her way slowly along the edge of the bed to the foot and then leaned down and reached for her coat and boot. "Should take the chairs out and shut the door," she told me. "Best to close off the heat. Hard to say how long 'fore somebody can get here to help George with the arrangements."

I moved both chairs like she told me to. But then she pulled on her boot and started on with her coat, and I didn't understand why.

"We can't go for anyone," I said. "There's no wagon."

"I just want to get outside, Juli. Help me."

I helped her into the sitting room and shut the door behind us. I figured maybe I could get her into a chair. "Emma, you should rest. It's awful cold and blowing snow—"

"I don't care if it's sixty below," she told me. "I'm goin' outside."

For a moment I was dumbstruck. Why go outside? What possible purpose could it serve? But I remembered George. Surely that was it. She was worrying for him, no doubt.

"Emma, he'll surely come back in soon—"

42

"There ain't no tellin' what he'll do, Juli. None at all."

It struck hard, knowing she was right. It was foolish and dangerous, what he'd done, and if he didn't care, that just made it all the worse. But there was nothing Emma could do, I was sure about that. "There's no sign where he went. You can't make it in all that snow."

"I know, child." She sighed, and it cut me. "There ain't no helpin' it, bad as I'd like to. If he comes back, he comes back, God love him. Help me to the door."

I wondered now if she was thinking right. "Why, Emma? Where are you going?"

"Just out, child. Just enough to see the stars."

Had it escaped her attention that it'd been snowing all afternoon? And snowing still? White in every direction, including up. Seeing stars tonight was about as likely as Wilametta Hammond rising up off her bed. "It's awfully cloudy, Emma."

"I don't care." She glanced over at the one frosty window and shook her head. "I need to look. I need to see clean up to God's own heaven, Juli. Help me."

There was a weight in her words pressing against my heart. I almost protested again, but the look in her eyes stopped me. She took my hand in hers. "If ever I'd had a daughter, she couldn't be no better than you. You brung me home, Juli, an' I couldn't be no more grateful."

"I'm the one should be grateful. Always. You didn't have to let us stay." Not even a year ago, my family had hitchhiked across the countryside on the promise of a job. But when that fell through and we were stranded with nothing, Emma had offered us her own farm, though she'd been longing for it so much herself. It had only been right to give her the chance to come home too.

She was looking up at me. "You're strong as the hills, child. Was the plan a' God havin' you here, to help all the rest make it through this. You can do it. I know you can."

Maybe she couldn't see how close I was to sinking into a sobbing heap right then. All those kids. It left me tight inside. "Oh, Emma—"

She pulled herself up but still looked so small. "I need to look out," she said again. "For just a minute. I got to see the sky." She stood there on her one old leg, and I wiped my eyes and took her arm. Determined as she sounded, she might just go without me, even if she had to crawl. I'd have to help her, whether I understood it or not. She was the only one I could do a thing for now anyway.

It was hard without the wheelchair and Sam's strong hands. Emma leaned heavily on me and one of her canes, hobbling slowly through the Hammonds' sitting room toward the door. She was weak, I could tell, and breathing hard. I longed for someone else to be here, anyone, just to help me, though what they could do, I did not know.

The blast of cold pierced us when we finally made it out into the weather. But Emma didn't seem to notice. She just stared into the swirling mass in front of us. Sky and yard and timber all blurred together till they were almost indistinguishable in the darkness.

"Please, Emma, don't you want to go back in where it's warmer?"

She didn't seem to hear the question. "Juli, you'll hafta see that Albert keeps his word to me, you unnerstand? You see that them Hammond kids get to keep this place, no matter what else happens. Their mama's gonna be buried out here. That's what she'd want. And it ain't right it ever bein' sold to no stranger after that."

Cold tears bit at my face, and I wanted to argue that she had no reason, no reason at all to be laying such a charge on me tonight. But she wasn't through. "Give me your word right now, Julia Wortham, that you'll speak for me if he comes down here thinkin' to sell this land."

I couldn't answer her. I just wiped at those cold, hard tears. I didn't want to think about Albert. He had nothing

44

to do with this. He was the only kin of hers I'd ever met, but he kept his distance. And she had no business thinking on him now when she just needed to get in by the fire and rest what little of the night was left.

"God, I pray you George is safe," she said. "Oh, Juli, I fear he's done himself in."

"No, Emma! He wouldn't! He's got the kids to think about!"

"He weren't thinkin'. An' it's been awful long."

"Let's go inside."

"There weren't nothin' I could do," she said. "Maybe nothin' nobody could do." She leaned to the side against the porch wall, ankle deep in frozen white.

"Please let me take you in."

"She was a good woman, Juli."

"Emma—"

"I'd a' told anybody she'd be fine, that I was gonna be the next 'un to go. Not her." Her right hand was shaking, and she was looking strangely sunken. Then I noticed that her left hand was clutching the cloth at her chest. "Gonna have to take Lizbeth under your wing, Juli-girl . . ."

I took her arm around my shoulder and pulled her away from the wall. Her cane fell soundlessly into the drifts, but I was too scared to care. "It's too cold, Emma! You can't stay outside!" With all my might I struggled to get her back toward the door, pulling her, carrying her along. She was nearly limp, not bearing her own weight.

"Juli," she whispered, "I'm so sorry."

"You shush, now," I commanded, tears streaming down my face. "You got nothing to be sorry about! You did your level best over here, and that's all anyone could ask. You've been the best, Emma, the very best you could ever be!"

Still pulling her, half dragging, half carrying, I shoved the door open with my foot. *God! Where are you tonight? Help me!*

"Can you get me to the bedroom?" Emma sounded quiet, far away.

"We're going straight to the fire! You feel just like ice!"

Somehow I managed to get her to the closest kitchen chair. I pulled the door shut. Then I ran for the rocker, shifted her into that, and pulled her just as close to the hearth as I could. I turned around long enough to poke the blaze and throw on more wood. Then I spun around again, the fear in me rising swift and horrible. Emma looked like a specter in the dancing firelight, all shrunken and gray. I pulled a frayed old lap blanket off another chair and spread it over her. She reached her thin hand to me but didn't speak.

"You want I make you something warm to drink?" I forced myself to say it, and to sound cheerful too. But she didn't even try to answer, just nodded and leaned her head to meet the rocker's high back.

She wouldn't let go my hand, though, not till I looked her in the eye.

"Psalm 46," she whispered.

I knew I shouldn't have left my Bible at the house. I should've known better than that. "I—I can't read it without my Bible. I'm sorry."

"Wilametta's got a Bible."

Something about the suggestion made me stiffen. It was there, all right. As always, right on her bedside table. And Emma just kept looking at me, waiting.

"All right," I surrendered with a sigh. "I'm certain she wouldn't mind. I'll put us on some tea and fetch it right away."

Satisfied, Emma turned her eyes to the fire. Her hands lay folded across her lap, and it suddenly seemed strange to see them like this—idle. It was so like Emma to always have some sewing or something at hand. I leaned and kissed her cheek, reluctant to leave her side.

"Apple mint," she said, and I smiled, taking the request as a hopeful sign.

I took a couple cups of water from the bucket, put them into the heavy enamel kettle, and set it on the stove. I threw in another chunk of wood and then went back to poke at the fire again.

"Did you see the stars?" Emma whispered.

I glanced her way in time to see her tiny, tender smile. *Stars?* I thought. *In that swirling, snowy mass?* It was clouds I'd seen, maybe all the way to eternity, and no relief in sight.

"Heavenly," she said, closing her eyes.

I stared at her, wondering what she'd seen or maybe what she was still seeing.

"Wila ain't sufferin' no more." Her voice sounded warm, accepting, like the Emma I knew.

"She's not. You're right. I hope George and the children bear that in mind." I didn't want to think about it. All those kids. But it was impossible not to.

"The stars is twinklin' finer for another saint upstairs. That's what my mammy used to say." She pulled the blanket a little closer. "So sorry, Juli."

"For what?"

"All a' this. You away from your family thisaway."

"Not your fault."

She laid a bony hand across the side of her face and relaxed against it. I looked at her a moment longer, then made my way back to the kitchen where my bag sat on the floor, leaning against a potato box. Emma wanted tea. Apple mint. Good thing I'd brought that kind with the others. She'd always loved it. It grew in dainty circles around the clothesline poles back home. Emma's home, which now seemed a million miles away.

I searched through cupboards till I found the cups and spoons, sugar, and a tray to carry everything on. I'd take it all to the fireside, just as soon as the water was hot.

But going back into Wilametta's room was a hard thing. The chill hit me as soon as I went through the door. Strange that it could cool down so fast. Or maybe it was just me, feeling the death in that place.

Wila lay there looking larger than life. Looking like she could just float away into the wintery clouds, her white covers spreading themselves into great feathery wings to lift her and all our worries straight up to heaven. I stood for a moment, stopped by such a thought. What was wrong with us? Emma seeing stars, and me—me fancying all the pain could just drift away so easily. For Wila it could, now that her struggle was done. But not for the rest of us. We had tomorrow, and all the tomorrows after that.

I turned to the bedside table. The Bible lay there with its edges bent and with one little tear in a corner. It had been read. It had surely been in Wilametta's hands many times. "Forgive me," I whispered, though I was doing nothing wrong by taking her Bible to comfort a friend. It was heavy in my hand, like an armload of bricks, and I turned as quickly as I could to go out. But I shut the door carefully behind me, not wanting to make the slightest sound.

Almost it seemed that death was a living thing in the house. It made me ache just picturing Wila on the other side of the door. She'd picked up hickory nuts with me in the fall. She'd gotten her share of blackberries, maybe more than her share, every morning bright and early while they were in season. It seemed I should've told her good-bye, still should, maybe. But I couldn't go back in and face her lying there. Not again. Not yet.

Bible in hand, I headed back to the fireside, seeing Emma sitting there so calm. I set the book on the chair nearest her and hurried to the kitchen for the tea fixings. How I wished George would come back in, or that I knew where to find him. Surely he was all right, despite Emma's worries. In the barn maybe. Or with Samuel and the children.

How I wished they were all right here, sharing this hearth and the psalm with Emma, wrapping each other's comfort around the grief they'd be knowing soon enough. We'd weather this. We'd have to. The good Lord would see us through it and give Emma the strength to help us along. She was the one Lizbeth would need to help her pick up the responsibilities left to her. She was the one strong as the hills. And she'd be there for us, as long as it took. I believed it. I trusted for it.

Pouring water over the tea took just seconds, and I was back by the fire with the tray, thinking to sit and read while the tea steeped on the hearth.

"Psalm 46. Is that what you said, Emma?"

She didn't answer, and I thought her asleep. She had every reason in the world to be exhausted, for sure. I turned and saw her head leaned back so serene, and my gut clenched tight as a clamp. She was asleep. She had to be! But something bitter and cold inside me didn't believe it.

"No." I stood, barely aware of the thump of Wila's Bible on the floor. "No, God."

In a panic I reached toward Emma but somehow couldn't touch her. I called her name, knowing already there wouldn't be an answer. Her quiet breath was stopped; her tender voice was stilled. For a moment I stood there, just staring. It couldn't be. Not now. Not Emma too, when every last one of us needed her so much.

I fell on my knees, forcing myself to reach and take hold of her hand. But it was not Emma's hand now. The life that had touched me so often was gone.

"No!" It had to be a mistake. It had to. She was just asleep! Sick. And so very tired. "Emma? Oh, please, Emma!" I laid one hand against the side of her neck, the other on her chest. "Emma?"

I knew. There was no thump of her heart, no weary little breath. Nothing but her coldness, her deadness, and the fury of my pain.

"No!" Tears clouded my vision as I reached for a cup of apple mint tea and flung it into the flames. "God, how could you do this? How could you leave me alone like this?" I pulled myself to my feet against the woven chair. One foot bumped against the fallen Bible, and I stared down at it, anger seething raw and vicious inside me.

"Why? Why Emma too? You're supposed to help people! You're supposed to care!"

The tears were so strong that no other words could come. I walked and I cried in the Hammond living room, almost wishing it was me sitting there cold in that chair.

The wind was howling outside, and I knew the sky was still spitting snow. It would be hours, maybe days, before Samuel could get through. But he was over there with all of the children, having no idea what he'd be coming to face. I wanted to go to them, but I wasn't sure if I'd make it through the cold and darkness. Where George had gone, I had no idea, but he wasn't with Samuel. Somehow I knew that.

I ran to the door, only to be nearly knocked over by the rush of furious wind, so much worse than before.

"Mr. Hammond!" I screamed. But the only answer was the distant low of cattle. *They're going to starve,* I thought. *They're going to starve if George hasn't tended to them. And then those Hammond kids will all starve too.*

"Mr. Hammond!"

I looked up at the sky, hoping to see some ray of dawn. Hadn't it been night for an eternity already? But there was only darkness over the swirling snow. No break in the clouds, no stars, any more than there'd been moments ago when Emma had so anxiously looked up.

It wasn't right. The stars should be out, like Emma said, to welcome not one but two dear saints. They should be shining for Emma brighter than they'd ever shone before, instead of hiding themselves behind the cruelty of the storm. I shut the door, feeling that I was walking in a horrible dream. It couldn't be real, this nightmare I was in.

I thought of Grandma Pearl and how we'd found her, dead in her bed all stretched out like the undertaker had been there already. I knew I should lay Emma down somewhere so she wouldn't stiffen, sitting like she was. But it seemed a sacrilege to move her, to touch her at all.

But what if George comes in and finds her there? There was no telling what he might do. Better that he not see her first thing. Better to soften the blow the best I could. Emma would want that.

Numb on my feet, I pulled the rocker with Emma in it toward the closed bedroom door. *Oh, God! Where have you gone?*

With my eyes ablur I wrestled that rocker to the side of Wila's bed. It seemed foolish what I was doing. Foolish. But I had to do it. Emma would want me to. She would do it if she were in my place.

I folded the covers back and struggled to lift Emma from the chair, feeling all the while that my heart was dying. She was small, surely lighter than I was, but there was nothing easy to it just the same.

I laid her there next to Wilametta, and they looked like sleeping sisters who shared some precious secret. There was no worry, no hurt on either one of them. I sunk away from the bed, breathing in short little gasps, wanting to scream and run for Samuel's arms.

For a moment or two I couldn't move. My chest muscles were stiff, clenched. I shook but could not shake away the horror. I tried to breathe more deeply, and felt like I was choking. But I still had to do what I could for Emma. She'd said I was strong. I wasn't. God knew I wasn't. But I'd act it, if I could, for her sake.

51

Carefully, I pulled off her coat, knowing in my heart that she would want Lizbeth to have it. But I couldn't put a Sunday dress on her. I sat on the edge of the bed, my vision blurred again. Emma had picked out Wila's finest right away, but I couldn't do that. There were no other clothes here for Emma. Still, I brought water and washed her face, wishing she could feel it, open her eyes, and give me some word of comfort. I let her hair down, combed it proper with Wila's comb, and then braided it and put it up the way she liked to wear it for church. I didn't have any nickels, but Emma did, two more of them and a penny in her pocket with a paper dollar. I put the nickels on her eyes the way she'd showed me, though I'd never before seen anyone do that. *There can't be any more dying now,* I thought. *Only one little penny left, and that isn't enough.*

I smoothed her dress and laid her hands against her chest, imagining her somewhere else right now, hugging on her long-departed husband, Willard. She wouldn't be missing us, not the way we'd miss her. I pulled the covers to her chin, though I supposed it didn't matter.

I couldn't cover her face. She'd claimed me for family many times, but I knew I didn't have the strength to do it. I backed out of the room, leaving the rocker there by the bed. I closed the door with shaking hands. I picked up the tray of tea things and set them on the kitchen table. Then I looked about the room, thinking to make myself useful again. But instead I sank to the floor, my heart pounding and my head aching with the hurt that would surely never stop.

F O U R

Samuel

I woke before light, something restless in me nudging me awake. The first thing I noticed was the calm outside. The wind had died down. The snow too, hopefully. Maybe the doctor would be at the Hammond house by now, or at least before long. Maybe Juli would be home pretty soon. I hoped she'd managed to get some rest.

I was quiet, slipping away from Sarah, who was curled beside me. All the kids were still asleep, sprawled in every direction, but most of them up against somebody else. I poked the coals in the fireplace, blew on them, and added a couple of cobs and some tinder to get the fire blazing again.

Lizbeth was the first to waken, anticipating by a fraction of a second the movement of the baby, who had somehow gotten to her side in the night.

"Gonna need some of the goat milk for her, aren't you?" I asked quietly, hoping the baby wasn't about to bawl loud enough to shake the heavens.

"Yes, sir, if you don't mind."

I set in a little more wood, lit a kerosene lamp from a shelf, and carried it with me to get the baby's milk. I knew Robert would be up before long. He was always an early riser, as I expected at least some of the Hammond boys to be. But I hoped that most of them would sleep in as long as possible. They might be itching to head home and check on their mother, and I wasn't sure yet what to tell them.

Franky was rolling over as I came back with the milk. He wiped his eyes and his nose on his sleeve and looked up at me. Lizbeth gave her sister the milk right away, and the baby started slurping it down hungrily. I'd been quick enough to avoid the otherwise inevitable wail.

"Got to milk Lula Bell," I told Lizbeth. "But I'll be right back in to start some breakfast."

She nodded at me, her eyes still on Emma Grace.

"Can I go with you?" Franky whispered.

"You better stay here. Liable to be pretty fierce for cold. You watch the fire for me and throw on a log or two. Can you do that real quiet?"

"Yes, sir." He slid away from his cover toward the fire, wiping his eyes again almost as if he'd been crying.

"Worried about your mom?"

"Yes, sir."

"We'll find something out before long. But I expect she's all right."

Robert rolled over, and I told him to feed the chickens. I went and lit the stove in the kitchen and stocked it with wood. Then I was ready to get the milk pail and head outside.

The wind was gone but not the clouds. It was just getting light in the east and trying to snow quiet flurries at the same time. It was hard to figure just how much it had snowed yesterday and through the night. In some patches there were just inches on the ground, but there were also drifts standing in great glistening piles higher than my head. It was a strange, sparkling-white landscape in which the trees stood like silent angels, their powdery wings lifted to the sky. The worst of the storm was past, at least for now, leaving this pure, cold beauty in its wake.

I prayed for Juli, that any storm was past in that house too, and all was well. But as I looked at the shape of the road, I didn't think it likely that the doctor could have gotten through. I wondered if Sam Hammond had even reached him, and where he might be if he hadn't. Our lane was drifted closed, and beyond that you could barely distinguish road from the flat fields stretching past it. There wouldn't be any automobiles through today. And Hammonds' wagon was stuck in a drift by the barn, its front wheels completely hidden in the snow.

I'd have to feed old Teddy first thing. But it took me a time just getting the snow cleared from the door to get into the barn. Our dog, Whiskers, jumped out at me with his happy tail bouncing. Dorcas the cat, with a kitten now as big as she was, came rubbing at my ankles. I expected they'd all spent the night snuggled together in the hay.

Teddy appeared to be asleep, standing up in the stall where we'd put him last night. I pulled the end of a bale of hay and threw it in at his feet. Lula Bell was calling me, ready for the milking to be over and done. I patted her soft neck and pulled up the stool. I'd never milked a cow before her, nor even touched one, but she and I had come to a pretty decent understanding in the seven months we'd been here.

I could hear Robert and at least one of the Hammond boys hollering back and forth in the general direction of the chicken coop. No doubt the better part of them would want to play a while in the snow, if they had decent clothes for it, which most of them didn't. It set me to wondering about the walk to school after New Year's. I'd still send my two, even in the cold, or probably walk them there myself. But maybe the Hammonds would be missing a lot of days through the worst of the winter. They seemed to miss a lot of days anyway. Especially the older ones, who hardly ever went.

And then I thought of Christmas. Only five days away. I'd made sleds for my kids, since buying anything was out of the question. But what about the Hammonds? Had George found a way to provide anything other than Patches the pig for their Christmas? He had more livestock than we did, but that was about all. I'd worked a part of the harvest for Barrett Post, and that helped us buy groceries at least, but I wasn't sure if George had gotten much cash for anything, even what little he'd managed to pull out of his and Emma's dry field. I thought maybe we ought to have them all over. With Wilametta being sick like this, they might appreciate somebody else doing a little Christmas for them. Juli could probably even turn out a cake good enough to suit Rorey if she had to.

I was almost done milking, with the cat rolling around my ankles, when Joe came out to the barn looking for me.

"Snowing," he said. "Starting to come down pretty good again."

I shook my head. That was about the opposite of what I'd expected and wanted right now.

"Was thinking maybe I oughta go over and see if Pa could use a hand with chores."

He was worrying, I could see it in him. But here was another thin Hammond boy in barely adequate clothing, about to head out through the drifts. "Better get something in your belly first," I told him. "It'll take a lot longer than usual getting through that timber today."

Robert suddenly showed up in the doorway behind him. "You gonna cook breakfast for all of us?"

"I guess I will. Unless you want to."

"There wasn't but four eggs. They's way down."

"It's the cold. Don't worry about it. I'll make pancakes. Get Whiskers that other bone your mother boiled for the soup yesterday."

Robert was quiet a minute, thinking. "You s'pose she'll be able to get home today with all this snow?"

"Remains to be seen, buddy." I picked up the milk pail, not near full, and started for the house with Joe and Robert following me. It was snowing harder, all right. Willy was sitting in the middle of a snowdrift, and Joe scolded him soundly with the reminder that they had no dry clothes to change into. And I thought of Juli, only a mile away.

But what a mile it was on a day like this.

FIVE

Julia

It was getting light, but not near light enough to lift my soul that morning. No more firewood in the house. Water bucket empty. Not a sign from George or anyone else through the many long, cold hours. I sat on the floor where I'd sunk last night, but there were no more tears, and I could barely put two thoughts together. I just sat staring at the grimy kitchen walls, the peeling paint and once-rosy paper border now curling downward from the tattered corners. Everywhere was loss. And decay. Everywhere I looked.

It occurred to me that I didn't have to stay here, that I could try to push my way through the woods to my family, snow or no snow. I was sturdy enough. I'd walked it several times in fine weather and always enjoyed myself. But Emma was here. Here.

She might've been in Belle Rive just a skip away from the doctor if she hadn't loved her farm so much. She'd come to live her last days and die at home and be buried next to her beloved Willard. But this was a cruel, ugly trick. Just a mile away. Just a mile. But she died here.

The thought gave me a deep, seething anger that scared me. I felt like throwing things at the faceless sky. I might have done it and felt justified too, if there'd been much of anything handy that was mine to throw.

It was plain unfair, and anyone could see it. Emma was good. The best person I'd ever known. She'd given her whole heart to people, and everything else she could think of to give, even though she never had much for herself. Emma was a saint if I ever met one. How could it possibly have hurt the plan of heaven to allow her to die where she wanted to die, right in her own bed, in her own house, on the farm that had been her life for more than seventy years?

I rose up off the floor, a darkness clouding over me like I'd never known before, a deep, searing hurt that soaked through me like oil. "She prayed to you, God," I said aloud, startled at the raspiness of my voice. "Why would you let this happen?"

My hands were like ice, and it was no help at all trying to rub a little warmth into my stiff arms. *It's so cold*, I thought. *At least there won't be much change to the bodies by the time someone finds us. Maybe I'll be dead by then too.*

I thought of George, still out there somewhere. He was the one who might be dead, and truly. Maybe I should've looked for him. Maybe I should've run over to Samuel, or somewhere, last night, trying to get help. Maybe there was something I could've done to save somebody. But now there were children to face. Children. *Oh, God, why?*

I pulled on my coat, not knowing why I hadn't thought of that before. I'd been sitting half froze, with blankets and my coat just a few feet away. And there was wood outside, surely. George would have a stock of it somewhere. The barn, maybe.

Through the window I saw that it was snowing, and I wanted to curse. I didn't do it, but having the feeling shook me. I used to think I was strong. Even after losing our home in Pennsylvania and all we had, I'd managed to be all right. I'd felt God's protective hand. But this was different. Wilametta's was a senseless, premature death. Like my mother, so long ago. But Wila had left ten needy souls behind her, not just one. It brought tears to my eyes again, thinking especially of Rorey, who was about the size I was when I'd heard the news of my own mother. And then there was Emma. An angel on earth. If this could happen to her, then anything could happen. Lord have mercy.

I couldn't leave till someone came. I couldn't leave Emma here, even in death. But I knew I should look for George. Emma would want me to. I had daylight now if I had nothing else, and I could get to the barn at least, just to see if he might've gone there. At least I'd know that much.

But it was a terrifying thought, knowing there might be another body to face. Or he might just be gone, never to be found. What would I tell his children then? Might they look at me forever as the one who'd been here, the one who might've done something to make a difference but didn't? I couldn't think of anything I could've done differently, and yet I'd failed. Utterly and desperately.

I buttoned my coat, forgetting the hat and scarf that lay at the top of my bag. I'd never taken off the boots, the only pair Emma had kept two of. She'd said they were so nice they ought to be shared. I turned and looked at the door that separated me from the sight of her and Wila. I thought of them here, just this summer, enjoying sassafras together while Emma looked over Emma Grace with a smile. So much they'd shared. And they were still sharing, even now.

With the deepest breath I could muster out of lungs that felt like lead, I turned and shoved the outer door open. It wasn't as windy as it had been, but it was cold, and the snow was heavy again, piling on top of all that was already there. Barren, frigid wasteland as far as the eye could see. Quiet as the death that encompassed it. It seemed as if a spell had been cast over this place that had always before been boisterous enough to make a body tired.

My legs were like jelly. Pushing them through the drifts of snow was a torture. But the barn stood only a stone's throw before me, pale as the sky. I started shaking inside as I neared it.

"Mr. Hammond?"

I might as well have been talking to the wind. My voice just spilled out over the snow-flaked sky and went on endless without response.

"Mr. Hammond!"

Lord, have mercy. Lord, send Samuel to me. It's too late for the doctor. Oh, dear God, please send Samuel.

The barn door was open just a crack, and snow was blowing in. I had to squeeze myself through the opening because it was froze in place and there was no budging it. With some relief I heard the shuffle of animal hooves. I'd almost expected to find the place ghostly empty or filled with the dead, frozen bodies of George Hammond's forsaken stock.

I edged over the straw-strewn floor, looking in on three pigs in one stall and a big billy goat in another.

"Mr. Hammond?"

There was firewood along one wall, standing nearly as high as my head. More pigs were grunting from somewhere nearby, and I could smell them now too. That was the only thing that seemed familiar here. The only thing that hadn't changed.

The pigs started in squealing, and I figured that seeing me brought them the hope of breakfast. But I didn't know where the feed was, and I had other things pressing on me. Slowly I peeked in every stall, steeling myself the best I could for whatever I might find.

A sleek, gray barn cat peered up at me from a hole in the floor, a mutilated mouse dangling precariously from her jaws. Somewhere a cow was calling, and then another, and then the first one again. I sought them out, following the sound to the south end of the barn, where I could finally see old Rosey with her head down to the hay. There were at least half a dozen goats in with her, and a younger cow. This was the largest enclosure of the barn, and only a wire fence and a crooked unlatched gate separated me from the animals.

I put the hook in place when the goats started crowding toward the fence, pushing their noses at me, hoping for a treat. There was a stack of hay in one corner, but they ignored it to gather around me, all but Rosey and one little nanny goat that stood busily licking away at something I couldn't quite see. I almost turned away, but the nanny raised her head, and I could see then what she found so interesting. A boot. An old, brown, man's boot, well worn and patched.

George Hammond's. Sure as I was standing. Fear clutched at my throat so tight I could hardly breathe. I couldn't see but the bottom and one side of the boot sticking out from the edge of the hay. If he was in it, he was lying still.

I forced the gate open and pushed my way through the goats. The beasts kept on crowding me, getting in my way, and I shoved at them and hit one right between the ears, my eyes blurring and my breath coming in short, hard gasps. I couldn't call out to him now. I was too afraid, even at this distance, that there'd be no answer.

George was in the boot. Backed up in the hay with Rosey standing over him like a protective mother, a pair of goats cuddled at his chest and the nanny now nudging at his knees. He was blue with cold. I was afraid to touch him and couldn't help thinking of Joe, how he'd looked running to our house just yesterday, scared and urgent. I hadn't had the sense then to be worried for him. I hadn't had the faintest inkling.

Then George moved, just the slightest bit. Rosey leaned her nose down to him, but I pushed at her and fell down on my knees at his side. He opened his eyes and looked at me, but it wasn't him, really. Not the same as he'd been. He looked empty.

"Mr. Hammond, can you get up?"

He closed his eyes and turned his face away from me.

"Mr. Hammond! You have to get up! You have to come in the house!"

"No." He shook his head. "I can't."

"You have to!" I screamed, all of my anger pouring out at him. I grabbed at his icy arm and gave him a mighty pull. "You have to! You're gonna die if you don't! And one of your sons is gonna find you laying here and wonder why you wouldn't even try!"

He opened his eyes, and for a minute I thought he was going to come to himself. But he shook his head again, his voice now as cold and horrible as his touch. "Get away from me." He shoved me back against Rosey's leg, and she stepped away from us. The goats were crowding in again, and he let them. I pushed them back.

"Mr. Hammond, you got ten kids to think about! You're cold as ice. You got to get to the house. You got to."

I tried to grasp his arm again, but he pulled it away from me. "I can't go in there. Don't you unnerstand? I can't."

I stood. One goat came nibbling at my skirt, and the nanny commenced to licking at George's boot again. He curled his legs up to him, shivering. I could see that it wasn't his right mind, this thing that had hold on him. It wasn't his right mind to stay out here in the hay with the goats and the cows, despairing of life.

"Wilametta didn't ask to leave you this way," I told him. "She wouldn't want you just giving up."

"Get away from me."

He looked hard, vicious, and I knew he'd shove me again if I tried to touch him. There was nothing I could do to make him get up. I couldn't wrestle a man bigger than me and carry him in the house. I couldn't convince him, not with my rational talk. He was half crazed or more, whether from the grief or the cold or both, and not even looking on me as a friend.

But I couldn't let him die. I couldn't just wait around till somebody got through, and then tell them where to find one more frozen body. Not one more.

I'd get his coat. I realized then I should've carried it with me to the barn. I should've known I might've found him in here and he'd be needing it. Stupid, that's what I was. Stupid. But I couldn't make any more mistakes. Not now. George Hammond was all they had left.

I'd bring blankets too. Even if he wouldn't get up, they'd feel so good he wouldn't refuse them. I'd bring every blanket I could find, and his coat. I'd get a fire blazing again and heat him some coffee or something to warm his insides. I'd make him come to himself. God help me, I'd make him see.

I turned to the rickety gate, but the other cow was standing right in front of it. Two goats were trying to nibble at my skirt now, and I swatted them both away. I squeezed by the cow, and she stuck her nose against my neck and made me jump.

I ran out of the barn and into the snow, picking up my feet high in the drifts. But my boot stuck in one, and I fell face down in the snow and stayed there for a moment, stunned. *Oh, God, it would be so easy just to lay here, do nothing, and die.* It would be easy, but it wouldn't be right.

I got myself up with tears cold on my face and pushed on to the house. I was nearly inside before it dawned on me that I should've been carrying in a load of firewood as I came. Stupid. Stupid. People dying on me and all I could be was stupid. I grabbed George's coat off the floor and the blanket that was draped on the sitting room chair. I looked around the room. I should have another blanket. Maybe two. There were those in Wilametta's room. But no. There would be more in the loft.

I went up the ladder quickly. The loft was nothing much but bedding all over the floor. I grabbed the two closest blankets and hurried back down, too fast. One of the blankets caught under my foot and I fell, hard, from the second rung. Devil be hanged, I wasn't going to stop though. I wrestled myself up off the floor, grabbed those blankets and George's coat, and tore outside.

Right away I slid off the bottom porch step and into a drift. But I wouldn't yield to this either. I wasn't going to lose again. I wasn't going to give up and die or just stay here and bawl. I picked myself up all over again, brushed the snow off the blankets, and hurried as fast as I could back to Mr. Hammond.

He hadn't moved an inch. And just like I'd thought, he didn't refuse the coat or the blankets I tucked around him. I asked him again to come in, but he only shook his head. So I told him I'd be right back, and headed for the firewood. If he'd drink something warm, maybe it'd help him. Maybe he'd look different on things and come and get warm by the fire. I'd have to get some heat in the cookstove and fireplace both. Get the house real warm again in case he came in. He'd have to eventually. He'd have to face Wilametta in that back room and then go on with the life he had ahead of him.

I went and fed the coals in the cookstove first and put on water to heat. Then I got the fireplace going, and it looked like life in this place again. I thought maybe I should make more than coffee. Maybe I should cut up some of those potatoes for a broth. George would need his strength.

He'd need all the strength he could get to go over the timber and tell his children.

Nobody could come by the road; I was resigned to that. But somebody determined enough could get out on foot. I'd prayed for Samuel to come, but now I prayed he wouldn't. He had all the children over there to look after; he couldn't just leave them alone. And it wouldn't be right to send any of them out in this either. It was just getting worse. Thank God, at least, that last night's crazy wind had gone.

I carried in two more loads of wood, checking on George both times just to make sure he was still under the blankets. Snowflakes as big as my thumb floated down like they'd been asked for. *How ironic,* I thought. *After the dry summer, we'd prayed for Christmas snow, and now here it is. But Christmas. Oh, Lord. At such a time as this.*

I was peeling potatoes into a pot when the knife slipped into my finger. Seeing the red, oozing line of blood, I broke down. I'd come here to help, but everything I did was worthless. I was falling apart, bleeding onto George Hammond's potatoes. If it was me dead, only me, it would be so much better. Everybody would be all right. I got the blood stopped and made myself still stand there, though my knees felt like buckling clear to the floor. I made myself stand there and finish those potatoes with my tears dripping down. Emma wouldn't quit. Emma would be strong enough to do what needed done without complaining. Even Wila would rise to the occasion. They were so much better than me. They were so . . . so . . .

Gone. Just gone. And nobody else in this world even knew it.

It was too much. I dropped the knife on the countertop and looked behind me to the Bible I'd so irreverently left on the floor by the fire. Psalm 46. That's what Emma had wanted. For the first time I wondered why.

"God is our refuge and strength, a very present help in trouble . . ."

I read it out loud as though there were anxious throngs waiting just to hear.

"We will not fear, though the earth be removed . . ."

Tears clouded my eyes, and I could not read on. As I hugged the book to my chest, I cried for the dear soul who'd given me these words in her last moments. God was still here, somewhere, even in the pain that tore through me and the despair that clutched at my heart. Some way, his way, he would make things right again.

SIX

Samuel

I couldn't make syrup the way Julia did, so I served pancakes with the blackberry jelly she and Emma had made over the summer. The younger boys would've kept me busy a long time making more, but Joe was anxious to get going, and I didn't want another Hammond son going out alone. So Lizbeth took over flipping the pancakes while Sarah and Rorey played with the baby. And I piled on layers of shirts, my gloves, and Robert's hat, hoping that Sam Hammond, who had my coat, was warm and safe somewhere.

I told Lizbeth we'd be back by noontime, maybe with Juli if Wila was feeling better. I told Robert to keep a special eye on Harry, who was hardly ever in one place more than half a minute straight. I could see how that boy alone could weary Wilametta or Lizbeth, or both. But his older brothers paid him almost no attention.

Harry was out the door twice in the time it took me to button my top shirt, the heavy double flannel I'd used for a fall jacket. I pulled him off the porch rail, and he kicked me and told me he was a wild Indian on a horse and I couldn't stop him with all the soldiers in the county.

"Scoot into your teepee," I told him. "And stay out of the weather till you've got extra leggings."

He laughed. "I'll go upstairs. It's a mountain. And you can't climb it."

"Fine."

Sarah came to the door for a hug. I thought at first she was going to protest me going, but she was still wrapped up in the fun of having her best friend overnight. "Tell Mama we're playin' school today," she said. "Me an' Rorey is taking turns bein' teacher." I smiled and nodded, and she made me promise to give Juli a kiss from her.

Franky asked to come along, and Joe adamantly refused to let him. I had to agree, though I felt sorry for poor Franky. He was the only one taking our departure gravely, except maybe Lizbeth, but she was so busy with a houseful of kids around her that it was hard to tell.

"Tell Pa I didn't mean to break the clock," he whispered to me.

"I doubt he's fretting over a clock today, son."

He shrugged, doubting my words and still stewing. I could see it in his eyes. "Help your big sister," I said. Then I turned to Kirk, the oldest of the boys that would be left. "You too."

"I need water in," Lizbeth said. "Gonna have to boil the diapers I brung and hang 'em by the fire. All right with you, Mr. Wortham, if I use a dishtowel to put Emma Grace in till the others is dry?"

"Do what you need to. I'll get some more from your mother while we're over there."

"Ain't many clean," she admitted. "I was fixin' to wash yesterday."

I wondered what Juli would think of diapering the baby with dishtowels. Probably wouldn't bother her. She was always making do. I tried to think if there'd be anything they'd need from over here, but I couldn't figure what it might be. So we left, Joe Hammond and me, making just as quick of tracks as we could into the timber.

It wasn't long before I realized that most of the landmarks I knew in these woods were covered in snow. I might've gotten lost if Joe hadn't known his way so well. He never wavered from his direction, just pressed on through the drifts, and I did my best to keep up.

More snow was fluttering down on our faces, and I groaned inside, thinking of the long wait they'd surely had for the doctor, and were probably still having. Coming clear from Belle Rive by the road, the doctor would encounter even more difficulty getting through than we were having, if he'd attempted to venture out at all.

The pond lay buried and invisible, and I wouldn't even have known it was there if Joe hadn't pointed out the top corner of Willard Graham's grave marker on the hill above it. About then, the snow stopped coming down. Joe pulled his coat tight and hurried even faster. *Lord, may it warm enough to start things melting, may the doctor have a sleigh, or better still, may Wilametta have no need of him now.*

It was almost spooky when we finally broke through the trees into the Hammonds' field. The house and all the outbuildings stuck up from the drifts, stark and gray, as if they were features of the nature-claimed landscape, hugged in by the snow. The place looked like it had been long abandoned, silent as the timber we'd passed through.

"Pa must've fed the stock already, or they'd be bellerin'," Joe whispered. Somehow he sensed it right to whisper, as though out of respect for the silence that lay around us. "We oughta check the barn first, though, jus' to be sure.

Pa won't mind me comin' if he knowed it was for chores first thing."

The closer we got to the big old barn, the tighter I felt in my stomach. I turned my eyes to the house, hoping we'd find the best of news. There was just a thin trail of smoke out the chimney and what looked like tracks in the snow on the front steps. George had surely come out and fed the stock, just as Joe said. But then we heard the pigs start up squealing, loud and deliberate.

"Shoot," Joe said. He stopped in his tracks for the first time, and I could see his eyes turn to the house. He looked a man already, standing there with the worry drawing his face tight. He didn't say another word, but he didn't have to. If his father hadn't fed those pigs yet, pigs he prized, there had to be some reason, and it couldn't be good.

I more than half expected Joe to run for the house. But he kept himself moving straight to the barn. It was a strong thing for him to do. He was just a kid, but with one decision he was more a man, taking on himself what needed to be done.

He went straight for the hogs, pulling a bucket down off a hook on the wall and filling it full of corn from a huge barrel. "You ever milk goats?" he asked me.

"No."

"Well, there's two to do, plus old Rosey. I'd thank ya to take one of 'em."

I didn't know why I didn't go on to the house. Joe knew far better than I did what to do out here and would've managed without me. But I didn't want to leave him; I knew it wouldn't be right. And he didn't seem to want me to, either. He was going to need my help with something more than milking, I knew that in my spirit somehow. Strong as he was, he was still a kid.

We found George in with the milk cow, wrapped in blankets and with three goats snuggled against him. He was staring up at the rafters, blue with cold.

Joe dropped his feed bucket and ran to him. "Pa! What you doin' out here?"

George wasn't of a right mind. I could tell it. He didn't even look at Joe, didn't blink his eyes.

"Let me alone, boy," he said, his voice raspy. "Ain't nothin' you can do."

"You sick, Pa?"

No answer. George shut his eyes and didn't help in the slightest when Joe tried to lift him. I leaned to help, and we finally got him to a sitting position but had to hold him. He couldn't, or wouldn't, stay up on his own.

"C'mon, Pa. We gotta get you inside."

He didn't look at either of us. He just said no, plain as day and incredible as snow in the summertime.

"What do you mean, no?" I asked him. "You can't stay out here."

But my words sounded hollow. Obviously he'd been here quite a while, cold as he was. He'd decided to be, planned to be, heaven knows why. George wasn't brilliant, but he wasn't out of his head normally, either. What had happened to drive him out here and befuddle his brain? I felt squeezed inside thinking of Juli. Did Wilametta have some contagion? Was he staying out to be clear of it?

Joe was trying to lift again, and I cleared my head of those thoughts to help him. It couldn't be that. If Wilametta was contagious, it was too late for him to stay away. He and all the kids had been exposed long before this, so then every one of us would've been, and it wouldn't make a bit of difference.

"George," I told him straight, "we're taking you to the house whether you like it or not. It's too blame cold out here."

One on one side and one on the other, we pulled him to his feet, but he jerked his arm away from Joe and slammed it into me like a club. We fell together into the pile of hay, and I rolled and grabbed hold of him by both arms.

"You listen to me!" I yelled. I was aware of Joe standing over us, eyes wide and scared. George looked up into my face, and what I saw scared me too. He was like a shell, empty inside, worn and wasted and void of hope. Something was dead in him. Dead. And I knew.

"Pa?" Joe's voice was broken. "What's happened? What're you doin' out here?"

He didn't say "How's Ma?" He didn't ask anything more. He just stood there, looking almost like his father, pale and lean, his jaw set tense and his eyes washed with worry.

"Regardless of anything that's happened," I told them both, "we have to get to the house. George, I mean to take you if we have to carry you. Don't fight me."

He shook his head. "I can't go."

"You have to. I'm sorry, but you have to. You're ice cold, and it's a blessing of God your boy insisted on coming over here. You got your family to think about. You stay out here like this, you're gonna freeze to death."

I pulled him up out of the hay, and he didn't fight me. "Bring the blankets, Joe."

I managed to get George to his feet, but he could barely stand. He was bigger than me. Too big for me to carry alone, truth be told. But I could hold him up and half drag him and get the job done. Joe got on the other side, the blankets all bundled up under his other arm.

The trail to the house was a sorry one. It was plain to see where somebody had fallen in the snow and left a chunk of wood behind. Juli, surely. God help her. By the porch steps it looked like she'd fallen again. I could see a handprint in the snow on the bottom step, still clear even after more snow had fallen. And then I noticed the crook end of one of Emma's canes on the porch, nearly buried in snow. Why on earth would she go out? Why on earth would Juli let her?

The door opened abruptly, and there stood Juli, no hat, no gloves, a steaming cup in her hand. She saw me, she saw George, and she made one choked little sound and went back in just long enough to set the cup down. She came rushing out, tears in her eyes, and took all the blankets from Joe's arms. I thought she was going to say something when her sad, green eyes met mine, but she didn't. She just got out of our way and held the door so we could get George into the house.

"Thank God you've come," she finally told us as we propped George in a chair by the fire. "I couldn't get him in by myself." She spread one of the blankets over him and hurried to retrieve the cup. George wouldn't hold it, so she handed it to me when she saw Joe on his way to the closed bedroom door.

"Wait." She took his arm and pulled him back toward the fire. For just a second, she glanced at me again, and I saw the pain in her like it was in George, stark and huge. But there was no void in Juli. She was filled with something I hadn't seen in her before. Some kind of deep, consuming resolve.

"Joey, your mama was talking about heaven yesterday."

He hung his head for a minute and then stared back at the bedroom door.

George clamped his eyes shut, suddenly shaking.

"She was assured of it," Juli continued. "She would want you to know that."

Joe's mouth dropped open, and he stared at his father. "You can't tell me she's gone. She wouldn't a' died! She weren't that bad, was she?"

Juli reached for my hand, and I set the cup down.

"Last night, Joey," Juli said gently. "Past suppertime. She was real bad. But she was peaceful. She went on home."

Joe took straight for the door again, but Juli grabbed his arm as she had before, and I went with her, wanting to

74

hold her and wipe away the tears that coursed down her cheeks. "Oh, Joe, I'm so sorry," she said. "We did all we knew. We sent for the doctor. Emma did her best, but—but . . ."

Joe reached his hand to the doorknob. Juli couldn't stop him. She knew she couldn't, but she wasn't finished. "Oh, Joey! Sammy! Emma's—Emma's . . ."

Joe pulled the door open and just stood there. I could feel the cold draft of that room; I could see both of them lying there. My breath stopped. I couldn't imagine what Joe must be feeling.

In a moment he rushed forward and collapsed at the side of the bed.

I started to move toward the room, but a voice behind me stopped me short.

"Leave him be," George commanded. "Leave him be."

I could see the boy's shoulders sag and heave, and I knew he was weeping now. But George, so far from a decent state himself, was right. There was precious little any of us could do for Joe but let him grieve. I took Juli in my arms, and she seemed to break. She felt so small.

"Sammy, I'm so glad you came, but what about the kids?"

I kissed her smooth, brown hair, held her tight. But I looked past her, feeling numb on my feet. I'd known. With Wila I'd known. And miserable as it was, there'd have been some way to manage it. But Emma too! It was like taking the very world away. Nothing would ever be the same.

SEVEN

Julia

We didn't want to go. We didn't want to leave Joey in the cold horror of that house with his father so distraught he hadn't moved from the chair we put him in. There was life in George's body, plenty of it. He was a tough one, tough enough to withstand a night in the cold barn without even frostbite. Warmed by the fire, he might've seemed like himself again if it weren't for his eyes. Soulless they looked. Bottomless. It scared me to look into them now, as if they were a pit that I might fall into and not arise from. I knew I had to get out of here. I had to get back to those vibrant children, even if I was the bearer of such news that would tear their little hearts. But George would not come. And Joey, once he left the bedside and shut the door behind him, would not leave his father's side.

"You go," he told us. "I'll stay in case the doctor comes. Got the chores to finish too."

He clutched Samuel's arm with urgency. Fear. And I knew in my heart what he hadn't said. The doctor didn't matter, the chores didn't even matter so much now as his father did. He was staying because someone must, to make sure George was still here when we got back, to make sure he didn't do something stupid again in the desolate state he was in.

George said nothing to us, not even when Samuel asked him who we needed to reach with word of this. He didn't even seem to hear. He just stared at the fire, his tight jaw quivering.

"The preacher," Joey said after his father's long pause. "He'll know what to do."

He took my hand for just a moment, a gesture I couldn't begin to understand. He wouldn't look at me plainly, and it was just as well, because I wasn't sure if I could have stood it anyway.

Samuel wanted to carry me back over their boot-tracked trail through the woods, but I wouldn't let him. He tried to get me to talk, but I wouldn't do that either. I knew Emma would want me to talk about heaven right now and keep talking about it like it was the most joyous occasion any of us could imagine. But I was failing her and failing Samuel too. He was so worried about me, he was barely paying any attention to where he was going. He held my arm, and I could feel his eyes on me almost the whole time. But I wouldn't look at him. I didn't want to break down and cry again. I didn't want my face to be all red and puffy when we stepped foot back home. Maybe I couldn't be strong for Samuel. But I'd have to hold it together for the kids. I couldn't fail them too.

We marched on through the snow, and I realized suddenly that Sammy was talking, so soft I could barely hear him. He'd taken to praying so much in the past few months. And he was praying again. For me. Almost I stopped and whirled on him. Almost I shouted that he had no right, no right to decide that I of all people needed his prayers, or deserved them! He should be praying for Joey, for George, for the children we had to face. He should be praying for their futures. For their sad little hearts about to be shattered into a thousand pieces. Oh, Lord, and Christmas just around the corner!

I couldn't say any of it. He was right to be praying at all. I knew that. Sure as I'd read Emma's psalm not even an hour ago. God was our refuge, our strength. Even in this. But I wasn't comforted, thinking about Rorey and Harry and Bert. I wasn't joyful that Emma's days of weak heart and wheelchair were over.

They were gone too soon, both of them. Emma away from her beloved home. And Wila while she still had a baby yearning for her breast. My heart warred with my mind about it. Knowing God as good, I was still shaken by the unfairness of it all. How could he—he who controls the universe—let this happen?

"Juli?" Samuel's voice was as cautious as I'd ever heard it. "Honey, I'll have to go on to the Posts to get the word out. Ought to ask him to keep his eye out for Sam Hammond too, I think, and the doctor. I'll be right back as soon as I can. Might have to go and see about George after that. Didn't want to leave you there. You need to be with the children right now."

I thought of Sarah, and tears filled my eyes again. She was only six and loved Emma as dearly as if the woman had been her own grandma. I couldn't imagine how she'd react, couldn't picture it for all the world. And she was only one of ten there waiting.

Walking into that house and telling those children would be the hardest thing I'd ever do in all my life. I knew it. I hadn't the strength for the task. Emma'd been wrong about that. God was wrong. This was just plain too much.

It was just how you might picture it. They heard us coming before we got in the door, and every last one of them was in the kitchen waiting for the word I'd bring them. Samuel squeezed my hand, and I knew he was about to talk, to say the things I needed to say. But I couldn't let him. Not yet. Not till I'd told them everything I could think to tell about heaven. That's what Emma would've wanted. Wilametta too.

But Franky had hold of my arm already, and Lizbeth didn't wait two shakes before asking about her mother. Lord, how she suddenly looked like Wila, though I'd never thought it before, Lizbeth being so much skinnier.

"Mama, I missed you!" Little Sarah ran up and threw her arms around me. Her best friend, Rorey, stood beside her, her dark eyes looking up at me in question. And I almost lost it. I was weak from the walk and the worry and the pain. Samuel got me a chair, and I wondered if he knew just how badly I needed it then.

"What's wrong?" Lizbeth pressed. And I knew I couldn't hold back anything from them. They could read me like the Marion newspaper, and I had precious little time to touch them with a shred of the glory that Emma had wanted. Maybe, maybe, they would forgive me if I started with her.

"You all know how Emma talked so much about Jesus and the things of God?"

"Yes, ma'am," Kirk answered for all of them, looking painful fierce.

Bert tried to climb on to my lap but slid back down. Sarah and Franky were flanking my sides so close they hardly left him any room.

"She told me to tell you something. She wanted me to say that heaven is a beautiful, endless place where no one is ever sick. People who have struggled with pain or sorrow don't have to struggle anymore, because in heaven they're whole and happy and all of their needs are supplied."

All of the children waited, surely wondering what I was going to say next and why. Except Lizbeth, who was turning white as a new lamb. Baby Emma Grace wailed from somewhere in the house, but Lizbeth didn't move to fetch her. She looked frail, young as a baby herself, not half able to take on all that was left to her. *Oh, George!* I lamented in my heart. *You're going to have to find your will! You'll have to be strong, because this poor, dear soul can't carry all the mothering Wila left behind!*

"Children, you know Emma's been sick a long time," I told them, hoping I could tell all before any of them managed another question. I wasn't sure what I would do, what I would say, if they did. "She told us months ago she'd be moving on, and she was right. Emma passed on last night. She's in heaven now."

I could see the fear fall away from Lizbeth, and Kirk too. But Sarah was struck hard. Tears were soon streaming down her face. I put my arm around my baby girl, wishing I could comfort her proper, but the rest of them were still staring at me, stunned and silent and only knowing half. I looked at the boys' faces. Willy and Kirk. Franky, who'd melted to tears like Sarah. And the little ones, Harry and Bert, who scarcely understood. My own eldest, Robert, had turned his face to his father. And Samuel, seeming to understand the mission before him, spread his comforting arms not only around his own son but three of the Hammonds as well.

"What about Mama?" It was Franky asking, somehow looking like a ghost, his face nearly as drawn and hollow as his father's.

I tried to take a breath, but it wouldn't come. I made myself keep looking at them, knowing that what I was about to say would tear their little hearts apart. "Your mama was very sick too." I tried, oh, I tried to keep my voice steady for their sakes. "She loved every one of you. I know she did. We wanted her to get better, but she—she couldn't—"

"No!" Lizbeth screamed. Somewhere Emma Grace was wailing, louder now, as if she too had heard.

"She ain't dead," Kirk said. It was the same reaction his father'd had, and I feared lest he too might disappear out the door in despair. But he wasn't minded to let me off so easily. "You tell us!" he demanded, his face torn with a fierce, raw anger. "You tell us she ain't dead!"

Like the kick of a horse or the impact of a cannonball, the pain knocked away what little air I had left, and it was all I could do to draw in enough air to answer him. "I can't. I—I can't tell you that, because she's with Emma. They're not hurting anymore. They—they both passed on—last night . . ."

Lizbeth sunk to the floor, and I couldn't tell if she'd fainted or not. Willy and Kirk both took off in the direction of the baby's cry, but the crying didn't stop. Pretty soon I heard the footsteps of at least one of them going up the stairs. Rorey and Sarah were next to each other, next to me, both crying now. And Samuel had taken Harry and Bert, who both looked utterly lost, into his arms.

It was Robert who finally went and got the baby and brought her to me. His eyes met mine as he set the child on my lap. It was a terrible thing, to see all the pain and uncertainty alive in him again. I could see the question in his eyes. *What will become of us now?*

I had no answer. I hugged at little Emma Grace, nuzzled her soft hair with my face and cried. Not until I heard Kirk slamming something against the wall in the next room did I realize that it was Franky, quiet, backward Franky, who had disappeared.

Samuel wouldn't leave until the boy was found. We searched everywhere, and finally we found him outside in the filthy, frozen crawl space under the porch. He wasn't crying anymore. But he wouldn't move. Samuel had to haul him out by one leg and carry him back inside.

Samuel hated to leave me then, I knew he did, but I made him go. The sooner he got to Barrett Post's place down the road, the sooner he could get back again, and the sooner he could check on George and Joe, maybe get them over here with their family where they belonged.

There was so much to think about, but I could barely manage to think at all. The preacher would come when the weather allowed. And all the church folk. And Albert. Oh, Lord, we'd have to send word to Emma's nephew Albert, her nearest of kin. I shuddered thinking about what she'd told me. Don't let him sell the land. Don't let him make the Hammonds move. But who was I to stop him? If Albert hadn't gotten Emma's intentions set forth legal as she'd asked of him, there'd be nothing I could do. Albert Graham could throw us all out on our ears, despite her wishes. I wondered if Samuel had thought of that.

He kissed my cheek before he left and whispered he was sorry, as if there were anything his fault about all this. I wanted to curl up someplace, cover my head and hide, but I knew I couldn't. Kirk was still angry, mostly at me it seemed, and furious now too that Samuel hadn't let him go with him. He yelled at Rorey for crying like a baby, at Robert for picking up his little sister, and at Lizbeth for letting him do it. I was hoping he would calm down and offer some support to his brothers, but for the time being he ignored them all to glare at me.

"You were supposed to help her," he said. "You went over there to help her."

"We tried." That was all I could tell him. "We did everything we could. We even sent for the doctor, but he couldn't get through for the snow."

Lizbeth was wiping her eyes and looking around at all of us.

"You oughta get the kids' coats," Kirk told her. "We need to be gettin' home."

"No," Lizbeth insisted. "Pa told us to come here, and we ain't leavin' till he tells us differ'nt. You know better. He'll come for us when we's supposed to come."

"Maybe not." It didn't sound like Kirk now. It didn't even look like him. He gave a glance toward Franky, who was sunk now against the pantry door. I knew how his little brother needed his help. Needed somebody's help, but Kirk just stood there as if paralyzed. And here I sat, the baby on my knee and four other young ones crowded around me.

"Let me take her," Lizbeth suddenly offered. "Prob'ly due for changin'." She leaned to claim Emma Grace from my arms but turned her face away from me at the same time. Little Berty grabbed hold of her clothes with a shriek, and Harry plunked his thumb in his mouth and stood there looking bewildered. I would've gone to Franky, who had bowed his head clear to the floor, but before I could get up, Rorey climbed on me. She buried her face into my blouse as Sarah clung tight to my arm. It was too much without Samuel here. Too much grief. Too many to comfort.

Franky let out with a wail, sudden and piercing. It nearly stopped my heart from beating. Clutching the baby tight, Lizbeth turned and looked at him, herself as white as lily root. Bert was bellowing loud now, but Franky got strangely quiet. Rorey was quivering in my arms, and Sarah stood looking at me and biting away at her lower lip. It was Harry that finally walked over and sat down next to Frank. With one thumb still in his mouth, he put his other little hand gently on his brother's back and just sat there.

"Get Berty, Kirk," Lizbeth commanded. "I gotta change and feed this baby." She wiped at her face with one sleeve and turned to me with a look of utter dismay. "Oh, land! Mrs. Wortham, did your husband remember the diapers? The others ain't dry yet."

"Diapers?"

She didn't have to answer. I knew her predicament. The poor child had been sent off in a hurry unprepared, and she was still unprepared. Numb or not, I had to roust myself out of the gloom that was swallowing me up inside. There was so awful much to do just to get these kids through a day of normal living, and I had to do for them. Emma was right in what she had told me. I had to help them all through this. It might be a while before George was able.

"I used a dishtowel already," Lizbeth told me, her eyes near closed and puffy. "I hope you don't mind."

"We'll use another one for now, and I'll cut that old linen cover for you." I stood, pulling Sarah and Rorey along with me. "You girls want to help? Bert, you come too. You want to help me measure?"

Of course, it was far from a practical notion, asking a three-year-old to do any measuring, but at least I could pull him off Lizbeth for a while and get him to quit his bawling. He was looking at me like he was suddenly afraid of his shadow, but at least he was quieter. I looked over at Harry and Frank but decided it best to let them be.

Robert had gone upstairs, presumably after Willy, his best friend, and I thought it better to leave that alone too. Kirk was watching me with his angry eyes as I grabbed one of Emma's old dishtowels for Lizbeth and began to lead the little girls into the other room.

"Do you suppose we ought to start some lunch before long?" I asked him, hoping to find a way to enlist his help. That's about the only thing I could think of right then—get them all busy at something.

"I doubt anybody bein' hungry," he said. "Ain't nothin' you can do to make things all right, Mrs. Wortham. No sense even tryin'."

"We have to try," I countered. "We have to do something."

I scooted Rorey and Sarah and Berty into Emma's bedroom while Lizbeth went to change the baby. I hated being in Emma's room; it rubbed me raw inside to see her empty wheelchair by the window, the pretty, hand-sewn quilt on the bed, the little silver bell and all of the other treasures on her dresser. But the sewing things were in here, and all the extra cloth things in the house were on a shelf in Emma's closet.

Blinking away tears, I reached the scissors and measuring tape out of Emma's woven sewing basket and pulled down the heavy linen sheet that she had told me once would make decent tea towels. I gently spread it across her bed and asked the girls to smooth the corners. I could barely see what I was doing, but I knew I'd have to be all business and find a way to keep them from breaking down all at once again.

I let Bert unroll the cloth measuring tape and had Sarah fetch me straight pins, and then I measured out four squares, letting Rorey read off the numbers. She was still trembling, looking at me with eyes deeper than Willard's pond, surely wondering what I would do next. What any of them would do next.

I marked the squares with straight pins and started cutting.

"Mama was real sick," Rorey said so softly I could barely hear her.

"Yes, honey."

"I holded her hand."

"I remember. I bet she was real glad of it too."

"Will we ever see her anymore?" Her lip quivered when she said it, and I looked at Berty. He was wrapping himself up in the tape measure but watching us at the same time.

"Yes. Yes, honey, we will. She's waiting up in heaven now for the day when you and all the rest will join her there. You'll see her again, and it'll be a joyous good time."

"Will it be a long time?" Sarah asked me.

"I don't know. Nobody really knows."

"I wish we could all die," Rorey proclaimed. "Right now, and go and see Mama."

Berty suddenly banged his head against the hard wood at the foot of Emma's bed. At first I thought it was an accident. But then he did it again. And again. "Mama," he muttered. "Mama."

I dropped the scissors and picked him up. He clung to my neck so tight it hurt. But his little legs were kicking at me just the same. The poor thing didn't know what he wanted. He just knew that for some terrible reason things were not the same. Emma Grace was wailing in the other room as if she knew it too. I tried to look at his forehead to see if he'd done it any real damage, but he kept his head ducked and wouldn't let me see.

Suddenly I heard the back door open, and for a minute my heart leaped with relief, thinking it might be my husband. But it was far too soon. With Bert still in my arms, I rushed to the kitchen. Harry was leaning his head down against Frank now, who hadn't moved a solitary inch. But I saw the blur of a head out the window and rushed to open the door.

"Kirk!"

He was standing in the yard in his coat, his whole face red and his fists clenched as if he were ready to fight me. "I'm goin' home."

"Please, Kirk. I need you here a while. Your brothers and sisters need you here."

"They need their mama! Or at least their pa! I'm gonna fetch him to get us home. We don't belong up here no longer. You ain't workin' down there no more!"

I'd have to talk to him like he was a man. There was no other way around it. "Your father's grievin'. He'll be up here when he's able. And Joe's over there to help him. At least till my husband or your brother Sam gets back, I need you to help me. You're the oldest boy here."

The anger drained away from his face. "Sammy ain't home?"

I hadn't given that a minute of thought. But we had no way of knowing how far Sam Hammond had gotten in the storm, or where he was. Lord have mercy. Such a thing to worry Kirk with now.

"He's probably in Belle Rive," I suggested. "Or with the doctor on the way. It's so much slower going with all this snow."

"All night, and he didn't come back?"

"He probably got to town and was stuck there till this morning. He might—"

"Shut up! You don't know! You don't know nothin'!"

In my arms, Berty started bawling again. He was hearing too much, little as he was, and he didn't know how to handle any of it.

"Did Mama go peaceful?" Kirk suddenly asked, his voice cracking just slightly.

"Yes. She was peaceful. She asked me for a hymn last night. She told your father how much she loved him. And she loved all of you too."

Kirk was quiet for a moment, standing there in the snow, and I hugged Berty closer, knowing I should take him back in. But I didn't want to go yet, not without his older brother.

Kirk was only twelve, too young to take on the business of what had to be done. But he was thinking along those lines anyway. "That hymn you did," he asked me solemnly. "When it comes time for the buryin', would you do it for her again?"

I only nodded. There was no way I could talk.

His fists unclenched. "If Pa and Joe don't come by supper, I'll have to go home for the goat milk for Emma Grace. Your husband give the rest of us what the cow let, but she ain't never had cow. Mama was nursin' her and just give her goat milk for extra or if she took sick. She said goat'd set better on her stomach, but we'll be outta what we brung before long."

"All right. If they're not here by tonight, you can go for the goat milk. Joe might appreciate your help with the milking anyway." I turned to go back in the house, confident now that he would follow me.

"Mrs. Wortham?"

"Yes?"

"You want I grab a armload or two a' wood while I'm out here?"

My Samuel kept the basement stocked, and I knew it wasn't near empty yet. But this was what I'd wanted, what Kirk needed. A way to push on, do something useful, go on with living.

"Yes. Thank you so much. It's under the overhang at the east end of the barn."

He took off at a run, his too-long hair flipping behind him in the sudden breeze.

"Let's get you inside," I whispered to Bert.

"Kirky!" the little boy said.

"He'll be right in. He'll be okay."

Willy and Robert had not come downstairs, and I just let them be. With a prayer for strength, I opened the potato bin that Emma's husband had made long years before and got Sarah and Rorey started on counting out potatoes into a dishpan. I sent Frank to the basement for an onion, and he seemed shocked that I would speak to him. But he went quickly, with Harry following on his heels. I tried to set Bert down, but he started wailing, to which teary-eyed Rorey just shook her head.

"Is he used to being held?" I asked her.

"No, ma'am. He ain't been held hardly since he learnt to walk, not that I remember."

Of course, that didn't seem likely, but a six-year-old's memory could be pretty short. With three of his fingers in his mouth and his nose running, Berty looked close into my face and then laid his head on my shoulder. Oh, how Emma had loved these kids! How I needed her help with them right now! It wasn't right that they'd lost their mother this way, without even Emma to fall back on. *It's not right, Lord!*

I watched Lizbeth across the room, talking to her baby sister and offering her a bottle. She seemed calm, remarkably so. But there was a hollowness about her now too. Some special spark was gone, leaving her looking almost unreal.

She began to sing, whisper soft, but the sound of it drifted over the room like the ripples of a stream. Everyone else was quiet as Kirk came back in with wood for the woodbox. His cheeks and fingers were red with cold. No gloves. Had he had gloves when he left home yesterday? Oh, dear God, why did they have to be so poor? And we had nothing to give them.

It was a chore, supervising those little girls at cutting potatoes with Bert still clinging to me. I let him sit on the counter close to me just so I could have my hands free to get the pot and the parsley and everything else I'd need to throw together potato soup enough for everyone. Franky was a good long time getting back with that onion, but I didn't say a word about it. He stood by me for a minute, watching me with bloodshot eyes until I realized it wasn't me he was looking at but Emma's old cuckoo clock on the kitchen wall. He stood a long time, motionless and silent, just watching the little brass pendulum swing.

"It's running," he said.

"Yes. Emma said it always did run well. Same as the mantle clock."

"It oughta stop. Don't you think they oughta stop?"

He had such a strange look on his face that I wasn't sure at first how to answer. "No. I don't think there's anything to a notion like that. I hope they both keep right on for a long time yet." I thought of Albert Graham suddenly. Would he want them, perhaps, or more of Emma's things? He had every right, of course.

"If they keep runnin', would Emma like that?"

"Honey, she'd have no need thinking on such things. I bet she's so happy to see Willard, she's fairly dancing, and with two feet too."

But Franky just shook his head. "I think she'd like it." He didn't say anything else. He just walked away from me.

I had the potatoes in the pot and had started mixing cornbread batter, so I turned back to my fixings. Harry had set himself down on the kitchen floor at my feet, and Berty was still on the counter beside me. There was no sound from Robert and Willy upstairs. Kirk was holding the baby now, and Lizbeth was washing all of their breakfast dishes, silent as a stone. Little Rorey was standing on a chair, fishing one dish at a time out of the rinsepan to dry. Then she would hand her dishes to Sarah, who was standing on another chair, putting things away in the cupboard for me. We were all quiet. Methodical. As if somehow life depended on us just pressing on this way, whether we felt like it or not.

We were all completely unprepared for the sudden crash from the next room. Something heavy, shattering glass. I handed Berty into Lizbeth's wet hands and ran for the sitting room.

Franky stood beside the fireplace. He didn't look at me. He didn't look up at all. He just stared at the fragments at his feet. Emma's beautiful Seth Thomas mantle clock. Ruined.

"Franky!" Lizbeth hollered from behind me. "What in tarnation was you doin' with that?"

90

"You done it now," Kirk added. "You know you ain't supposed to touch nothin' that ain't yours, stupid."

The little boy didn't say a word, just kept staring. I moved closer. Franky didn't move a muscle, didn't make a sound.

"What happened?" I asked when I was close enough to see the tears glistening on his face.

"Mama's dead," he said. "Now Emma too."

I stood for a moment, unsure of his thinking. He already knew Emma had died. That clock was one of her prized possessions, precious to her because it had been a favorite of Willard's. But the breaking of it couldn't affect her now.

"Franky—"

"I was just meanin' to wind it. I knowed you gotta wind 'em."

He shouldn't have touched it. He had no business even trying, and it angered me that he had dared to do so without saying so much as a word to me about it first. But thankfully I had the good sense not to let my anger show.

"I didn't mean to bust it," he said, looking ghostly white. "I liked Emma plenty good."

His ankle was bleeding where a shard of glass must've struck him, but he stepped away and wouldn't let me touch it.

"Franky . . ."

His lips were quivering, and suddenly he turned and fled, past all of us and back to the kitchen.

"Franky!" Lizbeth hollered after him. "You come back in here and help clean up the mess you made!" She turned to me with a frown. "So awful sorry," she said more quietly. "He ain't thinkin' just right. Was it espensive?"

Before I could answer, I heard the back door slam shut. I ran for the kitchen, hoping I'd be quick enough to see where the little boy was headed. But by the time I reached the door, he was already out of sight.

In a moment I could hear a faint sort of sobbing coming from almost directly under my feet. So I stepped off the porch in a cold wind and looked down through where one of the lattices had come loose from the porch front.

"Franky?"

He was under there, all right. Just where Samuel had found him before, snuggled up to the back wall and crying his eyes out.

"Franky, won't you come out?" I asked him gently. "Accidents happen."

Kirk was right behind me, having left the baby in the house with Lizbeth. "Get your sorry self outta there!" he commanded. "It's bad enough, what all we gotta think about, without you carryin' on, makin' it worse!"

I looked away from Franky and over to Kirk. "Kirk," I said, "check the soup pot for me and make sure the oven's got good and warm."

He looked at me skeptically.

"Go on. Please. I'll talk to him."

Shaking his head at me, Kirk went back in the house.

Franky hadn't moved.

"Honey, I know you didn't mean to. It's awfully cold out here. Won't you please crawl on out? We can sit inside."

He turned his back to me and curled up in a ball. *These Hammonds*, I thought. *What is it about them, anyway? For their thinking to get so befuddled, Franky and his father both.* I knew it was the grief doing it to them. But I resented it almost like Kirk did, because you had to stop what you were doing, just to save them from themselves. You couldn't even do your own grieving. You couldn't take the time.

"Franky?"

He wasn't paying any attention to me. So I got on my hands and knees in that snow and crawled underneath, thinking to pull him out the way Sam had. But something in his choked sobs stopped me. He was calling on God.

"Franky?"

"I didn't mean to hurt 'em, Jesus. I didn't mean to do it. I wish that Mama and Emma ain't never had 'em no clocks. Then I couldn't hurt 'em none. Then I couldn't bust things up."

I crawled in quickly and laid my hand on his arm. "Oh, honey, you didn't hurt them. The clock had nothing to do with any of that."

"But I busted Mama's clock too," he sobbed. "I knew she was gonna die. It's true what Arthur Whistler told me. And it's my fault! I know it is!"

"Franky—"

"I wanna be dead too!"

"No, you don't."

He grabbed me so suddenly that I almost fell on my side. He was clinging to me so tight it hurt, and crying into my collar. He seemed small as a baby just then, and if I could've stood in that crawl space I might've picked him right up and carried him inside.

"Franky . . ."

He didn't even seem to hear me. "Jesus," he was crying. "Jesus. Jesus."

I had to take a deep breath. "Your mama and Emma are with him now," I whispered. "And they're happy."

"I don't want 'em to be mad at me . . ."

"They're not! None of it's your fault."

"But I know—"

"No. Honey, you just heard some foolish tale, that's all."

He looked up at me. "But they died!"

"Because they were very sick. You had nothing to do with that. Do you understand?"

"Kirky and Joey and all them is gonna hate me."

"No, they won't. Not if they have the slightest bit of sense about them. That's enough of all this. It's too cold to stay out here. Come in and help me with your little brothers."

He sat up and wiped at his face with his sleeves. "Why do they need help?"

"*I* need your help, honey. Just to play with them and keep them occupied and happy for a while. Please?"

When he nodded, I sighed with relief. We came crawling out from under there and went straight for the kitchen. Franky took Berty's little hand importantly and pulled him toward the sitting room door.

"C'mon, Harry," he said. "You too. Let's play Injuns in here."

I stood by the warm stove for a minute and looked down into my soup pot. All these kids. All these needs. I'd managed to get one of them to dry his eyes and come out from under the house. But what about the next problem? And the one after that? Could I really handle half of what would come upon us now, what with funerals to deal with and the long winter after that? And Christmas. Lord have mercy. I wasn't strong enough to carry all this, not even with Samuel at my side.

EIGHT

Samuel

Louise Post saw me coming and hollered for Barrett with something frantic in her voice. I guess she figured I wouldn't be walking two and a quarter miles across fields and snowdrifts to their place if something weren't wrong.

"It's Emma, ain't it?" Barrett asked as soon as I was close enough. Louise stood behind him, scrunching up a dishtowel in her hands.

I told them everything—about Mrs. Hammond's passing, and Emma, and the children all over at our house, and the way young Joe and I had found George. "I'm going to need your help," I said then. "Got to get word to Albert and the Hammonds' relatives and the preacher."

"I'll take you," Barrett said.

"Mercy me!" Louise exclaimed. "How's Lizbeth managing? And Julia?"

"Best as can be expected, I guess."

"You better hurry on," Louise commanded her husband. "Don't be waitin' a minute to get that preacher out to 'em. He'd be comfort at a time like this."

I was almost surprised to hear her say it. The Posts were not churchgoers and had always resisted Emma's attempts to influence them in that direction.

"Emma told me she didn't want the undertaker," Barrett added solemnly.

"She told me too. Way back in June, I guess."

"What about Wilametta? George say anything to you about that?"

"I don't think he's framed it in his mind to consider."

"He can't afford them things done, anyhow," he told me with clear sympathy. "We can do for him. That's what neighbors is for."

I was glad for Barrett. Though his wife was already fretting for all those children and exclaiming for Emma, a dear friend, he hitched his team to his forty-year-old sleigh and continued talking to me about arrangements.

"Too much a' today gone to 'complish much, after lettin' folks know. Better plan on payin' respects tomorrow. Don't be worryin' about the graves, Sam. Me an' Clement'll take care of it. We done it in the wintertime b'fore."

Barrett was ready to go right away, and I sat beside him, glad the snow had stopped again but wishing his team could manage to move faster. He wouldn't push them, though, because it was hard work pulling us through the drifts. But at least it was faster than walking.

"You makin' the coffins?" Barrett suddenly asked as we passed Grover's Corner, hardly recognizable in the snowy white.

I hadn't thought on that, though Lord knows I should have. "I'll have to do Emma's. She asked me to, though at the time I was hoping it would never come up."

"Yeah, she said you was good with wood. Ever since making her that chair." He nodded. "Might as well plan on Wilametta's too. George and his boys hadn't oughta be worried on somethin' like that. Got wood enough?"

"I don't know."

I wondered that he could be so matter-of-fact about it all. But he and his brother, Clement, had buried their parents, their sisters, a brother, and two children.

"I'll bring you some good pine out tonight," he promised. "Louise'll have a batch of food cooked up by then, I'd wager, so's none a' you have to think about cookin'."

Right then, I couldn't even imagine being hungry. "We thank you for your help."

"Ain't nothin' but neighborly. Ain't a soul round here that wouldn't do what they could for Emma. And Wilametta—criminy! Thinkin' on George is enough to sorry anybody! Sure hope her family can take in them kids."

That was a strange thought to me. Why wouldn't he expect the children to stay with their father? Because of what I'd told him? Sure, George was a mess. But I'd be in an awful shape too, if something happened to Julia. There was no reason to expect that he wouldn't come around. Was there?

"Wilametta was the glue, Sam," Barrett told me, as if he'd heard my thoughts. "George ain't none too bright upstairs. Might seem like he gets along all right, but he ain't never been good on decisions. Wilametta used to work side by side with him when she could. She'd be the one always tellin' what to do."

I'd seen her doing that very thing. But I'd thought it more bossiness than necessity. Why wouldn't George know what to do on the farm he was so familiar with? They'd been living there almost twenty years, and he more than that, as a kid years before.

"Need to keep an eye on him," Barrett continued. "He gets ahold a' any drink, he'll really fall apart. Can't handle it. Some say his father was the same way afore him, an' his grandfather too. Hate to say it, but Wila makin' him go to church was a good thing on account of it stopped the drink in him. They'd a' never made it this far, otherwise."

He sighed. "Prohibition ain't stopped them that wants to brew an' sell it themselves, you know. There's plenty a' liquor out there, if you know where to find it. Pity the folks that drinks the stuff they makes nowadays, though. 'Nough to strip the linin' right out your gizzard, you know what I mean?"

I just nodded, and he rode in silence a while, until Covey Mueller's house came in sight. Another large family, but their house was far bigger than Hammonds'.

"Might as well stop and give them word," Barrett said grimly. "If we could get the telephone line out this far, we wouldn't have to go to town. Ain't likely to ever happen, though. Nobody wants to do all that work for a few a' us farmers out here."

Covey and Alberta reacted about the same way Louise had. Barrett stayed to talk a minute, but I was anxious to move on. The quicker we got into town, the quicker we could get back, and I was plenty worried for Julia and the kids.

"Some folks wait till thaw," Covey said, not meaning a bit of disrespect. "When my aunt Mabel passed on, they closed her up careful in a shed till they could get at the ground. 'Course, that was northern Minnesota."

"Better not to wait with all them kids around," Barrett maintained. "Hard as it sounds, the quicker we can manage, the better. So's George an' the little ones can go on from here."

Covey nodded. "We'll help ya."

"We'll be settin' fires tomorrow, to warm the top layer," Barrett explained. "Won't be hard once we get below the freeze line."

I didn't want to hear any more details. I didn't want to hear the same things repeated over and over every place we stopped. Just thinking on all the hurt I'd seen buried under Julia's determination made me want to rush back and hold her. I hadn't had the chance. And all those kids! How I'd like to sit down with my two and explain things the best I could, hug them a minute, and make sure they were going to be all right. I hadn't had a chance to do that either. When would I? And who would do it for all the little Hammonds?

"You need a cup a' coffee?" Mrs. Mueller suddenly asked me. "You're not looking so good."

"No," I told her, but I couldn't manage to say more.

"Why don't you take him home?" Covey suggested. "Needs to be with his family, I expect. Me an' Orville, we'll go to town an' get the word out."

Bless you! I thought. *Bless you to heaven, Covey Mueller!* Barrett hadn't wanted to go into town without me. Whether he just didn't want to talk to the preacher alone or what, I didn't know, but he nodded to the Muellers and quickly agreed.

"You gotta call Albert up to Chicago," he instructed them. "And Fedora Bates and Chloe Adamson over to Farmington. Wilametta's sisters. Cryin' shame they ain't likely to make it over here in all this weather. And be looking out for young Sam too, will ya? He was headed in for the doctor yesterday, and there ain't nobody seen neither of 'em so far."

I was glad to be leaving there, glad to be headed back. And Barrett was too. He told me that much, and then he was quiet.

We went by the Hammonds first, because Barrett thought another neighbor talking to George might help. The house was still quiet when we got there. I climbed out of the sleigh and went to knock on the door, but Joe opened it before I got to the top porch step.

"Makin' coffee," he said. "Want some?"

"Sure," Barrett answered from behind me. We followed Joe inside, both looking to see what kind of shape George was in.

He was still by the fire, looking almost as if he hadn't moved. But one of them had. Two chairs were overturned in the middle of the room, one with its back legs busted up like somebody'd slammed it against something. Everything from the mantle now lay shattered and strewn across the floor, along with two dented pots, quite a few dishes, and Wilametta's Bible.

I looked at them both, wondering which one of them was capable of such a rampage. George, almost surely. But neither of them said a word. Joe brought the coffee and handed one cup to me and one to Barrett. When he tried to give one to his father, George pushed it away.

"Go home, Wortham," he suddenly said. "You too, Post. Ain't needin' ya in my face right now."

"Soon enough, I'll go," I told him. "But I'd like to take you with me. Your children need to see something of you right now."

"You drug me back in this dead house!" he hollered. "That's where you wanted me! An' I ain't goin' no place!"

"Now, George—" Barrett began.

"Shut up and leave me alone!"

"That ain't gonna solve nothin'," Barrett said. "An' Samuel here's right. Your children is gonna need somethin' of ya. All you can manage. You want we bring 'em here?"

Joe spoke up right away. "You hadn't oughta bring the younger ones just yet." He looked at me anxiously. "Kirk and Lizbeth might could come, though. If you all don't mind keepin' the rest a while."

"Don't want nobody comin'!" George yelled at his boy. "You hear me? You oughta go join 'em. Get outta here. There ain't nothing here to stay for, anyhow."

"But, Pa . . ." Joe turned to Barrett and me with what seemed to be fear in his eyes. Much quieter, he said, "I can't leave."

I had to nod at that. Someone should be here if the doctor and Sam Hammond made it through, or the preacher, or whoever else. And we couldn't count on George even staying if we weren't here to watch him.

"Don't you worry, boy," Barrett told him. "You're thinkin' right not to leave him alone."

George stood up and glared at us. "I didn't ask for no comp'ny! Why don't you go and tend to your own business?"

"We got a bit more to do considering yours, George," Barrett told him gently. "I know you ain't wantin' to talk about it, but I'm needin' to know where you mean for Wilametta to be buried. We have to discuss them things, bad as we hate to."

"Ain't nobody movin' Wila from her bed," George said softly.

Barrett shook his head, and Joe sat down, looking weak at the knees.

"We can't pay no undertaker," the boy told us. "I'll dig on the grave when the time comes. That's what Mama would want. Over by that birch grove where the bluebells come up."

Barrett sipped at his coffee. "Don't you worry on it. We'll take care of it. Just show us the place in the morning, if you would. Your mama'd be proud. You're bein' right strong."

Joe must not have felt it, because just hearing such words made him look about ready to fall apart.

I took a big drink of my coffee, hot as it was. I'd hoped George would be able to come with me to give his children the fatherly strength they needed right now. But he had none to share. And I didn't like just standing there feeling useless. "Stock need water?" I asked Joe. "Anything else I can do while I'm here?"

"Be all right." The boy gave me an appreciative nod. "If you don't mind it. You oughta take this morning's milk over to Lizbeth too. I shoulda sent it with ya before."

"She needs diapers for the baby," I suddenly remembered.

"Shoot. I don't know where they're at." He looked over at his father and sighed. "Pa, where's Emma Gracie's diapers?"

George was staring into the dwindling flames in the fireplace. He didn't answer.

Joe stood up and took a step in his direction but then stopped. Something in his expression changed. Hope. Or relief. Something new glimmering in his eyes as he rushed to the window faster than I'd ever seen him move.

"Did you hear that?"

I hadn't heard anything. And Barrett shook his head.

"Another sleigh comin'."

George stood to his feet. Joe was out the door in an instant, and I followed him. Soon as the rig was close enough, I could see Sam Hammond in it with an old man who was almost surely Dr. Howell. No wonder Joe was relieved. Young Sam had been gone almost twenty-four hours without a trace. And now he was back in one piece. But God help him, the news he had to hear!

Sam jumped out of that sleigh in a hurry and moved toward the house, his face looking raw and red from the cold. "Mama any better?" he asked before Joe or I had a chance to say anything. George hadn't come out, and Barrett had stayed in there with him. I could see the oldest Hammond boy glancing over at Post's little sleigh. He knew it wasn't mine and was surely wondering who else had come and why.

"Sure glad you're back," Joe told his older brother, barely able to contain the tears in his eyes.

"Better not to stand here jawin' then," Sam declared, looking a little shaken at his brother's expression. The doctor was just getting out of the sleigh behind him, and they both turned toward the house.

"Wait." Joe grabbed his brother's arm but couldn't seem to find the words. He looked at me in desperation.

"Good what you did, bringing the doctor," I told the boy. "But we're past the need of him now."

Young Sam just stared at us for a moment. Our faces surely didn't show that to be good news.

"I'm sorry," I told him, wishing I had something comforting to say.

"What's this?" Dr. Howell asked immediately.

"Mama's—she's—she's gone," Joe stammered, looking at the doctor. "We—we're sorry you had to come out."

Sam stared hard at me, as if daring me to confirm what Joe could barely manage to say. He was shaken, no question about that. He reached to the side of the sleigh frame to steady himself.

"I'm sorry," I told him again. "There was nothing any of us could have done."

Dr. Howell hung his head. "Is it all right if I step in?"

Joe looked at him in bewilderment, the tears now plain in his eyes. "But there's no use. She's passed on . . ."

Howell nodded. "I'm sorry, son. Comes my unpleasant duty to confirm the cause of death."

"Emma Graham," I said quickly. "She was here to help Mrs. Hammond, but she—"

"She's gone too," Joe said. "Both last night." He looked like he could barely stand. And young Sam, having such a shock after going all that way, was in even worse shape. I wished I could take them both in my arms, but they were as big as I was and didn't even hug each other.

Dr. Howell was standing still for a minute, digesting the bitter news. "Both of the same ailment?"

"I don't think so," I answered. "Emma'd been weak several days with her heart, same as before. I wanted to send for you, but she kept telling me no."

"I'd a' put her to bed. She knew that. Wasn't much else I could do for her most of the time. She come to the end of her days." He started for the house with slow steps.

"George is inside with Barrett Post," I said. "He's not taking this well. And he may not be pleased to see you now."

Sam Hammond sunk back against the side of the sleigh. "We're too late," he said, as if he were just realizing what we'd told him.

"There's nothing you could have done," I said again.

"You don't know that! If we'd a' been here last night—"

"There was no helping the snowstorm. You did the best anybody could do."

"I stopped," he said in a trembly voice, looking at his brother. "Couldn't make it after Birdie stepped off in a hole. I couldn't get her up. Had to leave her. Would a' been worth it to help Mama, but now—"

Joe looked ashen. "You lost Birdie?"

I knew what he was thinking. It was another blow. If Bird was gone, they were the same as stranded even in good weather. George's tired old horse Teddy couldn't possibly pull their big wagon alone. How would they manage without it? What would George do?

Sam's head sunk down to his hands. "I shoulda gone another way. I shoulda judged the road better and kep' Birdie outta the hollow. Then I mighta got through! I kep' fallin', on foot. Couldn't see nothin' for the blowin' snow. Had to stop at Tom Welty's. But I shouldn't a' stopped—"

"You couldn't have helped it," I told him. "It was too dangerous in that storm. I shouldn't have let you go."

"I had to. Pa said—"

"No." I almost told him his pa should've known better. He should've known it was too late, once the storm started beating down in its fury. But I couldn't say those words. "There's no use thinking on what might have been. We did the only thing we knew. Don't be blaming yourself."

104

George was suddenly yelling in the house. We all knew it was him, though it was impossible to make out just what he was saying.

"Is he drunk?" Sam asked.

"No," his brother told him. "Out of his head, though. Hard tellin' what he'll do."

The eldest Hammond shook his head, pain working deep in his eyes. I wished he would cry. At least Joe had done that. But Sam pulled himself up and looked at the house. "The kids over to your place still?" he asked me.

"Yes. And they'll be glad to know you're back safe."

"Do they know? 'Bout Mama?"

Joe looked at me again and sighed. "Yeah. By now they know."

Sam shook his head. "What're we gonna do now? We could lose this place without Emma."

"Pa said that," Joe acknowledged. "He said there weren't no use the kids comin' back, 'cause it weren't gonna be their home no more anyhow. I didn't know how much a' what he's sayin' to believe, though, with him like this."

I could see their eyes meet. The two oldest boys, and here they were talking this out like everything would be up to them now.

"Without Mama, we 'bout got nothin' left," Sam said.

"There's Aunt Chloe."

"No. With Dude and Rachel, and Simon sick all the time, she ain't gonna be much help. And Aunt Fedora won't do nothin' for Pa without Mama around."

I wondered about those two boys. They'd always respected their father. He was always working at something, and they'd always done what he'd said. But right now they were expressing no confidence in him at all.

"We'll be all right," Joe said, trying to sound certain. "Lizbeth knows most ever'thin' what to do with the little ones anyhow."

105

"We'll make it one way or another," young Sam added gravely. "But it ain't all right."

Dr. Howell was already starting back from the house. "Wasn't anything contagious that I can see," he said as he approached us. "Rest assured of that much at least. I knew to expect it of Emma. Awful shame about that Mrs. Hammond, though. She been sick long?"

"Two or three days, maybe," Joe told him. "Off an' on the whole fall, afore that."

Dr. Howell looked from one boy to the other. "Can't be helped, then. Mighty sorry for you, sons."

Sam only turned his head.

"You gotten a chance to send word to the undertaker?" the doctor asked me.

"Don't need no undertaker," Sam said immediately. "Can't afford him. Don't hardly know him anyhow. Mama'd want seen to by the folks that knowed her best."

Dr. Howell didn't respond to that. He only turned to me and solemnly shook my hand. "Shall I notify Emma's kin for you when I get back to town?"

"Covey Mueller is supposed to be doing that. But you've known her a long time. I'd appreciate you checking to make sure he got through, and letting her friends know, at least all that you know of."

He nodded. "Rita McPiery, of course. And Miss Sharpe from her church in Dearing."

Of course he'd think of Mrs. McPiery right away. But Miss Sharpe? She was the crotchety old lady that had thought Emma was crazy for moving back home. She'd despised Juli and me from the start and tried to turn Albert Graham against us. But Emma loved her anyway. Emma loved everybody.

"So sorry, again," the doctor was telling the boys. And then he glanced at me before making his way back to the sleigh. "Tell George I said I was sorry. Will you do that?"

He never said anything about what George had been yelling about. He didn't say if he'd tried to talk to him or not. He just gave us all another nod and started off through the snow.

"Yes, sir," I told his back, though I knew he wouldn't hear me now. "I'll tell him."

Young Sam headed for the house then. Joe followed him, and so did I, not knowing what else to do. "He's made a awful mess," Joe told his brother. "He was crazy mad a while ago."

"He hurt you?" Sam asked immediately.

And I was surprised at the question. I knew George spanked his children. Fiercely, sometimes. But I'd never heard any of them express any concern about abuse.

"Nah," Joe replied. "He weren't mad at me especially."

"Who's he mad at? God?"

"An' Emma. An' Mr. Wortham." He glanced at me. "Whole world, I guess. Mama too."

"That don't make no sense."

Joe's reply about broke my heart. "I don't guess nothin' does."

When we went inside, George was sitting at the table with his head in his hands. He didn't look up, but Barrett, who'd been sitting across from him, stood. "Good to see you're all right after such a trip," he told the oldest boy. "Weren't a fit night for a beast out there."

Sam stopped and sighed. "Thanks for your concern, Mr. Post."

"I want you to know that me an' Clem'll take care a' what all needs done for your mama, so you boys don't need to be concernin' yourselves."

"It's our job to take care of," George's eldest protested. "Our mama raised us to do what we could for ourselves."

"But she'd want you havin' help, boy. That's the way things is done. You let us see to the buryin'. You'd do us the favor. And maybe one day you'll hafta do the same for us."

Both boys nodded. Then they walked together toward their mother's room. I waited with Barrett.

"They should be all right here, hard as it is," he told me. "We need to get goin' afore long and see to what else needs done." He looked over at George. "It ain't a good time just yet bringin' the other children through the snow, if they's okay with you a couple a' days. George promised me not to go off half-cocked and not to touch no bottle. We can settle 'em back in over here day after next if the weather don't worsen."

After the funerals were done, I supposed, though Barrett didn't put it that way. But didn't the kids need their father before that? I thought they'd need him now more than ever. "Nobody has to stay here right now," I said. "It might be easier not to for a couple of days. George, I'd like you and the boys to come with me tonight. It'd be a comfort to your younger children. They don't know what to expect, things as strange as they are like this."

"You'd think strange." That was all George said, and I had no clue what he meant by it.

In Wilametta's bedroom, the boys were just standing still. Both bodies were covered now. Everybody was suddenly quiet at once, and the silence was hurtful. I wanted to say something to them, anything that might help, but there was nothing to say.

Sam Hammond didn't touch the blankets. He didn't touch the bed at all. He didn't sink to the floor and sob the way his brother had. He just stood. And there was nothing any of us could do but wait.

"Emma birthed pert near all of us," he finally said. "She was better'n a grandma to have next door. Even said I'd make a fine gent one day." He laughed. "Imagine that."

He didn't say anything about his mother. Perhaps he couldn't. And in just a little while he came out of the room, looking young and scared. Thinking deep, the same as Joe'd been doing, taking things on himself. "Mr. Wortham, you're awful good with makin' things. Would you think to make the coffins for us?"

My heart ached inside. He was sixteen. Joe was thirteen. It wasn't right that they should have to think on things like this. "Yes," I said quickly. "I should've told you already I would do it. And anything else you need help with."

"Get out," George suddenly growled at me. "Don't need your help, Sam Wortham. Not with waterin' stock or nothin'. Get out."

The oldest boy shook his head and walked toward the door with Barrett and me. "It's all right," he said. "I'll come see the kids later. Good you keepin' 'em."

"You don't have to go through the snow later," I told him again. "You can come now."

"I best see to Pa a little while. Ain't had time to speak with him yet."

"You tell us," Barrett said, "if there's anythin' else we can do."

"Just you see us through the buryin'," Sam said somberly. "That's more'n enough. Most a' what else we're gonna need, there ain't no helpin' anyhow."

Joe, standing behind him, just nodded his head.

I'd never seen a more defeated pair of young men in all my life.

NINE

Julia

Nobody'd eaten much lunch, so I had plenty to save back for Samuel. But I was fixing again, making a pie, just to have a way to keep the little girls busy alongside of me. I wanted to keep my mind only on that, but I couldn't seem to stop thinking of Emma. She'd made the best pie I ever tasted. And she'd helped me finally learn a really good crust. I remembered her laboring in this kitchen the day before Robert was baptized in early October, turning out one perfect crust after another to fill and bake. Six apple pies and six pumpkin we'd made that day, enough to feed all the church folk that came out to the baptism. Such a time that was, with all the dressed-up ladies and the men in suits or clean overalls. Robert had acted so proper, so grown up. And Emma'd been proud as could be, just the same as if she'd been kin.

Now Robert was upstairs with Willy, all this time without a single sound. They'd been down two minutes, I guessed, when I called everyone for lunch, but they hardly ate anything and went right back up. I thought I should go see to them, but I had to get the girls to a stop first.

Sarah was sprinkling cinnamon and sugar on the cut apples while I helped Rorey roll the crust with Emma's old rolling pin. Nearly everything we had was Emma's. Right down to the apron I was wearing. It was enough to make me want to sit down and cry. But I kept going and got the bottom crust in a pan, and the apples into it. When the top crust went on, I had a time of it trying to show the girls how to pinch the edges together to make a good flutey pattern. And then Rorey, a first-grader who did some struggling with her letters, cut a big "M-E" on top with the butter knife. I thought she was just showing me one of the few words she could spell, but I soon learned different.

"*M* is for Mama," she told me without looking up. "And *E* is for Emma."

I almost dropped the bowl I was holding. Rorey set the knife down slow, and I hugged her. Then I hugged Sarah, and soon we were all three crying. But I knew we'd have to stop that. And quick too. I dried my face with the nearest dishtowel and told the girls to wash up and go play with Sarah's doll a while. Lizbeth had seen our outburst, of course, but she didn't say anything. She just watched me put the pie in the oven and cooed something at little Emma Grace, trying to coax her down for a nap. She was going through the motions, trying to act the same as ever, but when I looked her way, she turned her head.

I was glad. I didn't want to see the hurt in her right then. I didn't want her seeing it in me. If I could go on pretending we were both strong, maybe things would be all right. She was her mama's best helper. And I needed her to be mine too, as long as they were all here. Or I'd simply fall apart.

Harry and Bert seemed happy enough now scampering around, playing wild animals. But Lizbeth told them it was about time they settled for a nap, and I wondered what Franky would do. He'd started the game and kept it going, though he still was looking white as a sheet. I wiped my hands on the towel and asked Lizbeth to please get him to lie down too.

"He don't nap," she declared almost sharply. "He's all of eight years old."

"I know. But he's little and looking mighty tired today."

She shook her head. "It ain't tired he's lookin'."

I felt my hands start shaking, I was so surprised at her words, her tone. "Lizbeth, please. I need to go upstairs and see about Rob and Willy a minute. They haven't said hardly two words."

"I'll take Franky outside," Kirk offered. "We'll bring more wood and maybe cut some if you don't care."

I hesitated, but the sun was bright now and Kirk seemed to like an outside chore. "All right. But don't stay out too long. And don't be hard on him. Don't let him out of your sight. Not for a minute, all right?"

"Yes'm."

"Check to see that Lula and Sukey got water, will you please?" I added. He knew Emma's cows. They all did.

"Yes'm. Franky, get your coat!" he hollered. "We got work to do!"

Oh, he was so abrupt with his brother! Even when I'd warned him. "Kirk—"

He saw my concern and shook his head. "Franky wouldn't know what to do with me pussyfootin' him," he said. "It ain't the way we do, that's all."

They were out the door in a minute, and I was up the stairs, hoping to find Robert and Willy peaceful for all their quiet.

I found them side by side against the wall in the children's room, on the floor because we had no chairs

112

upstairs. Both with pocketknives in their hands, they had their heads low over a pile of wood shavings on the floor. I couldn't tell what they'd been carving on until I saw the remains of the hickory wood horse Samuel had whittled out of a chunk of firewood one rainy evening.

Robert looked up and saw me. "It's all right, Mom," he said quietly. "I said he could have it."

"No! It's not all right!"

Willy's head jerked up at me. No tears. Nothing readable in him at all. He had what was left of the horse's back in his hands, carved to a jagged swayback. I wanted to yell at both of them. It wasn't a fancy horse. A quick one, Samuel had called it. Not worth much. But it was in ruins now, as if these boys had wanted an object lesson about the state of their lives. We were all broken. Beyond repair, it seemed. And about to face God's own Christmas without a reason to rejoice.

"Don't you destroy anything else," I told them as calmly as I could. "Don't carve on another thing in this house unless you ask me first."

"We won't, Mom," Robert assured me. "We'll clean up too. I promise."

Almost I turned to go. But Robert stood up suddenly, and I could see the fear in his eyes. "Will we all be homeless, Mom? Willy says we'll be homeless."

Robert knew what it was like, of course. He knew about sleeping wherever we could find a place and eating whatever we could manage to scrounge up. Bringing Emma home again had made a way for us to stay too. So it was no surprise that he would worry.

"Honey, Emma talked to Albert. I believe he'll let us stay on."

"Maybe you," Willy said bitterly. "But he hates my pa. I know. I heard him say it."

"Will he make them move?" Robert asked me, his deep eyes brimming wet.

"Don't be fretting over such matters, all right?" I told them. "Why don't you come down and draw me some fresh water for washing out the diapers?"

Robert stuffed his jackknife in his pocket but didn't take a step. He was waiting for Willy, who made no move.

"Kirk'll draw the water," the boy declared.

"He's seeing to the cows," I said, impatient about being put off. "And bringing firewood."

Finally Willy stood up. "I don't feel like doin' nothin'."

I could understand that. But it wasn't helping him to sit here all day, whittling things to pieces. And thinking too much, surely.

"You aren't the only one that feels that way," I admitted. "But it won't help us. We have no choice."

"C'mon," Robert told him. "We can go in the loft when we're done." He stopped suddenly, hearing something outside. A horse's whinny maybe. We both looked out the window to see Barrett Post drop Samuel off on the snowy lane before going on in the direction of his home.

"Dad!"

I hadn't expected Robert to be so excited to see him. It hadn't occurred to me that he might worry now with one of us gone. But it was genuine relief on his face.

"Dad's home!"

Willy didn't share his enthusiasm.

"C'mon," Robert tried to coax him. "Let's go outside like Mom said."

Willy got up reluctantly, closed his jackknife, and shoved it in his pocket. "Anybody with him?"

"No," Robert answered, and I felt sorry for Willy, who was surely thinking on his older brothers or even more likely his father. But he went along without any comment, and they clumped down the stairs together, completely forgetting the mess of shavings they'd promised to clean up.

For no reason at all I kicked at the stuff, and the bigger pieces went tumbling across the room. A little puff of saw-

114

dust lingered in the air a minute and then dusted down over the floor. *We're no better than that,* I thought. *Nothing but sawdust. And most anything can happen to scatter us hither and yon.*

It was foolishness, but I stood there and cried. Samuel was outside, and I was so glad of that. He'd want to talk to me. And the baby was wailing again downstairs, and I knew I should do something to relieve Lizbeth. But I only turned toward the next room and stood looking through the doorway at the other thing Samuel had carved on a stormy night. A little oak cross with a pair of flowers at its base. I had it sitting on top of the overturned crates we used for shelves. A wonder the boys hadn't carved it up too.

I stood looking at the little cross, the same question still driving itself into my mind. *Why, God? Why Wilametta? Why now?*

And why Emma over there, when she'd only wanted to be right here, in this house that whispered of her everywhere you turned? Emma's curtains on the windows. Emma's quilting keeping us warm at night. Oh, Lord! We owed her everything, and now there was no one to thank, no one to gratefully take care of. She'd always said what all we'd done for her, doing the work of the farm so she could come home again. But we'd been the ones with nothing.

I must've stood there several minutes, just crying and feeling foolish for not going down and greeting Samuel. Then Sarah and Rorey snuck in behind me, one on each side.

"Mommy?" Sarah asked timidly.

I dried my eyes and tried to stifle the tears. "Yes, honey?"

"Are you gonna die too?"

"Oh no, honey." I took her hand, seeing how scared she looked, the precious child. And seeing me in tears surely hadn't helped any.

"She might," Rorey said darkly. "You never know."

"Nonsense," I told her.

"It's true! I heard the preacher say it once! We don't never know when we's gonna die. We could fall down them stairs or catch the house afire or eat somethin' spoilt and be gone as the breeze! That's what he said!"

Her eyes looked sharp and angry, and I wondered if the same question I'd just been tossing about was burning inside of her too. Why, God? Why the unfairness? Why the uncertainty?

"We needn't borrow worry over such things as that," I told them. "If something were to happen to any of us, we'd be in fine hands. But there won't be anything to happen. We just go on living, that's all."

"You never know," Rorey repeated. "And I wish somethin' would happen. I wish we could go to Mama. If it don't hurt."

I started for the stairs, and Sarah stayed right at my side. "Your mother would want us to make the best of things, Rorey," I insisted. "Now, tell me, do your brothers all like ham and beans?"

"Berty don't. But he's a baby. He don't like nothin' but plain bread and butter."

"Rorey threw Bessie-doll down the stairs," Sarah said so quietly I barely heard her. "She said she was dead."

I stopped and sighed. "Rorey, honey, Sarah doesn't like you mistreating her things. Please tell her you're sorry."

"Sorry. But she just falled." The little girl skipped past us on the steps so she could turn and look at my face.

"Have you ever helped wash diapers before?" I asked her.

"No'm."

"Well, you're going to help me."

Sarah squeezed my hand. She didn't question whether I'd let her help too. She seemed to know she could stay right where she was, right at my side, as long as she wanted

116

to. But she sure didn't want to play with Rorey for a while. And I didn't blame her. Rorey was a good enough girl most of the time. But right then when we didn't want to think about death, didn't want to talk about it, she was a little hard to take.

Samuel met me at the base of the stairs, and I stopped, wanting to hug him from now until forever. But the girls had a hold of me again, one at each hand.

He looked so cold, so tired, and there was something else, something unreadable in his eyes.

"Young Sam's back."

Thank the Lord for that mercy! I almost said it out loud, but Samuel had stepped toward me, looking so deep.

"Are you all right?" he asked.

"Yes." What else could I tell him, with Sarah and the others looking on? "So glad you're back." I wanted to ask him how George was doing, if he was coming over, or if he would send the boys to fetch the rest of the family back. But I couldn't ask, because whatever the answers might be, I wasn't sure the children needed to hear. And they shouldn't go home now anyway. Not until the bodies were gone from the house over there.

"Barrett's coming back in a while. I wouldn't be surprised if Louise comes too, or at least sends food."

"Surely she wouldn't want to get out in this snow."

"It's not a matter of want to, Juli. It's a duty to them. And they loved Emma."

"I keep expecting the boys to be hungry, but they're eating like birds, Samuel, all except Harry."

"Don't worry about it. They'll be hungry eventually."

We went into the kitchen, and I fed Samuel, even though he wasn't hungry either. For one brief moment, all the children were gone from the room at the same time, and Samuel looked up at me.

"I'm going to make the coffins, Juli. Tonight and tomorrow."

I remembered the muggy summer night when Emma had asked him to do that for her. I couldn't imagine such a chore back then, and now with it upon us I didn't see how he could do it. My brain would be so befuddled just thinking about it that I wouldn't be able to see straight to saw or hammer or anything.

"Oh, Sammy."

"It's all right. Somebody has to do it."

He'd made one once before, for a neighbor family in Pennsylvania whose daughter had died. They had no money for a boughten one. That was bad enough. I wondered if George had asked him about Wilametta's.

"Is George doing better?"

Sarah came back in, right up to my side like she'd been away from me for too long. "You all right, honey?"

She nodded, biting down on her lower lip. But then she spilled out what was on her mind. "Rorey said you and Daddy might get sick, 'cause you was out in the snow so long."

Rorey. Not more of this. Lord help me with that girl! "Honey, don't pay any attention to her when she talks like that. She's just sad, so she's saying sad things. But that doesn't mean any of them are going to come true."

"Are you sure?"

"Very sure. Yes."

Sarah looked at her father, who gave her a reassuring pat. "We're fine, and we're going to stay fine."

That should've made little Sarah smile. But it didn't. Not on a day like today.

"I wish Rorey's mommy was fine too. I wish Emma was still here."

I had to swallow the bitter lump in my throat, but Samuel answered her without wavering. "We all do, pumpkin, but they're happy. They're well now too, with Jesus."

"Emma got both feet on?"

That made me smile. Emma used to say such things. Heaven was so real to her. *"Won't it be grand,"* she'd say, *"to wake up in the mornin' with both feet on! Oh, there'll surely be mornin' in heaven, even if there ain't night, 'cause mornin's fine as God's gift anyhow!"*

"I'm sure she's got both feet on," Samuel confirmed. "She's probably dancing on them."

"I'd like to see her dance," Sarah mused.

"So would I," Samuel said. "And we will one day."

Lizbeth came in to get Berty a cup of water. "Did you bring any diapers?" she asked.

"Joe couldn't find but two to send over. And the goat milk."

I was glad we'd cut that old cover for more diapers. Even with some hanging to dry, we'd need more before long.

Robert came back in with the water bucket for me. "We're gonna be in the loft," he said.

"Just don't get too cold."

"Okay. We'll be in pretty soon." He turned around and walked right back out. And Lizbeth had gone to take Berty his drink.

"Nobody really knows what to do with themselves," I told Samuel. "We're just trying to act like we do."

"Maybe that's George's problem," he said solemnly. "He doesn't act."

"Is he any better at all?"

"No. Not really."

He didn't have a chance to tell me anything more before children needed our attention. And I wondered how long it would be this way. How long would it be before George dried their eyes, held them in his arms, or just did what it took to get them through a day?

T E N

Samuel

Barrett came back before dark with lumber loaded on an old-fashioned bobsled. He was a surprise to me because he kept things that might've been his grandfather's but wanted all the new equipment he could manage too. He was always prepared. And far better off financially than most of our depression-ridden neighbors.

It was good pine he brought, just like he'd said. Straight, clean lumber, and its arrival drew Robert and Willy out immediately, their curiosity piqued.

"What's the wood for?" Willy asked.

I groaned inside, wishing I'd thought to head off that question somehow before it came.

"Well," Barrett began, not sharing my hesitation, "at times like this, somebody's got to make the departed loved ones a casket. It's a necessary service, and Samuel's gonna be givin' himself to the job."

Willy looked at me for a minute. His expression soured, as if he were suddenly seeing me as a conspirator with the enemy.

"Let's go back inside," he told Robert sullenly.

"My dad can't help it," Robert said. "Somebody has to, an' he's just trying to help."

Willy turned back to the house. Robert looked at me. "I remember the Willises, Dad," he said. "I know you gotta help."

"Thank you, Robert," I told him, wishing Barrett had come up with something else to say. To my mind, it would've been better if none of the kids knew what I was doing until all of it was done.

"It's good for 'em, havin' other kids 'round to talk with 'bout all this," Barrett told me when they were gone. "Ain't easy alone."

"It didn't help him to know about this."

"He's family. And family's got a right to know. They have to know, Samuel; that's just the way it is."

He helped me stack all the wood in the workshop I'd made in the sturdy west end of the barn. We could've used some boys to help unload, but I wasn't about to ask them.

"Louise wanted to come," Barrett said. "But there weren't no place to ride a woman on this contraption. It's made for hauling winter wood. She sent you some good eatin', though. And she'll be here tomorrow for sure."

"She doesn't have to—"

"Pshaw! Her conscience would bother her for months if she didn't! She'll be here, just as early as I'll bring her."

Barrett took two dishes of something into the house while I started sorting the lumber and thinking on a day already almost gone. It was warming up, and I was glad of that, but it would take an awful lot of warming to melt all the snow scattered over the timber and fields. Barrett would light fires, he'd said, to warm the ground for digging. Surely they'd want to shovel snow out of the way just to get to bare ground first. I knew I should help with all of it, and I would if I could get this job done soon enough.

Before long I heard Barrett leaving. I'd picked out the longest pieces and was sorting the rest by size when I heard Kirk and Franky talking over by Lula Bell. I hadn't even realized they were outside.

"She's a purty cow," I could hear Franky say. "How come our Rosey ain't as purty as her?"

"A cow's a cow," Kirk answered impatiently. "What matters is how much milk they give. And Rosey beats 'bout any for that."

"She's old, though. Pa says so."

"Not that old. Or she'd be dry as a desert well."

I was glad to hear them talking of everyday things, glad they were talking at all. I hadn't been comfortable with all my thoughts crowding the quietness, and the job at hand wasn't helping me any.

"Whatcha doin'?" Franky asked as soon as they were near enough.

I didn't want to say. Willy's reaction had been bad enough. What on earth would Franky do? So I hedged. "Always got work around here to do."

Kirk looked at the boards around my feet, and his cheeks slowly drained of color. "Franky, I'm gonna do the milkin' for Mrs. Wortham, an' I told you to fetch in a armload a' firewood."

"I wanna stay here. Can I stay here a while, Mr. Wortham?"

"No!" Kirk declared. "You'd just be in the way."

"I would not. I'd help. Just for a little while."

"You're s'posed to stay with me," Kirk protested.

Franky looked at me with his strange, sad eyes. "Somebody'll have to make Mama a coffin now. Is that what you're doin'?"

Kirk's face got even more pale. "Franky—"

But I held up my hand, and Kirk stopped whatever he was about to say. Franky was different somehow. Maybe he needed a little different treatment. "You're right," I told him. "Somebody has to. And I'm sorry over it, but it'll have to be me. Wouldn't be right to put it off to anybody else."

"Will they be purty?"

Kirk was looking at both of us in surprise.

"Not like some are," I said. "But I'll do the best I can."

"Mama likes flowers," Franky volunteered. "Can you make flowers on it?"

I bowed my head, thinking about that. What could make this eight-year-old who was barely bigger than six-year-old Sarah suddenly seem hardly a child at all?

"I'll try," I told him. "I expect Emma would like that too."

"I'm gonna stay here," Franky told his big brother. "You can tell Mrs. Wortham if you want, so she'll know I didn't run off or nothin'."

Kirk looked over at me. "Are you sure?"

"I think it'll be all right."

He went to milk Lula Bell, though it was generally my job. Franky was eyeing my tools, and I wondered if I was doing the right thing, talking to this boy so straight about this and letting him stay. But I didn't know what else to do. Something about the way he looked at me had made me think that refusing him would've just made things worse.

"You'll have to go in before long," I told him. "Still pretty cold."

"Don't seem cold to me," Franky said.

"Well, your ears look it. Don't you have a hat?"

"Left it someplace, I guess. Maybe in the side garden back home." He stuck his hand in his pocket and pulled out two fat, round bulbs. "Mama said day afore yesterday that she forgot to dig the glads outta the ground. So I went an' dug 'em afore the snow, but I couldn't find but two. Reckon they's not been froze?"

I couldn't picture him in the cold dirt, trying to fulfill what he must've thought was his mother's wish. But Wilametta would've known that the cold nights we'd had were enough to do in her precious flower bulbs. Forgotten is lost, I was sure, though I didn't have the heart to tell Franky that the bulbs he'd carefully salvaged were likely worth no more now than the dirt he'd dug through to get them.

"Maybe Mama would like it if we plant them right where—"

He stopped and looked at me, his lower lip quivering. And I nodded. "If that's what you want to do, I think she'd appreciate your efforts."

It was all I could say. He sat quietly and watched me, his nose tipped red with cold.

"Why don't you go back in?" I asked him. "Sit by the fire."

"No. I owes it to Mama to see this through."

I didn't know what to say to that. But he was determined, and far more settled about it than any other time I'd seen him that day. So I let him stay, longer than I'd anticipated. He turned out to be good help, measuring and marking for me and then planing some of the boards smooth. I'd never seen a child his size handle a wood plane so well.

But then Robert came in and just stood for a minute, watching me working with Franky at my side. "Mom said to tell you there's food when you want some."

Something was strange in his voice, and I looked up to see his eyes on Franky.

"Are they all gonna stay over again?" he asked me, the look on his face plainly showing his displeasure.

"As long as they need to," I told him. "And you watch your manners." Then I felt bad for scolding him. It was

bound to be tough on him at such a time as this to be sharing his parents the way he was doing. I tried to say something else to him, but he ran on ahead and I didn't get the
chance.

"Time to quit for a while," I told Franky. "Sounds like
Julia wants to feed you."

"I ain't hungry."

"Better to eat anyway right now. We're not in much
condition to judge if we're hungry or not."

"And we got a lot a' work to do?"

"Yeah. There's a lot to do."

His silvery eyes were shining like the moon, reflecting
the light of the coal-oil lamp I used to see by in the old
barn workshop.

"Why do you want to help me, Franky?"

"I told you, I owes it to Mama."

"I don't expect she'd think you owed her anything."

"To do a good job. She always did say do a good job."

I could only give him my nod at that.

Covey Mueller brought the pastor by that evening in
the same big green wagon he always used, only he'd taken
the wheels off and set the whole thing on runners. I'd
never seen that done before. But I was mightily glad to
see them, hoping for word from Wila's or Emma's relatives and wanting Pastor Jones just to be there a while,
especially for the older kids.

They'd already been to the Hammonds'. They brought
the evening's milk, some clothes that Joe had stuffed in a
bag for the kids, and the news that George's horse Birdie
had come limping home. They also had word from Wila's
sisters. Neither woman could come, and they'd both made
a point to say that they couldn't afford to take in any of
the kids.

I wondered why it so quickly occurred to them to consider that. But these were poor times. Hard for anybody

to see how George, when he'd already been struggling to make a living, could possibly manage ten kids alone.

"We need to pray for Albert Graham," Pastor was telling Juli and me. "He can't come down right now either, much as he'd like to, because his wife is sufferin' pneumonia. He's takin' it hard about Emma and fearin' to lose another one."

He prayed for Albert and his wife on the spot and then added George and the children. The pastor told us George had said he didn't want a funeral, didn't want anything at all, but his boys felt differently. They knew that if they didn't do the best they could, they'd regret it years down the road. But George didn't want anybody coming, not a soul.

"I already talked to Albert about this, and he said Emma would want to be home," Pastor Jones told us carefully. "We need to perform a funeral, for everyone's peace of mind. But it would be more difficult to move the bodies into town and back, not to mention the children. Albert said we ought to have the funeral right here—that is, if it's all right with you folks. And if Lizbeth and Kirk feel the same as their brothers, to include Wilametta here too might go a little easier on George."

Julia didn't cry at such a thought, the way I might've expected her to. She just sat down and looked around a little. I thought she must be thinking how awfully hard this was going to be for the children. But then she turned her eyes on our kind pastor and startled him badly, I'm sure.

"It's not right! None of this is right at all!"

I took her hand quickly when she said it, but there was no stopping her from saying the rest.

"Emma should've died right here where she wanted to die, Pastor Jones! Not have to be carried back in somebody's wagon! Why couldn't God grant her something so small as that? Why? And Wilametta! George knows it's not right. That's why he's gone near crazy. It's not his fault he can't handle it. There ought to be some things right in this world. There ought to be some kind of sense to be made of it all!"

Lizbeth turned and looked at Julia with the pain so awfully sharp in her eyes. I was glad the rest of the children, except the baby on her lap, had gone upstairs.

"Julia," Pastor said in a gentle voice, "we don't understand it. I can't argue that. But we know the Almighty has a good plan for each of us and that our loved ones are better off than they were here below."

"You just make the best a' things," Mr. Mueller added. "You'll get through. George too. You'll see."

But there was no question that George wasn't near through it yet. Maybe moving Wilametta and Emma from that bedroom might help.

I looked over at Lizbeth. She should've cried with all this talk going on in front of her. She was the oldest that wasn't with her father, and Pastor wanted to include her because her brothers had asked him to. But she shouldn't have taken it all so silently.

"Mama wouldn't mind a funeral 'long with Emma," she finally said. "There weren't nobody she admired more in this whole world." Baby Emma Grace was twisting away at Lizbeth's long hair with her pale little fingers, but Lizbeth didn't seem to notice. "By the birches," she added. "That's where we oughta put her. She always did like the birches."

I walked outside with Covey and the pastor when they went to leave, and they were both so solemn and quiet. I knew they had something more to say to me. But I wasn't expecting to hear what I heard.

"George threatened to light the house afire and burn himself up along with it," Covey told me. "I never did know anybody quite this bad."

"No use the rest of the kids seeing him this way," Pastor told me. "They don't need that on top of everything else. We need to pray it'll be different after the funeral."

"Yes," I said, wondering how near to such an action George could possibly be. Hard to believe he'd ever do such a fool thing. Surely it was just the hurt talking.

"Samuel," Pastor said solemnly, "he won't eat. He would scarcely talk to me. As soon as tomorrow he'll have to face all this, the funerals the day after that. He needs to face his children at the same time and see that they're hurting just as much as he is. But he might need help—he might need you and Juli to keep on watching at least part of them sometimes, at least for a while."

"We'll do what we can."

"Thank you. You've been a godsend, Samuel."

I had a difficult time picturing that. I hadn't done much. Certainly not anything worthy of special notice.

"I'm going back to be with George and his boys overnight," Pastor told me. "Pray for me, please. He may be less than pleased to see me again."

"Threw his wife's Bible at him," Covey added, though the pastor gave him a reproachful look.

I wondered how we were going to face the night and the next couple of days. Louise had wanted to come, Barrett had said earlier. And maybe it would've been a good thing if she could have, or the pastor's wife, or some other woman the children knew.

Juli and Lizbeth were both quiet when I came in the house, as if they were too numb for words. But then all of the children came downstairs, asking questions or sitting and sulking or, in the case of the two youngest, bawling their eyes out.

Harry and Willy were both complaining that they hadn't been able to go with Pastor and Mr. Mueller. And I could see that Juli was just about at the end of her rope.

I knew I should offer a story. But my mind was blank. What could I possibly say? Any of my little stories would seem so frivolous and cheap. Franky had quietly gone and seated himself in a corner, his head down across his folded arms. Juli had the baby now, and Berty was fussy in Lizbeth's arms. Willy and Robert just stood by the fire, as if they were waiting for it to need something from them, and Kirk was pacing, first in one room and then in another, like a caged beast. Sarah and Rorey were mercifully quiet, sitting on the floor with Sarah's doll between them, both looking up at Juli and Lizbeth as if they were waiting to be told what to do.

"Let's get the beds ready," I said, and at first no one responded to me.

Then Sarah stood up. "We gonna all sleep downstairs again, Daddy?"

I wondered for a minute. It sure would be nice to be alone with Julia a few minutes in our room upstairs, to talk things through a little. And some of the children would be fine in the other room upstairs, with the rest down here closer to the fire. But it was strange and different and sad and probably scary for the Hammonds. Not one of them should really be too far from the rest, or from us, tonight. I looked at Juli, and she nodded. "Probably we better," I told Sarah. "So we can all be close."

I got the big boys to help me again, getting mats and bedding and everything to the living room floor. And then sudden as anything, we heard a vigorous knock at the back door.

Barrett Post. Followed immediately by his wife and their sister-in-law, Elvira, the schoolteacher, both carrying more food.

"Louise plain insisted," Barrett explained. "Said we had no excuse, us having a sleigh. An' you all hadn't oughta be alone on a night like this."

I wasn't sure if Juli or Lizbeth was glad to see them or not. They both looked so exhausted it was hard to tell.

Louise and Elvira set their dishes down in a hurry. Louise grabbed the baby and took her straight to Emma's rocker by the fire, and Elvira offered to read Harry and Bert a story.

"Lizbeth!" Berty insisted. "I wan' Lizbeth t' read!"

"Well, then, you'll have to be good and quiet, won't you?" Elvira maintained. "Nobody, nobody wants to read to boys who holler and yell."

She took off her coat after producing two thin books from one pocket and sat on the long side of a mattress. Even though she wasn't Lizbeth, Berty went to sit beside her and look at the pictures. Sarah joined them, and across the room Franky raised his head, watching all of us and listening.

But Rorey folded her little arms and stamped her foot. "Why are you all here? I don't want you here!"

"I want them here," Juli declared pointedly. "And that's good enough. Now go sit down and listen to the story!"

Juli turned away from all of us as soon as she had said it. Her hands were shaking. Suddenly and without another word, she stepped alone into Emma's room and shut the door.

"Leave her be," Louise told me. "Sometimes a body's got to get alone and have 'em a good cry."

But I knew Juli. She liked being alone all right, in the happy times when she'd go singing around the kitchen or picking something outside in the summer sun. But not now.

I opened the door. I had to go in quick and shut it again, because Rorey and Harry wanted to follow me. Julia was sitting on Emma's bed, already in tears, bent down almost to the pillows. I hurried over to hold her. I climbed right up on that bed, boots and all, and took my Juli in my arms.

"I can't do this," she cried. "I just can't! I should never have talked to a little girl that way! She can't help it! But sometimes, oh sometimes—"

"Shhh, honey." I just held her while she shook and sobbed. I'm not sure how long we sat there. I could hear Louise singing to the baby, and a mingle of other voices, including Elvira's, reading now. Thank God they'd come. Thank God for people, people who just stepped in and cared, even these that didn't know the Lord.

"Now what'll they think of me?" Juli whispered.

"Doesn't matter what they think. You're entitled to grieve, honey. You have to, I can see it, or you're going to burst."

She took a deep, difficult breath. "Here we are in Emma's room." Her voice cracked, and I knew the tears were falling again.

"She'd be glad," I said. "Strange as that sounds, she'd be glad we're here."

"Are you sorry?" she suddenly asked. "Are you sorry you didn't take the deed when she offered it?"

"No. We need to show Albert due respect. This was his grandfather's place, not mine."

"Oh, Sammy, I miss her! Imagine what Lizbeth and Rorey and all the rest must feel missing their own mama! And here I sit just thinking on how much I miss Emma when she wasn't even family, not the same way—"

"She was family. The truest family I ever had, except you and the kids."

"I wish she'd lived a hundred and twenty years, like Moses."

"But she's glad. You know she's glad to be home now. It's not this home that matters so much as that one."

We had to rejoin the others. Harry kept tapping at the door. Rorey was sitting in the middle of a mattress, pouting, when we came out. Harry grabbed for Julia right away, but I took his hand and led him toward his brothers so Juli could sit down beside Rorey a minute and put her arm around the little girl's shoulders. Even Barrett stayed, eventually sitting down with Harry in his lap.

That night was hard, like nothing else we'd ever had to handle. We were laboring for hours just trying to get all the children to sleep. Then every little while somebody was awake, somebody was crying or just up walking around like they didn't know what to do with themselves. I wondered how Joe and young Sam were doing now and if our pastor, who was younger than me, was having a hard time of it over there with George. I wondered too how Wilametta had managed with ten at bedtime every night. But then it wouldn't have been like this.

Nobody asked me for a story. And I was glad, because I wasn't sure I could find anything to say to them. Franky came and curled up beside me, and I wondered if Robert would be upset about it like he'd seemed to be earlier. But I couldn't turn Franky away. He cried a long time, just lying there kind of quiet, and when I went to sleep, I wasn't sure if he weren't crying still.

E L E V E N

Julia

I'd been dreaming about Emma dancing around in the strawberry bed when her namesake, little Emma Grace, woke me with a wail so loud it shook me clear to the bone. Poor Lizbeth was so tired from soothing one sibling after another all night that she could barely turn over. But Louise must've been up already, because she got to the baby before I could stand up.

Samuel had already fed the fire and gone outside, even though it was still dark. Early as it was, I wondered how I'd been able to sleep that long. Especially since my outbursts of yesterday were plaguing me terribly. Nobody needed to hear any of the bitter stuff churning around in me, least of all Lizbeth. I'd have to keep my thoughts to myself or wait for a minute when I could share them with Samuel again. But maybe that wasn't for the best either.

I couldn't get the picture of Emma out of my mind—on the floor in Wila's room, utterly broken. She would've lived a little longer, I was sure, if Wilametta hadn't gone first. And that plagued me too. I should've been bolder. I should've insisted on going to see about Wila by myself, so Emma could've rested the way she needed to. She might've been here then, when I got back. She might still be here, to comfort all these dear souls.

I got myself up to make sure the kitchen stove was lit, but when I saw Emma's rocker across the sitting room floor, I just stopped. Louise came over beside me with the sniffling baby.

"Don't worry on breakfast," she said. "I'll start something. Got plenty of eggs?"

There were eggs. Yes. Because Emma'd brought four hens with her when she came back home. And there were sixteen chickens now. We'd raised the rest over the summer, even butchered some. Everything about us coming here had seemed touched by the hand of God. So why did God feel so far away now?

"There are eggs," I told Louise. "They're down in production since it's been cold, but there'll still be some out there. I'll send Robert to check pretty soon."

"Barrett's gone to tend the chores at home," she said. "Maybe he'll think to bring our milk and eggs back over with him too. They'll be gettin' an early start in the timber."

Digging. Of course, they had to do it, but I wondered how they could. And Samuel, with the job he had to do. He would do it well, I had no doubts about that. But I couldn't have done it, though I'd laid Emma out on that bed. I couldn't have made her a box nor set her in it, and I sure couldn't put her in the ground.

Somebody had already lit the cookstove. Robert, usually an early riser anyway, was stirring around pretty quick, and I sent him out to gather whatever fresh eggs there might be. Kirk wasn't up yet, nor were most of the others, so I decided to go ahead and rinse the milk pail and see to the milking myself. I sure didn't want Samuel to have to think about it this morning, with all he had to do. Tomorrow were the funerals. People would be coming, what people could get through, anyway, to pay their respects. How would I, how would we all, make it through seeing Emma and Wila in their stillness one last time?

All through the milking it bothered me. They'd be bringing Emma and Wila here. It didn't feel right. But nothing else I could think of came even close to feeling righter. Pastor knew going to town would be difficult, and not really like Emma or Wila, who both loved home so much. Oh, that it could've been spring, so we could all just be outside, surrounded by Emma's bounty of flowers.

I was nearly done when Franky came out to the barn, looking to help Samuel at his job. I made him come in with me, but he wouldn't stay. Had to help, he said. Owed it to his mama.

"He's worrying me," I told Samuel when I brought him coffee a little later and shooed Franky back inside to eat some breakfast. "He hadn't ought to be out here with you this way, watching this."

"What else is he going to do?" Samuel asked with sad eyes. "He's thinking on it, Juli. It'll be on his mind no matter what. At least he feels like he's contributing something."

"I could put him at something in the house. Louise is mopping in there to beat the band."

He sighed. "But we all have to deal with things in our own fashion. I don't understand it either, but maybe this is his."

Those simple words made me angry. We couldn't deal with things in our own fashion. I didn't even know what my fashion was. Maybe none of us did. We had to help rescue George and hold babies and try to keep from saying anything else as stupid as what I'd said last night. We had to be what everybody thought we should be and not fall apart any more than we had to. Just go through the motions, like Lizbeth was doing. I didn't even have a clue what I might be like if it was just me with this pain. Maybe I'd scream. Maybe I'd fling another cup of apple-mint tea into Wilametta's fireplace. Maybe it was better never to know.

Barrett Post came riding in with the milk and eggs from their place. He handed them to me to take inside, took a package of something in to Samuel, and then was gone, hardly saying two words.

When I went in the house, Sarah had broken a saucer and was sitting at the table in tears. Louise was doing her best to sweep it up with Harry crawling around all the chairs.

"Berty smelled up his pants," he announced as soon as he saw me. I took the milk and eggs to the cellar steps, thinking about poor Lizbeth. Having that to deal with, and baby Emma Grace too. But it was Elvira who had the baby just then, and I was grateful for that.

Rorey woke up sopping wet and crying, either from the shock or the embarrassment. And just then I might've screamed at George and Wilametta for having so many kids.

Where are you, George? I wanted to wail. *Confound it! When are you going to be here for them? When are you going to take care of your own problems?*

Before we had Rorey and Berty in fresh clothes, Kirk had decided it was time to take his father's other horse back home. I knew I couldn't stop him. There'd be no escaping the awfulness of the situation, regardless of which place he was at. "Just talk to Samuel first," I beseeched him. "He'll know if your father said anything about that."

They'll be moving the bodies today, I kept thinking. *What an awful thing to be in the middle of.*

Robert and Willy shoveled out Lula Bell's stall, God bless them, and gave her clean straw. Then they carted new straw to the chicken house too. Covey Mueller came back with Alberta as I was washing the big sitting room window. I hadn't seen a wagon on runners like theirs since Grandpa Charlie's when I was a little girl. Clarence and Pet, the Mueller's team, were the biggest horses anywhere in the area.

Alberta came charging straight in the house with her quick little steps, despite having her arms full with two covered pans. Chicken pie and a frosted cake. I set them on the counter and almost forgot to say hello. Mr. Mueller went straight out to the barn.

Alberta gave me a big hug, though I didn't know her all that well, and asked if I knew how many of the folks from the church in Dearing would be coming.

"We'll just have to see," I told her. "I don't know how there could be many with this snow."

But not twenty minutes later, Mrs. Gray, the Sunday school teacher, came riding up on a sturdy gray mare. Bundled in layers and carrying a sack, she came in the house looking like Santa Claus. She'd brought beet pickles and quince preserves wrapped up in towels, and a deep-dish apple crisp that I couldn't picture how she'd managed not to spill. She went straight for Lizbeth and hugged that girl's neck like I'd never seen anyone else do, ever.

"Oh, Mrs. Gray," Lizbeth said, but that was all. For a moment her face changed just a little, and she looked like she might say something else or even break down and cry. But the moment passed. Her eyes were soon hollow and hard again, and she was scolding Harry for pulling his socks off and throwing them in the potato bin.

"We let off Orville to help the digging," Alberta suddenly told me.

Her son, along with Louise and Elvira's husbands. Doing all they could, when they didn't have to do any of it. And these ladies didn't have to help clean this house that Emma'd called mine, though Louise and Elvira had already started. They didn't have to bring in food nor willing hugs. But for Emma they'd do anything, just like she'd have done anything for them. Even when it killed her.

Robert and Willy had started shoveling paths through the snow, and I wondered who told them to work so hard. I hadn't thought to, that was for sure.

Louise put on water to heat, and we were doing baths for the kids soon enough, though there wasn't a one of them that wanted anything to do with that in the wintertime. We portioned off a corner of the kitchen and no sooner had one child clean than we started in on another. Rorey cried when I brushed the tangles out of her hair, and Sarah sat as solemn as a stone.

"I don't want all these people," Sarah told me when I was almost finished with her. "I just want me and you and Bessie-doll all by ourself."

I had to hold her a minute. I surely understood. The poor child, used to being my baby and my shadow, had to wait her turn just to have me look her way. "I'm sorry, pumpkin," I whispered. "It'll get better."

"No, Mommy," she protested. "You haves to get wider and wider, to cover up where Rorey's Mommy used to be."

Such a picture. But surely it was true. At least for a little while.

Covey Mueller was helping Samuel with the coffins, and it sure speeded the job. Franky came in at one point and told me that Samuel had started carving flowers on the lids while Mr. Mueller was putting the boxes together. "The flowers was my idea," he announced. But I wouldn't go and look at them up close. It still bothered me that Franky was in the middle of all that. But there was nothing I could do about it. Samuel let Franky stay as much as he wanted to, and he'd let Kirk take the horse too, because the boy wanted to see his father so badly and be with his older brothers. Pastor was there, Samuel assured me; Kirk would be okay. I just hoped he was right.

Nobody wanted lunch, but Louise cut the chicken pie anyway, shoved a spoon into a potato casserole, and tried to persuade everyone. Once they got started, Robert and Willy could eat, after all that work they'd done. But nobody else had much, except maybe Bonnie Gray, who as soon as she finished, volunteered to carry food to the men in the timber. But Alberta told her that Covey would be going that way soon enough and could take the food then.

Sure enough, not long after lunch, Samuel and Mr. Mueller were loading the two long boxes into Mueller's wagon. It was hard to breathe suddenly, looking out and seeing that. I didn't know how they could've gotten it done so fast, even with the both of them working together. They had put brass handles along the sides; Barrett Post had brought them, and he wouldn't take any payment either, for that or the wood. I prayed for him and Louise, that God would touch them some way and bless them for their generosity.

Bonnie helped Alberta pack a generous amount of food in two baskets, one for the men in the timber and one for George and his boys and the pastor. Then they put their scarves and coats back on and charged outside with the baskets.

Samuel and the Muellers rode off together, and I felt a heaviness just watching them go. Everybody else seemed to change somehow too. Lizbeth sounded extra short trying to get Bert down for a nap. And Franky came in and just sat in a corner, staring into space.

Louise and Elvira were fluttering about, setting our house in shape and then picking out a few things Emma'd been especially proud of to set out and show. I didn't say anything, but I didn't like what they were doing, fingering her things and talking about her. They respected her, no way I could question that. And they were kind. But they didn't know her, not like they thought they did, because they didn't know it was God that had mattered most to Emma. They'd never understood that. All of the Posts were good enough people, but none of them concerned themselves with God at all, and they didn't seem to know what a burden Emma'd had for their souls.

I remembered what she'd told me once. *"Oh, Juli, Barrett's closed his eyes, and the rest of 'em ain't no better. They's turned their backs on the ever-lovin' Savior, and him all the while just a-callin' so fond."*

I prayed for them all over again, because Emma would've done it, and I wanted to do it for her. And then I told the Lord that there ought to be church ladies selecting some of her things, because they would understand what Emma would want people to see—and think about—at such a time as this.

As if in answer to my prayer, Mrs. Gray walked up to Elvira and suggested that Emma's Bible be placed right in the center of the little table they were going to use to display her things.

"Emma'd like that," Bonnie told them. "The Word of God front and center. She'd tell you the same thing if she were here."

Rorey came up to me in a blue dress of Sarah's, her wild curls waving every which way, just like her mother's. "Mrs. Wortham," she said solemnly, "what are we going to do about Christmas?"

She didn't ask about her birthday, though I knew it was only a day after the holiday. She didn't mention the cake her mother had promised to make, though I'd heard about it from Sarah, as much as three weeks before. She didn't say anything else at all, only stood there with her eyes wide and fearful, waiting to know what I would answer.

"The Lord will provide when the time comes," I heard myself tell her. "One day at a time right now."

Not two minutes later, Barrett Post came driving back in his sleigh with people bundled up in his back seat. Pastor Jones's wife Juanita and Delores Pratt and her teenage granddaughter Thelma. All from church.

"The preacher asked me to go an' get 'em," Mr. Post explained. "Best go and relieve him at the digging now, though."

The preacher? Digging? Almost I said something, but Mr. Post must've seen my expression.

"Oh, he ain't the only one, don't worry. He only come out to ask the favor and fill my spot till I come back."

"How is George?"

"Ain't seen him today. Ain't talked to him. His oldest boy never said nothin' either." He shook his head. "That'un can work, though, let me tell you. I tried to send him home after he marked the spot for us, but he stayed feedin' fires and then tore into that diggin' fierce."

Juanita and Delores were bringing beef stew, fried cabbage, applesauce, and a lemon custard into the house with them, and Thelma had two loaves of bread. Juanita gave me a tremendous hug, and Louise sat her husband down to a cup of coffee and a generous lunch.

"Everybody keeps bringing food," I said.

"That's what's done," Juanita told me. "Sit down, honey. We'll take care of this."

For the first time, it occurred to me that everybody was treating Samuel and myself as though we'd really been family to Emma, and doing most of what they did so I wouldn't have to. And I thought it was too bad about Albert and his wife. But then I remembered somebody else.

"Didn't Emma have a cousin somewhere?"

"Mary Lou Friday, her cousin Alice's girl," Mr. Post confirmed. "Albert said he'd tell them the news. And Ralph Watts, that's another cousin out West. I don't be expectin' them though, with s' far to come."

"Miss Hazel said she'd try to make it," Juanita suddenly told us. And I tensed inside. Hazel Sharpe? Lord have mercy. Right outside the church she'd snipped at us something fierce over our living here. She'd even told Emma it'd be the death of her to leave the boardinghouse and come back home. And it was.

I thought back over the months we'd spent, and I knew Emma'd been happy. Emma wouldn't regret a single minute of it. But what about Miss Hazel? What about other people?

Harry came and poked his finger in the custard, and I didn't have the energy to tell him no.

"You want some, precious?" Delores asked him. That was the way she talked. Anybody under six or seven years old was "precious," and most other folks were "honey" as often as not. She scooped Harry out a bowl of custard and set it on the table with a spoon. He sat right down and started eating with his fingers, but she didn't seem to notice.

"Time like this," she told me, "the important thing is to keep 'em eating. Don't matter so much that they have the regular time nor if they eat their dessert first nor nothin' like that, so long as they fill their bellies. Folks mournin' forget to eat sometimes, an' that ain't good for children. You got plenty down 'em today?"

"We tried."

She stepped closer, eyeing me sympathetically. "What about you, honey? You eat any lunch?"

I honestly couldn't remember if I had or not, though I wasn't pleased to be such evidence of her notion. I hadn't forgotten. I just . . . hadn't remembered to think about it when I was thinking about something else. She clucked her tongue and handed me a bowl bigger than Harry's. Then she sat beside me, though I really didn't want her there, and whispered, "We all loved Emma so."

"Yes," I said. I put my spoon in the custard bowl and then rose to see where Rorey had so quietly gone.

"Not a single bite," I heard Delores say sadly. But I didn't care. Let Harry eat it.

"Rorey?" I called softly. She was sitting on the floor by the fireplace in the sitting room. I hoped she wasn't upset with me for not giving her any clearer answers about Christmas. Maybe she just wanted to soak up the coziest spot in the house.

Sarah was coming downstairs with the little book I'd gotten for her once in Pennsylvania. I waited for her and sat with them both.

"Rorey, I didn't mean to stop talking to you if you had more to say. It's just the company coming. That's all."

"Okay," she said sadly. "Are *you* gonna have Christmas?"

It was still on her mind, and I didn't know what to say. Only four days away. "I guess we'll try," I said, though at the moment I couldn't imagine it.

"We can't have Christmas," she'd decided. "Not without Mama."

"Yes, you can," Sarah jumped in. "She's an angel now, and Christmas is angels too. Right, Mommy? Rorey's Mommy can be one of our Christmas angels! Emma too!"

Rorey looked at her in surprise, and I hugged them both, not knowing what else to do. Every year, Sarah and I made Christmas angels cut out of paper to decorate the wall behind our nativity set. I knew Sarah would want to do it again. But after Christmas last year, I'd given our nativity away because we'd been forced to move and there was just no way to carry it.

"Can we, Mommy?" Sarah pressed. "Can we make the Christmas angels? Can Rorey help?"

I was surprised at her, I really was, but ever so glad. Surely we could make the nativity from paper too. Maybe it would do them some good. "You can draw them," I told her. "You and Rorey can start today if you want. Color them pretty and get them ready. But we won't cut them out yet. Not with so many people here just now."

Rorey looked at me with her face all scrunched up, the way she got when she was puzzling over something. "Is Mama really an angel now?"

"I don't see why not. She's in heaven. I know that."

I got up and found some paper and Crayolas, and Sarah spread them out on the floor. I hoped Franky would be interested in joining them, but he only sat and watched.

The afternoon passed us in a slow haze, with the ladies cleaning all around me and trying to be of some comfort. They moved the bed out of Emma's room to make enough space for the caskets, and I wished I could sleep through all this like Emma Grace and Berty were doing. But even they were awake soon enough, crying for somebody's arms.

Before I knew it, Samuel and the Muellers were back. It was like a dream, those long boxes coming in the house. Not real. Not right.

Pastor Jones came with them, and I suddenly didn't want him in the house, though I dearly loved both him and his wife. *Don't talk to us,* I wanted to tell him. *Don't say anything at all, because anything you say will sound so final, so real. And I don't want it to be real.*

They weren't done with the graves yet. That's what Samuel said. They'd let a couple of fires burn all morning, and the digging still wasn't done. I didn't acknowledge what he said. I hadn't wanted to hear it.

It's too cruel, Lord. It's too cold, what we have to do. There should be something better for Emma. Not just a long pine box in her bedroom and a hole in the frozen ground.

Remember heaven, she would tell me. Remember the streets of gold where there is no sorrow, no pain. But here there was pain aplenty just looking into the wounded eyes of Wilametta's children.

"George wouldn't come," Alberta told me. "Not yet. I declare, I never seen a man s' outta his mind for grief. He musta loved her, surely, but what's ta come a' him, I don't know."

What's to come of his children? That's what I wanted to know. Like Franky, who rose up off the floor only when he heard the wagon, and now was sitting with his hand on the handle of his mother's coffin. And Rorey, solemnly drawing angels with tears streaming down her cheeks. And Lizbeth, who was once again consoling a pouting baby and looking nearly dead on her feet. And Willy and Harry, just acting as though they were trying to ignore it all. And little Berty, too confused by all the people to understand.

But I wondered about the big boys most. Sam and Joe, and now Kirk, perhaps with their father or perhaps digging in the timber, away from Juanita or Elvira or anyone that could give them a comforting hand.

By four o'clock it was dusky, and Barrett Post and his son, Martin, Elvira's husband, Clement, and Alberta's son, Orville, came up from the timber. The graves were done, and they'd already fashioned temporary markers until someone could arrange for ones of stone. The funerals would be in the morning, early, with a gathering at the graveside for anyone who could manage to get to us through the snow.

Louise and Bonnie tried again at feeding everybody, and the Muellers all went home. Frank Cafey and three or four other neighbors made their way out in the cold that night to pay respects. And after they'd all come and gone, the Posts went home too.

It was a strange comfort having Bonnie Gray, Delores and her granddaughter, and Pastor's wife, Juanita, stay the night. But Pastor Jones, after speaking to nearly all of the children, determined to go back over to see the night through at the Hammonds'.

As he was getting his coat, Samuel took me aside for a minute. "George asked if we'd see to the kids," he told me. "He said he didn't want to go on another day. Hard to say what he might do."

See to the kids? As if we hadn't already been doing that! I wanted to get a hold on George right then! What right did he have to ask us more? What right did he have to stay away so long in his pitiful madness, not even trying to be a comfort to his own flesh and blood? Those boys were over there having to be strong for their father, having almost to father him instead of the other way around! I wanted to shake him, knock his eyes open maybe, to make him see what he was doing to them.

Samuel wouldn't let the pastor head out alone through the snowy dark timber, though it was only a mile and Pastor Jones was young and plenty sturdy. Sam took a lantern, and they struck out together. It was a warmer night, and I was grateful for that. I stood out on the porch and watched them walk away down the trail already made by men's feet, Mueller's wagon, and Barrett Post's sleigh. And when I could see them no more, I looked up at the sky and saw the stars. Emma's stars, finally shining brighter than they had in a month of Sundays, just as if they wanted me to know they understood. Saints come home.

Reluctantly I turned and went inside, thinking how good it'd be just to stay under all that clear sky a little longer, to "see up to God's heaven" like Emma had said. I thought maybe I could lay the hurt aside a little and think about the good that was waiting for all of us somewhere beyond those glorious stars.

But my Sarah's arms were waiting for me inside, and Rorey's, and maybe more besides. Because even with the others there, the kids still wanted Lizbeth or me more often than not. And all of my thoughts, all of my sorting things out, could wait for their sakes. Surely it had to be so.

It was strange sleeping that night, knowing that Emma and Wila were with us. Willy had a hard time even managing to lie down. Franky wouldn't leave his mother's casket, and I had to wait till he finally nodded off, and then carry him to the other room. Harry, bless his heart, kept asking where his mama was. He and Berty still just didn't understand. Rorey cried herself to sleep for the second night in a row, and she and Sarah clung to me all night, just as I'd expected. I laid there and prayed for all of them, especially for Lizbeth, though she was seeming almost like herself again, bearing up surprisingly well.

Late into the night I dreamed that Emma had come back and was walking through the room, praying for each one of us in turn. But then I woke and saw that it was Juanita up and praying. I hugged her and cried till she cried too, and then I felt better.

Next morning was anything but real, feeding children and fixing them to look as nice as possible in their old clothes. The Posts were back before we were ready to see them, and then the Muellers too. Rita McPiery, Emma's dear friend from the boardinghouse, and her brother Daniel came out, both of them looking red-faced as though they'd cried on the way. Frank Cafey was back, smelling faintly of liquor. And other neighbors, and the Henleys, who lived just a mile outside of Dearing. When Pastor and my Samuel got back with Kirky and Joe, the service started, though George and young Sam had not come in.

It was like a dream, everybody stone silent. Even the baby. Nobody moved, nobody made a sound until little Berty fell off his seat and sat kicking furiously at a chair leg. Then whatever it was that got hold of him swept through the room, because Franky let out a wail, Harry ran in the kitchen to sulk under the table, and Lizbeth broke down in choking sobs that seemed to spread to almost everybody. I didn't see how we could manage getting out to the timber to see this through, but before I knew it, they had the coffins loaded in the back of Covey Mueller's wagon again, and folks were starting off in that direction.

It was a sunny day, not near so cold as it had been. Just the way it needed to be, I guessed, for what we needed to do. But I almost didn't go. I took a look at the children around me and cried out to Juanita in protest.

"It's too much for them. I can't expect more from them today. To see those boxes lowered into the ground. It's not right! I'll stay right here with all of them. We'll sing maybe, and work on our Christmas angels."

Juanita might've agreed. I certainly couldn't expect her to argue, but before she could say anything, Franky was shaking his head. "It's something we gotta do, for Mama."

His brother Willy agreed, and to my surprise, so did Rorey. "I'm gonna go," she said. "Hold my hand."

So we went, all of us but Harry and Berty, who we left at the house with young Thelma Pratt. We trudged down the path worn between drifts of snow. Every time I'd been out to the pond before, the half-mile walk had been easy. But this time it seemed to take forever. I was glad we'd delayed long enough not to see Mueller's wagon in front of us. Everybody was walking, though I wasn't sure why. We'd left at least three sleighs behind us in the farmyard.

But it had been the same way when Robert was baptized. All the church people walked out from the house, though at that time of year they could've gotten a car quite close to the pond. But Emma said it was the way things were done. For generations. Even at the TannyBrook Cemetery where her parents were buried, people stopped just off the road and walked the rest of the way. Maybe they figured it took a little walking in the fresh air to get your head together for what came next.

With Sarah on one side of me and Rorey on the other, I tried to keep some strength about me. I wanted to cry the way I had last night. I wanted to argue with heaven about all of this. But it wouldn't do. Not in front of the children.

I tried to look around and enjoy the timber a little. In the summer it was such a beautiful place, with wildflowers and willows swaying in the breeze. But now it was a wasteland of slushy gray and white, and when we got close enough to see it, Willard's grave marker stood up stark and cold. But no longer alone.

Samuel was already standing there with George's oldest boys and Mr. Post. I looked around for the pastor, knowing he'd gone ahead with the wagon and should be here. But he was nowhere in sight.

"Mommy?" It was Sarah talking, sounding suddenly frightened. "Does it hurt them to be put down in the ground?"

"No, honey. They aren't here anymore. They left right out of their bodies when they went to heaven. So they're with Jesus now, having more fun than we could imagine."

"Is it spring there?" Sarah asked me. "Emma told me she likes spring."

I couldn't help but smile, just a little. "I suppose it's spring there all the time. And anything else we could want it to be."

When we got closer to Willard's marker, Rorey squeezed at my hand, just staring at Emma's coffin on the lump of dirt, with the blanket stretched beneath it. I wished I could turn her attention away. But maybe it was better that I couldn't, so she wouldn't be looking off down the hill and toward the little grove of birch trees where her mother's empty grave lay waiting. *Lord God, how will we ever get through this day?*

149

George wasn't here. I should've seen it immediately and known it was why Pastor Jones wasn't here either. He'd be off somewhere, trying to coax enough strength into George to stand beside his little ones at such a time as this.

I looked around at Louise Post, Elvira Post, the Muellers, Juanita Jones, Bonnie Gray, and all the rest. It was a marvel to me that they all had taken the trouble to get here, cold as it was. But Emma had given them all cause to love her, and they'd have gotten here if there was any way at all.

I didn't expect anyone else. There were already quite a few people, all the ones that had been at the house. But then I heard someone else coming on the path behind us, and I was amazed to see that it was Miss Hazel Sharpe, despite her advanced years, hurrying down the path with her usual quick step. Charlie Hunter was right beside her, looking as though he'd like to find some way to help. But Hazel hardly ever needed help with anything, though she was stooped so low she could barely look up.

I was grateful to Charlie for coming. He'd been so faithful to see that Emma, and all of us, got to church. And he'd always called Emma "Grandma" since having her in Sunday school years before.

But seeing Miss Hazel scared me. Things were already so difficult to manage. And I'd never seen her, not once in seven months, when she wasn't all worked up and snippety at somebody. Lord have mercy. I knew how she'd loved Emma, at least she'd said she did. They'd been schoolgirls together, nearly eighty years before. But she had despised us being here and had despised George Hammond's poor kind of ways, and I prayed right there on the spot that she would have the decency to hold her tongue.

Lizbeth came and stood beside me with Emma Grace all bundled in blankets. I'd wanted to leave the baby with Thelma too, but Lizbeth insisted on carrying her, saying she'd do nothing but cry without her there. Elvira and her husband came up on Lizbeth's other side.

I looked over at Robert, who'd had so little of my attention lately. He was with Willy and Kirk and Joe, all standing in a line. Franky had gone straight to my Samuel and stood clinging to his hand. I was glad we'd managed to leave the two little boys behind.

Somebody started singing a hymn, and I thought again of all the church folks that had come for Robert's baptism and how excited Emma had been about it all.

"Just like old times," she'd told me over and over. *"Ever'-body comin' to sing an' celebrate an' then eat till they could just about bust."*

We'd had tables set up back at the yard then, full of food the people had brought with them. And people had brought food again this morning too, mostly for George and his children, I expected. But it was no celebration. Should've been maybe, at least for Emma's sake; that's what she would've wanted. But even she had had a hard time swallowing it down about Wila.

Lizbeth was sniffing beside me, and Elvira put her arm around her. Finally Pastor Jones came up the hill, but there was no George. Sam Hammond, who'd been standing quietly beside the Mueller boy, looked white as the sky suddenly and disappeared, not getting back in time for one minute of Emma's service.

Paxton Jones knew exactly what Emma wanted in a sermon. He painted a picture of heaven so grand that all of us should've been fairly floating with assurance for her sake. But we stood there weeping or stone silent like the stubborn mortals we are, never really grasping the little looks at eternity we get. The sadness was so big it seemed like not even God could be bigger, that not even God would be able to fill up the void that Emma and Wila were leaving behind. Even if the whole world had stood still, things could not have been more strange, more fiercesome, or more final.

T W E L V E

$\mathcal{S}amuel$

"Though I walk through the valley of the shadow of death, I will fear no evil. Thy rod and thy staff, they comfort me, and I shall dwell in the house of the Lord forever."

We lowered Emma's coffin slowly with one silk rose resting atop it. Miss Hazel had placed it there because, she said, "Emma always did like a flower."

Most of the people lingered only for a moment before moving slowly down the hill toward Wilametta Hammond's grave. Beside me Franky was silent, his face showing no expression. I saw Robert nearer to the frozen pond, kicking at a clump of snow. Willy and Kirk were beside him, looking almost dazed, and I wished that they could just break down and cry. They were all still children, no matter how big and strong they'd gotten.

Miss Hazel looked at me for a second as she went past. Her eyes were stern, but not with their usual blazing fire.

She looked down at Franky hanging on tight to my hand and gave his shoulder a little pat. Maybe I shouldn't have been surprised. But I was, not recalling her ever extending an ounce of affection to any of us before this. *Bless her, Lord*, I prayed. *Despite her crotchety exterior, she cares down inside. Maybe she always has.*

I waited for Julia, who with Sarah and the Hammond girls was the last to leave Emma's grave. I wanted to reach for her, to hold her again for just a minute, but we both had children needing us to hold them a while longer first.

We had just started down the hill when I heard George's voice bouncing through the snowy trees.

"I ain't standin', I'm tellin' you! I ain't movin' again!"

I could see him sitting with his back against an old birch tree, and young Sam leaning over him, saying something I couldn't hear. Lizbeth, Willy, and the rest stared at their father. The first glimpse of him they'd had in almost three days, and there he sat looking wild and disheveled and shouting loud enough surely to scatter the wildlife in the timber beyond.

"Leave me alone!" he exclaimed, jerking his arm back from his son. "You been hoverin' over me like a mother cat! Just get!"

Young Sam stood there for a moment until Pastor Jones put an arm around his shoulder and led him away. That was for the best. We'd all tried, me and his boys, Pastor and Barrett and Covey Mueller. But George would have to see to George, because nobody else could. Much as we'd wanted to, he wouldn't have it so.

Paxton spoke of Wilametta as a kind mother and free spirit who loved to do things out of doors. When he said she was a good wife, George slowly rose to his feet and came close enough to touch the edge of the coffin. Franky let go of me and tried to get his hand, but he turned away too soon.

153

"I can't see it," George muttered. "I can't see you put her in the ground."

The words hit every one of his children like a gale force wind. Both of the girls broke into sobs, and poor Joe sunk to his knees in the snow. Willy turned on his heels to run, and when Robert tried to stop him, Kirk shoved him to the ground. "Let him go!" he hollered. "Just let him go!"

Robert lay there in a drift, looking stunned, and Kirk went running after Willy. They were going the same way their father had just gone, through the trees toward home. I half expected young Sam to go after them, but he didn't. Tears in his eyes, he took Emma Grace from Lizbeth's arms and gave a nod to the pastor. "My mama would want a song."

Pastor Jones, looking suddenly younger and pale with worry, turned to Julia and asked if she could sing "Blessed Assurance." I knew that had been arranged already, that one of the Hammond boys had asked her to do it when he found out she'd sung for his mama the night of her passing. But Juli could barely get the words out. She tried, she tried hard, but Franky's wailing was louder and there wasn't a person standing could keep an eye dry.

Paxton spoke a little more and prayed, but he must've known the best thing was just to have all this done. He dismissed everyone with a blessing, and people started moving away, those that could. Lizbeth was just staring at the grave, standing there shaking. And Joe was still on his knees, looking around like he didn't know what the world had come to. The schoolteacher went to Lizbeth and Pastor went to Joe and Julia tried to turn the little girls away to the house.

I wanted to send Franky with them and do my part to fill in the graves without him watching in anguish. But when the Post brothers started shoveling in the dirt, he wanted to help. He pulled those dead-looking flower bulbs out of his pocket and told us he wanted to bury them with his mama. "Emma had a nice rose," he said. "My mama liked flowers too."

Barrett took the bulbs from him with the greatest of care, glanced over at me for a second, and then patted the boy on the shoulder. "You're right," he said. "And it's the thing to do. You're a right fine boy."

Those bulbs were tamped into the ground right in front of the wooden temporary marker that Clement Post had made. None of us said a word about whether those flowers would ever grow, though I'm sure with so much of the winter left ahead of us, they knew as well as I did what chance there would be. Summer bulbs. Meant to be dug up and sheltered before the bitter wind hit.

It seemed to me that we were all a little like that. Hardy for our season and then gone. Emma had told us months ago that she was going to be dug up and planted in another place, and I could imagine her blooming there just as happy as anything. And Wila was there too, maybe even holding Franky's flowers in her hand.

THIRTEEN

Julia

We were in a strange fog the rest of that day and night. Most of the people went on their way, and we had tons of food and nobody much feeling like eating it. If I'd thought it would be just me and Samuel and our two children after the funerals, I was wrong, because we still had seven of the ten Hammond children with us.

"I'm not going home," Lizbeth maintained again. "Not till Pa says so."

Nobody argued with her. Kirk and Willy were home, presumably, and the biggest boy, Sam, had gone to see about them. But George in his sorry state had not acknowledged any of his children, except for shoving young Sam away. We couldn't send the littler ones home, not knowing what George would be like. Emma would want us to watch out for them, and I couldn't help but think Wila would too. So Samuel and I sat with them that night, me reading Bible stories to them first, and then Samuel telling a couple of stories that he made up on his own. They slept here and there, scattered about our sitting room, with only Robert and Joe upstairs.

"What are we gonna do with them?" I asked Samuel when the house was quiet. And he held me in his arms for so long I wasn't sure he would answer.

"I guess we'd better figure out how to give them Christmas," he finally said. "George doesn't have much, honey, even if he does manage to think about it."

I couldn't protest, though something inside me almost wanted to. We didn't have much either. We'd worked and worked and pinched what few pennies had come our way the whole summer long, just to get our small family ready for the winter. What could we do for so many?

"I've got the sleds," Samuel told me, as if in answer. "I'm sure Robert and Sarah would understand sharing one of them. I might even have time to make another."

"Oh, Sammy."

"What else can we do, Juli? They need our help. There's no escaping it."

"Emma was making a dress for the baby." My mind went racing over such things. Samuel had made the sleds, one for Robert, one for Sarah. And I had made a hat for Robert and a new dress for Sarah's doll. If we gave one of those sleds to the Hammond children, they should each have something more besides. "Does Rorey have a doll?" I asked out loud. The girl dearly loved playing with Sarah's Bessie, but it had never occurred to me to ask if she had a doll at home.

"You've been over there," Samuel said. "They have scarce little of anything. Except milk and bacon."

"I didn't see a toy or a book in the place," I agreed. Oh, we had so little time! What could we do? It was rousing in some strange way, knowing what a lot of purposeful work had to be done, trying to make them all something.

157

But still I knew that no matter what we came up with, it could never make up for what was lost. Wilametta's absence would eclipse whatever else Christmas might mean for them this year, and maybe for years to come.

And I would be grieving for Emma. Already we'd shared stories of Christmas—things she used to do when Warren and Albert were little and things I'd done with the children back in Pennsylvania.

"I already give Rita my nativity set," she'd told me once. "So sorry, honey. We'll come up with another'n by then."

Cookies were what she had wanted. Star shaped and cane shaped and sprinkled with red sugar. Oh, how I would've loved sharing a Christmas with Emma! Apple-raisin pie. Sprigs of evergreen and little paper stand-up angels on the mantle. Lots and lots of Christmas songs.

Do it for the kids, she would tell me. Every bit of it, for all twelve of them. There was a little hope thinking of it. And a little dismay. What if none of them wanted any part of it at all?

"We'll figure something out," Samuel said. "At least we can try to feed them something special. And make Rorey her birthday cake."

Oh, the dear girl. I'd make her a cake all right. I would do all I could. But it would not be, and could not be, enough.

"Sammy, it's too much!" I protested again. "How can God expect us to manage all this! It would've been bad enough, just losing Emma! But why Mrs. Hammond? Why not George? He's been the same as useless to his own family all this time!"

Samuel didn't say anything, and my stomach twisted tight as a knot. Here I was so resentful over George, and yet I was making things harder the same as he was. I was making things harder for Samuel just talking like this. When had I gotten so coarse and unfeeling that I could talk about a grief-struck soul so harshly?

"I'm sorry," I told Samuel. "Maybe I should get some sleep." I turned from him, my head suddenly aching. I was angry, that's what it was. Angry at God, and nothing would ever be good again as long as that lasted. But I knew no way to change.

He took my hand and pulled me back into his arms. Samuel, my saint. He understood, maybe better than I did. "You want to talk about that night, honey?"

"No. I don't think I can."

"It might help."

The tightness in my stomach was suddenly painful. "They just died, Sammy! What else can I say? They just died! And there was nothing to be done about it. Except fix them up nice as I could for the folks that might see. Oh, Lord, why do we do that? Why do folks come and look and walk around and say things that mean nothing and tell us what we already know? It's useless! It's all useless!"

"I don't know," he said quietly. "I guess it's the only way we can think of to say good-bye."

"Emma took such care," I managed to tell him. "She fussed over Wila. She did the best she could."

He tried to hold me close, but I pulled away. "I didn't get her a dress," I heard myself sob. "The best friend I ever had, and I didn't even get her a decent Sunday dress! I should've thought—when I first got back over here—"

Tears broke over me; I had no control over them whatsoever. Sammy hugged me, and I sobbed into his chest for I don't know how long, thinking of Emma in that rocker over there. I should've seen it coming. I should've never let her go to the Hammonds. She would still be here if I'd have just made her stay home and rest her selfless heart.

It was late before we got to bed. I ended up telling Sammy all of what it had been like. Admitting my anger was not easy, nor was my anger only toward God. Worrying about George and thinking he was dead had scared me dreadfully. And then to find him the way that he was! Better if he *had* been dead—that's what I'd come close to thinking. How dare he become such a broken vessel? If he'd been the one dead and Wila the one to go on, I could imagine her calling all her children in, telling them the news so gently, and then explaining to each and every one just what they must do from here on out. How dare he be so weak!

There was life to go on living. Despite all the bitterness in my heart about it, at least I was changing diapers, washing cheeks, cooking meals, and such. At least I was trying to do what needed to be done. But God have mercy on me. Even though it broke my heart to say good-bye to Emma, my pain was different from what George was going through. I wasn't losing a wife of twenty-some years. I wasn't George without his Wilametta.

"We have to have him over Christmas too," Samuel said gently. "We need to find something we can give him and get him with his kids all we can. Maybe I can talk to him tomorrow and see if he'll give Lizbeth word for them all to come home. Maybe that's what he needs."

"What if he says no? What if he won't even come Christmas?"

"He'll listen. Surely he will. It's just hard, that's all."

"He's not quite like normal folks, Samuel. There was something less than sane in him, and I'm not sure if he'll listen or not."

"Thank the Lord he hasn't gone to drink. The Post brothers say if he ever did that, there'd be no way to save him. He drank when he was younger, and it had him clear out of his mind. Wilametta put a stop to it then."

"Surely we don't have to worry about that. Where would he get it?"

"Barrett says some people make their own around here. Even sell it, not caring much for the law, I guess."

"Well, anyway, I don't know how anything could make him worse than he's already been. Not even drink."

"Maybe he'll be better from here," Sam said with hope.

I wondered what George was doing that night, the first night with the funerals done. I wondered if he was being warm and thoughtful toward his boys over there, or if he was pushing them away. Lord help him.

And help me. Help me forgive you, Lord, for what death has done to all of us. Even though it never was your fault, from Adam on down the line. Help me forgive you, anyway, for the sake of my peace and because I know you want me to. So I can love you again the way I want to love you. So I can rejoice in every rain-drop, strawberry blossom, and mustard plant, the way Emma did. I want to be like her, Lord. Because she was like you.

$\mathcal{S}amuel$

Lula Bell had never given generous milk, but she was down again the next morning, so I gave her extra feed, hoping it would bring production up. But Sukey was worrying me even more than Lula Bell, since I knew she was due to calve before spring. My city upbringing hadn't prepared me to work with cows, and I was glad that Julia'd had some experience at least. But I knew we could use some more help, especially when it came time for the birthing. Maybe if I could stir George even to give me some advice, it would help take his mind off his problems. Worth a try, at least.

Franky came looking for me in the barn as I was sorting through what was left of the lumber. I'd have to work on the sled at night or I'd never manage to make any kind of surprise with my new shadow right there looking on.

"Whatcha doin', Mr. Wortham?"

"Just thinking a while."

"Gonna make somethin'?"

I couldn't answer that. "Up early, aren't you?"

"I'm always up early. Pa says I'll make a good farmer if I can keep from droppin' stuff an' tippin' over the milk."

"You'll get over that. All boys are awkward some when they're young. I know I was."

"Yeah," he said with a frown. "But it's extra for me. I can't manage much a' nothin' right."

I hadn't seen that to be so. Not a whit. He'd been good help to me, first with the planing and then with the sand-papering right alongside Mr. Mueller to get those casket sides smooth to the touch. He had a gift. I had to consider it so when an eight-year-old boy takes so natural to work-ing wood, even pointing out a mistake I'd made while I still had time to fix it. Elvira Post had to be wrong about him, because he wasn't slow. I thought he was brilliant. She just didn't know how to see it.

"Franky, just because you don't do things like every-body else doesn't mean you're wrong. You've got a knack for making things, I can tell."

"You gonna do a coffin again?" he asked solemnly.

Here I was, out here with the wood. Like before. "No. No, nothing like that."

"You know what I think?"

I waited, knowing he would tell me.

"You oughta make a sled! I know you could! An' it wouldn't take long. You just needs a couple pieces curvin' just the same an' the crosspieces cross the top. I got it all figgered out, but Pa never did let me the lumber an' nails."

His words came out all a rush, and I stood there with a strange new quandary. How could I tell him my plan? But how could I do it and *not* tell him? How could I look at him and say no?

"Franky? Can you keep a secret?"

163

"Yes. What?"

"I *am* going to make a sled. Maybe two. But you can't tell the others. I'll probably work when everybody's sleeping so they won't see."

"Robert's going to love it!" Franky exclaimed, coming to an obvious conclusion. "Sarah too! I wish our pa made stuff like you do. You did the rightest, finest job on Emma's wheelchair. The whole country was proud of ya!"

I had to smile at such a wild exaggeration. "Thank you. But your pa's busy putting meat on your table, which is something I haven't been too good at."

"He says you're tool smart, an' he's animal smart."

"I consider that a fine compliment from him. And I suppose he's right, in a way. Everybody's smart at one thing or another."

"Nope," he told me. "Not me."

"Now, Franky, I can plainly see how smart you are."

But he only shook his head.

We went in the house together and found Juli making oatmeal. Sarah and Rorey were playing school practically under her feet, teaching Bessie-doll a few simple words they'd written on some old scrap paper. Right away when we came in, Sarah tried to get Franky to read along, but he got red-faced and flustered and ran off into the other room.

"He's always that way," Rorey told me. "He can't read a stitch, not even his name, an' he oughta be goin' to third grade! Willy says it's a good thing he's sturdy, 'cause he sure is stupid."

"Rorey!" Julia exclaimed.

"I only said what he said!"

"He's plenty smart," I told her. "Just in his own way. God gives every one of us certain things."

"He's got a double amount a' clumsy. Pa said that."

Juli turned from the stove toward Rorey, but I didn't stay to listen. I found Franky in the sitting room, poking up the fire, and I went and stood beside him.

"School stuff comes hard, I take it."

He didn't look up. "Worse'n hard. Ain't much use me goin'. All I do is take up a seat."

"I bet you could make one of those old seats, though, couldn't you?"

"Well, yeah," he said, suddenly brightening. "They ain't nothin' but a sanded plank an' a straight back with a ledge stickin' out for the folks sittin' behind ya to put their books on. Couple a' board legs too, curvin' thinner in the middle." He stopped and gave me an almost conspiratorial look. "Are you still tryin' to tell me I'm smart?"

"Yes. And don't let anybody tell you otherwise."

"But what if I don't never read?"

"Just don't give up. You may get it if you keep at it. But put in a good day's work and do a good job, and one day people may pay you a lot of money for the things you make."

"Why don't *you* do that?" he asked. "Make things and sell? And fix stuff too, like you fixed Willard's tractor for Pa?"

"Times are hard, son," I told him, as though he were old enough to understand. "Too many folks out of work. Nobody's got extra money to pay for anything they can possibly do without."

I turned around to find Robert behind me. He stood there for a moment and then walked up the stairs. And I knew he was hurt. That was plain in his eyes. But I wasn't sure why.

"Excuse me, Franky, okay? I've got to speak a minute to Robert."

He shrugged his shoulders and glanced over at Joe, who was cracking nuts in the corner. Joe handed him a nutcracker, and Franky sat down cross-legged on the floor to help.

Robert was sitting on the bed when I got upstairs, looking sullen. I sat down beside him and put my arm around his shoulder.

"I thought they'd be going home," he said.

"They will. Soon enough."

"Seems like they oughta be home. 'Least sometimes. What's wrong with their dad, anyway?"

"I don't know all of it," I answered honestly. "But it's the grief affecting his thinking. He'll get better in time. He needs to be with his children, you're right about that. And they need him. I may go and talk to him again today. But son, if he can't see to his kids for a while, it falls on us. Since their relatives aren't able."

"They oughta come."

"I don't know about that. I only know we have to be kind. I have to help them, and so do you, because we're who they have right now. Do you understand?"

He was quiet for a minute before finally looking up, his eyes full of emotion. "I heard you call Franky 'son.' But he's not your son."

Oh. No wonder he was sore. "That's just like saying 'young fellow,' or something, Robert. People do it all the time. Some of the older gentlemen around here even call me son."

"But he's always right next to you, Dad! And you don't hardly look at me anymore! I just want things to be the way they were."

"Yeah." I sighed. "The problem is, things will never be like they were. Especially not for Franky and his brothers and sisters. I bet they'd like to go home and have things back to normal too, but it won't be the same without their mother. They need help, and they probably will for a while."

"I still want you to do stuff with me."

"I know. And I will. Just give us all time."

He was thinking, I could tell. And I couldn't help but consider how much alike Franky and Robert were sometimes. Very sensitive. But good with their hands too.

"Hey, Dad, remember I told you I'd really like a sled?"

I nodded, wondering at his abrupt change of subject. I'd made his sled when the weather first started getting cold and had hid it in Willard's old tool shed. I wasn't going to say anything about it to him, though.

"I know something we could do together," he continued. "When everybody else is sleeping, we could sneak out an' make the Hammonds a sled for Christmas, maybe big enough for three or four to sit at once, and they can take turns. Willy told me they don't get much of nothing for Christmas. Like maybe socks or some candy. Don't you think they'd like a sled?"

For a moment I couldn't even answer. Here was God talking through a boy. How else could he know what I'd had in mind? Why else would he be so zealous for it, when only moments before he'd been upset?

"That's a great idea, Robert." And I thought of Franky again, who'd had the same idea. Only he thought I'd be doing it just for my own two.

"You don't mind if I stay up?"

There was no way I could deny him. It seemed fitting, for sure, that Robert should help me bring some blessing. "I don't mind. With so little time before Christmas, I could use your help. Maybe we can even make two, since there's so many of them."

"Did you make me one already?"

"I guess you'll have to wait and see about that."

He smiled, his clear brown eyes shining. "I know it ain't Franky's fault he's here."

"Maybe you could be as much his friend as you are Willy's."

"He's kinda odd, though, Dad. And littler."

"Still—"

From downstairs, Julia's bell interrupted me, calling us to breakfast.

"Okay," Robert conceded and then grew quiet a moment. "I'm glad it wasn't my mom. I don't mean to be self-

167

ish about that. But I'm still glad." He started down the steps ahead of me.

"That's no more than normal," I said to his back, suddenly hearing something move in the next room. Somebody else was up here. I should've thought to check.

Before I could reach the stairs, Harry sprung from the other doorway and grabbed me by the knees. "Got ya!" he yelled. "I'm a wild Injun and you're a bear, and I'm gonna eat you up!"

"I'd rather have oatmeal, wouldn't you?"

"Nah! I like bear meat! I'm gonna cook it and pick apples and stuff."

I had to smile at his make-believe. I could remember being an Indian too, when I was a little tike, even bear hunting in the backyard. "You just one brave, all by yourself?"

"Yup. Berty wanted to play with Lizbeth."

"You're gonna need a nice bowl of oatmeal, then, to give you strength for all the work you've got ahead."

"Really? What work?" He let go my legs and looked up at me. By that time Robert was already downstairs.

"Takes an awful lot of work to skin a bear," I went on. "Can't eat it with the skin on. Too tough. If you don't eat something first, you'll get mighty hungry before you get the job done."

He shook his head. "I'm just playin'. Don't you know I'm playin'?"

"Sure." I gave his brown hair a pat. "If you weren't playing and I was a real bear, I might have to eat *you* up."

He laughed and then took my hand. "Are you really gonna make us a sled?"

He'd heard. Oh boy. This was going to be a hard secret to keep.

"I was spyin' on you," he boasted with a chuckle.

"I see that. But don't tell any of the others, okay? We want to surprise them."

168

"Are you really gonna make us one?" His eyes were wide, as if it were a difficult thing to believe.

"You'll see. But you can't tell anybody. Are you a big enough boy to keep a secret?"

I'd made the right appeal there. "I'm a real big boy!" he declared. "I'm sure big 'nough! I can even chop wood an' feed hogs an' ever'thin'!"

I couldn't quite imagine George having his five-year-old at such chores, but it was all right for the boy to think he could do them, at least. "I guess you are a big boy then. But let's not keep Juli waiting. Maybe you'd like to help me fill the wood box after breakfast."

"Okay," he said with a sly grin. "But then I'm gonna be a wild Injun again, an' I'm gonna catch you an' eat you up for sure."

He ran on down the stairs, laughing, and I thought of George and how much he was missing. He'd scarcely seen his kids for three days now. But did he ever really play with them? Was he missing even more than that?

We weren't finished with Julia's cinnamon oatmeal when Kirk and Willy came with the morning milk from the Hammond place. Juli jumped up to strain it immediately when she saw that it wasn't already done.

Kirk scooped himself some of the oatmeal. "Sam sent us over here," he said. "To help out."

"What did your father say?" Julia asked with obvious concern.

"Nothin'."

She looked at me with a pained expression. Nothing. And neither boy offered a word of explanation. Willy reached for a piece of toast and went walking into the sitting room.

"Why we lib here now?" Berty asked between mouthfuls.

"We're just visitin'," Lizbeth said hurriedly. "Hush."

"I wan' more milk." Little Berty looked straight at Juli, who filled his glass and gave Harry, Rorey, and Sarah some besides.

Lizbeth didn't ask how her father was. Neither did Joe. The two of them had talked the night before, and Lizbeth had said precious little since. She was spooning milky oatmeal into Emma Grace's mouth now, her face expressionless.

"Do you think we'll be home for Christmas?" Franky asked me.

"We ain't havin' no Christmas," Kirk declared.

Rorey got up from her seat and ran into the other room in tears. Juli followed her, but there was no helping it. For all our assurances, most of the Hammond kids could not imagine the holiday without their parents. Us talking about decorations and cakes and whatever else just wasn't going to be good enough. And I didn't blame them for it, not one bit. I had to take a deep breath, remembering Juli's words without really wanting to. "It's not right," she'd told the Lord and Pastor Jones. "It's just not right!"

FIFTEEN

Julia

Two days now till Christmas, and nothing but sorrowful-ness in the house. It was almost more than I could take. Sarah and Rorey had already drawn some angels, and I started right in after breakfast to help them finish the rest. Franky and Harry and Bert came and joined us with some interest, but none of the older boys did. Joe had started cracking walnuts for me before, and now I set him and Willy at picking out the meats and Kirk and Robert at cracking the hickories. We'd make cookies, that's what we'd do. I'd keep every one of these kids busy doing Christ-mas, whether they liked it or not. Surely that would lift the awful cloud off the place. Surely that would help.

I had Lizbeth help the little ones cut out their angels and arrange them all on the largest open wall space in the sitting room and stick them up with thumbtacks. She didn't want to, I could tell, but she didn't complain. I drew little pictures of Mary and Joseph, a cow, and a sheep, and Franky showed me the baby Jesus he drew.

"That's very good," I told him. "We'll use yours."

"His is too big," Rorey complained.

"Big is good," I maintained. "He should be big and easy to see because he's so important."

"But a baby ain't as big as a sheep!" she wailed.

"He's closer," Franky tried to explain. "See, some a' your angels is bigger. They's jus' flyin' closer."

That seemed to satisfy her, and she went back to playing with two of the paper angels, swinging them around with her arms as though they were flying over our heads.

"Do we hafta put 'em *all* on the wall, Mrs. Wortham? Can we keep some of 'em just for play?"

Her question lifted my heart immensely. Thank the good Lord for simple desires! "Sure, honey. We can make extras if you want."

"Make me a horsey," Harry asked. "A angel horsey with real wings."

"There ain't no angel horses," his sister chided him.

"There is too!"

"There ain't. Is there?" She looked at me.

"Well . . ." I had to consider that. "In the Book of Revelation it says that Jesus will be riding a white horse. At least I think that was talking about Jesus."

"What's Rebbalation?" Harry asked.

"Part of the Bible, dummy," Willy said from across the room.

"Now listen here," I said. "You need to speak respectfully to one another. No calling each other dummy or any other name, do you hear?"

"Yes'm," Willy mumbled.

I turned my attention back to Harry. "I'll make you a horse, if that's what you want."

"With wings?"

"All right. I don't see that it would hurt anything. Would you like a cutout too, Berty?"

"Goats," the little boy said.

"There ain't no goats in heaven," Rorey protested again.

"I don't know about that one way or the other," I said with a sigh. "But it would be fine having one in the stable near the baby Jesus. That's a good idea, Berty."

Rorey scowled at me. "You always do what the boys say."

"Seems to me I'm trying to please all of you right now," I answered her back, but then I wished I hadn't said anything.

"How many nuts you need, anyway?" Kirk asked me.

"All of them. We're going to make cookies today, and I need some for other things besides. But you can take a break when you want to. We don't have to do them all right now."

None of them stopped.

"Cookies?" Berty exclaimed.

"Yes. Two or three kinds. What are your favorites?"

"Snickerdoodles," Willy answered immediately.

"Can we make shaped ones?" Rorey asked. "To look like angels and trees and stuff?"

"We'll try," I said, thinking of Emma. "We just got some red coloring a few weeks ago, to make red sugar."

"Emma used to make us cookies every year," Lizbeth suddenly added, almost whimsically. "Stars and canes too. The stars with all white sugar. That was before she ever went to Belle Rive."

Silence fell over the room for a moment and had me frightfully uncomfortable. "Well, you all know just how they should look, then. You'll be fine helpers."

"I don't want cookies," Franky remarked quietly.

"I do," Berty declared.

"Me too," Harry agreed. "Can you make 'em look like horseys?"

"Oh. That would be much harder than a paper cutout. How about we stay with angels and stars and trees and canes? And maybe some plain circles or wreaths. Okay?"

I could imagine Emma over here in her kitchen, making cookies one after another, and all of them looking just right. Everything she made had to be right, or she'd do it over. Rows of them, stacks of them, she'd probably baked, for the Hammonds and more than likely other neighbors and friends too. Plus all the clothes and quilts and things she'd made for them, besides.

And here it was, already the day before Christmas Eve. I had to find that dress Emma was working on for baby Emma Grace and make Rorey's doll and come up with something for Lizbeth and the boys. They might say they didn't care, if I were to ask them. But they did care. It would matter to them, I knew that, even if it was years down the road before they thought it through. This might not be a good Christmas for them, it might even be the worst they'd ever have, but it would be the most important, nonetheless. Because they would either find paralyzing despair or enough of the hope and love of God to go on.

"I wish we had a piano," I suddenly said out loud, surprising myself.

"Oh, me too!" Sarah agreed. "Just like in Harrisburg, so you could play and sing carols."

Across the room, I could see Robert smile.

But Willy was shaking his head. "Don't nobody get too excited. Ain't no use none a' us puttin' out socks."

Joe plunked a handful of nuts into the bowl I'd given him. "Pa got the Christmas candy a couple a' weeks ago. I seen it. A piece for every one of us, even Emma Grace, an' she can't eat it."

"You ain't s'posed to tell stuff like that," Franky objected.

"This year's different," Joe reasoned. "We might oughta know that he thought on us. 'Cause he ain't thinkin' on it now."

There was a sound logic to that I appreciated. What George might or might not do in the next couple of days

174

I could not predict. But his kids should all know that he cared, regardless of his behavior, that he'd had them in mind before being knocked flat through no fault of his own.

"Pa likes lotsa gravy," Rorey remarked quietly. "On his potatoes and his sweet potatoes and his meat too, at Christmastime."

"I thought we'd have you all over here, if you want," I told her and the rest. "You can help me make plenty of gravy."

Lizbeth nodded, but far from happily. She looked as if she was simply resigning herself to do what she'd have to do, no more or less.

But Joe nodded too, more brightly. "I'll get Pa over here," he promised. "Maybe then we can go home."

"I don't want to go home." It was Willy who said it. His words put a hush over all of us. I could see his brothers and sisters all turn to look at him, just as surprised as I was to hear something none of us had expected any of them to say. I wanted to assure him somehow that he'd change his mind. But I couldn't tell him a thing. He'd been over there, he'd seen his father's despair. But more than that, he knew the emptiness of that house without Wilametta. And even when George came to himself, which he surely would soon, that part wouldn't change.

"We'll go home after Christmas," Joe solemnly declared again. "Mr. Wortham's talking to Pa about that right now."

Samuel had gone to see George, all right, but there was no telling what he might accomplish. He'd taken cinnamon oatmeal and baked apples over there for George and young Sam. I was hoping that they'd both be back with him, but I didn't want to say so, in case it didn't happen.

Suddenly Lizbeth sniffed and looked at me. "I have to go home before Christmas," she said with tears in her eyes. "'Cause I know what Mama made for Pa, and I'm the only one knows where it is."

Baby Emma, who'd napped right after breakfast, started to cry, and Lizbeth went to pick her up. The big boys went back to cracking nuts, and the smaller children turned their attention to the paper again. The silence was as hard as it'd been before. I just sat there, cutting out an angel and praying. For George and for all of us.

SIXTEEN

Samuel

The snow was beginning to melt, leaving a few bare brown patches of ground dotting the timber. Nothing moved around me, and nothing made a sound except for an occasional sliver of ice falling from a tree limb. I had ample time to think about what I might say to George, to encourage him toward getting his family together again.

But when I came in sight of the Hammonds' porch, all the words I'd planned slipped away from me. George had been so miserable, lashing out at everybody. I knocked on the door, barely hoping for anything better.

I expected young Sam to answer. But it was George, looking haggard. It was a wonder he came to the door at all, as tired as he looked.

"What are you doin' here?"

"Came to talk a minute, if it's all right." Strangely enough, the usually messy Hammond home looked far neater than the last time I'd seen it. "Where's Sam?" I stepped past George to get inside.

"He took Teddy 'while ago an' went to talk to Buzz Felder at the lumber mill. Wantin' to see if Buzz'll use him again afore long."

Sam had helped Mr. Felder off and on before, and the little money he'd managed to make had been a real boon to the family. He was surely thinking of them now too, riding the almost seven miles on that old horse. And he'd left George alone to do it. Maybe George was doing better. At least he was standing before me, looking right at me, answering my question. That was a sight better than yesterday.

"Why's ever'body think they gotta talk to me, anyway?" he asked. "Barrett Post was by here a while ago, snoopin' around."

"Neighbors are supposed to care. We're just trying to be good neighbors. Are you hungry? Juli sent you some breakfast."

I set the food on the table, but he didn't pay any attention. "My boy Sam ain't a neighbor," he mumbled. "But he give me a earful this mornin', he did. Said he was gonna see 'bout his work, an' I could jus' sit here an' rot if I wanted to."

I couldn't picture Sam Hammond saying such a thing. He'd been fearing for George and what he might do, and before this had hardly left him alone because of it. He'd labored, that was for sure, trying to pull his father out of the gloomy pit he was in. But George wouldn't be pulled, not even to talk to his children. And maybe young Sam had had enough.

"He's pretty tired," I said quickly. "And hit pretty hard himself lately."

"Angry, that's what he is. Blamin' me that his mama's gone. But it don't matter."

I'd been worried that the boy might blame himself. "It's not either of your faults," I told George. "I hope you both realize that."

"Don't matter whose fault it is. She's gone and there ain't nothin' to be done about it."

He sounded so hopeless. Why couldn't he see all the life that was going on, with or without him? "You're wrong. There's an awful lot that has to be done. You've got nine other kids besides Sam that are wondering about the future, probably even more than he is. You have to tell them something. You got your house looking nice. You ought to bring them home and get things as normal for them as you can."

He turned his face away, shaking his head angrily. "Sam done the house up. An' I don't need you tellin' me what to do. There ain't nothin' for 'em here. Don't you understand that yet? And you ain't got no business in on it."

"Yes. I do. As long as we're seeing to your kids the way we are, I have every right to come and question you." I knew I was just angering him worse, but I couldn't help it. It needed to be said. "They need their father, George, and you need to take a look at your own responsibilities."

"I am lookin'! That's the problem! You an' me may be throwed out in the snow soon as Albert gets here. He didn't draw up them papers legal. He told me he didn't. Said he wanted to wait an' see what you done. And now both places is his, an' he can do what he wants with us. We ain't got nothin'!"

"He knows what Emma wanted."

"That don't matter. Not if he still figgers we been usin' her. That's what he thought last time I seen him, leastways 'bout me."

I didn't know how Albert felt. But I expected him to honor his aunt's intentions, though I couldn't know that for sure, one way or the other. "That doesn't change what

I'm telling you about your kids, George. It's bad enough not having their mother—"

"Shut up! What's the use bringin' 'em back here? Better for 'em to get used to bein' someplace else—"

"Even if that's true, they still need their father. Especially now."

"I ain't got nowhere to go." He looked absolutely broken and somehow terribly small. "Me an' Wila used to talk 'bout this, what we'd do when Emma was gone. Maybe go t' her sister's place, but Fedora ain't gonna have me around even for a visit without Wilametta. I knows her to be that much a shrew. Chloe might be the one to change her mind an' take maybe two or three of the kids. Don't know what the rest of us'd do, though, even if we was here."

He sat down, shaking his head.

"You aren't split up. You don't have to be. And about Albert—"

"He ain't gonna listen to me. Nor care nothin' for m' needs, neither."

"Maybe not. But God can make a way."

"Where would you go, Wortham, if he sold Emma's place?"

"I don't know. I'll cross that bridge if we ever get there. What you need to do right now is think of your kids and quit borrowing worry over things that haven't even happened yet."

He was staring at me with a frown. "Any of 'em sick?"

"No. Lonesome for you. Missing their mother. Needing you to be strong and be a father to them. When do you want me to bring them home?"

He didn't answer. He got up and walked across the room to the fire, and I followed him.

"Julia and I would like to have you all for Christmas," I told him, my patience wearing thin. "I'll bring you the children this afternoon, and then I'll be back to walk you all over to our place Christmas morning."

"I didn't say to bring 'em today."

"I don't care what you said. This has gone on long enough."

"You ain't—"

"I'm sorry for you, George. I am. But you have to go right on being a father. I can't do it for you."

He threw a log into the fire so roughly that coals and charred pieces of wood scattered down across the hearth. "Why not? You ain't got but two! You might could take on at least a couple more."

His words stunned me. Automatically I reached for the broom hanging next to the ash shovel, swept up the smoldering pieces, and threw them back into the fire. I could barely speak to answer him. "They need their own father."

"Maybe they think so. I dunno. They'd be better off someplace else. You know that. I ain't never had much to give 'em."

He was serious, and I could scarcely believe it. "You giving up, George? What are you going to do?"

"Don't much matter to you, that I can see. If you don't want 'em all, you'll send 'em where you have to send 'em."

"No. George—"

"Shut up an' go home, will you? I'm tired a' talkin'."

He was ashen-faced, standing and staring at me. And it was no wonder his boys hadn't wanted to leave him alone. I couldn't go, not while I was seeing what I saw in his eyes. A dark and dead determination.

"George—"

"I said shut up."

"They need you."

"You can say that. But I can't give 'em nothin'. I can't do it."

"You have to."

"Who says? God? Well, he makes mistakes, no matter what anybody says! He done this to me, an' what he wants now, I don't 'specially care! I can't make it without Wila!"

I wondered when Sam would be back, or when somebody else would be by. I didn't want to stay here, but this was the first time George had been really alone since Juli'd found him in the barn that morning. If I left, it might be one of his boys finding him after a while. Dead. In this frame of mind, he was capable of anything. Why had Sam left? Didn't he know the kind of shape his father was in?

"George, I want you to come to the house with me."

"Chloe's most likely to take Lizbeth an' the baby. I know her."

"They'll all want to stay together," I said. "And with you."

He was looking off toward the kitchen. "What did you say 'bout Christmas?"

I certainly hadn't expected that change of subject. "I said we want you all to come over."

"Wilametta was knittin'—" He stopped and shook his head. "I—I got sticks a' candy for the kids. Why don't you take 'em over to 'em?"

"Give them the candy yourself. Please. Christmas morning. And if Wila made them something, they'll treasure it, George, sad as that's going to be. You could have your own Christmas right here and then come over for dinner."

"No," he said, his face tightening. "You take 'em the candy. I can't do that, Wortham. I know good and well I can't."

"You can. It's your job. A man does what needs to be done. But if you don't want to do it here, then bring everything with you when you come. It'll mean a lot to them, George. Don't make them feel abandoned. You've got to care."

"Did you come over here to tell me that? Is that why you come?"

"Yes. And to make sure you had breakfast. And let you know the little ones ask about you. They want to come, but Lizbeth won't, not without your word. She's trying to obey what you said in sending them over there, but they'd be glad, I know they would, if you'd tell her to come home."

"I can't," he said. "I just can't. But I see where you're right about Christmas. I gotta give 'em that much, don't I? Wila'd want that much."

"George, they want their father back."

He was looking away. "They can come. They can come for now, if you say that's best, but I'll have 'em all back to you Christmas Day, Wortham. You gotta help me."

"I'll help you. But I won't help you tear your family apart."

He nodded. "That's 'bout what I'd expect you to say. Can't expect no differ'nt."

He wouldn't say anything else. But at least I'd gotten that much of a promise out of him. Christmas. But what he'd do after that, I didn't know.

SEVENTEEN

Julia

Back in November, Emma had made out a list of everything she could think of that we might need for Thanksgiving, Christmas, and some stock-up. She'd even insisted on giving us money to cover part of it, though that had bothered Samuel. "I'm eatin' here too," she'd said. "Ain't no more'n my duty."

So now we had every ingredient for her sugar cookies, and her handwritten recipe was stuck up right in the front of her little box like she'd moved it there special to make it easier for me to find. I had kids mixing the color into a bowl of sugar and other kids helping me measure and stir the big bowl of batter. I'd tripled the batch, because there were so many of us and because I thought it would be proper to give some to the Posts and the Muellers, as a thanks for being so helpful. And to the pastor. I thought we should give some to the pastor too, or a loaf of nut bread or something.

In between measuring ingredients, I thought of Samuel over at the Hammonds and wondered what the future would hold for all these kids. Would it be just our little family again soon? Or would we stay molded together like this? So much of that was up to George.

At least being occupied was helping. I'd given everybody some kind of job to do. Willy and Robert were chopping vegetables for a big pot of stew, but since they weren't too happy about that kind of job, I soon sent them outside to split logs by the shed. Kirk had the baby again and was holding her hands and trying to get her interested in walking, though she was only seven months old. With Emma's little turn-handle grinder, Joe was grinding up all the nuts they'd shelled. I really appreciated him, because he'd started in without me even asking, and he was being just plain decent to his brothers and sisters. Sometimes Kirk and Willy, and even Rorey, were not that way.

"Hey, Harry, you wanna pour some in the top?" Joe would say. And then when Berty crowded in, he'd give him a chance too and pick up the spilled pieces without saying a word.

Lizbeth took over the stew pot, seasoning it before I had a chance to see how much of what all she'd put in. Then she started in making corn bread, because, as she said, "If you got that with a stew, you don't need nothin' else."

There were no tears in the kitchen. We just all did what we were doing like there'd been nothing to yesterday, like we hadn't just put their mother and my best friend in the ground. What they were all feeling on the inside, I didn't know, but they probably just did the same as me—hid all that to go on doing. I guess we knew better than to talk about it, because nothing good would come of it. But to think too much, that could be a problem too, and there was no way I could stop them from doing that. I couldn't even stop myself.

We made triangles of the cookie dough for the angel robes and added on little circles for heads and bigger circles cut in half for the wings. Franky loved cutting all of the circles out of the dough with two different sizes of jar lids, and Sarah and Rorey dampened their fingers and stuck all the shapes together. I knew what a mess we'd have letting Harry and Berty help sprinkle the sugar, but I let them anyway, because they wanted to so badly. Before long, Berty's little fingers and all around his mouth were red from tasting the sweet stuff.

"Quit eatin' it!" Rorey complained. "We got lotsa cookies to pretty up!"

But when she thought no one was looking, I saw her sneak a taste too.

"These is beautiful, ain't they, Mommy?" Sarah asked me, and I was suddenly dismayed at hearing her sound so much like the Hammond children.

"Aren't they," I corrected gently.

She nodded her head. "Yeah. They are."

"Let's do canes now," Rorey piped up.

But Franky shook his head when I started to bend a single strip of dough into shape. "That won't look like Emma's."

That was the closest I'd come to crying in a while. I couldn't duplicate Emma's cookies. I'd never seen Emma's cookies. She was so good at everything when it came to baking, I couldn't hold a candle to it. There was so much to miss not having her here, and we'd be missing it all, over and over again.

"Take two strands," Lizbeth told me. "Roll one in the red sugar, and twist them together. You want me to help?"

She was looking at me funny. Maybe the sadness I felt was showing more than I realized. Hers was too. But only in her eyes.

186

"Please," I told her gladly and then let her and the other kids finish shaping those cookies while I mixed a batch with nuts and raisins and little chopped-up bits of candied cherry.

Lizbeth cut two triangles of dough and laid them across each other to make each star. She twisted together strands just like for the canes but joined the ends to make little wreaths. Then she made tree shapes and let the kids ornament the tops with pieces of the nuts, raisins, and cherries.

"Do you folks get a tree?" Lizbeth suddenly asked me.

Well, that hadn't occurred to me. Not even once. And I wondered why. "We used to. Last year we couldn't because of where we were staying."

"We never had one," she said. "Pa ain't again' it or anythin', he just says there ain't no place to put it that somebody wouldn't knock it over and muss it up."

Rorey asked to help stir the batter I was making, so I gave her the bowl, and she started in with her brow all furrowed in concentration.

"Maybe we could get a tree for you here," I told Lizbeth. "I'll ask Samuel about that."

"Good!" Harry declared. "Can I put candles on it?"

"Well, no," I said. "That would be a problem if it did get knocked over. That happened once when I was a little girl. Scared me awfully bad."

"Burn up the house?" Kirk asked.

I should've known better than to bring up a thing like that. They certainly didn't need anything worrisome to think on. "No," I said quickly. "They stopped it in time." I guess it was automatic to me, remembering that near fire every time I thought of a Christmas tree. Some things you just never forget.

Just then, Rorey slopped some of the batter over the side of the big mixing bowl. She tried hard to catch it, but it landed with a splot on the floor. She looked up at me with her wide eyes, waiting to see the sort of reaction she'd get. And as soon as she realized I wasn't mad, she set the bowl and spoon down, scooped the mess up off the floor with two fingers, and shoved it promptly into her mouth. "Umm. These is gonna be good cookies. Did ya put in honey?"

For a minute I wondered just what I should say. This wasn't my child, after all. But it was my kitchen, at least for now.

"Yes, they have honey. But Rorey, dear, please don't eat off the floor."

"Why not? Mama says it's a sin to waste food."

That created quite an awful picture in my mind, of the filthy floor at their house, far dirtier than this one. And children sitting, playing, even eating off it. Ugh. "It isn't clean, honey. That's why."

She shook her head, still not comprehending. "The ground ain't either, but that's where food grows up outta."

"But we wash the food."

"Oh." She started to reach for the spoon again, but I handed her a dishcloth.

"Please wipe your hands and the spot on the floor first."

Rorey complied, but with a look on her face that said I was asking too much. She turned to Sarah with a whisper. "You got some strange ways 'round here."

"We pick up things a lot," Franky told me, sharing his sister's wonderment. "We'd lose a lot a' good food if we didn't. Ain't hard to wash somethin' in the water bucket if it's got hair on it."

That wasn't a pretty picture either. "It's all right if you wash it. If it's something that can be washed," I said. "But that doesn't apply to unbaked batter."

I already knew that it didn't occur to most of these kids to wash up before a meal. And their table manners were atrocious. Those who'd slept on our mattresses didn't seem to know why I wanted to put sheets down beneath them.

And I couldn't help wondering how the Hammonds could be so backwards, when most everyone else around here was not that way. Maybe George and Wila had simply never been taught when they were kids.

Wilametta had made the best blackberry cobbler and the finest jam I'd had anywhere. She'd made her own butter and enough homemade bread to keep a troop this size happy. But they were never really neat. Not even at church. And if Wilametta hadn't known how, then none of these little souls did either. "They need us," Emma had told me more than once. "George and Wilametta ain't got enough to go around." Enough of what, I hadn't questioned. Hands, I'd figured. Or undivided attention. I could easily see how that might be the case.

But Emma'd meant something different, I knew that now, but I couldn't quite put a finger on what to call it. We were poor too, and Emma'd been poor, but with a difference. I could look at my two children and see all kinds of dreams, like they could be whatever they wanted to be. But I'd never heard George or Wila ever mention any expectations for their children, except when Wila, on her deathbed, had said she wanted the girls to sing, that she'd seen it in a dream. And maybe it was dreams that Emma meant.

Without a dream to strive for, maybe they thought it pointless to strive at all, even in everyday things. Maybe they thought it didn't matter how clean you were or how you conducted yourself, if nothing ever changed. God might have had all that in mind in bringing them here around Samuel and me this way. We could at least show them that when you're down and out, there's no reason to expect to stay that way. That what you do with the little details of your life really matters, not only in the way others perceive you, but even more in the way you perceive yourself. Because people generally live out the picture they have of themselves, good or bad.

189

"If we get a tree," Sarah said, interrupting my thoughts, "can we make popcorn ropes and stuff?"

"Well, yes. We'd have to make things."

But Rorey looked a little worried. "It might just get knocked over and mussed up."

"I never knocked over a Christmas tree," Sarah informed her.

Across the room, Kirk scowled at them. "I think you're dumb to even talk about it."

"Would it be easier not to?" I asked him. "We'll be talking about something, or at least thinking about something. And it may as well be something pleasant. Don't you think?"

He frowned, but he didn't argue. Emma Grace started bouncing up and down, and he tried walking with her again, holding her little hands.

"We had a Christmas tree at school," Rorey told me. "I helped dec'rate it, an' it was nice. Us younger wanted a angel on the top, but some a' the bigger kids wanted a star, so teacher let us make 'em both."

"I'll bet that was pretty."

"Better'n book lessons," Franky declared.

Before long the oven was full of shaped and decorated sugar cookies. But there weren't enough cookie trays to hold them all, so I used the metal lids from Emma's cake pans to hold as many as I could. My minced fruit cookies would have to wait until the sugar cookies were out of the way, so I set that bowl aside and started mixing ingredients for Willy's snickerdoodles. We'd had a neighbor in Pennsylvania that used to make those. So cinnamony good. Soon the whole house was smelling delicious, and I expected we'd done something at least to improve the kids' appetites. Who could resist cookies, after all?

We had three trays out of the oven when Willy and Robert came in, stamping snow off their boots. "Can I have one, Mom?" Robert asked right away.

"Sure. Have two."

He gave me a look, probably remembering me not being quite so generous with cookies, especially before supper. But he did exactly as I'd said and helped himself to two. Willy followed his lead and grabbed one in each hand. "They don't look too bad," he said.

Rorey took a table knife and carefully sawed the wings off an angel and solemnly whacked off its head.

"You're going to eat that, aren't you?" I asked her.

"I guess so. I like 'em in pieces."

Lizbeth let Bert and Harry help themselves, but she didn't eat one. Kirk gave a plain one to Emma Grace, but he didn't have one either. Before I could say anything, the baby just clunked her cookie against the table leg a couple of times and threw it on the floor. I picked it up without a word and set it out of her reach.

Sarah seemed like my sunny little Sarah again, helping me spoon out the drop cookies and then roll the snickerdoodles in cinnamon sugar. Joe came and helped, much to my surprise, and Franky sat there, right in the middle of things, watching.

"We're almost like a family," he said.

"Pooh," Lizbeth told him immediately. "We're good neighbors. Good neighbors always work together, no matter what they come to be workin' on."

We had the whole tabletop full of cookies and the last of them in the oven when Samuel came home. Everybody got quiet as soon as they heard him. I dearly hoped that when they asked about their father, he'd have something good to report.

He stood in the doorway a moment, just making sure he had all the snow brushed off outside. When he came in, he looked at the table full of cookies and then at us with a pleasant smile.

"You've been busy."

"We made umpteen dozen!" Sarah proclaimed. "That's what Mommy said."

"Well, it looks like it. Smells good in here too." He looked at me warmly. I could see the strain in his eyes, but his smile was larger, better than I'd hoped for.

"George is coming Christmas," he said. "And he said to tell Lizbeth that any of them can come over there until then, if they want."

"If we want?" Lizbeth questioned. "He don't mean some can stay here, does he?"

"Well, yes. Since you'll all be back day after tomorrow anyway."

"Seems like home is the place to be," she said, but without the smile I might've expected.

"Can we take cookies?" Harry wanted to know.

"Shush," Lizbeth scolded.

"Of course, you can take cookies," I assured the boy. "You all did such a lot of work making them, they're yours as much as mine anyway."

"We need to get our coats and ever'thin' together," Lizbeth said. "And we'll take some of Mrs. Gray's preserves too, if you don't mind me askin'. Pa'd like that, I'm pretty sure."

"Certainly," I told her, but I was looking at Samuel with questions swirling in my head. No more explanation than that? Was George all right, then? What if he changed his mind or carried on in some kind of way in front of the children? Was he really ready for this? Were they?

"No great hurry," Samuel was saying. "Let me sit and rest a minute first."

"I'll make you some coffee," I told him, wishing I could have him alone for a minute and get him to tell me what was said.

192

"He misses you," Samuel told the children. "I know he does."

"I'll stay here," Willy said. "Since we'll be back Christmas anyway."

"William George Hammond!" Lizbeth scolded. "Pa said to come home."

"He said if we want to!"

"An' he also said for me to see to you boys when we come over here! You know he aims for you to mind me, 'cause I'm older. We're goin' home, every blessed one a' us, just like Pa said. An' you can jus' want to, 'cause I said to want to! You hear me?"

Samuel was looking at her rather straight. "Be patient," he told her. "It's kind of a sad and frightening time."

"I know it," she said sharply. "'Course I know it. You'd have to be a blame fool to think I ain't noticed. No offense."

"Has the wind died down?" Joe asked. "It ain't too cold for Berty and Emma Grace walkin' the distance?"

"If we carry all the little ones we can move faster," Samuel told him. "It's pretty still right now, and warmer too. But we can wait till morning if you want."

"We got time before dark," Lizbeth said.

"Yes. If you want to go now." He looked over at me. "Don't worry, honey. Please."

I had to accept those words, without any more detail than that. Joe and Kirk were already going to collect all the coats and things, and I'd have to bag up some cookies and as much as I could of the other food that had been brought. But if all the bigger ones were carrying little ones, how would they carry the food?

Willy wasn't the only one not excited about going home. Surprisingly, Franky was reluctant too, though he didn't argue. "What about after Christmas?" he asked.

"One day at a time," I told him. "We'll work it out."

"It ain't too far," he said. "I reckon ever'body'd know that if we wasn't there, we'd be here, right?"

"You'll need your father's permission before just running back over here."

"Or Lizbeth's?"

"Yes."

He was solemn, standing so close to Samuel. And he'd been doing that every chance he got, I realized. He did need to be with George, to latch hold of his own father, where hopefully he could feel secure.

Before long they were bundled up, though I would've felt better about them waiting till morning. I'm not sure why. The weather was not a problem that evening, and it would be a relief in a way to have them home. But I fretted and stewed inside even as I wrapped another blanket around Emma Grace and got my and Sarah's scarves for Lizbeth and Rorey.

"Oh, Lizbeth! I left Emma's coat over to your house! I wish I'd thought to bring it. She would want you to have it, I know she would, and you're just not warm enough in your thin wrap. Take my coat for now, please. You've got a ways to walk."

"That ain't necessary, Mrs. Wortham," she told me. "I'll be just fine."

But I persuaded her, and she took my coat, promising to send it back with one of the boys tomorrow.

"Bring it Christmas," I told her.

"You been a fine host," she said. "We thank ya for all your help."

"You're very welcome." I was hoping she'd hug me. But she didn't; she wasn't one to volunteer a hug toward anyone. And I wasn't sure what she'd think if I approached her. She'd back away from it, that's what I expected.

But Rorey hugged me. "Bye," she said, and nothing else.

"Goin' home," Berty told me.

"I know."

194

"We'll come play Injun with ya some other time," Harry offered with complete seriousness. "We got cookies ready to take?"

"Right here." I handed him a paper bag and then gave Franky and Willy each a bag of other things. Lizbeth held Emma Grace. Joe picked up Berty. And Samuel lifted Harry and his bag of cookies.

Sarah came up beside me and took my hand, and Robert stood watching as his father struck out again through the timber with all those Hammond kids bundled as well as we'd been able.

"They'll be back," Robert said when they disappeared into the woods. "Before Christmas."

I didn't know why he'd say such a thing. I hoped he was wrong. But, oh, I hoped Samuel was right and that George was ready and they'd all be okay.

"Dad's gonna make 'em a sled," Robert announced. "And it's a good thing."

"Can we make them something too, Mommy?" Sarah asked. "Can we?"

"Yes, and we'll have to hurry. There's only the rest of today and tomorrow before Christmas."

It was getting dark when Samuel got back, and he was exhausted but happy to report that things had gone smoothly enough at the Hammond house. George was more like his old self than any of us had seen him for days. And though the kids were all quiet in that house that had always been so loud, they had all seemed to be all right with it. And young Sam had come back with Mr. Felder's promise to work him at least a day a week for a while, and that was better than a lot of men had right then, my Samuel included.

I stitched a scrap of an old linen sheet into a simple doll shape and then, knowing she'd approve, I stuffed it with some of Emma's old stockings cut in little pieces. I let Sarah pick out yarn for the hair and colored thread for the nose and mouth. Two buttons out of Emma's button jar would make the eyes.

"This is going to be so pretty!" Sarah exclaimed. "I just know she'll like it. But Mommy, oh! We need two presents for Rorey because it's her birthday too!"

I nodded. "I wish you had more clothes so we could share. But you need everything you've got to wear, and we won't be able to get more very soon. Maybe I could make something, though, if I work quickly enough."

We went to Emma's closet again, and I pulled out all the spare fabric we had to work with, which included what was left of Willard's old shirts and trousers and things. Emma scarcely ever threw out anything because she used so many scraps in her quilting. Then her blouses and dresses caught my eye. She would want them put to use too. Of course she would; that's the way she was. And she had been skinny, the way Lizbeth was skinny.

My hand went to a soft pink button-down blouse, and I knew what I wanted to do for Lizbeth. Of course, anything of Emma's I'd share with her or use for any of the rest of them. But for Christmas there ought to be something special. I carefully removed the regular collar from that blouse and then cut the lace collar and cuffs from a dress of mine that had torn badly. That lovely pink blouse with a new lace collar and lace edging around its cuffs looked truly pretty, and I was pleased with myself over it. But Rorey and the boys would be more of a challenge.

I finally decided to give Sam a hat that had been Willard's, and Willy Emma's garden gloves, because he was small enough to fit them. I could give Franky the shirt that Robert had outgrown; it wasn't worn too badly because it had been for school or church and not at home.

"I could give Rorey a book, Mommy," Sarah said. "I got three."

"Oh, honey, are you sure?"

196

"Yeah. If I want to read that one again, I can read it with her when we visit each other."

"Okay. That would save me a bit of time not to have to make something else. We still have to make the doll a dress."

And figure out something for Joe, Kirk, Harry, and Berty too. Then I remembered something Grandma Pearl had made for me when I was little. It hadn't taken long—I'd watched her do it. A little cloth ball, made from a towel on the outside, stuffed with rags. I'd had such fun with that, rolling and tossing it, and I even took it into the wash-tub with me. I would make two small ones, one for each little boy.

Samuel and Robert had brought in wood from the barn and gotten their start on a sled, working on the kitchen floor where they could benefit from the cookstove's warmth. But all our eyes were drooping now. We'd have to finish everything tomorrow. Rorey's doll dress, the sled, something for Joe and Kirk. And something for George.

Only when we were in bed did Samuel tell me the way George had been. We figured that having the children around him might be the only way to lift him out of his hopelessness and help him gain a renewed sense of purpose. They needed him. Surely he'd see that.

It was sunny in the morning, and I was scurrying about, thinking of the gifts and what we could make to feed so many. Christmas. Tomorrow.

Completely to my surprise, Barrett Post came with his team and sleigh before the morning was half gone. Samuel went out to meet him, and I thought he'd just come to talk, but pretty soon both of them came in the house, each carrying a huge bundle.

"You ever roast turkey where you're from?" Mr. Post asked as he came in the kitchen door. "Louise said it'll take a good three hours to roast this 'un, maybe more."

"Turkey?" I could scarcely believe it.

"I was by the Hammonds' last night, an' they said they'd be here Christmas, else I'd a' brought a lot a' this straight over there."

Sweet potatoes. Three pies. Cranberries. Oh, it'd been so long since I'd seen cranberries! Home-canned peaches and home-canned corn. And the turkey was one of the biggest I'd ever seen. "Oh, thank you! Tell Louise thank you!"

"Kinda figured you had potatoes an' enough flour for rolls an' such."

"Yes. Yes, we do." I was overwhelmed by this generosity, and Samuel must've been too, because he didn't say a word.

"Them Hammonds is a lot a' mouths to feed. They need help for sure this Christmas, an' it wouldn't be neighborly to leave it all on you."

"Thank you so much," I told him again. "God bless you."

"Now that's exactly what Emma would say," Barrett declared. "Only she'd say God was wantin' to bless me more, if I'd let him." He was quiet a minute. "You all believe like she did, don't ya? You all believe she's in a real heaven right now, singing with angels or some such?"

"That's what the Bible tells us, Barrett," Samuel said. "That they who believe shall receive eternal life."

"What if you don't know if somebody believed or not?" He was looking uncomfortable.

"God knows their heart," Samuel told him. "We don't know for sure, but we can hope that God touched them and that they received his grace and are with him right now."

"My pappy was a good man," Barrett said. "Never went to church, though. He was killed by a couple a' crooks when he wouldn't let 'em steal his wagon team. Don't know if I ever tol' you that."

"No, I don't think you did," Samuel said.

"Mama grieved pitiful, said she couldn't stand to think a' him burnin' in hell, an' I couldn't neither. Couldn't stand to believe God'd do that when he was a good pappy to me. I never went to church with her again. Guess that grieved her too."

"It surely must have, but we don't know the workings of God with a man when he comes close to his death," Samuel said. "We don't know but that maybe God was talking to his heart, and maybe your dad cried out to him, even just before he died."

"But you reckon that'd count for anything?"

"Of course," Samuel assured him. "Scripture says that whosoever calls on the name of the Lord shall be saved."

"They shot him four times. You sayin' he might a' called on God while he was layin' there bleedin'?"

"It's sure possible. Likely, even. I'd have been calling on God if it was me."

Barrett looked especially somber. "Can't say that I wouldn't. That much is true. Things looks differ'nt when death is starin' at ya." He turned to the door. "Better be goin', I guess. We all got our work to do."

"Thank you again, Mr. Post," I said quickly.

"Yeah." He nodded. "You was about to say God bless me again. But you know, he has. For a lot a' years now too, an' I ain't exactly figgered out why. Emma prayin' for me though, that's prob'ly what it's been."

"And your mother's prayers," Samuel added. "Even if it was long ago."

Barrett looked struck suddenly, more than I'd ever seen him. He didn't even try to say anything else, just tipped his hat hastily and headed back out our door.

"Every one of the Posts is going to come to know the Lord because of all this," Samuel told me when he was gone. "I can feel it in my bones."

EIGHTEEN

Samuel

I let Robert pick the length of the sled we were making, and true to his word, he wanted a long one. It would fit three or four Hammonds easily. I just hoped it would be good and fast. Without metal runners, I'd used a couple of planks about an inch by three inches and five feet long, carved them down some, and then left the ends to soak overnight. Now we had to put the bend to them with the help of a vise and a couple of clamps. Sanded smooth and greased slick, they would do just fine, provided they took the bend. I hadn't had any trouble with that before, but I'd had more time for it too.

Robert seemed happy, helping me piece together the top, but he must've been thinking too, because it didn't take him long to start asking questions.

"Are we gonna stay here?"

"I don't know how long we'll be here, Robert. But you shouldn't worry."

"But where would we go if we left?"

"Well, there's all kinds of options. Mt. Vernon, Vandalia, Springfield. Maybe even Pennsylvania again—"

"I'd rather stay close around here."

"Well, I like it here too, but there's not much for work or housing around."

"What about Grandma in New York?"

I was surprised he would ask, surprised he would remember her. I'd talked to her with a telephone once and written letters a few times, but we hadn't seen her since we made the trip from Harrisburg to show her newborn Sarah when Robert was almost five. "We won't be going there," I told him.

"She's not like Emma much, is she?"

"No. Not hardly."

"Does she make cookies?"

"Can't say for sure now. She didn't use to, but that'd be a pleasant change if she's ever taken it up, don't you think?"

"Yeah, I'd like it." He was quiet for a second. "Dad, why don't you like her?"

Such a question. "I like her. I love her, more like. It's just hard to be around her sometimes."

"Why?"

He didn't remember. Probably a good thing. "She's not very patient with kids, son. And she drinks too much. At least she used to."

"How come she doesn't write?"

"I don't know." It wasn't something I really wanted to talk about right then. My mother would visit my older brother in the penitentiary but scarcely give me the time of day. Been that way for years. *You think you're something, Sam Wortham,* she'd said once. *You think you're better than us. But you're nothing but Bible-toting trash.*

How I'd prayed for her. But she didn't want anything to do with God, and she didn't want anything to do with me. Or my children.

"I'm gonna miss Emma," Robert suddenly said.

"Yeah," I agreed. "Me too."

Juli called us for lunch, and we all sat down to a hodge-podge of things the neighbors had brought that we hadn't had room to carry over to the Hammonds.

"I know what I'm going to make for Joe and Kirk," Juli announced happily. "And George too, I think. You know the tie Emma made you, Robert?"

He nodded. Cut from sturdy old green drapery, it was one of the nicer ties I'd seen, and with interesting texture.

"There's enough of those curtains left," Julia said. "I don't suppose they'd mind having matching ties for church?"

"I don't think they ever had no kinda ties for church, Mom," Robert said.

"Well, then, this'll be just the thing. Maybe I can make the rest of the boys some another time."

"Mommy made the doll dress!" Sarah exclaimed. "All pretty with rickrack and ruffles! Rorey's really, really gonna like that! Her new dolly's just as pretty as Bessie!"

It was nice to have the kids so excited about giving. It was nice to be able to give. Though we had, by last count, only forty-three cents to our name, we had willing hearts and Emma's legacy.

Julia must've been thinking the same thing. "Emma would be pleased," she told us. "She said we're always rich when we have faith, so we can always find a way to give."

I couldn't deny the truth of that. Emma had tried to give me this farm. She might even have her way still, though I couldn't let that concern me one way or the other at the moment. She'd long decided to forgive George Hammond's debt and give him his farm too. She hadn't really held anything to be her own, just had it in her hands as long as she needed it, until someone else needed it more.

We scarcely did anything then but the necessary chores and finishing up our gifts for the Hammonds. And it was a good thing we'd been so diligent with what time we had, because at no later than two that afternoon, we heard something off in the timber. I looked out the window and saw Franky come crashing through the trees. At first I thought something was wrong, but he didn't seem to have anything distressing to report.

"We—we come back early, if you don't mind," he told me, all out of breath. And I didn't have to wonder who the "we" was for long.

Joe came stepping out of the trees with Berty on his shoulders, followed by Kirk and Lizbeth with the baby, then Willy, Harry, and Rorey all in a line. Everybody but the big boy, Sam. And George.

"Pa said it'd be all right to come back over here," Lizbeth told me with something distant and strained in her eyes. "He's still plannin' on comin' in the mornin', far as I know."

"Is everything all right?"

She assured me that it was, though I knew it wasn't. Juli rushed out the back door of the house and helped get all the little ones inside to sit down, unbundle, and warm up a bit.

"How's your father today?" I asked Joe, hoping for more detail than Lizbeth was willing to provide. But it was Kirk who answered me.

"He's got him a bottle. Said he weren't gonna do nothin' but sip off the top, but it's more'n half gone by now."

"Let's play school again," Rorey said to Sarah, not appearing touched by the worry burdening her older brothers and sister.

The little girls ran off together, and the little boys were soon scurrying around as well. But Joe was looking heartbroken. "I knew it was better to get the little ones away, Mr. Wortham. You don't mind, do you?"

The despair in him made me wonder what the older kids may have gone through that the younger ones were too little to remember. And I was angry at George for putting them through it again, especially now. "Where'd he get a bottle?" I had to ask, finding it hard to imagine that George would just go off somewhere, especially after I'd brought all his needy children home. And liquor was illegal. Where could it have come from?

"I dunno where he got it," Joe confessed. "He ain't been no place. I jus' hope he ain't got another'n hid back."

I was hot inside, and I knew Julia could tell. She was looking at me with worry.

"Samuel, what are you going to do?"

"I'm going over there."

"He ain't gonna listen to you," Joe said. "Nobody but Mama could keep him sober. If his babies can't do it, nothing can."

Those were hopeless words, and I didn't want to acknowledge how true they seemed. If George wouldn't abstain for all his children who needed him so much, why did I think he'd hear a word I said? But I wanted to see young Sam as much as George. He'd been to Buzz Felder's, less than a quarter mile from town. Might he have brought his father liquor? Could he have?

"Samuel . . ." Julia started to say something but stopped.

"I need to talk to them," I said. "I won't be gone long."

But Lizbeth shook her head. "Be all right if you'd stay a while. Keep 'em from hurtin' each other." She didn't say anything else. She just walked off, but not before I saw the tears in her eyes. The poor girl, over here like this with all her younger brothers and sisters to take care of. Christmas Eve. God help her.

204

I walked that mile faster than I'd ever walked it, or so it seemed to me, seething the way I was inside. How could he do this? Bad enough the way he'd already been, but to pour drink on top of it! No wonder Juli was angry at him! No wonder his boys hadn't trusted him! But was Sam part of the problem in this? It was hard to believe.

I saw somebody moving around in the farmyard when I first approached and thought it was George, as big as he was. But it was young Sam, pacing around like he wasn't sure what to do with himself. For a moment I wondered if he might have been drinking too.

"What'd you come for?" he shouted. "Ain't no use you comin'! Might as well go to Mr. Post's an' get him to haul all the kids he can to Dearing! Mrs. Gray might take some of 'em, an' Mrs. Pratt, an' Pastor hisself, one or two apiece maybe, and if you'd—"

"Sam." I wasn't sure what I'd say to him, but it was clear how distressed he was. Crying, the tears surely cold against his angry, red face.

"He hit me," he said, "an' shoved me out the door an' tol' me to go with the rest of 'em, not to stay around him no more." He looked toward the house, the pain and something almost like hatred suddenly vicious in his eyes. "I oughta kill him. Oughta trounce him good."

Oh, how right Lizbeth had been. "Sam, none of that will help him. I expect he even knows he deserves it, but it wouldn't do nothing but make things worse. Did he ask you to bring him a bottle yesterday?"

"Me? You think I'd do it? You think I'd help him go stinkin' crazy even if he did ask me?"

"No. I just—"

"He used to beat us. When Mama was off anywhere or outside or anything, he'd be drinkin' an' cut loose on us afore long. But she slugged him good one day, and I oughta do the same thing—"

"But it was her getting him to church that stopped the drinking, wasn't it?"

"Maybe so. But she slugged him first. Made him go."

"Your father gave his heart to God, didn't he?"

"We thought so."

"He did. I know. And it'll be God to get him through this. Will you believe that with me?"

He was shaking. "I don't know. I don't know if nothin'll get us through."

I put my hand on his shoulder. "It doesn't seem so, when you're in the middle of things, but he's here with us. He's going to help your father and all of you. Trust him, all right?"

"You don't know what it's like."

"No. Not with your mother dying, I don't. But I know about the drinking part of it. My father would come home violent, till one night he left us altogether. My mother drank too, and soon got us a stepfather as bad as she was. I pretty much learned to stay out of their way. But your father's different. He already knows better, down inside somewhere. He knows God cares."

Young Sam was quiet, looking down at his snowy boots.

"Will you go inside with me and talk to him?" I asked.

"He don' wanna talk to me no more. He done tol' me that."

"It's not up to him. Nothing's up to him right now. Not until he gets himself straightened out."

George was at the table. We kicked the snow off our boots, shut the door behind us, and took off our coats before he even looked up.

"Get out."

He was drunk. I knew from the way he was sitting, the way his words came out, before I even got close enough to see his eyes.

"I thought you were going to give the kids Christmas."

"I will. I'll be there."

"Uh-huh. Do you think this is what they needed? To see you like this and come running back, scared of what you might do? What is that, George? What are you trying to do?"

He slapped his hands down on the table and then his head down on them. "I didn't mean to scare nobody." He looked like he was going to cry.

Young Sam stood and stared at him, clearly surprised that he wasn't raging.

"Where's your bottle, George?"

He looked up at me, shaking his head. "I—I finished it. I chucked it out the window."

"Got another one?"

He shook his head. "You wantin' a drink or aimin' to take it from me?"

"Where is it, George?"

"I'm gonna need it. I—I ain't meanin' to be drinkin' all the time now. Jus'—jus' fer a day or two. I done told you I couldn't handle it. Ever'body knows that. Can't nobody expect me to—"

"People expect you to care for your children, George. I expect you to."

I moved for the cupboards, and he jumped up. "What're you—"

"Just looking for your bottle. Where'd you get it?"

"Frank Cafey brung it after you left yesterday. He unnerstands me. He knows what I was a-needin' to manage with all them kids, jus' lookin' in their sorry faces."

"Frank doesn't know anything. But he'll know soon enough not to be spreading his poison like this. You know better, George. You know exactly what Wilametta would want from you."

He sunk back down in his seat as if I'd hit him. "I know. I know. But I can't. I can't do it. I ain't able—"

"Where's the bottle, George? For Wilametta's sake." I opened one cupboard, then another, and then found it in the third. Some cloudy-looking home brew in a quart jar sticking up behind the tea and baking soda. It didn't take me long to have it open and poured into the remains of Lizbeth's filthy dishwater.

"Wait a minute! Wait!"

"I'm doing you a favor. Maybe you'll sober up and be in some kind of decent shape by tomorrow."

"I hate you, Sam Wortham."

"No, you don't. You don't know what you think right now." I lifted the soupy dishpan and handed it to Sam. "Dump it outside for me."

The boy's eyes were fairly glowing with appreciation. He moved to the door quickly, avoiding his father's reaching hand trying to catch him by one arm.

"I wasn't meanin' to be drunk, now you know that," George blubbered. "I was just—"

"I don't want to hear it right now. I'll be talking to Frank Cafey and letting him know that if you decide to defy the law and all rational sense it may be your business, but if he gets himself involved in it again he'll have me and your boys to face."

"You're a hard one, you're hard . . ."

Something about those words kindled the rage in me. "You're the hard one, George Hammond! If you'd been looking at your children's faces when they came back over to us today! Lizbeth and Kirk and Joey looking like they hadn't a hope in this world. You've given them nothing to stand on. You're their father, for God's sake—"

"Shut up! Just shut up! Leave me alone."

"No. I'm sorry if I seem hard to you. I know you're grieving, but you're going to do right by those kids so far as it's in my power to see that you do! I'm staying right here until you sober up, and then you're coming home with me, like it or not, to give them a decent Christmas. If we have to trounce you like your boy said, that's the way it's going to be."

208

NINETEEN

Julia

I wasn't sure I could break the gloom off everybody this time. Even the younger children who'd gone playing were more solemn than usual, sensing what the older ones felt. Rorey stood grimly upbraiding Sarah's doll for some nameless infraction, and Harry and Bert were crawling up the staircase on their knees, in retreat from some unseen foe.

Lizbeth, who'd carried a cloth bag in addition to the baby, now sat with the bag between her feet. She leaned forward in the old kitchen chair and started to cry.

"Oh, shoot." Kirk got up and moved away from her, clear to the other room where he wouldn't have to see. But Joe scooted his chair up close, and I wondered if I should leave them alone or try to help him comfort her.

"I thought we'd make it," she said. "I thought we could do it, almost the same, if he was the same."

"We'll make it," Joe told her. "Without him if we hafta."

"Look what I brought," she cried, opening the sack at her feet. "Look!"

Joe didn't look. "We'll give the kids their candy in the morning. An' if Pa don't want his present, that's his business. Maybe he can't even think about Mama right now."

"Maybe that's why he don't hardly look at us."

"The Posts sent a turkey," I said, hoping it would cheer her. "Lots of fixings for the rest of the meal too. It's for you, only they brought it here when they found out you'd be here."

"We's a pity to 'em all, I guess."

"Oh, Lizbeth, they care about you."

"You was right the other day, tellin' the preacher it ain't fair. Pa don't want us, Mrs. Wortham. He plain don't want us, an' I ain't sure God does neither."

"Lizbeth . . ."

But what could I say? My words had done this to her heart, just as much as her father's behavior had. *God forgive me. I know you love them. You love us all.*

"Lizbeth, I'm so sorry I said what I did. I was just feeling overwhelmed, that's all. Your mother was absolutely sure of God's love, I know she was, and she would want you to be. He's going to provide for you. He's going to work everything out all right."

"You have a mama?" Her words sounded like an accusation.

"In heaven," I said. "Years ago. She passed on when I was five."

She looked up at me, startled. "I didn't know that."

"Not something I talk about much."

She was looking at me differently. Like maybe she thought I understood at least a little of what they were going through. "Did you stay with your pa after that?"

"Not much. He was gone a lot. And then he died when I was nine."

She sniffed and wiped at her eyes. "What did you do?"

"Stayed with Grandma Pearl. And she was wonderful. She taught me about faith and shared so much."

"We ain't got a grandma. They's both gone."

"But God will work out something wonderful for you. I know he will. Don't give up on your father, honey. He's going through a rough time."

"So are we. But I don't see him studyin' on that none, Mrs. Wortham. Maybe he'd like to be gone off like your pa was."

"I don't think so. Give him time."

She shook her head. "Ain't got nothin' but time, I guess. But that don't help matters." She stood up. "Ain't doin' squat jus' sittin'. I'll help you fix on somethin' if you want. Mighty sorry to trouble you for the holiday an' not have nothin' to give none a' you all. You been so kind."

"You're a wonderful help, Lizbeth. That's enough."

Sarah was singing in the next room, faintly at first, and then louder. "Hark the herald angels sing . . ."

Nobody else joined in.

"I make good stuffing," Lizbeth told me. "If you got bread enough, I could cut it to dry for crumbs. That's somethin' we oughta have done ahead."

"Let's make some more bread then," I agreed. "To make sure we have enough."

We were occupied at that, Sarah still singing, when somebody knocked on the door. I wondered who in the world it could be. Not Samuel. He wouldn't knock.

Kirk opened the door for me, and Pastor and Juanita stood there on the porch, their arms full of packages.

"Julia, honey," Juanita said right away, "I hope you don't mind the intrusion."

"Oh, come in! Goodness! You're never an intrusion. You're welcome. Come in!"

"It's just too far to get up to our families in Iowa this year, and we wanted to spend some more time with you tonight anyway, if it's all right."

"Oh, yes," I assured them, feeling relieved. Maybe with Pastor here, with Juanita here, I could get us through this holiday. "Can you stay over till tomorrow?"

"Well . . ." Pastor looked at Juanita, and she looked at him, and they both nodded at the same time. "If you want us to."

Harry had run up and taken Juanita's hand. "I know a secret," he chuckled, trying to pull her into the sitting room.

"Harry, let her get her coat off," I scolded, hurrying up to take the big cloth bag she was holding.

"Something for the kids," she whispered.

"God bless you," I said. Oh, God was good in the most amazing of ways! We had a feast, courtesy of the Posts, and Barrett Post was even thinking on God. Now here were these dear souls bearing gifts when their presence alone was gift enough right now. Bad as we hurt, and even though I'd been handling it all so poorly, God was trying extra hard just to let us know he was here with us. I hoped the kids noticed, especially Lizbeth.

Lizbeth noticed that Juanita had brought presents. "Why? Pastor Jones, why'd you come out? I don't recall no other pastor comin' out Christmas Eve."

It was hard to remember that Pastor Jones hadn't been in the Dearing area much longer than we had. He seemed such a natural part of the surroundings.

"We wanted you to know how much we care for you," he said. "And not just us. The things we brought are from other members of your church family, in town." He set his two bundles on the table. "Would you mind me unhitching the horse and finding a place in the barn—"

"I can do that," Kirk offered immediately. He took Willy with him to see to the chore.

Pastor started unbuttoning his coat, and I looked out the window, knowing that he and Juanita didn't own any horses. Charlie Hunter's sleigh was sitting in the lane, with the same strong mare he'd used to bring out Miss Hazel. *Bless him, Lord. What would we do without the dear friends you give us!*

"We made cookies for you," Lizbeth told the pastor timidly.

"Well, that sounds good right now. With coffee, if you have some."

"Yes, sir." She whirled around automatically, all set to get it for him, and then turned to me with a funny sort of look. "Oh. Oh, Mrs. Wortham, do you have coffee made?"

"Let's get him a fresh pot. I'll do it."

For a minute there, she almost seemed embarrassed, like she'd forgotten this wasn't her own home. Strangely enough, I was kind of glad about it. I wanted her to feel at home here.

I soon heard Juanita's easy laughter from the next room, along with Harry's. And then she was singing with Sarah and prompting the others to join in, something I couldn't have done.

Pastor was sitting at the table, enjoying the cookies Lizbeth had hurriedly set before him while I made the coffee.

"Got a tree?" he asked me.

I shook my head. "No, I forgot. We talked about it. And then I forgot all over again."

"It isn't necessary," Pastor said. "We just had a few things to put under it, that's all. But we can set them wherever you like."

"I know where there's a tree," Joe said. "In the timber. Not too awful big."

"Where's Samuel?" Pastor asked me.

"With George."

He nodded but didn't comment. Instead, thankfully, he turned to Joe. "You want to get that tree?"

"I don't much care, but some a' the younger ones might get a kick outta havin' it."

213

Pastor's eyes suddenly glistened. "Julia, would you mind me taking an ax and some of the children and getting us a tree?"

"No. No, I don't mind." How could I possibly mind? This is what I'd wanted—for Christmas to absorb us enough to find a little happiness, something good to remember.

Before he'd even had a chance at the coffee, Pastor got up and asked how many of the children wanted to go walking into the timber after that tree. And he ended up taking six of the eleven children in the house. Joey and Harry and Bert and Rorey and Sarah. Franky didn't want to go, but I talked him into it. Robert would've gone if it was his father, and I tried to get him to go anyway, but he chose to stay with Willy and Kirk, who'd just come in and declined to go back out again. Lizbeth and the baby stayed too, which was about what I'd expected.

Juanita had barely gotten her coat off but put it right back on again when she saw how many youngsters her husband would have on his hands.

"Let's make snow angels," she suggested while struggling to help wiggly little Bert with his buttons. "It won't be dark for a while yet, and it's a little warmer again today."

"We should make some in a circle," Franky suggested. "All around Mama's grave."

I wasn't sure how Pastor would handle that one. And maybe he wasn't sure either, because he didn't answer right away. Instead, they all went trooping out the door, some looking excited and some still uncertain. But thank God for Pastor and Juanita! Bless them! They would know how to make this Christmas as close to a celebration as possible under the circumstances, and that was what Wila and Emma would've wanted.

"Why don't you go on and join them?" I suggested to Kirk. "You can help Pastor with the little ones."

"Joe can do that." He looked out the window with a frown.

"But it wouldn't hurt you to be a part of it."

"Wouldn't help me none neither, that I can see."

"Kirk—" But I stopped. What right did I have to insist? Robert and Willy were already starting a checkers game. Lizbeth had gone back to cutting the leftover corn bread into cubes. Maybe I should just leave him alone. But he was looking so . . . lost.

"Why don't I spread a blanket on the sitting-room floor for Emma Grace," I suggested. "And bring her some cups and spoons to play with. Would you mind keeping an eye on her so she doesn't scoot too far?"

"I guess."

He was far from pleased, but at least he didn't argue. After I got them situated, I went back to the kitchen, trying to figure in my head how much stuffing we'd need if Pastor and his wife stayed for Christmas dinner, which I dearly hoped they would.

"Sure glad we made them cookies," Lizbeth said. "With Pastor here an' bringin' us things, wouldn't be right not to give 'em somethin'. We can heap a plate up. Too bad we ain't got more'n that."

I nodded my head in agreement. I'd have to think on it. Maybe we had something.

"Oh, Lizbeth, I know!" The thought came so sudden it surprised me. The little oak cross that Samuel had carved, sitting upstairs in our room. Of course, I'd have to ask Samuel about it, but I was sure he'd be willing. Maybe it'd look nice on a table or something at their house. Samuel could make me another one sometime.

I ran right upstairs to get it, surely making Robert and Willy and Kirk wonder what I was about.

"It's perfect," Lizbeth told me when I brought it to her. "If you don't mind it bein' gone, it's just the sorta thing for a pastor's mantle. Or in a winda or somethin'."

I started to put it in a drawer, under the dishtowels, but Lizbeth protested immediately.

215

"Mrs. Pastor might find it there if she goes to helpin' us with the dishes tonight, an' you jus' know she'll offer. We oughta wrap it in paper afore they get back so there ain't no chance them seein' it. You got paper?"

I was a little surprised at her enthusiasm. "I've got paper. Plain brown or white, though. Not colored, unfortunately."

"That don't matter so much. It's havin' somethin' to give 'em that's important." She grew quiet, looking at me. "I wanna give my Christmas candy to your two, and I sure wish I had somethin' more for you all."

There were tears in her eyes. Seeing it, there were very nearly tears in mine. "Lizbeth, thank you. But what came from your father, you need to keep. Samuel and I have something for the children."

I was glad that we had worked so hard last night and all that morning getting things ready for the Hammond kids. I'd finished Rorey's doll dress but not the ties. And Emma Grace! I'd completely forgotten to locate the dress Emma'd been making and see if it was finished. But there was nothing I could do now until the kids were asleep.

"You're kinda like Emma," Lizbeth said when I brought her the paper. "I can tell you're fond a' givin'."

I smiled. That was about the highest compliment I could imagine. "You too, Lizbeth. You're fond of giving too."

She continued cutting the corn bread, and I started making a double batch of Grandma's soda bread, because it was faster than yeast and would do fine for stuffing. "Oh, what should we serve for dinner tonight?"

"Let's heat all the leftovers and make a dishpan full a' popcorn." She made me smile again. There'd always been some unspoken distance between us, but now, like a miracle, that distance was gone.

Kids and snow and the fresh smell of pine all came bursting through the door together. It was a fine tree, not too big like Joe had said, but plenty big enough when we didn't have much to decorate it with anyway.

Emma Grace laughed when they came tramping through with their boots and their coats still on to see how it'd look by the sitting-room window.

"Oh!" Pastor exclaimed. "I completely forgot to think how we're going to get it to stand up."

"If Samuel were here, he'd nail a couple of boards to the base of the trunk, like an X," I offered.

"I can do that!" Franky exclaimed and headed straight for the door.

Juanita looked at me in question, but Lizbeth shook her head. "Let him do it. He prob'ly can."

I had to agree. "He knows where Samuel's tools are by now too."

Lord, how we were all like one big family. But such a thought frightened me, and I wished Samuel would get back. I wished George were here. But they'd come. Samuel had promised me they'd come. At least by morning these children would have their father again.

"Now we gotta trim it pretty!" Sarah exclaimed. "Mommy, are you making popcorn?"

"Not yet, honey, but I will. We can make a paper star for the top too, and you and Rorey can color it bright for us."

"Do you have any buttons?" Juanita asked me. "Or yarn?"

"Well, yes. We have both. Not much variety in yarn, though. Only three or four colors."

That was enough for her, and she sat down with Harry and Bert to sort out the biggest and brightest buttons while Franky made the tree stand and Robert helped him sand the base of the trunk smooth so the tree wouldn't lean.

I set out food for everybody to help themselves when they were ready for it. Then I helped make popcorn chains spiraling all the way to that little tree's top. Sarah and Rorey did the star up with yellow and orange, just as bright as they could make it. And Juanita showed the kids how to thread three buttons on colored yarn so they'd look real pretty tied with a bow and dangling from the tip of a tree limb. I wished we had pinecones and dried milkweed pods, because Grandma had made some nice ornaments with those too, but it'd be hard finding them now, and we'd lost our daylight anyway. Seems like I could've thought about all that earlier in the season.

Juanita had started braiding yarn, and I had no idea what she was doing till I saw her tie off the head part and slide in one braided section for the arms. A yarn doll. The littlest one I'd ever seen. When she was finished, she pulled out a loop in back and hung it front and center on the tree.

"Oh, make more!" Berty shouted. "Make more! Looky, Rorey! It's a people!"

Rorey was looking somber. "I just wish it was for keep." One little tear trickled down her cheek, and I remembered Samuel's observation—not one plaything in all their house. Juanita's little yarn doll was enough to make her cry.

"They're for keep," Juanita said. "We won't need them after Christmas. Do you want to make one?"

The little girl's eyes went wide, and she didn't say anything but stepped just as close as she could get. Juanita was busy for what seemed like hours then, helping one child after another and making yarn dolls enough for the tree and several more besides to jump and dance across our sitting-room floor. Finally the yarn was running low, and her fingers were tired. Pastor pulled out his Bible and read the Christmas story from the Gospel of Luke.

I started worrying just a little, with it dark outside and getting so late. Samuel must've decided to stay over at the Hammonds, but I knew better than to think that was good news. Pastor knew it too, I knew he did. But he kept on reading, letting the little ones edge up closer until the whole story was done and eyes were getting droopy.

"Oh," Juanita said. "Paxton, look at the wall."

We all looked. Apparently she'd just noticed our paper figures. They seemed brighter now in the flickering light of fire and kerosene lamps than they had when the sunshine was pouring through the windows.

"That's our Christmas story," Sarah said.

"You've done such a wonderful job." Juanita was looking at me. "Oh, Julia, you're a marvel."

"It was mostly the kids."

She got up and went straight for one of the bags we'd left in the kitchen. "This hadn't ought to wait till morning," she said. "Because the Christ was really born at night."

She came back with something small wrapped in tissue. She tried to hand it to me, but I gave it to Lizbeth, as the oldest child there. Juanita hadn't said anything, but I knew this gift was meant for all of us.

Lizbeth unwrapped it carefully, with her youngest siblings leaning impatiently into her. She gasped when she saw what it was. "Look. Look," she told the kids. "But don't touch."

It was a tiny glass nativity, the prettiest thing I'd ever seen, and my eyes filled with tears.

"We can put it in front of the wall, Mommy," Sarah declared with delight. "So the angels can be flyin' around it!"

"No," Lizbeth said. "This here's too perfect to risk gettin' broke. It oughta go up on the mantle where everybody can see."

After all the children had looked at it up close, we set the precious little nativity in the center of the mantle above the fire, where Emma's Seth Thomas clock had been. I got two little candles, set one on each side, and lit them.

"That's Christmas," Lizbeth said, having a hard time getting the words out. "Thank you, Pastor, Mrs. Pastor."

Harry wanted to sneak a look and see what else was in those bags. But we settled him and the rest of the little ones down for bed, upstairs this time, divided between the two rooms and bundled warm under blankets.

Kirk and Lizbeth and Joe were up later than the rest. I had a lot to do, but I didn't try to hurry them away.

"We don't know if Pa'll really come or not," Lizbeth finally said. "But we want to thank you for making it a pleasant time when it mighta been somethin' awful over here."

"Pa was drinkin' hisself drunk," Joe told the pastor. "He ain't in no kinda shape, an' we maybe won't be able to stay with him, 'least not when he's like that."

"I understand." The pastor got up, and for a moment I wondered if he was considering going over there, even in the middle of the night. But he just turned and asked the kids a question. "Do you know what a foundation is?"

"What you put a buildin' on," Kirk volunteered. "To make sure it goes up solid."

"Yes. But people have a foundation too. What they stand on in times of crisis. Their faith in all that is good and orderly. Their trust in the God who holds the future in his hands." He walked over to the tree. "Your father's foundation has been shaken, because so much of what he knew was wrapped up in your mother, even what he knew of God. He feels like this tree, cut off from the world he understood, but he doesn't see a purpose in it, or a hope. That's where we'll have to help."

"I don't think I can," Kirk said. "'Cause I don't see no purpose neither."

"We may none of us see it. But we don't have to see it now, as long as we believe there is one. As long as we know God is still in control."

"Well, he ain't been real good to us lately."

"Shut up, Kirk," Lizbeth said.

But Pastor wasn't ruffled in the slightest. "It's natural to be upset. Don't worry about that. It's an awful thing that's happened, there's no denying. But I want you to know that God sees every bit. All of you, how you just go on. And your father, how he needs your prayers. God is our hope, and your father's hope and comfort if he can accept that. I know that he knows the Lord. I made sure of that myself. But he needs to understand God's presence with him as his sure foundation."

"Because Mama ain't here to be it," Joe interjected.

"Yes. Yes, that's right."

"It don't none of it make any sense to me," Kirk stated. "I don't feel like trustin', 'cause there ain't nothin' sure. Mama trusted, an' she's gone. An' we don't even know if we'll make it t' spring or where we'll be if we do."

"God knows. You'll make it. Every one of you will. George too, if he can plant his feet on the solid faith that God will never leave you nor forsake you, that he will always provide."

"He's provided you," Lizbeth whispered. "An' that little nativity set."

Kirk turned on her, his eyes flashing. "That ain't nothin'! You know that! That ain't nothin' by next week some time when we gotta live an' eat and see if Pa's gettin' hisself another drunk!"

"Whether he stays drunk or not," Joe told his brother, "we gotta have confidence to make things work out. That's what Sam says. He's gonna work. We'll all work. We'll do what we hafta and be all right. You gotta live that out of ya, Kirky, or you're gonna scare the little ones awful bad, an' they don't need no more a' that."

Kirk was silent, but after a moment he gave a slight nod. "I know. I shouldn't be bellyachin'. We's supposed to be thankful. In ever'thin', Mama said. An' she tol' me that one time when she had the stomach trouble an' poison ivy all over her back, to boot."

That was a picture of Wila I'd never gotten. I'd seen Emma struggle through so much and still praise God. But Wilametta had done it too. And it made me glad inside that these kids remembered. They would help the little ones remember too. And that would help the same faith grow solid in them. Because nothing helps you gain something more truly than having to teach it.

It must've been nearly midnight before all of the children were asleep. I went into Emma's room, lit her lamp, and started searching for that baby dress. Juanita came up behind me.

"I've finished Rorey's gift and most of the others," I said. "But I've a couple of ties yet. And Emma was making something for Emma Grace. I've just got to find it." Finally, I pulled down a box from the top shelf in her closet. There were two pillowcases on the top. Embroidered. It wasn't till I set the box on the bed, closer to the light, that I saw one said "Samuel" and the other said "Julia."

"Oh." I sat clutching them to me. "Oh, Emma! Oh, look what she's done!"

There were pillowcases for Robert and Sarah too. Each with their names, Robert's in blue, Sarah's in cheery pink. Beneath the pillowcases was Emma Grace's dress, looking finished except for the bottom hem. And twelve sturdy little mats made from braided strips of cloth the way Grandma used to do rugs. When could Emma have done all this without me knowing?

"Placemats, maybe?" Juanita asked. "For the Hammonds? It would've been the right number."

"That must be it," I agreed. "Oh, Emma, you were always so kind."

But there was something else at the bottom of the box. Another box, as long as a child's shoe box, but not so tall. I opened it carefully, and we were both hushed.

Balls. Little glass ornament balls. Tiny and delicate and all the colors of the rainbow. Each with its own tiny ornament hook. "Oh, Juanita," I said. "If we'd have known about these when the kids were awake—for the tree—"

"Better that we didn't. Better to see their faces first thing in the morning when they see. Magical, Juli. Like a kiss of God."

My heart was thundering with excitement, and I knew she was right. My children were expecting something sure, but not such a surprise on our homemade tree. And the Hammond children were expecting nothing at all, except their father's candy and whatever they might conceive to be in Pastor's bags. They would remember this Christmas, I could not doubt it.

Juanita hemmed Emma Grace's dress for me so I could finish the ties. I pulled out the bag of things I intended to give the children and what I had of brown paper. Pastor started wrapping things carefully, though I never would've dreamed of asking him to.

I told them about the sled Samuel had worked on and that I didn't know if he'd had time to finish it or not before the Hammonds all came that day. But he'd give it to them anyway and finish it Christmas Day if he had to.

Juanita admired the blouse I'd modified for Lizbeth, Rorey's doll, and the ties I was working on. When her husband picked up Harry's little cloth ball, she shook her head. "You're just amazing, Juli, what you came up with for the kids."

"I didn't know you were coming. There had to be something for them." For some reason I wanted to cry, but then I wouldn't be able to see to sew that way, so I fought back the feeling of tears and kept right on working, saying nothing more.

"Some of the church ladies made up the most wonderful candies you could ever hope to see," Juanita told me. "Made me wish I was that handy in the kitchen. Delores sent you a fruitcake, and Edith sent a canning jar of mincemeat and some peach preserves."

"I couldn't ever imagine you all being so good to us."

"You're family. That's the way church family's supposed to be." She smiled. "Wait'll you see what Bonnie and Erla and Betty Jaynes did. Knitted scarves, every one of them with different colors. One for each of the Hammonds."

I smiled. "You picked out the nativity, didn't you?"

"Tell you the truth, it was my Aunt Jane's. We didn't have a penny, honey, to shop with, or we'd have bought out the store."

"Oh, Juanita. Oh, Pastor! I didn't know you were in need."

"There'll be money from the church when we're able," Pastor said quietly. "But right now, I didn't want to receive much for ourselves when there are so many needs in the congregation."

I didn't know what to say. How far did their need go?

"Say, do you have something here for Samuel?" Pastor asked me. And I had to get up to get it because I'd almost forgotten. When I handed him the jar of sloshy brown stuff, he gave me a strange look. "What's this?"

"Walnut stain. I soaked the crushed outer hulls. My Grandpa used to do that." Neither of them said anything, and my mind turned again to their situation. "Do you have food at home?"

Pastor chuckled. "We're not home at the moment to be concerned about that."

That almost got me riled at them. "You should've told us! You shouldn't be going in need like this. People will help!"

224

"That's just it. People can't afford to help. They can't afford to put much in the offering either, right now. And I don't want to take what I know they need."

"You're not the only ones with a gift from the church family," Juanita added. "We tried to take at least something to every family where the father isn't working." She tied off her thread and held up the dress to show me she was done. "Edith was generous with her peach preserves. And I forgot to mention there's a tin of homemade crackers from Doris and Wayne Turrey. Better than store bought, I think. We do have some of those at home. They insisted."

"I love you," I told them. "Both of you. And Edith and the Turreys and all the rest."

"We know you do."

"Even Miss Hazel," I added, not sure why I would bring her up.

"Wait'll you see what she sent," Juanita said with a mischievous smile. "But that can wait till morning."

TWENTY

Samuel

George was sick when he woke up, leaning over a bucket in a matter of minutes.

I sat up, not feeling particularly sympathetic. "Liquor doesn't agree with you, does it?"

"Shut up."

Young Sam rolled over on the floor in front of the fire-place where he'd slept, took a quick look at us, and jumped up. "I'll feed the stock and start the milkin'," he said. "We got to get an early start 'cause they'll be waitin'."

George wagged his head back and forth, still leaning down on the bucket. "I can't go."

He was miserable, no question about that. But I wasn't about to give him a choice in the matter. "You have to go. If you can't even crawl, we're taking you. You promised them."

I expected his argument, but he only shook his head sadly. "You think I'd do any good at all?"

"At least you'd show them you're willing to keep your word."

He leaned over farther, and I thought he was going to heave again, but he didn't. "Dad blame it, you might hafta carry me, then. I'll go if you're s' all-fired sure they even want me."

He'd have to see that for himself. "Did Joe take the Christmas candy with him?" I asked.

"I think so."

"Well, be sure. And you said Wilametta was making something?"

"In a box. Unner the bed."

He was looking almost green. So I went for him and pulled the box out of the bedroom. It was full of hand-knitted things. Mostly mittens.

"There's hats in there somewhere, for Willy an' Kirk," he said. "Mittens 'nough for the rest. I guess we'll tell by the size."

"She knew what they needed."

"Yep," George acknowledged. "Stayed up late doin' it too. Prob'ly oughta rested more." He set the bucket down hard on the floor in front of him and ran his fingers through his tousled, dark hair. "You're hard, Wortham. But I unnerstand it."

"Good. See if you can get your boots on."

While George struggled with his boots, I went out to help Sam with the chores. The boy had been right. The sooner we got going, the better. It was just beginning to dawn; the kids would be waking up at the other house, and I didn't want to leave them wondering for long.

By the time we were done, George had stuffed all the mittens and hats into a canvas bag.

"Easier to carry," he said, fumbling with his coat sleeve that had turned partially inside out.

"Thanks for thinking about it. Anything else we need to bring?"

He was quiet. I didn't really expect him to answer, except maybe in the negative. But he took hold of the back of a kitchen chair like he just needed to steady himself a minute and gestured toward the cupboard with his other hand.

"Jar a' candied cherries," he said. "Your Juli's got the rest a' the 'gredients for cake, don't she?"

Rorey's cake. God bless you, George, for remembering. "Yes. It may not be the same, but—"

"I dunno where the recipe is. But we'll come up with somethin'. She'll unnerstand."

I liked that he said "we." That was the best thing I'd heard from him in days.

"Guess we oughta bring that ham we saved back for the purpose," he added. "Don't need to leave ever'thin' on you all. The milk an' eggs too. Ain't no use for 'em here, an' them kids can't never get enough."

In minutes we had everything together and started on our trek through the snow. The timber was colder than yesterday, at least while it was early, but George seemed to liven a little because of it. The sick look was leaving him as we walked, and he only had to lean against a tree once, thinking he had to lose something that never did come out.

"Don't know if I oughta give 'em these." George gestured to the canvas sack of gifts. "May be too hard on 'em."

We hadn't told Sam what was in the sack. He was standing there looking at us, but neither of us tried to explain.

"You've got to give them, George. That's what Wila wanted to do."

"She woulda liked better to get store stuff," he mused. "But there weren't no way for it."

"Whole lot of the country's in the same shape as you on that."

"Yeah, but I always been that way. Year after year, an' I can't buy hardly nothin'."

"Looks like you may be better off than some then, just for knowing what to do."

"Ah, Wortham! You always got some cheery kinda spin t' put on things?"

"Not always. But lately. Thank God."

"You oughta be a preacher. I ain't never heard the like 'cept outta some preacher."

"Well, maybe we're all called. In our own way."

"Yeah," George scoffed. "I'm called to feed hogs, I guess. Put bacon on the table."

"Somebody's got to do it. That's honest work."

He laughed. "An' I'm just fine, to hear you tell it."

"I reckon it's up to you whether you're fine or not."

He shook his head at me and didn't say anything else. Young Sam was quiet too, and we walked a long way with barely a word among us.

Lord, I prayed, *let George treat his children right and not say or do anything too awfully dismal. God, let it be your day. Use our giving, though it is small, to show the greatness of your love.*

TWENTY-ONE

Julia

Pastor, Juanita, and I had all slept downstairs, partly so we wouldn't wake the children as we went to bed, and partly to be sure that they woke us as they came down in the morning.

Robert was the first one. He came halfway down the stairs and stopped for a moment, just looking at the tree in the first dawn light from the window.

"Mom," he said when he finally got closer. "Where'd all that stuff come from?"

It did look rather full beneath the little tree. With all the packages Pastor had wrapped in paper for me and everything they'd brought along, one might think we were rich indeed. I hoped the children would feel that way.

"I guess Pastor brought it all," Robert concluded. "'Cept the stuff we made." He knelt down a minute, inspecting the packages. But then he looked up at me with alarm.

230

"Mom!" He checked himself and started to whisper. "The sled's in the barn. We were going to sand it better and grease the runners slick."

"Don't worry about it. If that's all you have left to do, your father can show them when he gets here, and it won't take long to finish."

Robert didn't say anything, didn't smile. He might've been looking for a sled-size package under the tree for him. I knew where it was, but I hadn't carried it in. Samuel could get that too, when he got here. And he would get here. Even if George didn't.

Franky was halfway down the stairs before any of us even heard him. Quiet as a mouse, he came the rest of the way down and sat cross-legged in front of the fire, just staring at us and the wonder of that tree.

Then the quiet was done. Harry, Willy, Rorey, and Berty all came thundering down the stairs at the same time, with Harry yelling war whoops all the way. "We get candy! We get candy!" he exclaimed. And then he stopped at the base of the steps and stared.

Kirk came clomping down the stairs, already in his boots and looking as tall as a man. "We got chores to think about," he said.

But Berty was dancing back and forth in front of the tree. "Looky! Looky! Santa Claus gived the tree people a bunch a' purty balls t' play with!"

"Did they really come from Santa?" Rorey asked, her eyes wide. "I didn't think there was any Santa."

"I'd say they came from Jesus," Juanita told her. "Through Emma. She had them saved back for us."

"Is there somethin' from Mama too?" Franky asked wistfully.

Sarah came hurrying down the stairs in her bare feet. And then Joe carrying Emma Grace, who surprisingly wasn't crying, though she hadn't been fed or changed yet.

"Where's Lizbeth?" Rorey asked.

"I'll get her!" Harry hollered and started for the stairs, but I grabbed him on his way by.

"Now, hold on. No need to hurry her if she's trying to rest. We won't open anything anyway until the chores are done, like Kirk says. And when Sam gets here."

"Which Sam?" Sarah asked with a chuckle. "Daddy or Rorey's brother?"

"Both of them," Rorey answered her. "And Pa too."

"Hope there's somethin' under there for him," Franky added. "Did you bring him somethin', Pastor Jones?"

"Yes, as a matter of fact, we did." The pastor was feeding the fire, and I got my bedding cleared out of the way in a hurry and went to put the turkey in the oven. I should've been up earlier, but it was no wonder I wasn't, as late as we'd worked.

"Ever have apple coffee bread?" Juanita asked me.

"I don't think so. Sure sounds good, though. We've still got apples down in the basement. They need to be used."

"Don't worry about breakfast," she said. "I'll make the coffee bread and . . . do you have sausage?"

"Yes. Some. Canned on the pantry shelf."

"I'll make sausage pie then."

I smiled at her. "Good having you here, Juanita."

"Thank you. Can't really think where I'd rather be."

I put the Post's big turkey in the oven, and Robert and Kirk went out to see to the animals. I could hear Pastor in the other room, reading to the kids again.

"Maybe you should check on Lizbeth," Juanita suggested. "Is it like her to sleep later than the rest?"

"No. Not at all." Juanita was right, I knew. Lizbeth was generally among the first up, along with the baby. Maybe coming down to face Christmas was a little much for her this morning. I wiped my hands on the nearest dishtowel, though there wasn't a thing on them. Lizbeth wouldn't have been able to sleep through all the racket the others ncaused. She was worrying, somehow I knew that, and I wasn't especially anxious to face her.

I got the baby's bottle and carried it to Joe in the sitting room. I knew he was glad I was going to check on Lizbeth, even though he didn't say anything.

"You gonna get Lizbeth?" Bert asked me, tugging at my dress.

Harry ran up behind him. "Oh, good! Tell her come see all the presents! I never see'd so many presents! Tell her come see!"

Both little boys tried to follow me, but I told them no. Berty, with a shake of his head, turned his attention back to the paper-wrapped packages, lifting up two and giving them a squeeze.

"Be careful with those," Pastor admonished.

Harry gave one present a pat, then another one, and then started looking over the little name tags, trying to determine which might be for him. But of course, he didn't know.

I sighed, thinking what it must be like to be Lizbeth, left in charge of all these siblings, most of them so young. Maybe I wouldn't want to come down the stairs either.

I found her sitting on the edge of the bed springs Samuel and I generally slept on, since we were short a mattress. And I didn't know what to say. She was staring out the window at the sparkling white trees outside and didn't turn her head when I stepped into the room behind her.

"Lizbeth . . ."

I heard her sigh. "You need my help with somethin'?"

"No. It's not that. Juanita's making breakfast."

"The baby ain't cryin'?"

"No. Everybody's fine."

"That's good." She hung her head for a moment.

"What about you, Lizbeth? Are you all right this morning?"

Finally she looked at me, and I could tell from her face that she'd been crying, though she somehow managed to squelch the tears before I got there. "What if he don't come, Mrs. Wortham? What are we gonna do?"

I sat beside her. "We'll eat Juanita's cooking and open presents, honey. Maybe we'll sing some songs with the pastor or something, and have a big dinner."

"I don't mean that. I don't care about that. If Pa don't come, if he don't want us or he can't keep us, what are we gonna do? We can't stay here forever. You been better'n oughta already."

"You can stay just as long as you need to stay. But I think he'll come. Your brother and my husband will find a way to convince him. I just believe they will."

"But don't you see? That he need convincin' . . . that he ain't already been here all this time, or us over there . . . that's just what I'm meanin'! I don't wanna go off an' live with nobody else. Especially if we can't all go the same place. An' who's gonna take ten? Nobody would!" She shook her head. "Sam says he's old enough to be on his own. He says me an' him an' Joe an' Kirk can handle it, but he's foolin' hisself, Mrs. Wortham. We can't do it. I can't see no way we could, especially if we don't even got our home. An' that's up to Pa an' Albert Graham."

I put my arm around her, and she didn't shrug it off.

"Why don't he want us?" she begged to know. "Why don't he wanna be around us?"

"It's not so much that he doesn't want to," I tried to explain, hoping that my words were true. "He just doesn't know how to handle things yet without your mother. But he'll be all right soon."

"What if he ain't? What if he gets worse? Can we stay here, Mrs. Wortham?"

I'd already told her they could. But I knew she was really asking for something else now. For more than a temporary refuge. "Honey, we just have to believe he won't get worse. He loved your mother so much. That's why it's hard. But he loves you too. He'll want you with him, where you belong."

"I'm not so sure anymore," she said quietly. "I ain't even sure if he'll keep on livin'."

She started to turn from me and then sat stark still, her hands clutching tight at the quilt we were sitting on. "He said he'd make sure we get through Christmas. Then he asked me to help the other'uns remember him fond."

George, how could you do such a thing? How could you burden this girl so? "I'm sure he doesn't know what he's saying," I heard myself tell her. But I knew she didn't believe me any more than I did. Whether George meant to give his children up to other homes or whether he meant something even worse, I didn't know. But I was shaken inside even thinking about it. And poor Lizbeth started crying in my arms.

"I tol' him we love him, Mrs. Wortham. I—I tol' him how glad we was to be with him. But I don't know if he even heard me. He—he jus' tol' me to be sure we thanked you for all the favors an' not cause you no trouble when we come back. First he just sit, an' then he started his drinkin' an' got real sore if anybody come close or made a sound. But I can't keep them kids quiet all the time! I jus' can't. I didn't know what to do but come back! And he was glad, Mrs. Wortham. When I told him we was leavin', he was glad!"

I only held her, knowing there was nothing else I could do until her tears were spent. And there was nothing I could say. But the anger seethed in me again at George, mixed with a concern for him and his children. How could he leave them? How could he think such thoughts? But I knew it would do no good to voice any of that. I just hoped George had been talking as plainly to Samuel as he had to Lizbeth. Maybe Samuel had already managed to straighten him out some. Maybe George would walk through the doorway in just a few minutes—sober, revived, and ready to be a father again.

Lord, let it be.

TWENTY-TWO

Samuel

Christmas Day. My mind was full thinking of the children as we made our way through the timber's remaining snow. George was in no hurry, judging by the way he walked, but young Sam kept moving so fast that he had to stop every little bit and wait for us to catch up. He had goat milk in one hand and cow milk in the other, and I had a few eggs, the ham, and Rorey's jar of cherries. George was carrying the sack of gifts. At least no one could say that he wasn't providing something with all this.

But I hadn't finished the sled. Oh, it was done enough to look like a sled. It was all put together. But it needed careful sanding and a good rub of the runners with axle grease. I'd show them what I made, and maybe they wouldn't mind waiting the time it'd take to finish the job right. Juli'd worked so hard getting every last one of the

Hammonds something special. Maybe it would help them just to know we cared enough to try.

George stopped for a minute and swung his sack down to the ground. "What if they don't need me over there?"

"You're talking foolishness, George. Of course they need you. You're their father."

"Yeah." He shook his head. "But they been makin' it fine."

"They've been surviving, George. One day at a time. That's about all."

"Your wife made some good sugar cookies. The little boys was happy 'bout that."

"I'm glad. Juli's trying to do her best with the situation."

"But you're good with kids, Wortham. Both of you are."

I didn't want to hear any of that again. "Pick up the sack, George. Let's go. They're waiting."

Young Sam glanced back at me for a minute and then at his father and then trudged ahead of us through the trees.

"You gotta stop talking like that," I admonished George. "You're worrying your boy, and it's not right."

"Talkin' like what?"

"Like you're not needed. Like you're thinking to just let us deal with it instead of facing things for yourself."

George shook his head again. "He knows how it is."

He seemed cold when he said it, cold as the drifting snow blowing around us. "I'm not so sure you know how it is," I told him.

But he just picked up his sack and started moving again, keeping just ahead of me and not saying another word. We reached the edge of Emma's pasture fence before long, with the barn just ahead of it and the house beyond that. Just seeing the place was like a weight lifted somehow. But another weight remained. How would George conduct himself? How would the children be at this most precious of holidays, without their mother's arms?

As we came along the side of the barn, I noticed a little red-and-black sleigh in the yard not far from the house. But who might've come? It wasn't Barrett Post's sleigh or Covey Mueller's wagon contraption. I couldn't figure who else would venture out on Christmas.

Quiet as the cat, Kirk came out of the barn almost in front of us. He stopped for a moment with the milk pail in his hands and looked at his father. "This cow's almost dry," he finally said.

"Happens this time a' year," George replied immediately. "Don't worry 'bout it. We brought milk an' eggs from over t' home."

Kirk stood in an awkward silence, as if knowing there should be other words between them. Why they couldn't seem to say anything else to each other, I didn't know. George just looked away toward the toolshed. He ought to have hugged his boy, I thought. He ought to have told him he was glad to be here.

"Appreciate you doing chores," I told Kirk just to cover up the silence. "Everything done?"

"Yes, sir. Robert was out a minute ago." He turned toward the house. "Pastor's here. They spent the night."

"Well," George drawled out, "can be thankful he was here and not with us. Don't s'pose he'd a' been too pleased at me submittin' to a little drink like I done."

"He knows about it," Kirk said.

"Might espect he would, boy. You'd tell him, wouldn't you?"

"It weren't me. I ain't likely to go tellin' anybody but you what I think."

George almost laughed. "Well, Merry Christmas anyway, Kirk Howard. Ain't too pleased with your pa at the moment, are you?"

Kirk looked suddenly sunk. "At least you come. I'm glad for that." He turned away from us, and I knew George had hurt him, talking the way he had. If Kirk was disappointed, if he was dismayed by his father, he had a right to be. But he didn't need chided for it when we were supposed to be having a holiday.

Kirk went on toward the house, and after one glance back, young Sam was right behind him. But George just stood there.

"Are you coming?" I asked, far from patiently.

"I didn't know Pastor would be here."

"I didn't either. It's nice of him, though. I expect he knew it would be a difficult time."

"Ain't no easier with him here!"

"No harder either. Come on."

"He don't unnerstand. He thinks we oughta go right on praisin' the Lord like nothin's happened."

"Well, it might help you feel better about things, just acknowledging that God's still with you, George. That he's good and hasn't changed."

"I told you you sounded like a preacher! An' I ain't 'specially needin' to hear it!" He slung the sack over his shoulder. "Let's get this over with."

I almost objected to that statement of his. When it comes to your children, you don't just get it over with. You go on with them because that's what a father does. But at least he was headed to the house now.

We were only to the base of the porch steps when the door came swinging open.

"Pa! Pa! Come see the tree!" Harry came rushing out on the porch in his stocking feet, followed closely by Berty saying, "Looky! Looky!"

The rest of them hung back, not approaching George even when he stamped his boots off and came in the house. I set George's ham and the eggs and Rorey's cherries on the table and wondered if I should go straight back out to get the sleds.

Juli hugged me. "Thank God you've come so early," she whispered. "Wait'll you see what Pastor and Juanita brought us."

239

Juanita was busy cooking, but she turned to greet me merrily. "Be just a little while before breakfast. Do you think the children might want to go ahead and open a present or two?"

She made it sound as if there were surely more than that, but I was still surprised when I stepped foot in the sitting room. A tree with the finest little glass ornaments and some very nice handmade ones. And scads of presents underneath. Enough for an army.

George was standing there with one boy on each side of him, just looking at that tree and then the wall of paper angels. "You do purty well, Mrs. Wortham, not havin' a lot a' cash on hand."

"Oh, most of that the pastor brought out from the church folks," she said quickly.

"Can we open somethin'?" Harry was asking. "Huh? Can we?"

"I—I brought somethin' more," George said and stepped forward to set his sack beside the tree. "They ain't all wrapped individual, though."

"I thought we already brung the candy," Willy said.

"This here's from your mama."

Everybody was quiet for a minute. Pastor stood up. And from the bottom stair step where she'd been sitting, Lizbeth stepped forward to the tree and fished around till she found one certain package. With her face all red and her hair pulling out of its braid every which way, she turned around and handed her father the gift. "This is from Mama too. For you."

I thought he'd turn tail and run. He looked like he might. But he just sunk down to sit on the floor next to Rorey. "Guess I better open it, then," he said weakly. "You all get somethin' to open too."

"Mama's first," Franky said.

George nodded. "Ain't no more'n fit." He reached for the sack and pulled the whole pile out on his lap at once.

Mittens, bright red and warm as anyone could ask for. There was a pair for every child except Willy and Kirk. For them, Wila had knitted two blue-green caps.

"These is nice," Rorey said and immediately started crying.

Nobody said anything. Lizbeth leaned and kissed her sister's forehead. Little Emma Grace threw one of her tiny mittens on the floor and commenced chewing on the other. Franky lifted his to his cheek and just rested his head against their softness.

Knowing the need at such a moment, Pastor quietly said a prayer, brief and gentle. George pulled the paper off the package Lizbeth had given him and stopped as the cloth lay revealed on his lap.

"What is it, Pa?" Rorey asked.

"Appears to be a vest, true enough," he said. "Don't know when she managed to stitch this together."

"Clear last October, Pa," Lizbeth said. "When you was harvestin'. She done the boys's caps then too, but I didn't know where she put 'em."

"Well. She was a fine one. That she was." George looked around for a moment at all the faces in the room and then settled his eyes on the tree. "I reckon we got a lot more ground to cover, thanks to the good pastor and the Worthams. Might as well start in."

Some of the children put their mittens aside, but Rorey put hers on, and Franky stuffed his carefully inside his shirt. Every child, even Robert and Sarah, had a package from the church ladies: a multicolored scarf, every one of them different.

"Pretty," Sarah said, reaching to find her mother's hand. "When are we gonna open the stuff you made?"

"Oh, we will," Juli told her. "Be patient."

There were twelve little bundles all tied up with dainty ribbon—fudge, divinity, and little nut clusters of some

241

kind. Homemade candy for each of the children, except the pastor gave Emma Grace's to George.

"Oh! Oh!" Berty exclaimed and popped a piece in his mouth before anyone could stop him.

"Not no more," Lizbeth told him sternly. "Not till after breakfast."

"Look what a bunch a' presents is still left," Rorey told her sister.

"Yes," Lizbeth agreed. "Seems like folks outdone theirselves."

With Juli's help, Pastor distributed the things she'd come up with. Young Sam's fine hat that made him look like a grown man, and one for Robert, just like he'd hoped to have. Gloves for Willy, ties for Joey and Kirk. And a tie for George, who shook his head and said she shouldn't have. Robert's old shirt was a little big on Franky but looked all right. The little boys were so delighted with their cloth balls that they soon had them soaring past our heads or rolling around our feet. And Rorey couldn't do anything when she saw her new doll except hug it and whisper, "Oh, she's the bestest little baby." Our Sarah was just as pleased with a new dress for her Bessie and ran immediately to get the doll and try it on her.

With her own package untouched on her lap, Lizbeth opened Emma Grace's little dress and gently fingered the fabric. "It's beautiful."

"Emma's handiwork," Juli said softly.

And then Lizbeth opened her own. She sat for a moment as if transfixed by the soft pink cloth and the delicate lace collar. Tears started running down her cheeks. "Oh, Mrs. Wortham. Mrs. Wortham, I never had somethin' so nice."

Juanita poked her head in with a smile. "Maybe we should go ahead and eat," she suggested. "Since everything's done and hot. We can finish the rest afterward."

Slowly, everybody got up, surprisingly quiet, as though awed by all there was to see.

But I found myself thinking of the day we first met George, when we rode in his wagon that was headed into town with a pig's head for a widow lady.

"You two's bound to come better'n ordinary friends," Emma had insisted once. *"You's called to be brothers."*

Called. Maybe she was right. Maybe I should've been praying all the time I'd been here that the Lord touch George, help him, prosper him somehow. Emma'd had confidence for him, even if nobody else had. She'd wanted me to have it too. And she'd be happy today, seeing how many people had lent a hand.

The kitchen smelled of bread and sausage and roasting turkey. Kids came after their plates more eagerly than usual, but there was nowhere near enough room at our table, so most of them took their food back into the other room and sat on the floor. George's ham was sitting on the counter now, to be served along with Mr. Post's turkey later that day.

George was quiet, watching everybody and looking especially somber. I went and sat beside him. "Merry Christmas, George. I didn't mean to be unpleasant earlier."

He was watching Willy and Robert in the corner comparing scarves and each sneaking a piece of divinity when they thought no one was looking. Then Willy put his new knit cap on his head and left it there.

"They miss her," George said. "I know they do. But they're all right. The church folks is done fine by 'em, an' I didn't even e'spect that."

"We all care about you," I said, hoping he understood that I really did mean *him* too.

"Uh-huh." He turned to his food, still somber. There was something in his eyes I couldn't name, except to say that it worried me as much as anything I'd seen in him so far.

Juanita and Sarah were singing "Hark the Herald Angels Sing" by the time the rest of us were done eating. And George just sat cold as stone.

When we'd all finished breakfast, Juanita passed out the rest of the presents, starting with jars of mincemeat and peach preserves for George and for Juli and me. Then a basket full of the same candies the kids had already gotten. Then Juanita lifted one of two stacks of identical gifts, small rectangles with the only store-bought wrapping paper under the tree.

"Miss Hazel bought these," Juanita said softly. "She said something about a legacy."

Twelve Bibles. One for each child of both families, regardless of age. And in all of them, "In memory of Emma Graham" was written inside the front cover.

I didn't know what to think. It would never have occurred to me, even dreaming, that Hazel Sharpe would buy our children Christmas presents. But Juanita was handing me a small rectangle too. For Juli and me, a book from Pastor. *Pilgrim's Progress.*

"In Des Moines about four years ago I gave them to graduating seniors," Pastor told us. "I had four left."

They gave George one too. But he set it down, barely looking at it. Instead he was watching Rorey now, who had her doll wrapped in her new scarf, rocking it just as vigorously as she could without tipping herself over.

"That dolly ain't gonna nap much thataway," he said.

"Oh, Pa," Rorey responded. "I'm playin' I'm the swing." She kept right on rocking while Juli presented Pastor and Juanita with two gifts, to their obvious surprise.

"How could you manage?" Juanita asked. "You didn't even know we were going to be here."

I wondered the same thing until I saw that the first gift was a box of cookies. And the second was Julia's cross that I'd carved for her from seasoned oak months ago.

"I hope you don't mind," she whispered to me. "Didn't have time to ask you."

"It was a fine idea," I told her. "I'll make you another one."

"It's wonderful," Pastor said, looking at us both. "You don't have to do this."

"We want to."

Juli went right on from there and gave me a jar wrapped in a dishcloth and tied with a yarn bow. The strange, dark brown liquid almost made the jar look like it was brown glass.

"Walnut stain," Juli explained. "It should work for wood. Or your boots."

I smiled. I knew she'd stuffed the outer walnut hulls into a bag last fall, but I just thought they might be useful kindling. This was better. "Thank you." I kissed her cheek and stood to my feet. "Now I've got some things to get outside."

I saw the smile spread across Robert's face like sunshine. Pastor picked up the bundle of Christmas candy that George had bought and passed it all to him. Reluctantly George handed it out to his children as I pulled on my coat.

"Want to help me, Robert?"

"Yeah!" He jumped up with more enthusiasm than I could muster, and Julia smiled.

"Can I come too?" Sarah asked me.

"Sure. Why not?" I figured maybe it would be better to present these two with the sleds I'd made for them first and bring in only the one for the Hammonds.

"We got a lot this year," Robert said when we were outside.

"Yes. You both need to write a letter soon and thank the church people. They've been more than generous."

"We ain't done, though, are we Dad?"

I smiled a little, enjoying putting him off. "Well, no. We have to give the Hammonds their sled. And I have something for your mother too."

"You do?" Sarah asked with her eyes wide. "You made something for Mommy?"

"A curio shelf. I've had it done for almost a month."

"That's not what I meant," Robert said in dismay. "Is there something else for me?"

Instead of going all the way to the barn, I stopped in front of the shed first, pulled the latch, and opened it wide.

"Wow," Robert said.

Sarah said nothing at all. I pulled down the two sleds from the roof rafter and presented one to each of them.

"I knew it," Robert said. "Can we sled today?"

"Maybe. After we give the Hammonds theirs. And I have to finish it a bit."

Robert was looking over his sled front and back. "Thanks, Dad."

Sarah nodded her head. "There's room for Rorey on mine. And our dolls too."

Robert frowned at the mention of the girl. "Do you think they'll ever go home?"

"Yes. Maybe not tonight. But we'll see."

"Their dad ain't happy to be here. Everybody else is thankful, at least. But not him."

Not something I'd expect a child to notice on Christmas. But Robert was old enough to know.

"At least he's here, son. That's a start." I pulled the gunnysack with Juli's shelf out of the corner and handed it to Sarah. "You want to carry it?"

"Yeah!"

"You can carry the other sled in if you want, Robert."

"Okay. We gonna leave ours out here?"

"For now."

Somehow just coming outside with me this way made my kids feel good, and they loved the idea of carrying the gifts in. "They'll think they're from us!" Sarah chuckled.

We made quite an entrance, me holding the doors, Robert dragging the big sled, and Sarah hopping up and down with the gunnysack, shouting "Santa's here! Santa's here!"

Everybody gathered around, and the Hammond boys were especially taken with the sled. Franky was fairly glowing. "I knew you could do it!"

"For us?" Willy asked, incredulous.

"For us?" Harry echoed.

"For you," I said with a smile, but then I saw George hanging back from the others. And I knew down in my gut that I'd made a serious mistake.

"And this is for you, Mommy!" Sarah exclaimed, thrusting the gunnysack in Juli's direction.

She pulled out the shelf, looked it over front and back, and reached for my hand. "Sammy, it's beautiful."

But I could barely acknowledge her. George had retreated even further, to a chair in the far corner of the room. He was watching Lizbeth with haunted eyes as she held the baby and shook a rattle that someone must've given her while we were outside.

He saw me looking at him and gave just a hint of a nod. "Merry Christmas," he said, but his voice sounded hollow, soulless. Something like fear tensed inside of me. *He's going to kill himself. He's going to try.*

I knew it as sure as I stood there, that that's what he'd been meaning all along. And what could we do? If he hadn't listened to a word any of us had said so far, how could we hope to stop him?

TWENTY-THREE

Julia

"This is too much," Lizbeth was protesting over her gifts. "We ain't never had so much."

Juanita put her arm around the girl. "Maybe you all are needing it this year. You think?"

"It's nice," Lizbeth admitted. "You all been real nice. Still, I'd trade it all an' a whole lot more to have Mama here."

"I would too, honey," Juanita acknowledged. "She was a good lady."

"Say," Lizbeth said, seeming to brighten, "I was thinkin' we ain't never had Christmas away from home before, but we did! Right here one time! Emma had us over. We was littler then, an' she helped us act out Christmas. You remember that, Joey?"

Her brother nodded. "I was Joseph. You was Mary. An' Rorey got to be Jesus."

"Nah," Rorey shook her head. "I ain't never been Jesus."

"You don't remember," Joe informed her. "'Cause you was just a baby."

"Then we oughta do it again!" Rorey exclaimed. "I wanna be Mary this time! Emma Gracie can be Jesus!"

"But she ain't a boy," Harry pointed out.

"It's just for play," Rorey told him, suddenly an expert. "An' I weren't a boy neither when I done it."

"Then I wanna be Joseph," Harry declared.

"Can we, Mrs. Wortham?" Rorey persisted.

Their enthusiasm surprised me. And I thought it a grand notion. With Emma all those years ago, it would've been a fine thing to see. "Sure, why not?" I'd noticed George sitting in the corner. Maybe seeing his kids at such a project would lift his spirits some.

"Put on a show for your father," I told the kids. "It'll be fun. You two can be Mary and Joseph. Franky and Willy and Robert would make good wise men."

"Huh-uh!" Willy protested.

"Mom," Robert echoed his dismay. "We want to go sledding."

"This won't take long, honey, and the younger ones want to. It won't hurt you to indulge them a little."

"I wanna be Jozep!" Berty hollered.

"Honey, we need you to be a shepherd, to take care of all the sheep and goats and such."

Berty smiled brightly. "Okay. That's importan' too, ain't it?"

"Yes. Very."

"What about me?" Sarah asked. "What can I be?"

"An angel."

Joe graciously volunteered to be Berty's herd of animals, and it was decided that Lizbeth becoming the manger would be the only way to keep "baby Jesus" lying still. It was a cute little show for George and Pastor and Juanita and the rest, and it lasted maybe all of ten minutes. By then, I could smell the turkey coming along and knew I'd better start in with the rest of our big meal, so I agreed to let all the kids go sledding with Samuel.

Samuel, however, didn't seem to want to go. I wasn't sure why not. But he agreed to put the finishing touches on the Hammond sled so the boys could all go.

"Won't you come?" Samuel asked George.

"Nah. I believe I'll set right here."

"Want to sled with them, then, in a little bit?"

"Nope."

"They'd like your company."

"I'll be right here when they come in fer dinner." He folded his arms and leaned back, and that was it about it. Samuel went on out, and every one of the kids but Lizbeth and the baby piled out of the house with him, leaving the place suddenly quiet.

"Don't you want to go?" Juanita asked Lizbeth. "I'll watch the baby."

Lizbeth glanced at her father and shook her head. "They won't be out long. Not with a turkey comin' on." She started singing to the baby, and from across the room I could see George's pained expression worsen. Lizbeth noticed too and abruptly stopped.

"Oh, I'm sorry, Pa. I wasn't thinkin'." She looked up at me. "That was Mama's song. Her favorite."

"Go on an' sing it," George told her. "I always did like it too."

So Lizbeth sang, looking unsure of herself. And before long, little Emma was sound asleep in her arms.

"You're good with that baby," her father told her. "Like you was born to it."

"Maybe I was, Pa. There's always been a baby 'round, 'long as I can remember."

"I got somethin' special for you, girl."

Lizbeth looked at her father in surprise, and he started fishing something small out of his pocket.

"Your mama tol' me to do this. I almost forgot it, but I got an obligation to fulfill."

Lizbeth stepped closer, and he presented her with a shiny chain—a tiny gold locket.

"Gramma's necklace." Lizbeth stared at her father, making no move to touch it. "Oh, Pa!"

"Your mama wanted you to have it. And it's right, on account a' you bein' the oldest girl." He looked down for a minute, fishing in a pants pocket. "An' I need you to do me a favor."

"What, Pa?"

He pulled out a pocket watch on a leather fob. "I want you to save this back an' give to your brother Sam. I'd do it m'self, but he prob'ly wouldn't take it just yet, on account a' he's sore at me."

"But he'll get over that, Pa! 'Specially if you don't drink no more!" She stopped for a moment, gauging his reaction to such words. But his expression did not change. "Pa, there ain't no hurry."

"It's Christmas," he said. "An' besides, you two been right grown up 'bout all this. I oughta show you how's I 'preciate it."

Lizbeth took the locket and the watch in her hands and stood there looking at them for a minute. Then she turned her eyes to her father. "We love you, Pa."

"I know you do. An' I love every one a' you." Then he suddenly lifted his voice. "Mrs. Wortham! Come put this on my girl an' see how grown-up an' purty she looks!"

I did as he said and quickly saw how worried she was. But she didn't say anything about that. "Thank you," she murmured, reaching up with one hand to touch the delicate golden locket at her throat.

"I b'lieve you're purtier'n your mother was," George said. "Oh, she was purty enough. She used to say, though, that she weren't built for lookin' at."

"I'd like to see her right now," Lizbeth said softly.

"So would I, girl. So would I."

Pastor was picking up the scattered paper all over the sitting room and looking to be praying at the same time. Juanita had gone back to the kitchen and was working on fixings for dinner.

"I should be helpin'," Lizbeth suddenly said. "I s'pose you're plannin' to fill the table with food."

"There'll be plenty," I assured her. "With what the Posts brought and your father's ham. But I'll see to it. You stay here with your father." I turned to George with a question, but his eyes were so stormy strange, I wasn't sure he'd hear me. "Will Rorey expect her cake today, Mr. Hammond, or tomorrow?"

"Tomorrow." He breathed a heavy sigh. "I 'preciate you bein' willin' t' make it, Mrs. Wortham, even if I didn't say so before. Lizbeth, you need to be 'bout helpin' her. That's the thing to do, even if she says she don't need it. You be good as gold for her, just like you always been for me an' your mama."

"Yes, sir." Lizbeth was looking at me, her hand still on her locket.

"Keep the watch back now for Sam," he told her again. "Till he's good an' ready for it. You'll know when that is."

"Yes, Pa." She turned and walked away into the kitchen because she knew it was expected of her. And I just stood there looking George in the eye, and him looking right back. I wanted to reprove him. I wanted to tell him exactly how I felt about him worrying Lizbeth so. But I couldn't say a word. Finally I just turned my head to the pastor, and he gave a solemn, understanding nod.

No wonder she thought he didn't want them. He hadn't said a word about taking them back home. Now that he'd fulfilled his obligation to Wilametta, it was almost as if he believed he could just turn his back on them and walk away.

Lizbeth was cutting sweet potatoes with her head down. I knew she was trying hard not to cry. "My mama's only necklace," she told me.

"It was good of your father to give it to you."

"It weren't good about the watch. That was Mama's pa's watch that he wanted kep' with his children. Pa knows he ain't got no business keepin' it, 'less he stays with us, an' no reason not to keep it, 'less he's fixin' to leave."

"Now, Lizbeth, it's natural to pass things along as soon as the next generation is old enough to appreciate them, and you certainly are." But my words had a hollow sort of sound, even to me.

"You know what Sam said?" she asked me.

"No."

"He said we can't make Pa do nothin'. Not have us home nor stay around nor nothin' else. We gotta jus' let him do what he's gonna do and make the most of it."

"I suppose he's right up to a point. But your father does love you. I expect that, given time, he'll make the right choice."

"Sure," she agreed. "To his mind. But his mind ain't thinkin' like yours."

As we got food on the table, Emma's favorite Scripture floated through my mind.

"To every thing there is a season, and a time to every purpose under the heaven."

So many times she'd quoted those words to me!

"A time to be born, and a time to die; a time to plant, and a time to pluck up that which is planted."

She'd been so careful to let me know what those passages meant to her, as if she were a pansy or something, plucked up by God's gentle hands and added to a flower garden in heaven. But while everybody filled their plates with that fine dinner, I couldn't help but consider one of the passages that came next:

"A time to weep, and a time to laugh; a time to mourn, and a time to dance . . ."

Nobody was dancing here. Nobody was laughing, though they'd had a fair enough time trying out the sleds. Most of the kids were eating better now, and at least that was a start. Maybe they would laugh before long.

And George was seeming suddenly more cheerful, much to my relief. He ate heartily too, and just seeing him seem so nearly like himself was putting all the children at greater ease. Except maybe Lizbeth. She seemed genuinely surprised when he accepted Willy's challenge of a game of checkers.

"Pa's doin' better," Kirk told me a bit later in the day. "Reckon we'll go over home tonight?"

"I don't know," I told him. "You all can stay here if you like. Him too."

"Nah. Got the chores to think about."

Harry and Bert were busy throwing their cloth balls up and down the stairs to each other. Franky had moved from Samuel's side to his father's. Rorey and Sarah were sitting under the wall of paper angels, rocking their babies to sleep. I sat down in the kitchen for a minute, feeling numb on my feet.

"Wish we could stay longer," Juanita told me. "You could use the help."

"You have to go?" The news was dismaying.

"We promised Oltmeiers we'd stop in tonight. Better to go before dark."

"Well, you've been so much help. A godsend."

"That's what I think of you."

Strange to hear her say such a thing. I'd been wondering what they must think of me, with the attitude I'd had.

"You've been my honest-to-goodness friend, Julia, when some of the ladies of the church seemed afraid to be that. You were pure blessing to Emma too. She told me. And now, helping George—"

"I'm not helping George," I blurted without thinking. "I'm helping his kids." Immediately I regretted opening my mouth.

"Now, Juli, it comes out about the same, doesn't it?"

"Yes. And I'm sorry. But you ought to know, I guess, that I'm not so good as you think I am. It's too much that he doesn't even try."

"Maybe he's trying, in his own way. It takes time, sometimes, settling everything in your heart when hard things happen."

"Well, he's had time to think, that's for sure. But we haven't. Not without a hundred other things going on around us. Juanita, I just want to sit in the quiet and think on Emma a little, if that doesn't sound silly."

"Oh, Juli, I know." She reached out and took my hand.

"She used to talk to the Lord like she could see clear to heaven or like he was standing right at her elbow or something. I'm needing that. Lately he seems so far away. And I've come close to being too tired to care."

"It'll get better. George knows he can't just keep leaving it all on you. Don't feel guilty about sending them home when you get the chance. You made it, Juli. And they'll make it too."

I'd made it, losing my mother young. Yes, they'd make it too, though I was not much comforted by her words.

Samuel went out to hitch the horse to the sleigh, and Pastor took the time to speak with George. "Just try," I heard him say. "Give the hand of the Lord a chance."

"He don't need nothin' from me," George replied stubbornly. "He's the one ain't give us much a chance, seems to me."

"You know what I'm saying," Pastor persisted. "Trust him. Believe he'll provide for you and the children and—"

"Right fine bit a' Christmas they've had," George interrupted.

"Yes. And God has plans to take care of all of you beyond this."

"He can get to doin' it, then."

Pastor was quieted a moment by George's embittered words. When he spoke again, his words were quiet. "He's available to you. But it's not all on him. You're their father, and you'll have to do your part. Your kids need you to do what's right by them. They need to know they'll be taken care of."

"They will be," George promised. "I been doin' plenty a' thinkin' on it, an' I'll do the best I can for 'em. You got my word."

I sucked in my breath, hoping he meant those words as much as he seemed to.

"We have to be going," Pastor was telling him. "But we'll be looking in on you again in a few days."

George nodded his head and shook the pastor's hand. I gave Juanita a hug. "It'll be all right," she whispered in my ear. "He's going to be okay."

But as soon as Pastor and Juanita left, George was looking just as gloomy as he had a while before. "Be better t' have the kids here another night," he told me. "Seein's it's Rorey's birthday tomorrow an' you're bein' so good as to fix the cake. No sense walkin' 'em over an' back in the cold."

"We could bring the cake to you there," I offered.

"Oh no. Rorey's enjoyin' bein' with yer little Sarah, anyhow. That's the kinda birthday she'd want."

I didn't feel like arguing, though I could almost shake him silly for going back on his word so soon. How could it be best for the kids to keep on staying with us and not go home? It just left them wondering if they really had a home anymore. "After a birthday dinner, then," I told him, "you need to take them all back. It's hard on them, missing their own house."

256

"Ain't nothin' 'bout that to miss," he maintained. "Nothing but their mama, an' there ain't no help for that."

He started to go. He would have gone. But Samuel stopped him when he went to put on his coat. "It's still Christmas," he told George. "And tomorrow's like a holiday for your family too. If you want the kids to stay for it, then you ought to stay and keep the day along with them. That's the way it should be. So long as they're here, George, I want you here too."

He obviously wasn't happy with that. "You're doin' fine," he told us. "Better'n I could do."

"No. We can't replace you." Samuel was adamant. "And we won't."

George didn't make any effort to reply to that. But he stayed. He sat in the corner by the fireplace hearth and watched the boys in one checkers game after another. He let Berty sit on his lap for a little while, and I was glad of it. But Berty went to Joe when he needed the outhouse, to me when he wanted a drink, and to Lizbeth when he started to get tired.

We made popcorn. We read the beginning of *Pilgrim's Progress* out loud, up to the point where Pliable abandons the truth at the Slough of Despond.

"That's the most tomfoolinest story I ever heard," George complained.

"I think it's sorta wise," said Lizbeth, surprising me. "It shows pretty plain that we hadn't ought to just quit and go back when things gets hard."

George looked at her. "What do you know about it? That Christian fellow's as much the fool as t'other one, goin' off on some journey without his wife when she didn't even want him to go!"

"He had to, Pa!" Franky added. "He couldn't help it if she wouldn't go! Besides, it don't mean a real journey, like going up to Belle Rive or somewhere."

Franky looked at me as if he were hoping for verification. And I was even more amazed at him than I was at Lizbeth. How could an eight-year-old who couldn't read have such a grasp of John Bunyan's sometimes difficult wording? To my astonishment, Franky continued.

"It just means the kinda stuff that happens when we're doin' what we're suppose to. Right, Mrs. Wortham? All a' that journey stuff might a' been goin' on and him still in the very same house as his wife the whole time."

"That's a bunch a' baloney!" Kirk declared. "It plain said he was out across the field, didn't it? You're jus' ignorant!"

Not wanting to take sides, I tried to be as gentle as I could. "Now, we could consider you both to be right. It does say he was walking in the fields and then fell into a bog. But it's also true that the whole journey represents our Christian walk, whether we leave our houses or not. The author says that too, in his apology at the beginning."

"I never heard a' nobody apologizin' for his book," Willy said. "If he thought it was so bad, why'd he write it?"

I almost laughed. "Not an apology like saying you're sorry. It means an explanation, a defense. His book isn't bad at all. It's helped a lot of people for hundreds of years."

George shook his head. "Don't much see how them crazy kind a' words can help anybody."

"It's Old English."

"I'm not old," Rorey said quickly. "I guess that's why I don't unnerstan' it."

Several other children nodded in agreement. But not Franky or Lizbeth.

"Can't we read some more?" Franky asked timidly.

"No!" Harry protested.

"I'll tell you what. It is a little hard for children to grasp." I glanced at Franky, who truly looked puzzled. "I'll read something else now and then read more of this to whoever wants to hear more later."

258

Franky smiled, and Willy elbowed him in the ribs. I read the story of Jonah from our Bible storybook, though some of the bigger boys paid precious little attention.

What a mixed bag they were! Ruffians and sensitive sorts. Loud, quiet, insulting, insightful. How could George and Wilametta have come up with a lot like this? I looked over to George and realized that his children were well on the way to surpassing him. He had no education, no ambition, and didn't seem particularly concerned that they acquire any either. What would they do, this whole family, if they were left alone?

TWENTY-FOUR

$\mathcal{S}amuel$

I rose up several times in the night, restless. And then in my dream I heard the door. I woke up in the stillness, and the first thing I did was check to see if everybody was still there. Juli and the children all slept peacefully. But in George's place there was only an empty blanket.

I pulled on my coat and boots in a hurry. The boys had planned on chores this morning, his farm and ours, so he didn't have any need to be up and gone without saying a word. I ran out into the cold and was surprised to find fresh snow almost to my boot tops and more coming down. Much of the snow had melted in the warmer spell we'd had. But here it was, back again. It was dark with no moon, but there was a faint glow to the east, enough for me to make out George's fresh tracks heading off into the timber toward home.

"Let him go," some people would've said. "Maybe he just needs to be by himself a while longer."

But I had a nasty feeling, a burning in my gut that I knew wouldn't leave me alone.

The wind was picking up. Juli and the kids would be waking any minute. I knew I should go in and tell them what I was doing, but I didn't want them worrying all over again. I didn't want them all rousting out and trying to come with me to see whatever it was I'd find. *Oh, Lord, help*, I prayed. *Let me be wrong about all this.*

I tried to tell myself that maybe George just saw the snow and decided it was his job to get out and tend to his stock. Maybe he thought we'd know that, or that he'd get back before we were very many of us awake anyway. I didn't know how long it'd been since he left. I couldn't be sure exactly when I'd heard that door. But I prayed it wasn't long. Maybe he wasn't far ahead of me.

I hurried, wishing I knew what George was thinking about. I fell twice in the trees; it was getting harder to see my way. Just yesterday the trail had been plain, but the dry, blowing snow had covered it all up again and now was working at skirting away George's fresh tracks. I should've at least wakened Julia to tell her where I was going, but then others might've woken too. I figured there was no use thinking about it now. I could get to the Hammonds' house all right. And maybe I'd find George making coffee, just wanting to greet the sunrise in the home he'd shared with Wilametta for so long.

It was hard going after I lost George's tracks. What a fine sack of potatoes it would be if I got out here and got myself lost! The trees and everything looked just the same, and I knew it would be easy to get a little turned around in the whipping wind. But the hint of dawn in the east was enough to help my progress, and I thanked God for it.

"George!" I hollered, just hoping he might still be close enough to hear me. If he knew someone was out looking for him, maybe he'd have the decency to stop.

But there was no answer. I should've hollered sooner, maybe, whether I woke the others or not. But he was probably too far ahead then too.

"George!" I yelled again, hoping the snow would stop. I didn't want George isolated from us at a time like this.

When I finally emerged from the trees at the edge of George's field, I felt a whoosh of relief. Surely he'd be in the house. Just ahead of me now.

"George!" I called again, running up to the door. I found it hanging open, snow blowing right inside. He'd been here, surely he had. The snow tracked in all the way to the little wall cupboard behind the stove at the far side of the kitchen. I yelled again and checked Wila's room and the loft, but he wasn't in the house.

So where would he go? And what had he come here for first? Did he have another bottle hidden somewhere? *Oh, Lord, I should've turned this house upside down and not just assumed I'd found the only one.*

But then as I turned around I saw something I should've seen when I first came in. Wilametta's Bible on the table, and sticking out under it, the only photograph of George and Wilametta that I had ever seen. Maybe he'd come just longing to look at it. And maybe he'd finally chosen to find comfort enough in Wila's Bible to pick it up off the floor. But maybe, maybe he'd set them there for his children to find, something to keep and remember, something to hold on to.

I tried to shake away the thought. Surely George was in the barn right now, taking care of those chores. He'd probably think me foolish even following him over here. He'd probably be plenty irritated that I couldn't just leave him alone to tend to his own business.

My efforts to talk myself out of the worry did no good at all. On the way to the barn I prayed, begging God to help me find him, and quickly. But unbroken snow had drifted in front of the barn door. It wasn't likely he'd gone through there without leaving some sign, but I shoved the big sliding door open and stumbled in anyway, just hoping. A low moo and the sound of shuffling feet welcomed me.

"George?"

I looked in one stall after another, and the hayloft, but found only animals. Where could he have gone? Surely somewhere close. When I was outside again I thought I heard something just for a moment, above the wind. My eyes settled on the implement shed in the distance, where George kept the tractor that had belonged to Emma's husband. What earthly reason could he have to go there this morning? Maybe he hadn't. Maybe he'd done what he thought he needed to do already and started back. But I'd have to check, on the strength of that one tiny sound.

"George!"

No answer still. I ran through drifts almost to my knees, a tightness growing painful inside me. The large door was halfway open, and as I got close in the small light of morning, I could see a shadowy figure on the back of the tractor.

"Hey! George!"

He just stood there like he hadn't heard me. And maybe he hadn't, for all the furious wind. But when I stepped in the doorway, I could see the long, thin line stretched from where he stood to a rafter in the ceiling. A rope. And he was holding one end in his hands.

"No!" I ran forward screaming, but he wasn't paying me any attention. Just before he got the rope around his neck, just before his feet left the tractor to dangle in mid-air, I got to him. I rammed him, knocking the rope out of his hand, and him down to the hard dirt floor.

"What are you doing? Are you crazy? What are you doing!"

He tried to shove at me, and I hit him, hard.

"Don't fight me!" I screamed. "Don't you dare fight me!"

He lay there for a minute, and I could see the angry shadows etched across his face. I thought he'd say something to me. He was shaking.

"George—"

He didn't give me time to get another word out. He sprang up like a wildcat, knocking me into the dirt, and started pounding at me with his fists. I had to twist around, grab him by the waist, and pull him off balance. And still he wouldn't stop.

"George! For God's sake, listen to me!" I shoved him again, just to put some distance between us, and this time he didn't come roaring back.

"Why should I listen to you?" he demanded. "You don't know nothin'! Jus' get off your sorry duff an' get outta here! I ain't none a' your business!"

"You're all of my business right now! Your ten children in my house are my business! What in blazes are you tryin' to do to them, George?"

He stared at me. When he spoke, his voice sounded deathly hollow. "Jus' like I tol' the pastor. I aim to do right by 'em."

"You call this right? To hang yourself on your little girl's birthday?"

"Shut up."

"I won't. Is this what you want her to remember? Every birthday for the rest of her life, thinkin' that her daddy had more coward in him than care about her? That you'd rather die than be with your family?"

"You don't unnerstand! You don't know what it's like! I ain't got nothin' for 'em! I ain't never had nothin'! It'd be better for 'em to be with somebody else. You can see

264

that with your own eyes if you jus' take a look. But they won't want it! Not unless—"

"George, you can't think—"

"Shut up and let me finish! I seen it, Wortham. I seen how it is. All I ever did for them kids was set 'em about chores or whack 'em once or twice when they got outta line! Wila done everythin' else. They'd be better off with you. I seen it. You know how to make a kid smile, you do. Like you was born to be father to more'n two. An' Julia, she's good as gold, good as anybody could—"

"George—"

"I said shut up! They's happy with you! Can't you see that? They ain't never looked at me how they's already lookin' at you, you blame fool! What are you doin' over here, anyhow? I'm tryin' to give 'em a chance! You can't see that? If you don't take 'em all, there's the pastor. They ain't got none yet. He'd learn 'em plenty, I'm a-knowin' he would!"

"Now listen here—"

"No! I can't hol' a candle to you nor him when it comes to kids! I can't do it without Wilametta! I don' even want to. Can't you unnerstand?"

"I'm trying to, George. But your kids wouldn't agree with you. It's bad enough, the hurt of losing their mother. If you take away their pa, it'll tear them apart. That can't be what you want."

"They'd be all right. They's all right with you already. I seen it."

I had to protest that. "No, you haven't seen it. You haven't seen them crying themselves to sleep. Because when you were there last night, George, they didn't cry. They had their father. And I'll never be that. Neither will the pastor, no matter how good we can try to be as friends."

He was quiet for a minute, and I prayed that my words were soaking in. I'd managed to stop him. I'd gotten that far. But what could I do if he wouldn't let this madness go, if he just waited a while and then tried again? Lord have mercy.

"I figgered you'd be the one to find me, Wortham. I was hopin' it'd be you. But not this soon." He looked up at me, and I could see his eyes stormy in the dawn glow. "I care 'bout them kids. I do. Didn't want one a' the boys findin' me when they come to do chores or somethin'. You'd be the only one have call to touch this tractor. That's why I come in here. You or Albert Graham, an' it wouldn't bother him much t' find—"

"It'd bother anybody," I protested. "Don't kid yourself. It'd still break your kids' hearts, no matter who found you."

"You can give 'em a lot more'n I can."

"No, I can't, George. I've got no more money than you have, and no more claim to my home. Looks to me like we're almost in the same boat. We're in God's hands together."

"I wish you'd just leave me alone."

"I can't. And I can't be party to what you're thinking to do."

"What in blazes you gonna do about it, Wortham? Follow me around from here on?"

"If I have to."

"Precious little work you can get done that way."

"Not much this time of year anyway without getting hired on somewhere, and you know the chance of that."

He sat on the cold dirt floor, studying me. "An' what if I say I ain't goin' no place? Not for nothin'?"

I had to sigh. "Then I guess I'll be here a while."

"Well," he said real slow, "guess a man can 'preciate you carin' for the kids thisaway. It's kinda like I told ya."

"I reckon I'd be here to stop you just the same, even if you didn't have kids."

"If I didn't have kids, I wouldn't a' waited till Christmas was done."

"What about Rorey's birthday? You know it matters to her. Juli making a cake won't make a bit of difference if you're not there. She'll think you didn't care enough."

"If I agree on her birthday, then . . . willikers! There's Franky's in January, and then—"

"You ought to think about that. They need you now, and they're going to keep on needing you till kingdom come, George. What would Wilametta tell you? Would she want you abandoning them this way?"

His eyes flared at me. "She did! She abandoned us! By golly—"

"Not by choice."

That struck him silent. He stood up and walked toward the open door, where the snow was still swirling.

"We'd better go," I suggested. "Before we get stuck here."

"I won't get stuck. 'Long as you know which direction you're headed, a little snow don't have to stop ya."

"Will you come with me, then? You know the timber better than I do when it's snowing like this."

He bowed his head. "That I couldn't argue." He was quiet for a minute, and I came up beside him, waiting.

"You think it true she didn't choose t' go?" he asked me in a shaky voice. "I figgered maybe she was tired a' all the hard work. Tired a' me, maybe, not doin' no better'n I did."

"Everybody gets tired. But I don't think she had any thought to go just now, with all the little ones not even half grown. She wouldn't leave those children any more than she'd want you to."

"Then why'd God allow it?"

"I can't say. I just know the devil loves giving people grief. But God has a way of bringing peace and turning things around all right again."

"I ain't too pleased with him right now."

"But he's still with you."

267

I thought he might argue the point or demand to know why he couldn't feel God right then. But he only grew quiet, his head still bowed.

"I know," he finally admitted. "I try to shut him up, Samuel, 'cause I don't wanna hear it. But he won't let me alone. I knows he wants me right back over there, holdin' Rorey's hand. But Lizbeth's so much better at that than I could ever be—"

"Lizbeth's just a girl herself. She needs your hand as much as Rorey does."

"She's half a mama anyhow."

"No, she's not. Just a good big sister."

George acknowledged my words with a nod. "You know what she used t' wanna do? Teach school. But she ain't even been able to go so long, we needed her to home so much. Ain't no way for it now."

"Yes," I said. "There's a way. You only have two or three younger than school age. If we help you when you're in the fields and such, George, all the rest can go back when the new term starts. Lizbeth too."

He almost laughed. "You talk like I'll get to keep this place. That ain't near sure. But I got no fields nor nothin' else without it."

"You've got your family, and if it came to that, I'm sure your church family would help you find another place."

He didn't say anything, just kicked at a blob of snow in the doorway.

"It felt good to be working together when you let me help you with your fall butchering, George. I expect we'll need to keep working together from here on out."

He scoffed. "You're jus' talkin'. What do you need from me?"

"Help birthing Sukey's calf, for starters."

He turned around to face me, something new in his eyes. "You're serious, ain't ya?"

268

"The meat you gave us at butchering was a blessing,
George. And shares out of your cornfield for my work on
the tractor too. You know I've hardly had wages for
months. But we've been a good team already. We could
keep it up and get through most anything."

For the first time, I saw a little light in him, a hope trying to push through the doubt. "What if Albert throws us
both off?"

"We'll figure something out."

"You're serious! Dad-gum city boy! You think you can
make anything work!"

"We have to, don't we? We have our children to think
about."

He shook his head, looking at me and mulling it over
in his mind. "Yeah," he finally said. "Yeah, we do."

He took a deep breath, but I could scarcely breathe at
all. *Lord, touch him.*

"You really think we can make it?"

"Yes, George, I think we can. Emma did her best to give
us both a decent chance, and she'd be expecting us to make
the most of it. Remember how she used to say, 'You've
always got something, even when you've got nothing,
'cause that's what God hung the world on.'"

He shook his head but almost smiled. "Po-tential. Isn't
that what she called it?"

"Faith."

"Crazy lady. You ever think how crazy she was?"

"Crazy enough to love us, George. Not just the kids. You
and me. She could see past folks thinking us a couple of
failures. We're not failures. We don't have to be."

"You believed her, then?"

"It was hard at first. Coming here with nothing, having
nothing to give my wife and kids. For a while there, I felt
like you're feeling, that they'd be better off without me.
If I couldn't even put food on the table, what good was I?"

He was still staring at me, and I was feeling a strange heat

269

inside. "I had a friend back in Pennsylvania. When our plant shut down, we both lost our jobs and everything we'd invested. He jumped off a bridge. Left a wife and son. And for a while there, I used to think about doing the same thing."

"Guess you musta decided again' it."

"I realized Emma was right. We're put on this earth by a loving God. And he doesn't abandon us. We're more than our work or our money or lack of it. And our kids need their fathers. They need us to do our best and show them it's okay to need God. Just being with them, that's what they want."

"I ever tell you you'd make a good preacher?"

"Yes."

He was quiet for a moment. "I got a hard row to hoe, Sam, any way you look at it."

"I'll help you. Your church'll help you. You know your boys will. They're all primed to do whatever it takes."

He was quiet again, looking back toward Willard's tractor and that dangling rope. "I guess I owes it to 'em then, don't I? 'Least to give it a try a while."

"I'd say so."

He took two steps, picked his hat up off the floor, shook it off, and pressed it on to his head. Then he looked up at me for just a moment before turning to the doorway and stepping out into the blowing snow.

"Got chores waitin', Wortham. You gonna help me or what?"

TWENTY-FIVE

Julia

Samuel and George both being gone made me nervous. But not so much that as them not saying anything about it first. Joe and Sam and Robert brought water and took care of the rest of the chores, but I told them the men probably had chores well in hand at the other farm. Maybe seeing the snow they thought it best to take care of things themselves.

The children all seemed to accept that all right. For now. But I didn't believe it. Samuel would go outside in the middle of the night sometimes and think nothing of it. But it wasn't like him to leave the farm without saying something to me. Not unless he was in an awful hurry.

I did my best feeding everybody, oatmeal again because it was easy to make enough.

"It's Rorey's birthday," Sarah reminded me for the third time.

"I know, dear."

"Shouldn't we start on the cake? Mommy, shouldn't we?"

"Let me clean up from breakfast first," I said with a sigh. Some of the Hammond children had definitely gotten their appetites back. They'd eaten a lot. And I found myself worrying.

Thank God for all the food we'd been given the last few days. But except for leftover turkey, it was nearly gone, and our winter supply was not as plentiful as I would've liked it to be. I'd done some figuring on that in November, and Emma had scolded me for it.

"Sure," she admitted, "it don't look like 'nough for a long winter, there bein' four a' you. But the Lord'll provide."

Four of us. With her, it would've been five. But even then she'd known she wouldn't be here long. And this morning we were thirteen for breakfast. Lord have mercy. He'd have to provide if this kept up, or we'd be out of food by the end of January.

Such thoughts soon had me scolding myself. Why couldn't I be more faith-filled, the way Emma had been? I had been like that once, coming out here for the first time, picking the wild things that grew hither and yon just to put things on the table. I'd been the one assuring Samuel and the children that everything was just fine. What had happened to me? I couldn't seem to muster the same confidence now.

"To every thing there is a season." There came that same Scripture occupying my head again. And there was not one mention of a time to doubt.

I started in earnest mixing batter for Rorey's cake. It was to have a special frosting that was more like sweet cream and cherry sauce poured rich over the top. Lizbeth was carefully telling me how.

"Did your mother make cake for everybody's birthday?" I dared ask her.

272

"Nope. Pie sometimes," she said, not looking up from the potatoes she was peeling. "Let's make a turkey pie of the leftovers, Mrs. Wortham. Mama done that when she got the chance. Got carrots?"

"A few."

"They's good in it. You want me jus' to make it? I knows how all right."

"I'd appreciate that, Lizbeth. Very much."

I didn't expect her to say anything else. She wasn't much for talking most of the time, but this morning she seemed to need to. When Sarah ran off to play with Rorey again, we were alone in the kitchen, at least for a while.

"You seen what Pa give me. Now things ain't ever gonna be like they was. I don't know, honest, if we'll see him again."

"Oh, Lizbeth! Surely they just went to do the chores—"

"Your husband, maybe, Mrs. Wortham. That's prob'ly so. But Pa weren't minded to come back. I knows it."

I didn't know what to say. I marveled that she could stand there so steady, so strong, and tell me that.

"I can't show Sammy the watch he give me, Mrs. Wortham, 'cause he'd go off lookin' right now, an' I don't want him out in the snow again so long. Is that wrong a' me?"

"The weather doesn't look fit for anyone to be out," I said. I agreed with that much. "But they had to get over there to see to your stock. It'll just take them longer getting back."

She smiled. "You're awful much tryin' to be nice about this. An' I hope Mr. Wortham don't get lost or nothin', if he's out lookin' for—"

"Lizbeth—"

"I come used to the idea that things is gonna be different, Mrs. Wortham. I wish you'd think some more on all a' us stayin' here. Anythin' else is gonna be hard on the youngest ones after all this."

There she was, asking me again. "You can stay as long as you need to, like I already said, but that surely won't be too—"

"We'll just have to see, that's all."

What if Lizbeth was right? What if George just took off, and Samuel went after him? Should I send the boys to see? We'd know something was wrong if those chores weren't done.

They'd had plenty of time to get over there and back by now, considering how early they'd left. The snow was just slowing them down. Surely they'd come in any minute, more than ready for some hearty breakfast. But I'd gone and put everything away, as if I weren't expecting them.

Harry walked into the kitchen, eating a string of stale popcorn he must've pulled from the tree. "Can we make cookies again?"

"Goodness! I'm making cake! And we still have some left."

"I'm hungry. Can I haves one?"

I got him down a cookie, though he'd plainly helped himself to a snack already. And he'd just eaten. Suddenly there were three more boys underfoot, as though the cookies had brought them out of the woodwork. I put some on a plate and told them to pass it around.

"But only one apiece," I cautioned. "That's enough till after dinner."

"You're good, Mom," Harry suddenly announced.

His words twisted around in my insides, choking me silent. He hadn't called me Mama, but Mom, the way Robert always did. He almost seemed to be accepting me the way Lizbeth was, and I very nearly panicked. I hadn't bargained for this. I kept thinking how Willy had said he didn't want to go home. What were we to do? George had already been too distant for too long, and here he was gone again.

Rorey came in and watched me put her cake in the oven, but she didn't say a word. Twisting one wayward strand of hair around her pointer finger, she turned to where Lizbeth was stripping the turkey off the bone and swiped a chunk of the meat.

Emma Grace was suddenly wailing from the other room.

"Joey'll get her," Lizbeth told me. "He knows we got our hands full in here."

Joey got the baby all right, and young Sam helped Harry on with his coat and boots and took him outside a while. I was just starting the cherry frosting when I heard a dreadful thump followed by Berty's tearful bellow. Without thinking I ran into the next room.

Berty was lying on the landing of the stairs, crying his little eyes out. Kirk was beside him already, but the little boy didn't want anything to do with him. "Lizbeth!" he called pathetically.

But when he saw me, he reached out his little hand. "Mommy! Mommy!"

No! I wanted to run back to the kitchen and tell Lizbeth to go and tend to her brother. But the little tike was up and limping in my direction, and it was too late.

"I falled!" he wailed. "I falled on them steps ober dere!"

I knelt to his level, feeling suddenly very heavy. "Well, you look like you're doing all right, considering, Bert. Can you show me where it hurts?"

He pointed quickly to both knees and one elbow. Then he held both of his hands to his little head and begged, "Hold me!"

Oh, George! Why aren't you here for this?

That little boy's big tears compelled me, and I picked him up despite the turmoil in my heart. Sarah had said I would have to cover the ground that Wilametta couldn't. And I hadn't wanted to. I hadn't wanted to let these kids into my heart quite that deeply, even though Emma had

275

and I'd admired her for it. I wanted to love mine, sure. But all these? Oh, Lord! I just wanted them to be able to go home.

But Berty gently took hold of a fistful of my hair to rub up against his little cheek, and then he leaned his head against my shoulder, soft as anything. He sniffed a couple of times, but then he was quiet, just clinging to me. I sat in the nearest chair.

"He okay?" Sarah asked, suddenly beside me.

"Sure. He will be. He needs a little comfort for a minute is all."

"He's just a little kid," she said. "He needs to be helded more than us big kids."

"Maybe so."

Berty closed his eyes, and I could feel him relaxing against me. Three years old. He was little all right, far too little to understand everything going on around him. But if it was confusing to be here with me, he didn't show it. He just held my hair close to his cheek and looked for all the world to be sleeping. My eyes filled with tears. He was so cute, in a way I hadn't noticed before. And so dependent. And trusting.

"We're kinda like one family now," Sarah said.

"Almost seems that way today." I sighed.

"If they go home, they're gonna miss you *and* their mama."

I looked up to see Willy watching us, and Franky too, over by the fire. Neither of them said a word, but Franky hugged his knees up to his chest and wiped his nose with one shirtsleeve.

She might, oh, she might be right. And what about me? I'd wonder every day how they were, if they were eating good and if George was being decent to them or shoving them away. *Lord, help me! Surely you never meant for us to get so attached! Of course, we're supposed to love, we're supposed to care, but we just can't stay involved forever. Can we?*

276

We were two families, so different. And Sam and I shouldn't have to do George's job. I knew I should give Berty to Kirk or call Lizbeth from the kitchen or just set him down and tell him he was all right now. But Sarah had one hand on his back and one on my arm, content with things the way they were. And it felt so strangely good, with his warm little body snuggled against me and my little princess standing there giving us both her support.

I put my hand on Berty's head and ignored the single tear drifting down my cheek. *To everything there is a season,* I thought. *To love. To love more. To love all these, and even George, for their sakes.*

I knew in my heart we couldn't just send them home and have that be the end of it. It was never the end of it for Emma when she'd gone over and brought another Hammond baby into the world. She was there for them always. And she would want us to be too. She'd left us that, just as surely as she'd intended to leave us this farm. But without Wila's passing, without that, I would never have let it be so.

TWENTY-SIX

Samuel

The snow was stopping, and I was grateful. Two of the goats had gotten out, and instead of just standing by the barn, like I might've expected, they took to frolicking in the drifts. It took a little while getting them in again.

"I'm tellin' you," George said, "nothin' beats goats for wantin' to play. It seem warmer to you?"

"Not really."

"Well, they're sure kickin' up their heels."

We rounded them back in again and finished the milking and feeding. Then with the milk and only three eggs, we started back across the timber.

George had grown quiet again. But when we got closer to the graves he said, "I wanna talk to Wilametta when we get there. If you don't mind waitin'."

I wasn't sure that was a good idea. But I figured maybe he needed to do it. He'd hardly been able to manage much

278

on the day of her funeral. And I could really do nothing but agree, anyway. "I don't mind, George."

We trudged through new-drifted snow that had almost completely covered our tracks. But the wind was down now, and suddenly the sky burst clear in the west with a stunning blue.

"Don't see that too much in winter 'round here," George said. "Sky stays white most a' the time, seems like."

"I'm glad to see it. Maybe the kids can get out more."

"You fixin' to send 'em home with me, ain't you?"

"Going to have to, one of these times. You all need to be together."

"Don' know if they'll wanna leave you now, after such a Christmas as that was. Land, but you went all out! I s'pose you got some birthday somethin' up your sleeve too."

"Just the cake. That's all I know about."

"I can't do birthday presents. Not for so many. I jus' can't."

"You're not the only one. You can be sure of that."

"You reckon that Herbert Hoover'll ever lift a finger to help the strugglin'?" he asked me almost angrily, but then he shook his head. "'Course, they wouldn't do nothin' for me anyhow. I was strugglin' 'fore I ever heard a' Hoover or no market crash. None a' that don't mean much a' anything to me."

"We can't really blame the president for what happened," I told him, though I never cared much for a political discussion. "We likely won't have him a second term, though. With an election before the new year's out, there's bound to be some change."

"That'll be a good thing. Be more help for farmers, good Lord willin'."

It was strange to hear him talking that way, as if nothing at all had happened out of the ordinary that morning. "You all right, George?"

"Well, sure I'm all right!" he exclaimed. "Didn't even get the rope 'round my fool neck afore you knocked me in the dirt. Some bruises maybe but can't blame you for that. What about you? Clipped you pretty good the one time, didn't I?"

"I'm fine."

"You look kinda mussed up. Like you been fightin'. I look that bad?"

"Yeah. I guess you do."

"They's gonna wonder then. You gonna say anythin' to 'em?"

"Not to the kids. I'll need to explain myself to Juli. And maybe, eventually, to your oldest boy. He knows what you've been about anyway, doesn't he?"

"Don't think he cares no more. Don't think he thinks I'll be nothin' to 'em."

"Then you need to show him different. Let him see it's not going to be all on his shoulders. He's tryin' to be a man and needs you to show him the way."

George didn't answer, just headed in front of me straight to the barren white birches. Before I knew it, he was standing there looking down on Wila's grave.

And he looked so broken again, sinking to his knees. I wanted to lift him up and make him go on, but then I figured maybe this would be good for him somehow. At least this time he was doing what any man might do—just grieving at the side of his wife's grave.

I walked away from him, just a little ways around the hill where I could see Emma's wooden grave marker next to Willard's stone one above me on the rise.

What must Juli be thinking, us gone all this time? And no telling how much longer exactly. I couldn't go ahead without George. I sure wasn't going to leave him alone. But he needed his time, and thank God he was through the worst. He was doing better.

Stepping into smooth, untouched snow, I realized I must be on the pond. There were no weeds sticking up here. The brush stopped in a neat circle around where I stood, leaving a clean, unbroken surface of white. If we had ice skates, what a time it could be skating under a clear sky like this! That is, if we could skate at all with snow drifted this deep over the surface. A person might not even know there was a pond here if they hadn't been out to see it before.

I got to wondering if there was a way to make skates. I thought I'd ask George about it later. I went on toward the hill, thinking those thoughts. It never occurred to me how thick the ice was. It never entered my mind that cold enough to snow again might not be cold enough after the bit of melt we'd had. But I only took two more steps before hearing an ominous, almost echoing, crack.

And then my foot was sinking. It happened so fast. Pitching to the side with the cold shock of water rising over me, my head struck something hard. And then all I knew was chilling blackness.

TWENTY-SEVEN

Julia

When the cake came out of the oven, I started to really worry. There was no way under God's heaven it could take two grown men so long to get a mile through the woods, do a few chores, and come back. Especially since the snow had stopped. Something else was keeping them, I'd known it all along, and it pained me not to know for sure what it was.

The kids were wondering too, by now. I could tell. And it wasn't long before young Sam was pulling his coat back on.

"It's time I checked about my business," he said.

Joe, Kirk, Willy, and Robert were all ready to go with him, but Lizbeth protested. "Only one a' you," she insisted. "It don't take more'n two to go see 'bout nothin'. All right? Least ways till we know somethin' about it. Jus' go see if chores is done. See if they's over there. An' come right back."

I had to agree with her, knowing nothing else to tell them. Sam appointed Kirk to go with him, to Joe's disappointment and Willy's disgust.

"Maybe they went to Post's house for something," Robert suggested. "Or maybe one of the stock come up lame, needin' their help."

I didn't venture a word, and young Sam and Kirk were soon out the door. Lizbeth turned her face from me, and Rorey sat down on the floor and cried.

"I don't want cake! I don't want cherries! I don't want nothin'!"

I tried to comfort the little girl, and so did Sarah, bringing her new doll. But Rorey only set it on the floor beside her and went right on crying.

"Rorey, honey, there's no reason to cry. I'm sure they're fine."

"Then why ain't they home?"

I couldn't tell her anything she'd accept. I knew I couldn't. She'd seen her big brother's worry, and she was only thinking the worst. They thought their father was gone. They thought he'd left them somehow, and my Samuel was out there trying to find him. *Lord help them, they've suffered so much already. Can't they have good news, just this once? Can't Robert be right, perhaps? Maybe ol' Rosey was needing extra attention. Or one of the pigs. Anything but more trouble with George.*

"Is Daddy okay?" Sarah suddenly asked me.

"Of course, he's okay. He just went with Rorey's daddy to do the milking and such." Of course, that was all it was. The men would explain their delay as soon as they got here, which was bound to be any minute.

But Sarah just looked me, less than satisfied. She had no reason, no reason at all, to seem so worried all of a sudden. But she was. And Rorey had no reason to be crying like this. At least no new reason. I caught myself impatient with the both of them and took a deep breath. *Lord, we're all in your hands. Wherever the men are, they're in your hands too.*

Suddenly a song seemed to be filling me from the inside. Like it was Emma singing it, like we were back to the day she'd sung it before, coming home from church in the sunshine, with me knowing how poorly she'd felt that day.

"Great is thy faithfulness, O God my Father . . ."

She'd started so quiet. But she seemed to just gain strength as she went on, and she wasn't quiet for long. *"Thou changest not, thy compassions they fail not! As thou hast been, thou forever wilt be . . ."*

I could almost hear her resonant voice singing the glorious hymn. *"Great is thy faithfulness! Great is thy faithfulness! Morning by morning new mercies I see! All I have needed thy hand hath provided! Great is thy faithfulness, Lord unto me!"*

How Emma had loved that song! It summed up the way she'd looked at everything, her answer to anything that came her way. God's presence. God's provision. God's mercy.

Why can't I be more like her, Lord? After all you've done to bring us through such terrible trials so smoothly, why haven't I rejoiced? Oh, God, you know what the future holds. You know our days and all the good that you have planned. I rest in you. The way I should have been doing all along, I rest in you. We'll manage, no matter how long the kids are here, no matter what happens. Because you are here, faithful Father God. You are here, and I cannot doubt it. I cannot doubt the goodness that brought us here, that put so much of Emma in my heart and made me love this sometimes difficult family.

I wasn't prepared when the boys came bursting in, carrying someone between them. I thought it was George. But George came in right behind, shouting out orders, taking charge.

"Get him by the fire! Quick! Get them wet clothes off him! Get blankets! Go on! Hurry!"

He was talking to everybody more than anybody in particular. For one quick, irrational moment, I thought, *Where's Samuel?* And then I saw that the icy gray figure they were hustling past me *was* Samuel.

"Mommy!" Sarah screamed.

"Get towels," I told her. "Run now." She was scared, but I couldn't address it. "Robert," I ordered, "you run up and bring down every blanket you can carry!"

I saw myself then in Emma's room, yanking all the covers off her bed, without even knowing how I'd gotten in there. And then I was running to the fireside, where George and his big boys were pulling off Samuel's dripping coat and boots.

"He broke through the ice, ma'am," George was saying as I struggled to pull the covers around my Samuel. *Oh, God, how could this happen?*

"I—I shoulda been watchin' where he walked to," George said on. "But tell the truth, I wouldn't a' known neither that the ice weren't solid. Awful sorry, ma'am. Truth told."

He looked pretty pale himself and was at least partly wet. He must've managed somehow to pull Samuel out, God have mercy.

Mercy. Faithfulness. Yes.

"Sammy? Can you hear me?"

He was shivering. He was breathing. But he didn't answer, and I couldn't be sure he'd heard me. He hadn't opened his eyes.

"Lay a couple a' them towels right along the edge of the screen here, right close to the fire to get 'em warm," George was telling my daughter. Then he turned to me. "Got to pull ever'thin' off him, ma'am, 'fore the fire an' the blankets can do their job. He's soaked clear to the skin."

285

"Yes." Feeling numb, I helped him pull the wet things off my husband, cover him again completely, and start rubbing warmth into his arms and legs.

Oh, God, I thought. *Emma rubbed Wilametta so fruitlessly. We tried so hard. And now Sammy is laying here all pale.*

Sarah came up at my shoulder, her teary eyes just glancing at mine before she started in rubbing her father too. Robert was throwing more wood on the fire. Seemed like everybody was doing something.

"He gonna die?" Rorey asked timidly.

"Nah," George answered immediately. "Nah, he's a tough bird, this 'un. He'll be up again afore long, keepin' an eye out for me."

There was something about the way he said it. And the deep look in his eyes. I wouldn't have imagined it to be so, especially after the way George had been lately. But he really, really cared.

"Was he under long?" I dared ask him.

"Didn't seem like long, ma'am, but I can't say. Done the best I could. Breathed on his own, he did. That was the most a' my worry."

To think of Samuel in that icy pond! It was shallow enough around the edges, but ten feet in, it was deep enough to baptize, and in the middle easily over a man's head. He might've been lost. He might've slipped beneath the ice, where George couldn't reach him.

"Thank you," I managed to tell him. "I'm so glad you were there."

He shook his head. "He wouldn't a' been there if it weren't for me. Dad blame it all if we ain't some kinda brothers after today."

Samuel didn't wake. And I kept thinking, *Shouldn't he? Shouldn't he have already, even before they got him to the house? In a near-drowning, once the person's breathing, doesn't he wake up?*

"Sammy?" I tried whispering to him.

"You know," George told me, "if it weren't for those two-by-sixes stuck out there to the post, I couldn't a' reached him without falling in my own self. Give us a safe track clear to the shore. Lucky there was snow knocked off, or I couldn't a' even seed where they was."

Two-by-sixes jutting out over the water instead of a dock. The Hammond boys fished from them in the summertime. But snow knocked off? Maybe Samuel had tripped on them. Or worse.

"Was he right next to them?"

"Yeah. Arm's length. Good thing too."

A chill working through me, I reached my hand ever so gently to the back of Samuel's head. Under his thick, dark hair behind his left ear I felt what I'd dreaded. A welt, long and swollen, where he must've struck his head. Pulling my hand away, I saw just an inkling of blood across my fingers, and it turned me cold.

"George, see if you can get Barrett Post to fetch the doctor for us."

He looked at me first in surprise, then with a sturdy sort of resolve. "Yes, ma'am."

He was up and almost out the door when Joe stopped him. "Your coat's wet, Pa. I'll go."

George shook his head. "I'll be fine. But you can come with me."

It seemed like hours before they returned. Samuel didn't stir, and we were all pretty restless in the interval. Sarah cuddled up against her daddy, crying. I felt like crying too, but strangely for her pain more than for Samuel. He'd be fine. He had to be.

"Mom?" Robert was asking. "Why does bad stuff keep happening?"

I didn't really have an answer for that, but I had to tell him something. "I don't know, honey. But your father'll be all right. I know he will."

"We better pray for him," Franky said.

"Yes. That's the thing to do." I looked around at the little faces around me. "Don't be afraid, all right? God is still here with us."

"That didn't help Mama," Willy said cynically.

"Yes, it did. She had perfect peace."

I prayed with children gathered all around me. Lizbeth was giving the baby a bottle, and Sam Hammond was holding little Berty in his lap.

"I don't want my birthday cake," Rorey said for the second time. "Don't want turkey pie neither if he don't wake up."

"He'll wake up," Robert insisted. "He'll be up before the doctor gets here."

We were all relieved when George and Joe came back. Of course, the doctor wasn't with them, not yet. But that he was sent for was some comfort at least.

"He any better?" George asked right away.

"He's warmer," I told him, but there wasn't much else I could say.

"Barrett's gettin' a move on pretty quick. Weather's good an' clear now too. His sleigh'll get through no problem. Doctor oughta be here some time this afternoon."

I just nodded.

"Why don't you sit down, Mrs. Wortham?" he suggested. "You're lookin' kinda tired or somethin'."

I shook my head. "I'm not the one that just walked all that way through the snow."

Just the same, he brought me a chair, but I didn't sit in it. "I have to get dinner for all of you."

"I'll set everything out, Mrs. Wortham," Lizbeth said quickly. "Don't you worry about it."

I went over to the fire where Samuel still lay with pillows propped under his head and shoulders. Sarah was at his side, and I knelt beside her. "Sammy," I said. "It's time you wake up. You're worrying the children."

"Why's he sleepin' so long?" Sarah asked.

"Sometimes that happens when someone hits their head, honey."

"Berty didn't sleep at all when he fell on the steps. And he bumped his head."

"That's some different."

"But, Mommy—"

Samuel moved his hand, just a little. Sarah saw it too and didn't finish what she'd started to say. He opened his eyes slowly, looking first at her, then at me.

"Daddy!" Sarah squealed. "Is you all better?"

Sam looked a little confused. "Did . . . George . . ."

He couldn't seem to finish.

"Yes. Two of the boys helped, but he already had you out of the pond." I took his hand, delighted beyond measure that he was conscious and talking.

"You okay, Daddy?" Sarah asked.

"Head's pounding, pumpkin." He looked at me. "Ice wasn't solid."

"I know. George told me."

"Bet you didn't know . . . you married somebody so stupid."

"Oh, hush. I'm just glad you're still here." Tears filled my eyes. I couldn't help it. I wiped them away, but he'd seen.

"Sorry, honey. For worrying you."

"It was just an accident, Sammy! You don't have to be sorry! I'll make you some tea a minute."

He didn't answer me, just seemed to be looking around the room. "Where's George?"

"Right here . . ." He'd been behind me, but when I turned around, he wasn't there.

"On the porch," Franky reported. "I seen him go out."

"He went and sent Barrett Post after the doctor for you," I told Samuel.

He tried to sit up, but I saw the pain in his face.

"Please lie back, Sammy. He's all right."

Kirk went to the back door, and I knew he was checking, just to see. But I didn't expect to hear what he said when he came back.

"He's cryin'." He didn't seem to know what to think.

Lizbeth nodded, as if she had more of an understanding on it than the rest of us did. "Maybe he'll be ready for some birthday cake afore long. If he can cry, he can feel better after, and then we can go on with today, like we're s'posed to."

"He ain't gonna feel better!" Willy protested. "It ain't fair, that's what! For Mr. Wortham to get better when Mama didn't!"

Lizbeth shook her head. "Hush! Folks is funny sometimes. They can cry happy an' sad at the same time. Sure, he's hurt over Mama! But he's glad it's comin' out okay today, an' so am I. Our Pa's a hero, ain't he, Mrs. Wortham? He saved Mr. Wortham's life! Mama would be proud a' him. She'd want him to stay right here an' be a protector for every one a' us—you all too. Ain't that right, Mrs. Wortham? Mr. Wortham?"

I looked at Samuel, and he looked at me. "He's a hero all right," I told her.

Samuel managed a nod. "Looks like I could use all the help I can get."

"Pa!" Rorey hollered, suddenly excited by such words. She picked up her doll and raced for the porch. "You's gonna be our portector, Pa! You's gonna be a hero!"

I had to smile, and Sammy squeezed my hand. "Thank you, Jesus," he whispered.

Much to Samuel's delight, the children were all over George for the rest of the afternoon. And when Barrett

Post and the doctor finally came in, we were all in one big circle spread across the sitting room floor, eating Rorey's birthday cake.

I'd gotten dry clothes for Samuel. He wasn't quite feeling like eating yet, but he was strong enough to hold Sarah on his lap. And for a moment, Barrett and the doctor just stood there looking at us.

"Feeling better, I take it?" the doctor asked Samuel.

"Yes, sir. Hurting still. Light-headed if I try to get up. So I haven't moved much."

"Pa's a hero," Harry carefully pointed out.

Doctor Howell barely glanced his way. "I heard some such." He knelt beside Samuel, took a good look in his eyes, and carefully examined the goose egg on the back of his head. "Shouldn't move much for a few days," he told Sam. "Got you some concussion here. Doesn't seem to be any ill effect from the ice water, though. You're a lucky gent, you are."

"Wasn't luck," Samuel told him. "Providence. We've had God's help this whole day." He looked at George. There wasn't a word between them, but somehow there didn't need to be.

"The Almighty has a way a' showin' his hand," George said in agreement. "Even when we's too dull to wanna look."

I saw Mr. Post swallow hard and look down at his boots. He didn't say anything, not until the doctor was done and gone back out the door.

"Mama said once . . ." he started, and then hesitated. "Mama said when things is hard, that's when God does his miracles, 'cause there ain't nobody standin' in the way thinkin' they can do better."

"Your mother knew what she was talking about," I agreed with him. "He does the most for people who know they need him."

"Want some cake?" Rorey offered. "It's my birthday."

Barrett looked like he could almost sink into the floor. "I been angry forty years, George Hammond, an' here you sit eatin' cake an' celebratin'! Blast it all! I unnerstood what you was going through before, but . . . but—"

"Had to lay it down," George said. "Or die."

"But how d'you lay it down?" Barrett asked, looking truly shaken.

"I dunno. An' I ain't sayin' I'm doin' so well. But if God can handle Wilametta up there, maybe he can handle the rest a' us too. Maybe there's some reason me still bein' here."

Barrett shook his head. "I didn't know how long it'd be afore I'd hear you in your right mind."

"Don't know how my mind is yet," George admitted. "But I'm here. Gotta be a pa again too."

Barrett turned his eyes to me. "You been prayin' for us, ain't you, Mrs. Wortham?"

"Yes," I admitted, wondering why he would think to ask.

"Louise said you'd take it up, now Emma's gone. Shoot, Louise said she's feelin' like prayin' too, just thinkin' a' Emma takin' so much stock in it."

"Can't hurt ya," George told him. "Maybe you'll quit bein' s' angry, you ol' cuss."

His words surprised me, but then I remembered how they'd bantered in easier times, in the summer and at harvest, ribbing each other like enemies though we all knew they were friends.

"Maybe I'll come to church one of these days," Barrett said. "See what all the fuss is about."

"Thanks," George told him then. "For the Christmas turkey."

"An' the fixin's," Lizbeth added.

"Yeah," said little Harry. "Yummy!"

"Our pleasure to do it," Barrett said and turned to go.

But Sam Hammond, leaning against the door frame, suddenly spoke up. "Maybe you oughta pray while you're here. Seems like in this world there ain't nothing sure."

His words so surprised us that the whole room got quiet.

"I know one thing," Sam continued. "Mama wanted me to believe, an' it sounds like your mama wanted the same thing from you. It prob'ly ain't gonna set real well either one a' us decidin' we know better."

"You all plan this out ahead?" Barrett questioned.

"Nope." It was Willy that answered, and Barrett just looked at the boy a while.

"I do gotta do it," Barrett said finally. "I know I gotta do it."

Franky suddenly rose up on his knees, excited. "Mrs. Gray says you jus' tell Jesus you wanna be his instead a' your own. Jus' tell him you's glad he died for ya."

Barrett just stood and stared. "What are you doin', George? Raisin' up a whole passel a' preachers?"

"Nah. That was Wila's doin'. Always said it sure would be nice if one or more of 'em took to the cloth."

And just like that, Barrett prayed. Right there in front of all of us. He prayed and accepted the Lord and told George how much he cared and Samuel how glad he was that he was doing all right.

"Keep up the good work," he told me as he left. "I'll tell Louisey 'bout this. Don't know if she'll laugh or cry."

George went out with him to the sleigh. And when he came back inside, he stood in the doorway for a minute, shaking his head. "Barrett praying," he said, looking at Samuel. "If that don't beat all."

TWENTY-EIGHT

Samuel

Albert Graham came two days later and got his car stuck in a melting drift about a quarter mile down the road. I was asleep on a pillow when the noise of the door and the commotion woke me and set my head to throbbing again.

"Oh!" Juli exclaimed when she saw him. "Mr. Graham, how's your wife?"

"Better. Much better, thank you." He seemed surprised to find me, and a mattress, on the floor. And to see Lizbeth and the baby there, along with Rorey and Sarah and Berty in the corner playing with a cluster of paper angels.

"We're so sorry about Emma," Juli was saying. "So sorry you couldn't be here."

He nodded his head. "I wanted to come. She was a wonderful aunt. I would've liked seeing her again."

He came and stood over me. "Heard in town you had a close call."

"Yes, sir. Guess I did."

"Don't have to call me sir. I'm not much older than you are."

I smiled at that and thought of the last time he'd come, when he took hold of Emma's ax and whacked at the log right next to me without a word of warning. Hard enough to make me back up a couple of steps and wonder at him for sure.

"Left the car stuck down the road a piece," he said. "I could use a shovel. You still got Uncle Willard's in the tool-shed?"

"Yes."

"You don't have to be doing the shoveling," Julia protested. "Robert and Willy can do that." She called for them up the stairs.

"You got all the Hammonds here?"

"No," I told him. "Exactly half of them over home with George right now. They all come shifting back and forth."

"George all right?"

"It's not been easy. But he's all right."

Robert and Willy came tearing down the steps like wild horses but stopped in their tracks when they saw Albert.

"Mr. Graham's car is stuck on the road," Juli told them. "He needs some help shoveling."

"Okay," they said almost in unison. But both boys turned their eyes to me before going for their coats. They were worried. They'd been worried for days about what Albert would say when he got here.

"When I get the car in, will you be up to walking with me out to Aunt Emma's grave?" he asked me.

I pulled myself to my feet. "I'll help you with the car."

"No. You stay here. You're not supposed to be doing much is what I hear. Clement Post says you almost died, and now you and George's boys are preaching to the whole countryside."

"That's a little exaggerated."

There was a certain softness about his expression. "It's been a hard winter so far. And I mean more than the weather."

He went with Robert and Willy and let them ride back with him the short distance to the farm. I got my coat and hat. My head hurt, and I was still having trouble being light-headed when I was up too long, but Albert wanted me to walk with him. Nothing would keep me from it.

"Sit down," Julia urged him when he came back in. "Warm up a little with a cup of tea."

Albert shook his head. "You and Emma and tea." But that was all he said. He sat down and let her fix him a steaming cup and looked all around him at the house while he drank.

"You haven't changed the place much. Where's the mantle clock?"

"It was broken accidentally," Juli said quickly. "We'll replace it, if it was important to you."

"If that one was important, some other one bought to replace it wouldn't quite fit the bill, now would it?"

Neither of us said a word. It was impossible to tell whether he was bothered about the clock or not.

"The preacher do a good funeral?"

"He tried," Juli said timidly. "He did very well. It was just . . . so hard, Mrs. Hammond's being on the same day."

Albert sighed. "Yes." He was quiet, looking into his cup, and then drained the rest of it in one gulp. "You folks have any new plans?"

Julia looked at me almost nervously. It would be far easier for me to go, if it came to that. To do something else if we had to. But Juli loved this place. She'd connected with it, and with Emma, right from the start.

"No," I told him. "We don't have any certain plans."

He stood up. "You sure you're okay to walk?"

"Yes."

"Get one of Aunt Emma's canes, will you?"

"I don't need—"

"It won't kill you now just to be a little cautious. You don't have to act a hundred percent if you're not there yet."

So I took a cane. And it helped, just knowing it was in my hand when the world tilted a little.

We were out of the farmyard and well into the trees before he spoke again.

"What kind of shape is George's place in? Gone down pretty bad? I didn't even go over and have a look at it last time I was down."

"Needs work. Quite a bit of work, to be honest. But so does this one. But we've tried to keep up, and I expect he has too."

"You think so? He feeds his hogs. Milks the goats and such. But he's never been one to fix on a place. It was sturdy enough once, but I've heard it's not far from falling around his ears."

"It's not that bad."

"You've come to be a friend of his then?"

"Yes. I have."

"No more than natural. Under the circumstances."

He was unreadable, at least for the moment. Hard and soft at the same time. No telling which way the water would run.

I followed him up the little hill above the pond, where you could still see the place I'd gone under, a jagged hole glazed over with a fresh patch of too-thin ice.

He stopped in front of Willard's grave, but he was looking at Emma's. "I'll have a stone marker sent out," he said. "But it might not be till spring." He was so quiet then, for the longest time. "Did you understand her?" he finally asked me.

"I tried to. She was a good woman. But it was Julia that was closest to her. Seemed like they'd known each other for years."

He laughed. "Two of a kind. Just as soon be barefoot in the garden or picking some kind of leaf to put in your teacup. Rather do that than go watch a picture show."

"They're funny sometimes," I agreed. "Practical, though." Too late I realized I'd used the present tense.

"Seems like she's still here."

"Yes. I guess it does."

He sighed. "She wanted you to have her farm when she found out I wouldn't move back down from the city. She said you needed it. And you'd appreciate it."

I didn't say anything. I couldn't say anything. He had his right, whatever he chose to do. And I had no right to influence him.

"She was strong-willed. Heart of gold. But no business sense at all. You know? Do you have any idea what this farm is worth?"

"No," I answered honestly.

"Well, I don't either in today's market, but in 1928 it would've brought a fair price. She didn't care, though. She didn't care about stuff like that."

He glanced down the hill toward Wilametta's grave in the birches but turned his head away again.

"How do you figure a person that'll throw away thousands of dollars over a lifetime? Giving all the time? Huh? What do you call that?"

Saintly, I was thinking. But I couldn't say it. I figured he didn't really want to hear it.

"I tried. Over and over I tried to explain to her the way financial matters are supposed to work in this world, and that it isn't a sin to look out for yourself. But she was too busy looking out for the likes of George Hammond to listen to me."

"She listened," I ventured. "She just had to follow her own heart. It beat a little different than most people's, I think."

He turned and looked at me, making me wish I hadn't spoken. "She told me she used to be greedy when she was younger. Like the rest of us, I guess. But she couldn't be that way anymore. Tell me. You still want the place?"

"I can't tell you. I can't be swaying your decision one way or another."

"Tarnation, Sam Wortham! Aunt Emma tried to give you the deed, and you wouldn't take it! Now you won't tell me. What is it with you? Does it go against your nature some way to get ahold of what's in front of you?"

"No. I just don't want to be taking what's yours."

"Emma didn't count it mine. Not since I told her I meant to stay in the city."

I bowed my head, looking down at Emma's grave. *Lord, please show me what to do, how to talk to this man.*

"So if I straight-out offered you the deed, same as Emma did, would you take it now that she's gone?"

I wrestled with the question, though Julia's answer was sitting there on the tip of my tongue, tingling to get out. It was too easy. Sure, I'd worked. I'd have to keep working. But I wasn't like somebody who had struggled for years to keep a farm in the family or managed to save back wages to buy the ground with cold, hard cash. I hadn't had a steady job for almost two years. I didn't deserve this. Just like I'd told Emma. I didn't deserve this.

"Well . . . would you take the deed or not? Why's that such a difficult question?"

I swallowed hard, thinking of Julia, Robert, and Sarah, their happy voices floating across the farmyard and joining with Emma's. Oh, she'd loved them. They'd loved her. It was right. It was God-ordained.

"Yes," I said, barely able to get the word out. "If you mean to give it, I'd take it."

"Well, now. We have an answer." He was looking at the sky and then the timber all around us. "I used to play with

Warren out here. Emma's boy. Did she ever tell you about that?"

"She didn't talk about him very often."

"I expect not. Hurt awful bad losing him." He turned to me again. "We used to fish down there, and swim too, in that pond where you were almost lost, Wortham. Emma used to tell us to be careful. Be careful. Well, we weren't. But nothing ever happened out here. Not to anybody but you." He shook his head. "Pretty spot in the spring. Used to picnic out here. I think I'll section off a square and keep it. You don't need it, anyway. You sure don't need the graves."

"No," I agreed. "I don't."

"I've thought on this a lot. Can't see clear to buck against Aunt Emma's intent, though it doesn't make any real sense, you understand that? She only knew you, what, seven months?"

"Yes, sir."

"Well, it seems mighty foolish, but it was Emma's place. It was her choice. And I'll fix you the deed before I go back north."

I almost could've fallen over, knowing the relief Julia would feel. Of course, I didn't know if it was the news or being upright so long that was making my head feel like it was swimming.

"You all right?"

"Yes. Thank you. Yes."

He grew quiet a minute. "What would you do about George?" he finally asked me.

"Well—"

"No. Wait a minute. I've got to say something about that. It's different. That farm was never Emma's home. It was just something Willard bought to make a profit. George was supposed to pay. Long time ago he agreed to pay. And as far as I see it, he hasn't put in a dime, not one dime, for at least eight years."

"He's been struggling just to make ends meet. Emma told him to put feeding his family first. She didn't—"

"She made it easy for him to cheat her. It was different with you. You were supposed to keep up the place and take care of her so she could come home. You did that."

"It's the only home his children have known."

"That don't give George an excuse."

"She loved them too."

"She loved everybody. Fools as much as anybody else. That was Aunt Emma. I'm getting cold, how about you? Let's head back to the house."

There was no stopping him, no persuading him, the way he looked just then. He marched away from me down the hill and straight back over the trail to the farmyard. And my heart pounded just thinking of George. Why should I gain a farm and him lose one? Why should I be spared and his precious wife go on to be with the Lord? Sure, he'd been slack about upkeep, but maybe he wouldn't stay that way. *Lord, give him another chance.*

But Albert didn't give me another chance to talk to him before we got to the house. As soon as we came in, Lizbeth offered him cocoa and some of the Christmas cookies they'd made, but he paid her no attention at all.

I knew it bothered Julia to see us coming in looking so grim. I wanted to tell her he'd already decided to honor Emma's decision about us. But that wasn't the foremost thing on her mind. Something was working in her, I could see it, and it had her flustered some way. She dropped a dish, picked it up again, and then couldn't help but come at us looking as scared and as determined as I'd ever seen her.

"Mr. Graham . . ."

He looked at her in surprise, as if he didn't expect any of us to say much of anything unless he spoke first.

"Mr. Graham, I have to talk to you."

"Well, go ahead." He seated himself in a kitchen chair, looking almost amused.

"Mr. Graham," Juli began, "I was with Emma when she died. I was the only one. And she told me I had to talk to you when you got here. I don't know what you've decided. But I have to tell you what she said." She took a deep breath. This was hard for her, I could tell.

"She told me not to let you take George Hammond's farm—"

"It's not his farm." Albert was definitely not amused now.

"Maybe not," Juli persisted. "I guess I can understand that, to your mind. But it's his children's home. That's what she was thinking about. Wilametta is buried in that ground over there—"

"I didn't approve that."

"Emma did! She told me the land shouldn't be sold to anybody else. Not ever. She wanted George and especially the children to have it, Mr. Graham, because their mother is buried here, and because she loved every single one of them like they were her own. Most people don't understand that, I know. But you were so far away. And her son was gone. They were family. She wanted them here. She wanted them around, whether they could pay anything or not. Just for love! Just because that's the way she was!"

Behind her, Lizbeth burst into tears, and I saw that Juli too was crying. Dear, strong Juli. When there was so much at stake for our own family, to be standing here presenting a case for the Hammonds. I was proud. I hoped she knew that.

"Oh, Mr. Graham," she went on. "Forgive me, but it's not your decision. Not really. It was Emma's. And she made it."

He leaned his head against one hand. "I can't say it's anything I haven't heard before."

"We know," Julia told him pointedly. "She asked you to draw up papers for her."

"She didn't always know what was best for her own self," he defended. "I wanted to be sure, before I did any-

302

thing, that she wasn't going to be hurt by it. Or change her mind if she finally got tired of him using her so long."

"She didn't change her mind."

Juli looked as unmoveable as brick, and I smiled. "I can witness to that."

He looked up at me, his face still unreadable. "Well . . ."

He didn't say anything else. He picked up one of the cookies that Lizbeth had set on the table and sat a long time not talking, just slowly breaking that cookie up into bits and not eating a crumb. Finally he looked up.

"You're Lizbeth, aren't you?"

The poor girl jumped, she was so startled that he would address her. She shifted her baby sister to the opposite hip and timidly nodded her head. "Yes, sir."

He glanced up at her for a moment and then turned his eyes back to the table with a sigh. "Aunt Emma told me once you were the one that started it all. She didn't always feel so close with you, you know. She said once you were nothing particularly special and none of the other families she helped were either. She just midwifed and went about her business. That's what she said. But after helping your mother bring you into world, and then you being so sick that winter they didn't know if you'd make it— that's when she came to care. She took to praying. Took you to heart. And she kept right on caring all this time since. And not just for you. Like to drive me batty sometimes, not knowing what she'd do next. Give away a registered bull or a wagon or part of her corn crop. I couldn't keep up with her."

Lizbeth nodded, though I didn't know if she'd ever heard all this before or not. She didn't say a word.

"I can't give your father that land," Albert told her. "I don't even want to renew the contract and give him a chance to come up short on it like he did before." He brushed the cookie crumbs away from him with one sweep of his hand. "He doesn't make much of an effort, so far as

I can see. He's lazy, shiftless, not worth the paper we'd sign. Do you understand what I'm saying?"

"I don't be seein' him to be all that bad," Lizbeth said, calm as a breeze. And I was proud of her too.

"You wouldn't. And I guess that speaks well of him, of a sort. He's not been too ugly to you at least. Has he?"

"No, sir. He's not been too ugly. Nor so lazy, neither, if you don't mind me contradictin'."

He smiled. "You take care of your brothers and sisters, don't you?"

She wiped at her cheek with a sleeve. "I try."

"Been to school enough to read well?"

"Haven't been in a while, sir. But I can read, yes."

"Then I think I'll make this little agreement between me and you. For Emma's sake, you understand? Because she felt so strongly about it."

"I'm not sure I do unnerstand. No, sir." She was looking bewildered and more than a little scared, and I could understand why.

"I'll draw up a paper," he explained, his expression clearly softening. "It'll say your farm is yours to live on as long as you want to. Or your brothers and sisters. If ever any of you should manage to turn a profit off it, well, I'll get percentage payment. And if ever the time comes you all move away before it's paid clear, the land comes back to me."

She seemed almost breathless. "Then you'll let Pa keep the farm?"

"Not your pa. You."

"Me?"

"That's right. And your older brother after you. He was the only one of you Emma didn't midwife into this world, I understand."

"Y—yes, sir."

"Well, it becomes his if you ever choose to leave it, and the others after him. Of course, as young as you are, I'll have to set up the whole thing in a trust, in my own name, I guess, till you come of age."

"What about Pa?" The girl was looking truly shocked.

"You can choose to keep him if you want to. I don't have any particular say in that matter."

"He's a good pa! A' 'course we'll keep him. And he'll be in charge too. He's our pa!"

He nodded. "It's your farm. If you want him in charge, it's your business."

I had to smile at that, and Juli did too. Her eyes twinkled with relief, her cheeks glistened, and I reached for her hand.

"Thank you, Mr. Graham," Lizbeth was saying, still in shock. "We thanks you so much."

"Well, you're welcome. I suppose I have very little choice in the matter if I want to honor Aunt Emma's memory. But I already told Mr. Wortham here that I'm keeping some of the land for myself."

I could see how those words jarred Juli. She must've been thinking he meant Emma's farm. This whole farm. But before I could tell her different, Albert was talking on.

"I'll have it surveyed to put the measurements on paper. The pond, Aunt Emma and Uncle Willard's graves, and the land around them."

Lizbeth drew in a quick breath.

"But not your mother's grave. That'll be your side of the line. I don't mind you using the pond, but don't do it any damage, and don't let Wortham here sink his bones into it again."

She stared at him, then nodded her head. "Yes, sir. Thank you."

I could feel Julia's tension beside me, but Albert had turned his eyes back to her too.

"Mrs. Wortham, you surprised me. When I told your husband you and Emma were two of a kind, I didn't know how true that was. I thought you were going to beg me for this farm for yourself, not plead for the Hammonds' sakes. No wonder Emma loved you. You almost think alike."

"No," she stammered. "I haven't been—"

"Don't worry. I'd have a hard time with myself if I didn't accept Emma's last wishes. Everybody that knew anything of it'd have a hard time with me too, I expect. I already told your husband I'd fix you a deed. She had a right to her decision, just like you said, whether it made any common sense or not."

Then Julia breathed easy. "Thank you, Mr. Graham. She would be so glad."

He nodded, gave Lizbeth another glance, and then another one to Julia. Then he fixed his eyes on me and smiled. "Didn't somebody say something about cocoa?"

TWENTY-NINE

Julia

Albert was true to his word. Within two days, we had a deed, and Lizbeth had her contract. George had some mixed feelings about the arrangement, as is understandable. But he was more grateful than anything else. And he swore to Samuel on Wilametta's Bible that he'd never drink again, and never try doing himself any more harm.

Sam Hammond's job at the mill didn't last very long. The mill closed, and the Dearing grocery, and more businesses than I could count. My Samuel too continued without work, though he would've loved to find anything at all available. But the southern Illinois mines were failing, and there were no other businesses anywhere near us hiring. Samuel couldn't even find many odd jobs, because we were too far from town to make that a practical option without transportation of our own.

It wasn't long before we were hurting, and the Hammonds as well as us, needing things we had no money to buy. But we prayed. We shared things. We got by.

Franky came over almost every day, trying to get Samuel to keep on working with his wood.

"You can sell stuff 'long the road when there's more folks out come spring," he told us. "I'll help. We'll make lotsa money. You'll see."

At least it was something for them to do. With Franky and Robert and sometimes Willy watching or helping, Samuel made a porch swing, two upright chairs, and half a dozen little carved-top boxes for jewelry or keepsakes. I didn't know if they'd sell or not, but it was all good work, and I was glad to see those boys growing so close and eager to be working in the shop with Samuel that way. I knew he felt good too, just to be able to accomplish a task, to create something beautiful while the weather was too cold to work the ground.

"You don't wanna ever be idle," Emma'd said once. *"A good rest is all right, but don' let the devil catch you idle! Oh, but he'll play with you then!"*

I took such words to heart and worked hard that winter teaching Rorey and Sarah to sew. Soon they were doing mending for me, sewing buttons and the like. And when I wasn't busy with children or anything else, I got out the quilt blocks Emma had already cut and started piecing, determined to finish for her what she'd barely had time to start. She'd done so many beautiful quilts in her lifetime, but this would be my first. Working in the lamplight while the children slept, I decided to give the quilt to Pastor and Juanita. They'd blessed us so much and continued to look out for us the best they could. I knew Emma would be pleased. She would be glad to see us all working together this way.

Even Hazel Sharpe, who found it in her heart to give every child a Bible. That was a miracle from heaven, and we all knew it. Though she still barely spoke to us when we saw her at church, we knew things had changed. Miss Hazel was family too, though she'd never be one to come out and say so. I picked out Emma's two prettiest lace doilies, perfectly matching, beautiful work, and gave them to Hazel one Sunday morning. She just stood there the longest time, fingering Emma's fine work and avoiding my eyes.

"Land, she was patient, wasn't she, doin' the like a' this?" Hazel finally said.

"Oh, yes," I ventured bravely. "Very patient. With people too."

Hazel looked up at me, her tiny gray eyes seeming to sparkle without the hardness that usually masked them. "I'll say. Where would you be without her?"

That was all she said and all she did, except to hug the doilies to her breast and hurry away, almost as if she couldn't risk another moment of someone peering into her soul. Emma used to say that the very thing Hazel wanted most was what she tried the hardest to push away. So every time after that when Charlie Hunter came to get us for church, I would sit with Hazel if I could, even though I knew how she'd behave—like I was irritating the daylights out of her. I even hugged her once or twice, though she never hugged me back. It made me feel good inside to love her right over top all the rough edges.

Sukey's calf was born in February. And Samuel was so nervous about it that little Franky, who'd spent the night, just sat there and laughed. "You can read all right, huh?" the little boy said. "But you don't know nothin' 'bout them cows? Guess there's all kinda smarts to this world!"

It was a difficult birth, and Samuel and I were glad that George and his boys were there to help us. I'd been just a child the last time I'd been in on a calving, and Samuel had never seen such a thing before in his life.

Sukey was bawling, and I knew it bothered Samuel not to know anything he could do to help her. But she did all right, her calf was strong, and George seemed especially glad to be of such service. Not long after, his milker Rosey took sick and died, and from that point on we shared everything, from either farm, as if it were all one.

I soon discovered that George didn't read a bit better than his son Franky did. But after hearing me read from *Pilgrim's Progress* a few more times, he took to liking it. Even seemed to understand it better than he had at first. Several times I caught him with Franky discussing this or that part of the tale. Or with Willy or Kirk, though they always had their minds on something else.

George and Samuel did most things together, an arrangement that Samuel really seemed to like. He told me he might learn a thing or two yet about livestock, at the very least. And I marveled that he didn't see the progress he'd already made to seem so at home on this farm where at first he'd been so uncertain. I prayed that we could manage a good crop from the fields next season and turn a profit by it. Maybe we could turn Albert Graham's opinion of George too. Maybe.

All the Hammonds that were old enough went to school more regularly than they had before. Of course, that kept me busy with Harry, Bert, and Emma Grace, but seeing the change in Lizbeth, I didn't mind.

"You think any a' us'll go to college?" she asked me one day.

"Well, I don't know. Maybe. If you really want to."

She stared at me for a minute, then shook her head. "I can't hardly b'lieve you said that! Don't you think there ain't no way? We ain't got no money atall for that!"

"That doesn't matter," I told her with confidence. "None of us knows what God has in store for tomorrow."

"You're the strangest lady," she told me. "Even when you's poor, you don't know you's poor."

She studied more than the others, late at night when her younger siblings were sleeping. Her older brother had given up on school and declared he was only going till some job opened up. But Lizbeth, though she started the term almost two years behind, was determined to end it on the same level as students her age. She was like a different person, a Lizbeth I'd never seen, with a book in one hand and a bottle for Emma Grace in the other, taking full advantage of a chance she'd thought she lost. And she loved me for it.

"You don't have to watch the kids, Mrs. Wortham," she told me more than once. "I'm old enough. I can stay home with 'em."

And every time when I told her no and sent her on to school, she hugged my neck and very nearly cried. She loved her family. She truly did. But they all thought she'd wanted to stay home from school. No one had seen how much it had torn her heart to do so.

I tried to help Franky with his reading sometimes when he came over. But I didn't get any further than Elvira Post did. But we did discover that he had a propensity for math, at least if he could do the figuring in his head and not on the chalkboard or paper. I wondered for a while if he might need glasses. But Samuel said his eye was far too good working with wood for that to be the case. We prayed about it, but none of it was bothering Franky anymore.

"I'll keep tryin' to learn it," he assured me. "But I'll jus' be the bestest at woodworkin' in the whole country! I can do that!"

And I could believe him. Samuel said it wouldn't be long before that boy could build whatever he wanted to build.

I could believe for Lizbeth too, that she could go to college and be a schoolteacher or whatever else she wanted to be. And the rest of them could dream whatever they wanted to dream too. Not that times weren't hard. The kids would still cry sometimes, especially at night, especially on special days when they missed their mama. But there was always a ray of God's hope shining through, breaking through the darkness of grieving, worry, or doubt. Like Franky's dead flowers that came up by Wila's grave in the spring, surprising us all with their little green shoots and blossoming promise.

Only later did we learn that Barrett and Louise Post had gone and gotten new bulbs and planted them fresh so there'd be life when Franky came to look. It made me think of how God does the same thing. When we have nothing left, he hands us something new, something beautiful, that we could never have managed on our own.

To everything there is a season. A time to every purpose under heaven.

Emma's time was Emma's time, and Emma wouldn't have changed a thing. She gave us something stronger than the memories, better than her house and all the land around it. She gave us peace, deep and eternal. And trust, knowing that even when it looks like there's never enough, God always has plenty to share. So do we, when we look with an eye to eternity, with the loving, giving, selfless heart of God.

I found it's not so hard to love the unlovable or open our arms or our homes. I came to respect George much more deeply than I'd ever resented him. It thrilled my heart to see Emma Grace's first tottering steps angling in his direction. And Samuel and I stewed with him for several days over what to do about headstrong little Rorey causing fights after school.

Kissing cheeks, passing plates, even listening to George pour out his woes one more time over a late cup of root coffee—it was all the work of God. Because people need each other. And sometimes we don't realize how much we have to give until we've started giving it.

Perhaps the best thing of all was knowing that Barrett and Louise were family now. Both of them turned their hearts to the Lord. And then their son, then Clement and Elvira too. How Emma must be dancing for that news!

"Couldn't a' been done," Lizbeth said, "without Emma an' Mama. We miss 'em. We'll always miss 'em, but good's come."

Yes. Good's come.

This world has its time to weep and time to laugh. Time to mourn, time to dance. Not long ago, I didn't think we'd ever dance. But then one night early in the spring, Barrett came by just to bring us his old battery radio. Didn't work anymore, he'd said. He had an inkling, I think, that Samuel could fix it. And he did fix it. But the Posts claimed they didn't need it back. So we turned it on that first Saturday night and got some bubbly horn music and toe-tapping rhythm.

Little Emma Grace on her tiny, tottering feet was the first to start swaying. And then she danced, this way and that, pumping her little arms up and down, laughing all the time. It was such a sight to see that I nearly cried. But before anybody could say anything, Berty and Sarah and Rorey were up and dancing with her.

"Look at us!" Rorey cried. "Dancin' angels! Jus' like Mama!"

"Emma too," Sarah added, looking at me with a confident smile lighting her face. "Emma's dancing too, with both feet on! And her hands holdin' Jesus' hands!"

When we get there, I'm sure we'll see it to be so. Emma and Wila and my mother and Grandma Pearl and everyone else we've ever loved and lost. Dancing. Happy. With their hands in Jesus' hands.

It doesn't take away the pain of this world. But just knowing the outcome can stop the ache that comes in the middle of some lonely night, or can give you words to make a crying child smile again. God is faithful. Our shelter in the time of trouble. Our refuge in the time of storm.

We don't always know what he's given us. When we're deep in the hurt of some awful moment, we don't always know what good things God has prepared for the days ahead. But we do know so much of himself has been given to our hands. To cherish. To rest in. And especially to share.

To everything there is a season. To dance. To laugh. To rejoice again. To pick up a child and go swirling around the room the way George did when he got swept up in the music. Life goes on. And on. For eternity. And just gets better, if we have each other. If we have God.

Albert sent out a marker for Emma's grave, just like he said he would. And right under her name, it said, "In God's Garden Now." I couldn't think of anything more appropriate. Except, perhaps, what he'd had engraved on the one he'd also gotten for Wilametta: "Waiting to Greet Us in Our Heavenly Home."

And so it is.

Amen.

Leisha Kelly is a native of Illinois and grew up around gardens and hardworking families. She and her husband, K.J., have two children, eighteen peaceful acres, and several pets.